PRIESTESS OF SHADOWS

LUNA LEWIS

Copyright © Luna Lewis
Dust Jacket Design by: @Niru.Sky
Cover Design by: @Shaked_Creates
Cover/Dust Jacket Copyright © Luna Lewis

HB ISBN 978-1-7398676-0-7
PB ISBN 978-1-7398676-1-4

v.2

For the ones who fight against the darkness and those who learn to embrace it.

CHAPTER 1

*M*y stomach growled as the burning ache of hunger twisted deep inside my gut. It was a feeling that I had grown used to by now, that hallow emptiness that has plagued me for longer than I can remember.

The last time I ate was yesterday morning when I had gotten lucky enough to find half a loaf of stale bread that the baker had tossed out to the bin.

Groaning with relief, I remember quickly grabbing it and scurrying to the nearest alleyway before I tore it into chunks and scoffed it down. I had eaten it so quickly that my stomach had swelled up to the point it was painful.

I couldn't remember the last time I had a full and proper meal, not since my mother died and I was forced to survive on the streets of Ghislane City to fend for myself. It has been so long since then that the days seemed to blur together to the point where I didn't even know how old I was anymore. It was safe to assume I was around thirteen if I compared myself to the other homeless children who had parents.

Ghislane City was the main centre point to the Kingdom

of Ghislana which sat on a small island surrounded by rough ocean that stretched on as far as the eye could see.

The city itself was sectioned into two districts, the Noble District that surrounded the main palace and the Commoner District that was on the outskirts. The living conditions between the two districts were like night and day.

The Noble District was polished looking with its immaculate cobbled streets and tall stone houses, whereas the Commoner District was decaying with crumbling brick shops and nailed together wooden houses.

I'd heard that Ghislane had once been fair with no segregation and everyone lived in harmony but when king Embram took the throne, he grew greedy with his riches and raised the taxes whilst also raising the trade charge for the distant continents. It was only a matter of time before the poorer people of the city came together and created a civil war, demanding the taxes be lowered for the non-nobles of the kingdom.

Years of bloodshed and resistance followed and when the king learned that the commoners where being supplied with help from other continents in hope of lowering the merchant charges, it made him go into a frenzy.

He closed the port down completely and put a border around the nobles, leaving the commoners to fend for themselves.

Without the steady supply of foreign merchants, the supply of weapons and help also came to end which meant the commoners eventually had to admit defeat and accept the now total divide. With this crushing defeat also came the now common knowledge…

If you weren't born into money, then you weren't likely to survive long.

I hated it—detested the fact that you were either noble or commoner your life decided for you, before you can even figure it out for yourself. It was the bitter truth, and you had no choice but to except it.

I slumped against the wall in the alley I was in and thought over all the stories my mother had told me about Ghislane. So much could be different if we had a better king, a *fairer* king.

"Clear the way!" A man yelled in the distance, I slowly peeked out from behind the wall of the crumbling stone building I was beside.

The main trade square of the Commoner District had now become crowded with floods of angry people which meant only one thing. The royal carriage was about to be passing by.

That was the only reason a large crowd would swarm the uneven streets of the main road – it sent a wave of adrenaline through my body. Occurrences like this were rare, but it was a great opportunity for me since everyone was watching the royals pass by, they were less likely to be watching their shops and stalls.

The King rarely left the comfort of his palace to journey out into his vast Kingdom of Ghislana anymore and I'm sure it was because the scarce towns and villages that I heard scattered the countryside were in just as bad of a state as the Commoner's District.

Not missing this rare chance, I quickly began to run down to the small bakery I had tried to scavenge from multiple times. I felt a huge smile crack across my face as I saw the back door had been left open. I hugged the chipped brick wall as I spied the crowded main street, a wash of excited nervous energy running through me as I spotted the baker standing in amongst the crowd.

This was it! A chance of a lifetime.

I snuck round to the back again and made sure that beyond the back door was clear before I shuffled in. I was small and thin but had always been quick and light on my toes which came in very handy for times like this.

The smell of freshly baked bread and pastries filled my nose and my mouth immediately began to fill with saliva. I shook my head to clear my mind and focus as I found the source of the delicious smell. Rows of freshly baked bread lined the back wall of the kitchen – I almost wept at the sight of it.

Without hesitation, I grabbed a discarded sack near the exit and began to fill it with the golden loafs of bread, my body trembling with adrenaline.

I heard the crowd beginning to boo at the carriage from the streets outside and my stomach lurched at the thought of the baker coming back. It wouldn't be my first beating from getting caught stealing, but I didn't think my frail body could take much more than a few punches before it crumpled.

After almost filling the sack to its fullest, I quickly swung it over my shoulder and stumbled backwards from the weight of it. I grunted as I pushed myself from the back door and began dragging the sack towards the alleyway where all the homeless people stayed. It was there that my little tent made of discarded blankets stood, my home.

My mother had brought me there after she had given birth to me. She had no family and nothing to her name, except me. She raised me the best she could in the alleyway, feeding me until I was full and only then would she eat what was left.

The families that lived in tents in the alleyway shared around tattered story books for the children to read. Even though my mother couldn't read, she would pretend to and make up wild and crazy stories that I used to love hearing.

This carried on until my mother suddenly became sick. It was common for the homeless to become sick with their poor living conditions and frail bodies, but it was still no less surprising and upsetting.

It began slow and then progressed until she couldn't keep down food or water anymore. Day after day she withered away as I tried desperately to find someone who could help. Crying out for someone, anyone to come and save my loving and kind mother. No one ever came. Except the city guards when they came to take her stiff and lifeless body away.

I grew hardened after that day and as the days turned to weeks, months, years...

I realised that life in the Commoner's District was a game of survival and if you lost, you die.

I continued to haul the heavy sack of bread down the back streets when a chill shot up my back and the hairs on my body stood on edge.

An eerie feeling of someone watching me filled my senses and I began to move faster. There was no way I would lose this precious food now, not when this bag of bread was all that stood between life and death for me.

I would fight for it if I had to. The almost translucent skin that hung to my bones was evidence of my near death. I wouldn't give up.

Not now, not ever.

Cursing under my breath with sweat running down my face, I hurried my pace and let out a breath of relief when I finally reached the familiar walls of my alleyway.

"Renetta! Renetta!" I called out as I dropped the bag in front of my neighbour's tent. Renetta was the mother of Luca and Brendan, my two best friends.

She and her boys had only arrived at the alleyway a few weeks ago and I had been helping them to settle in as much as I could. Luca and Brendan were maybe only a year younger than I was and they reminded me of little puppies, always excited and jumpy that I could almost imagine two little tails wagging behind them.

"Nevara?" Renetta peeled back the tent entrance and looked curiously at me. When her golden-brown almond shaped eyes spied the large bakery sack in front of me, her mouth fell open.

Renetta was young in appearance and looked out of place amongst the homeless with her sleek and shiny dark brown hair and soft skin.

"I got bread for us all," I whispered excitedly as I opened the bag and showed her what was inside.

"Nevara…" She was speechless as she looked inside the bag. "How did you…? No." She shook her head and closed the bag, shoving it back towards me. "I cannot take any of this. This is all yours Nevara, you need this." Her eyes shifted to my too thin arms and frowned. With a sigh, I put my hand in the bag and handed her one of the loafs, still warm and soft.

"You are my friend, Netta." I called her by her nickname and her eyes gleamed as she smiled at me.

"You are too kind to be where you are, Nevara," she whispered as she took the bread from my hands, her own enclosing around mine for a moment. I gave her a small nod and her smile grew as she examined the bread. When had she last eaten? When had any of the other homeless people last eaten?

With that thought in mind, I quickly began distributing the bread down the line of tents. There were two types of people who settled here, those who were rich and for whatever reason lost their fortune or those who had been born with nothing. This alley was filled with all kinds of people because it didn't matter about the diversity when it came to this place, we were all in the same position. Fighting for survival. Fighting to *live*.

"Thank you," said a woman with a small babe clutched to her chest as she took the bread with a grateful smile. An elderly woman squeezed my face in her hands as she rubbed it endearingly which made me giggle.

"Hey!" I heard a boy shout and I stood up from the elderly woman's tent to see Netta's two sons, Luca and Brendan thundering down the alleyway, a worn red ball in hand. "Mother told us you looted the bakery and were giving it all away," Luca accused as he looked down at the nearly empty bread sack.

"And?" I asked, looking at them confusedly.

"Well...why are you giving it away? Why aren't you keeping it for yourself? You know no one else shares what they find," Brendan queried, brows furrowed and after a long moment of silence I lifted my foot and kicked him in the shin earning a yelp from his mouth.

"I share because we are all stuck here," I said angrily. "I don't care if no one shares with me, I won't let my greed stop all these desperate people from eating." I stood there scowling as Brendan rubbed at his leg.

"But..." Luca began and I cut him off.

"Do you think poor Edin can go out and find food for herself?" I pointed my hand at the kind elderly lady I had just given the bread to. She looked up at the boys and gave them a smile, her body trembling from her age. "Do you think the young mothers and disabled men and women have the means of going out of this alley and fighting for food?" I asked them and their faces paled as they looked at each other and shook their heads sheepishly.

They shared the same honey-coloured almond eyes as their mother but their hair was a pale hay colour that they must have earned from their father.

"That is why I share my food," I said proudly, then continued to give away the bread until there was only one loaf left for myself, just enough so that every tent in this alleyway had a portion. Brendan and Luca followed behind me, their heads hung low in shame.

Even though Luca, Brendan and I had become friends, they were still only newly living on the streets. They weren't settled down in the alley yet and I didn't blame them, being homeless wasn't something someone could easily get used to.

Netta had been living in the noble district as a mistress to a lord. After fourteen years, the wife apparently began to fear that Brendan and Luca would reveal her husband's adultery and forced him to get rid of Netta or she would leave him and reveal his secrets anyway. Of course, the lord chose to cast away Netta and his sons. I still couldn't believe how easily he had done it – like they were simply objects that he could just cast aside and forget about. It made me sick.

Netta had gone from a comfortable life for her and her boys to now living out on the streets in a makeshift tent. It just shows you how unpredictable life is – nothing is set in stone.

I frowned at that last thought as I walked towards my tent and a sudden change in the air had my body tensing. A thrum of energy had filled the narrow space around me and I gulped at the feeling of unease.

"What a brave young girl you are," said a man's voice from behind me, and my body trembled at the sheer power that emanated from his words. I was outside my tent now and I clutched the last loaf of bread as if it could ground me somehow.

I turned around slowly and hoped desperately it wasn't the baker coming to seek vengeance for his stolen produce. A short-lived breath of relief escaped me as I looked up and up and *up* at the tall, cloaked man that now stood before me. His piercing red-coloured eyes seemed to glow under the heavy hood of his cloak. A small raven was perched on his shoulder and it cocked its head in my direction, as if studying me.

"Who are you?" I asked breathlessly, my palms beginning to sweat around the loaf of bread. I had no idea who this man was other than he seemed important and very wealthy. I could tell by the heavy black velvet material of his cloak and the red embroidery that crawled up the fabric into designs that looked like flames. The cloak alone would probably cost enough that I could feed myself for many years and that was what scared me the most.

This man had no reason to come to a place like this and that made me question his intentions.

I felt Luca and Brendan cower behind me and I opened my arms slightly to block them against the mysterious man.

"So brave," he repeated and I could see a small smile under the hood as he lifted his hand. I tensed my body and shut my eyes as I braced for the impact of his fist, he must have seen what I did and was punishing me for it, but it didn't matter. I was doing it to survive and to help those who were struggling like me and I would do it again and again with the threat of getting hit and punished because I didn't have any other choice.

The man chuckled as his hand landed gently on my head, his fingers mussing my messy black hair.

"I think you will do," he said gently and a warmth began to spread from his palm into my head and then began to travel out to the rest of my body. What was this strange feeling?

The raven cawed loudly as it launched itself up into the skies, circling above where we stood. The man lifted his hand and then placed a finger to the centre of my chest and I sucked in a breath at the increasing buzz of energy around me.

"A time will come when I will require your help," the man

said in an endearing and soft voice. "For now, I need you to keep fighting and survive. Use my gift well, little shadow."

My chest began to burn, and I dropped the bread from my hands. The burning turned unbearable as the fiery pain made its way into my heart, unrelenting and consuming as my breath came in pants. My heart began to thunder beneath his finger as if it were fighting against whatever heat was trying to invade it and I suddenly came to a terrifying thought.

I was going to die.

"Let go of her!" I heard Luca scream as he and Brendan began pulling and hitting at the man. His eyes were locked on mine and a swirl of red was all I saw before the world around me turned to dark and swallowed me whole.

"Nevara!" I heard a familiar voice call. I gasped loudly at the ache in my bones as I opened my eyes.

"Netta?" I croaked and looked around, realising that I was now inside Luca and Brendan's tent. I put a hand to my chest remembering where the man had touched me, and I flinched at the tenderness of it.

"Thank goodness you're okay." Netta breathed out a sigh of relief as she helped me sit up. My mind spun slightly and I placed a hand to my head as if it would help steady it. "What happened to you? Luca and Brendan came racing to me as pale as ghosts, saying that a scary man was hurting you." She gently smoothed back my messy hair.

"I...I don't know," I admitted as I looked down to where the man had burned me. A glimpse of black lines caught my attention and I quickly pulled my top down slightly to reveal a black circle filled with writing and symbols that I had never seen before. He had marked my skin.

"What the..." Netta was speechless as she leaned in closer to see the mark. "That's a magic formation," Netta pointed out and her face paled.

"A magic formation?" I asked confused and I recalled my mother sharing stories of magic when I was younger but I couldn't remember what she had said.

"Luca and Brendan's father was a battle mage," Netta said, her mouth twisting as she said 'father' as if it was a foul word. "I remember seeing formations just like this in his study and in his books. But nothing as detailed as this," she murmured as she continued to study my chest.

Magic was something that had only been discovered in the last decade and the stories were so hard to believe at first that everyone had thought it was only a rumour – a myth. That was until the city guards began to use this so-called magic to keep the commoners in line.

I witnessed it myself in person once. A city guard had a man on his knees, accused of stealing. He drew water from the local well, flooding the man's mouth. I watched in horror and amazement as he pulled it from the man's mouth again and again only to force it down straight after.

The guard had slowly drowned the man as he sat helpless against the abnormal power of the water. It was just another thing that separated the commoners from the nobles, an incredible power that could kill with the flick of a wrist.

"What does it mean?" I asked, a little scared as I took in the incredibly detailed lines of the formation that now inked my skin. "Is it harmful?" I added, even though apart from a few aches around my body, I felt fine.

"I'm not sure." Netta shook her head. "Just be careful from now on, okay? It must be some sort of punishment for taking all of that bread." She sighed and fixed my tatty shirt.

"I would do it again and again," I replied proudly and she

opened her mouth as if she were about to argue when running footsteps outside drew our attention.

"Nevara!" Luca cried as they bundled into the tent, almost falling on top of me as they hugged me.

"I thought you died," Brendan sniffed and I rubbed their heads, their blonde hair soft under my fingers. Brendan and Luca were identical twins and most of the people in the alley couldn't tell them apart – but I could. Certain things like a small scar under Luca's eye or the way that Brendan had a limp in his right leg from an injury as a baby. I could always tell which one was which.

"Don't be so dramatic." I chuckled and they both looked up at me with those puppy-like eyes.

"We tried to follow the man but he disappeared," Brendan sniffled.

"You're our sister, we can't let anything happen to you," Luca cried and I stilled under their arms and looked nervously at Netta who looked surprisedly at her sons.

"I'm not your–," I began to deny their words before Netta put her hand on my shoulder to silence me.

"She is your sister, so you need to take good care of her. Ok?" Netta said gently and my heart thundered in my chest.

"We promise!" They cried as they hugged me tighter and my own eyes began to threaten with tears.

Ever since my mother had died that night and had been taken away from me, the cold feeling of true loneliness settled in. I thought I would never have that warmth again. I had fought to survive all these years on my own, surviving just to live another day in this awful city. The thought of having to do it for the rest of my life often kept me up at night, clutching the dirty blankets around me and crying softly so no one else could hear me.

I had hardened myself to this life but at the end of the

day, I was still a child and no child should be left to live all alone.

"Brothers." I tested the word quietly and then something broke inside my chest and began to warm my body. It seemed to blossom as I clutched Luca and Brendan to me and felt Netta's arms around all three of us.

"All we have is each other now," Netta choked, her tears falling freely. "We're a family now."

Family. The word sent another wave of warmth through me and it was as if the hardened exterior began to crack and soften from the embrace of these people around me.

"Here," Luca said as he placed a loaf of bread in my hands. He must have picked it up where I had dropped it before.

"Thank you," I said, wiping their tears with the back of my hands. I began breaking the bread into chunks and offered it to everyone else and we sat and ate as we talked to each other about miscellaneous things.

The two brothers bickered and Netta scolded them before laughing with me. My heart swelled with the whole scene. Finally, I had people around me. Not a family by birth but a family by choice and I would protect them with all my strength.

Not just them, but this whole alleyway. I would become stronger and fight until each and every one of us never had to worry about where our next source of food would come from.

CHAPTER 2

"Come and see what we found earlier." Luca grinned as he pulled me out of the tent that evening.

"Be careful out there!" Netta called out to us as I followed Brendan and Luca down the alley, people now waving and smiling at us as they ate their bread.

"What did you find?" I asked curiously as we weaved through the narrow back alleys behind the Commoners' Districts trade square. The smell of all the different foods filled my nose and made my stomach grumble.

"It's a surprise," Brendan chuckled. I narrowed my eyes at them as they continued to drag me over the uneven cobblestone floor.

I knew all of the back alleys in the Commoner's District of the city. I had spent many years memorising every location so I could always find an escape if I got caught stealing – which happened more often than not.

"Why are we going to the arena?" I asked as the familiar building came into view, the two brothers giggled to themselves, apparently enjoying keeping me in the dark as to what they were doing.

The arena was a crumbling coliseum type of structure where the Commoner District guards would train. I had always made sure to steer clear of them and the shining swords they always had strapped to their sides.

The brothers pulled me through one of the side entrances and the sounds of men yelling and grunting rang through my ears. We shouldn't be here – in fact I would rather be anywhere else *but* here. I was about to tell the brothers as much before they suddenly scurried forward and pulled me down behind one of the walls surrounding the open arena floor. The smell of sweat and metal filled the air and I scrunched my nose.

"We should leave," I whispered furiously to Luca who shook his head.

"You need to see this," Luca whispered excitedly as he pushed my face forward to look into the arena.

A man stood in the middle of the dusty floor, a crowd surrounding him as he faced a wooden target. He was huge and muscular and stared at the target with a deep intensity, his arm poised in front of him as he gripped a large sword with ease.

He was the sort of man that demanded attention, a leader where the rest would follow. His greying hair was cropped close to his head, and I could see his piercing blue eyes as they narrowed at the target in front of him.

He took a deep breath, and the crowd grew silent, only the wind making the faintest of noises as it whistled through the cracked archways of the arena. A build-up of anticipation filled the air and no one dared to move a muscle. What was going to happen? Was he just going to attack the target?

The questions in my head faded as a familiar energy filled the arena and my skin began trembling. The man lifted the sword high above his head and everyone, including myself, seemed to take a deep breath in. Sparks crackled along the edge of the blade before a burst of fire engulfed it entirely and I felt my eyes widen at what I was seeing. A moment later he brought the sword down upon the wooden target and the crowd let out a collective gasp as it too erupted into flames.

The crowd stood frozen in shock and then erupted into cheer as the man thrusted his sword up into the air.

He had just summoned fire out of nothing.

"That is what a magic swordsman can do!" The man bellowed and the crowd went crazy.

"Did you see that!?" Luca squealed as Brendan jumped up and down excitedly.

"I want to be a magic swordsman!" Brendan yelled and Luca nodded enthusiastically.

A magic swordsman.

My blood pounded through my veins as I watched the flames engulf the target. That man was powerful enough to summon flames and he *wasn't* a guard. Or a noble.

"When we came earlier, we saw a man who shot ice out of his sword!" Brendan exclaimed and I looked at him wide eyed. Not just fire but ice too? I remembered the guard who had summoned water as well and my mind spun at the possibilities of what other magic might be out there.

I looked back at the man who summoned the fire and watched as the group showered him with praise and a tug of jealousy pulled inside of me. If I had such power, then I would never need to fight to survive again.

My mind began to circle around the thought, and I solidified it in my mind – into my very soul – as I spoke the words, "I'm going to become a magic swordsman."

"Me too! Me too!" Brendan squealed and I hugged both of them tightly, thankful that they brought me here to see this.

This was how I was going to survive. I was going to become a magic swordsman even if it was the last thing I did.

～

MOONLIGHT FILTERED in through the gaps of the tent and I let out a sigh, unable to sleep.

I had moved my blankets into Netta's tent to make it slightly bigger to accommodate an extra person, but Luca and Brendan had still somehow managed to tangle themselves on top of me in their sleep and were now snoring deeply. I stifled a laugh as I looked down at their drooling faces.

I couldn't stop thinking about the magic swordsman and his fire. It consumed my every thought since we left the arena – I replayed the fiery scene over and over again in my head.

I had never given much thought to what the future might hold for me because I was always so focused on surviving that I never had any time to really think about it. But there was just something that clicked within me when I saw that man with his sword and then his flames. I knew that this is what I wanted, what I *needed.*

Netta lay sleeping to the side of the tent and once I saw that her breathing was deep and even, I began to untangle myself from the brothers.

I crept out of the tent and the cool night air nipped at my arms. It was the beginning of autumn so whilst the days were somewhat warm, the nights were getting cooler.

I made my way quietly down the alleyways, retracing my steps from earlier until I finally reached the arena again.

The streets were quiet now apart from the odd drunken shout from the local tavern that lay opposite the arena in the main commoners' trade square.

I crept in through the same side entrance as before and was relieved to see the arena was now empty. A new wooden training dummy stood in the centre of the floor with a discarded sword off to the side.

After double checking to make sure no one was here, I scrambled over to the sword and studied its rusted and chipped blade. I pulled it up by the hilt and grunted when I realised just how heavy the damn thing was and how it was also nearly as long as I was tall.

A caw sounded from my right and I jumped back from the sudden noise, falling on my behind in the process. A raven sat on the wall beside me, watching with its onyx eyes. I blinked and felt my blood grow cold as I realised where I had seen this bird before.

"You!" I gasped and it cocked its head to the side just like it had done earlier. It was the raven who was with that cloaked man from before, the one who had branded me with the mark that now inked my skin.

Even though it had happened today, I could feel the memory of the man fading in my mind as if it was being stolen from me.

My hand flew to my chest where I knew the black outline of the circle still inked my skin and I jumped quickly to my feet.

"Shoo! Shoo!" I hissed and flapped my hands at the bird. It let out a short repetitive caw and beat its wings back. Was it *laughing* at me?

I realised then that something shiny lay inside the bird's beak. Hesitating, I took a tentative step closer, and it lowered its dark head down to release the contents of its beak. I watched in shock as a gold coin *clinked* against the stone and settled on the wall where the bird was perched.

"Where did you get that?" I whispered and took another step closer to make sure what I was seeing was real. It was a gold coin! The kind I had only ever seen a few times when people traded in the trade square. It was rare to see gold coins in the Commoner's District, even silver coins were a luxury I've only managed to own a few times in my short life.

The bird hopped down the length of the wall, coming closer to where I stood and I leaned back wearily. I put a shaking hand forward to pet its head but the bird suddenly jumped and flapped its wings slowly as it landed on my arm.

I braced for the pain that would come from its sharp-looking talons but was surprised at how soft and smooth they were. It was like the raven knew not to squeeze too tightly.

"Is this for me?" I pointed to the golden coin that seemed to sparkle in the moonlight. It nodded its little feathered head and my mouth fell open. Did it understand what I just asked?

"Maybe you're not such a bad little bird after all," I said breathlessly. I knew it wasn't possible but it really did seem like it understood me. "Ok then, I forgive you for earlier," I grinned and it cawed in response.

I scratched behind its head and the bird shut its eyes and leaned into my touch. I chuckled as it hopped back down on the wall and I quickly tucked the gold coin into my pocket for later. What I needed to do now was focus on trying to use this sword.

"Be prepared to see the first day of my training," I called out to the raven. "It will be marked down in history one day." The raven cawed a laugh at me again and I narrowed my eyes at it before walking back to where the rusted sword lay. I reached down and pulled at its hilt again, grunting as I finally lifted the damn thing off the ground.

I felt unsteady under its weight and half dragged it over to where the wooden target was. Charred earth lay beneath it, the only evidence of the brutal flames from earlier.

"Ok." I let out a deep breath as I heaved the sword above my head and the smile on my face quickly turned to shock as the weight pulled me backwards and I fell, narrowly missing the rusted edge of the sword as it slammed into the earth beside me.

I let out a string of curses that I had heard other people from the alleyway use and stomped my feet onto the earth. I knew it wasn't going to be easy to become a magic swordsman but I couldn't even pick up a sword let alone swing one.

"How could such a little girl know so many bad words?" A male voice said and I quickly scurried to my feet. The raven cawed and launched up into the air, leaving me alone to face the man.

Traitor, I thought to the bird and it almost seemed to laugh at me again.

"I'm sorry, I didn't think anyone was here," I said as I focused on the man and my breath caught in my throat. It was the magic swordsman from earlier.

I got a closer look at his tanned face and saw it littered with scars that told me just how many fights he had been in. I started to back up against the wall, sweat slick on my skin as I pictured him cutting me down with flames like he did with the target earlier.

"Were you trying to hit the target with this sword?" He said picking up the rusted hilt in his hands as if it weighed nothing. I nodded sheepishly and he narrowed his sharp eyes at me again.

"The blade is almost longer than you are," he choked out, then tipped back his head to laugh and some of the tension fizzled out of my body.

His laughter quietened down and he proceeded to stab the blade into the earth again before he folded his arms, muscles twitching and flexing with the movement.

"Let me guess, you want to become a magic swordsman?"

I nodded my head eagerly as I took a small step forward.

"I saw you earlier with your flames," I said excitedly and a smile appeared on his face, the expression making him less intimidating. "I want to do that too."

"Magic has only entered this world for around a decade," the man said. "You're looking at one of the first graduates of the magic swordsman class from Ashwood Academy. I am Kain Manus." He stood proudly – I felt a rush of awe as I stared at him.

Ashwood Academy was founded just over five years ago and was where the city guards learned to awaken and use their magic. Regular people could attend the academy also but I had heard that it costed a small fortune to attend. This meant it was normally only the wealthy nobles that attended, alongside the hopeful guards.

I could only dream of what they learnt in there and it only motivated me more to become a magic swordsman, just like the man in front of me.

"Can you teach me?" I asked bluntly and Kain took a step back in surprise and then let out a roar of laughter.

"You want me, the great Kain, to teach you?" He asked and then he looked me over. I pulled nervously at the tattered shirt I wore and frowned. That's right, I was home-less and poor. Why would he ever teach someone like me?

Kain pressed his mouth into a thin line and let out a sigh.

"Listen." He scratched the back of his head. "Let's make a deal. I will train you until you're ready to go to the academy but it comes at a price," he said and I sucked in my breath in anticipation. "One gold coin," he said lifting a finger and his eyes shone with amusement. He obviously thought because of my appearance that I had no money to my name…and he would normally be right.

But not tonight.

The gold coin seemed to burn in my pocket as I thought over his words. A gold coin could feed the alley for weeks if not months... but then what happens when that food runs out and we must steal and beg again?

If I were to learn from Kain, then I would have a steady income in the future and never have to worry about buying food or other necessities again.

I thought of the raven again and wondered about this whole situation. How come the bird just so happened to drop off a gold coin before Kain came and offered his price? Did the bird somehow know that was going to happen?

No, the bird had simply found something shiny that caught its attention and just so happened to find me. That's the only sane reason.

"I know it's a lot to pay, but I am one of the greatest, if not *the* greatest–" I cut off his words.

"Deal," I pulled the gold coin from my pocket. I had never wanted something so much in my life. Sure I had always wanted and needed food, but this...this was something deeper, something that seemed to call out to me.

"Where..." Kain looked at me as if I had three heads. "Where did you get that?" He asked and I wondered if I should tell him that a bird gave it to me but decided against it knowing he would think I was insane. Which I probably was.

"Do we have a deal?" I asked, ignoring his question and he stared at the coin again before picking it up and examining it.

"How old are you, kid?" He asked as he looked over at me once more.

"I don't know," I answered honestly. "I think around twelve or thirteen. I'm not sure when my birthday is." Something like pity twisted his features and he let out a sigh.

"What's your name?" He asked after a moment.

"Nevara," I said nervously, wondering if he would accept or not.

"Well, Nevara, today onwards will be your birthday," he stated and a huge grin spread across his face. "It will also be the day you begin your training to be the best magic swordsman there ever was!"

CHAPTER 3

"Where are you going?" Netta asked as I crawled past the bickering brothers inside the tent.

Last night, Kain had agreed to train me to become a magic swordsman...well, at least until I was old enough to apply to the Ashwood Academy. He said anyone over the age of eighteen could apply, so that gave me a good seven or so years to train.

"Just going for a walk," I replied, trying to keep my face neutral as I lied because I was in fact on my way to have my first lesson with Kain. He told me to meet him back at the arena after sunset every weekday to train and I had agreed happily.

I didn't tell Netta the truth because I knew she would fear for my safety and I didn't want her to worry.

"Well, be careful. It's almost nightfall," Netta warned and I nodded with a smile before crouching out of the tent. It was nice to have someone worrying about me again.

I ran almost the whole way to the arena, a smile pinned to my face and excitement coursing through my blood with each step. A bird cawed above me and came to settle on my shoulder.

"Back again?" I chuckled giving the raven a scratch behind its head. "I guess I should thank you seeing as you made this all possible."

It cawed loudly in response as it launched itself off of me and disappeared behind some of the dirty buildings behind the arena.

All the traders and merchants were packing up their stalls around the main trade square now and people in tattered clothing were filtering towards the tavern or making their way back to their homes.

I wondered what having a home would feel like. A roof over your head and hot food on the table with a fireplace to keep you warm at night. I had looked in a few of the nicer houses in the district when I was younger out of curiosity and it always filled me with longing. I wanted that, a place to call home.

"Ah, there you are!" Kain shouted as he saw me entering the arena and I gave him a nervous smile. The arena was empty again apart from a few men chatting to each other in small groups.

Some looked at me with curiosity as I approached Kain whilst some looked with open disgust as they saw my messy appearance. "You didn't waste any time coming back, did you?" He chuckled and then slammed a hand on the shoulder of a man beside him.

"This is Derrick, he will be your sparring partner." Kain grinned and Derrick's mouth dropped open. Derrick was middle aged, like Kain, but with close to no hair and tattoos covering him in large patches. I cringed at the angry looking beast that inked his neck.

"She's a kid," Derrick choked out. "You didn't say she was

a kid... and one that looks like she could keel over at any second," he added with a scoff and I glared at him.

"Now, now. No need for that." Kain chuckled nervously and threw a bundle of clothing towards me. "Take those rags off and put some proper clothes on. Tie that messy hair back too, it will only get in your way," Kain ordered and I stared at him.

"But I don't have any more money," I said quietly and something softened in Kain's face.

"You've already paid your fees. Go on," He waved me away and I grabbed the clothes without having to be told twice. I couldn't remember the last time I had gotten new clothes, the ones I wore now were hanging together by a few threads.

The clothes Kain had given me consisted of a pair of leather breeches, a white cotton shirt and a pair of worn leather boots.

Tears threatened as I hugged the clothes to my chest, excitement bubbling in my belly. This was the first gift that anyone had ever given me and I didn't know how to deal with the flood of emotions that overwhelmed me.

I quickly found a hidden alcove and stripped down before I pulled on the new clothes Kain had given me. Everything was slightly baggy but the shoes seemed to fit at least.

I took the small leather strap and tried to pull my messy hair back as neat as I could. It took me a few attempts but I got it tied in the end.

"Now you look like a swordsman!" Kain clapped his hands together as I joined them back in the arena, feeling more confident now in my new attire.

Derrick looked away with disinterest and I wanted to thump him on his bald head.

"Thank you for the clothes," I said earnestly and Kain gave me a small nod.

"Now, I'm going to let you use one of the smaller training swords seeing as you could barely lift the two handed one yesterday." Kain stifled a laugh and my cheeks grew warm at the memory of how I had fallen backwards with the weight of the rusted sword last night.

Kain retrieved one of the smaller training swords from a nearby rack and held out the hilt for me. I took it excitedly and was surprised at how much lighter this sword was – it was still strenuous to keep it lifted off the ground but I was managing to do it unlike last night.

"I don't really have to spar with the little brat, do I?" Derrick sighed and my face heated again but this time with anger.

"You're in my guild so you're going to do as I say," Kain barked out and before I could ask what a guild was, Derrick scowled and pulled out his own sword that he had sheathed at his hip.

I lifted my sword in front of me and felt a nervous tremble run through my body as I realised this would be my first ever spar.

"Now, you're going to want to spread your feet about this far apart and angle your hips and arms like this." Kain moved my body into the right stance and it felt awkward, but I'm sure after time I would get used to it. "Now I want you to take turns in doing attack and defence. Derrick you can start with defence and Nevara you can go at him with all that you got."

"Also, the blades are dull but will still pack a punch, so be careful," Kain warned, a mischievous smile at his mouth as he took a step back.

"As if any attack she makes is going to hit." Derrick smirked and I let out an angry yell as I charged at him, using everything in my small body to shut that stupid mouth of his. Derrick lifted his sword in a last-minute surprise dodge and the blades bounced off each other, the vibrations seeming to hum into my bones as I stumbled backwards.

"You little brat!" Derrick yelped and raised his sword to swing back down.

"Lift and block, Nevara!" Kain yelled and I quickly obeyed but Derrick's heavy attack had my sword flying out of my hands as I fell to the dirt floor.

"What are you doing you bastard!?" Kain shouted as he stomped over and grabbed Derrick by his throat. "Using such a heavy attack on a child! Does that make you feel like a man?" Kain yelled into Derrick's paling face.

"Again!" I yelled and the two men looked at me in shock. "Again," I repeated, quieter now and Kain glared at Derrick again before shoving him backwards. Derrick scowled as he straightened himself and got back into defensive form.

"Cut from the side, feel as if the sword is just another part of your arm," Kain suggested and I took a deep breath before launching out and swinging sideways, Derrick deflected it easily before returning an attack, one that wasn't deadly this time.

WE SPENT the whole evening going back and forth with attacks until my legs trembled beneath me and my arms felt like they would fall off. I ended up with far too many bruises and cuts from Derrick's heavy-handed swings but other than that, I felt...good.

The mark on my chest burned, it began to radiate heat and I worried in case Derrick had made a cut in it.

"Not bad, brat," Derrick said and patted a hand on my shoulder. "Sorry for being a dick."

"I told you there was something about her," Kain said

proudly and put us both in a playful headlock. "Now that we're all friends, how about we go get a full meal at the tavern."

"That's the best idea I've heard from you in a while." Derrick laughed as he pulled away. "I'll even treat the little runt." Happiness blossomed in my chest as a smile stretched across my face.

"Really?" I asked and Derrick rolled his eyes.

"It's as if I told you I was going to give you a diamond necklace," he chuckled. "Come on."

I followed them as they left the arena and made their way to the tavern that I had seen so many times before but never entered. I could hardly hold in my excitement at the thought of hot food as we got to the entrance.

The smell of hot sweat and alcohol hit me first. It reminded me of the pint of beer I found discarded in one of the alleyways before and I wrinkled my nose at it.

"Kain!" Many people began calling out as we entered, he waved and greeted them as we made our way to an empty table at the back. My ears began ringing with the noise of everyone talking and I could barely hear my own thoughts as Derrick and Kain sat down opposite me.

"Who is this cute girl?" A woman called out as she made her way to the table. "You weren't stolen were you sweetie?" She asked, her brown eyes showing concern and amusement at the same time.

She was a beautiful woman with dark brown skin that seemed to glow golden in the light of the tavern. Her hair was a bundle of curls on top of her head and she had on a white and black simple muslin dress. I thought that she must have been the most beautiful woman I had ever seen, apart from Netta and what I could remember of my mother.

"This is Nevara, my new student," Kain exclaimed

proudly and the woman, who must have been Kiera, let out a chuckle.

"Oh sweetie, how did you end up with him as a mentor?" She teased and then turned her attention back to Kain. "What will it be boys?"

"Three ales and three stews please," Derrick said and Kiera looked at me.

"You do know children aren't supposed to drink alcohol?" Kiera said and Derrick scratched the back of the head.

"O-of course not!" Kain laughed awkwardly as he waved his arm, clearly not knowing that. "Just get her a water." Kiera gave me a wink before leaving for a moment and returning with drink and food on trays.

"I gave you an extra helping, you're looking a little thin." She gave me a soft smile and I could have cried with happiness as I looked down at the steaming bowl of stew.

"What about me?" Kain asked and Kiera flicked him on the nose before she was called to another table.

"Well, what are you waiting for?" asked Kain. I looked back down at the bowl of stew, the smell was definitely making me drool now.

With shaky hands I picked up a spoonful, spilling a little as I brought it up to my mouth. I couldn't remember the last time I held a spoon, I was used to just eating with my hands.

Flavour and heat erupted in my mouth and I let out a little squeak of joy as tears pricked at my eyes. It was delicious. The most delicious thing I had ever eaten in my life and I couldn't get enough. I shovelled the stew into my mouth, making a mess of the table.

"Easy girl, eat slower," Derrick grumbled and I made a grunting sound of agreement.

Soon, too soon, the bowl was empty. A pang of guilt shot through me as I thought of Ranetta and my brothers back in the tent, probably hungry again after the last of the bread got eaten.

"Here." Kain nudged his bowl towards me and Derrick scraped what was left of his on top of it and my mouth dropped.

"Are…are you sure?" I asked sheepishly as I stared at them. They both nodded their heads and I picked up the spoon ready to devour their leftovers but stopped before I took another bite.

"I should take this for my family," I said as I sat down the spoon reluctantly. "The only thing they've eaten today was some bread. I bet my brothers would cry with envy if they knew I had eaten stew. Hot stew at that!" I giggled. When none of the men said anything, I looked up and met their sombre stares. Surprise ran through me as I looked at them. Had I said something wrong?

"How many is there in your family?" Kain asked quietly, his tone serious.

"Well, my mother died when I was around six years old, but Ranetta has taken me in with her two sons. We spent all afternoon making the tent bigger." I smiled excitedly as I remembered that they were my family now.

"Damn this kingdom." Kain pinched the bridge of his nose in frustration. "Kiera!" He yelled and I jumped in my chair.

"What is it dear?" Kiera asked as she came up to the table.

"Prepare three bowls of stew and bread for Nevara to bring back to her family, she'll bring back the bowls tomorrow."

"Of course, I'll even throw in some pastries for free," Kiera said and she shared a sombre look with Kain before disappearing.

"You don't have to do that," I started to argue but Kain shot me a dark look and shook his head.

"My student and her family will not go hungry anymore. You need to eat if you want to gain muscle," he said sternly and I swallowed the lump in my throat. "Now eat up that stew before it gets cold, there's plenty for your family."

Worried that I might start crying in front of them, I nodded and began to scoff down the second bowl of stew.

"Brat," Derrick said after a large gulp of his ale. "Why do you want to be a magic swordsman?" I lowered the spoon from my mouth. I thought about my answer for a moment as images of my rough life on the streets filtered through my mind, the many faces of the other people in the alley, the people who didn't survive like I had. The last images left a sour taste in my mouth as I answered him.

"I want power – I want to be strong enough to support my family and friends in the alley; to not let them go hungry anymore. If I get to be strong like Kain, then the kingdom will be throwing money at me to hire me for jobs," I stated proudly before I continued to eat.

Derrick and Kain were quiet for a moment as they looked at each other and then burst into laughter.

"That's the spirit, brat!" Derrick bellowed. "By the time we're done training you, you'll be the best swordsman there is! You'll be the best graduate to come out of that damned academy!"

"You certainly changed your tune from this morning." Kain smacked him on the back with a chuckle.

"What can I say? The runt changed my mind." Derrick winked at me and I shot him a toothy smile. It finally felt as if my life was beginning to change for the better.

I LEFT the tavern with my aching arms filled with bowls of stew, bread rolls and pastries. The smell filled my nose on the way back to the alley and I had to resist hard against stopping and scoffing the food myself.

It was late enough now that all the others in the alley were tucked away in their tents and makeshift shelters. I quickly made my way past them towards the bright red and brown tent that I now came to know as my home.

"Netta! Luca! Brendan!" I half whispered, half shouted. They all stared at me curiously as I nudged my way past the blanket door.

"Is that..." Netta trailed off as her honeyed eyes fastened on the food in my arms. The tent was lit by only the filtering moonlight and it glinted off the hungry faces that stared at me.

"My teacher gifted them to us," I said excitedly as I handed out the bowls to the three of them.

"You're the best, Nevara!" Luca and Brendan said in unison as they began to scoff down the cooling stew without hesitation.

"How?" Netta asked quietly and she looked tearful as she watched her two sons eating.

"I'm training to become a magic swordsman so I can take care of you and my brothers," I said proudly and Netta opened her mouth as if to say something but then shut it again. She noticed the new clothes I wore and a warm smile crept onto her face.

"Is that so?" She whispered as if she doubted what I had said. "Here." She handed me her bowl but I shook my head.

"I already ate mine!" I said and pushed the bowl towards her. "Eat!"

"Ok, ok!" Netta laughed and it was the first time that I had such a happy noise come from her.

Something warmed in my chest as I watched the three of them eat. This is what I was going to fight to achieve, for them to never go to bed hungry ever again.

A bird cawed from outside and I quickly tore a chunk off the spare bread roll. I ducked out of the tent and a smile spread across my face as I saw the dark amused eyes of the friendly raven.

I quickly tore up the chunk of bread and held it out to the bird. It flapped its wings and then jumped to land on my shoulder and it pecked at the crumbs.

"It's all thanks to you, my feathered friend," I said as I rubbed my head against its side and I could have sworn it leaned into me too.

If it wasn't for the gold coin that the raven had given me, then all of what had occurred the past few days wouldn't have happened.

"I think it's safe to say we're friends now, right?" I asked and the bird made a little fluttery caw of confirmation. "I think that means we should give you a name. How about…" I thought about all the things that were dark like the raven and I remembered the small fires that would be lit in the alley in the winter to keep us all warm. It was a rare occasion that someone would be able to acquire some coal and I remembered how the hands and faces of the alley would blacken with soot.

"Soot! It's the same colours as your feathers. What do you think?" I asked and suddenly felt shy to learn what the bird thought. After a moment it gave an excited caw and a little jump.

"Soot it is!" I giggled as I scratched the bird.

"Nevara, come in now. It's time to get to bed." I heard Netta call from the tent and she was right. I quickly smuggled the bird inside and set up a little nest made of the edge of my blanket before tucking him in.

"Goodnight soot," I whispered as I snuggled down between the two snoring brothers.

They must have fell straight to sleep after having a belly full of warm food and I had to admit that I also felt drowsy. My body barely ached now from my first day of training and I fell asleep quickly, dreaming of what tomorrow would hold.

CHAPTER 4

"*Y*ou need to put more power behind your strikes, brat! It's like a damn kitten is swinging that sword," Derrick sighed as the setting sun casted gold rays across the arena. I huffed my breaths in and out, sweat sticking to my clothes from the hours of training.

It has been around a week since I started training and each day, wielding the sword became a little easier.

But only a little.

I would meet Kain and Derrick after the shops and stalls began to close and train with them until late into the night. Every evening without fail they would bring me to the tavern and feed me until I was full and then send me away with arms full of food for Netta and my brothers.

"Push the sword with the power from your core!" Kain tapped my stomach. "This is where the source of your magic is formed. Even though you can't use it yet, it's better to train as if you can." Kain nodded and I didn't have a clue what he was talking about but I would try anyway. I closed my eyes and took a deep breath as I swung down the sword whilst clenching my stomach muscles.

"Better!" Kain encouraged and Derrick gave me a nod of approval and I smiled proudly.

We continued swinging back and forth until Kain called it a night. I collapsed onto the dusty ground and gulped down greedy breaths, my lungs straining against the cold air.

"Is your body not aching all over? You've been training every day and that has to take its toll," Kain asked as he sat beside me, passing a small water canteen into my lap and I chugged it down. I focused on my body and flexed my arms and legs. Apart from a dull ache in my over-worked muscles, nothing else seemed to be wrong.

"I feel fine," I frowned. "Is that normal?"

"Ah, you're just too damn strong," Kain teased. "You would have to be, seeing as you survived on the streets for so long." He gave a shallow laugh and then sighed.

"What's wrong?" I asked seeing his frowning expression.

"We're not going to the tavern tonight," Kain said and I realised then that Derrick had disappeared. Whilst my heart sunk at the thought of going hungry tonight, I couldn't blame Kain. He had provided more than enough over the last week.

With the constant food every night I had seen Netta becoming happier and happier. Luca and Brendan even helped me distribute the spare bread rolls and pastries to the other people in the alley.

"That's ok," I said and gave him a goofy grin, hoping to cheer him up a little. He chuckled and rubbed the top of my head.

"I have an offer to make," Kain said after a moment and I went still. "I don't think any student of mine should be living on the streets – I haven't been able to sleep right since I found out." Kain scratched at his chin. "I was thinking about letting you and your family stay in my spare room. It's not much but it's warm and there will be food and water." The world slowed and quietened as the weight of his offer sank in.

A home.

"But…you hardly know me," I pointed out. "Why would you offer something like that to someone you've just met?"

"You are a child, Nevara," Kain said and then fell quiet after a moment as he seemed to choose his words very carefully. "I had a younger sister who passed a long time ago. My family didn't have much growing up and when she fell ill… we couldn't find the funds or the help to heal her before it was too late."

"I'm so sorry," I said after a moment of shocked silence, my eyes burning with tears for both Kain's sister and my mother who had both fallen victim to the horrors of the segregation in the kingdom.

"She was around your age when she passed, and I see her fiery spirit within you." He smiled warmly at me. "I don't want to see the darkness of this city sink its claws into you any more than it already does. So please, use my spare room. I'm usually out most days with my guild anyway."

"I don't know what to say," I choked out, a wave of different emotions washing over me. In all my wildest dreams, never did I think something like this would happen.

"I talked to Kiera, and you'll all have to help around the tavern to make some money," Kain explained and I was already nodding before he finished his sentence.

"Yes anything," I agreed excitedly. "We will do anything and everything to help out."

"No need to get so excited, just bring your family back here and I'll show you to my home. It's just a few streets from here," Kain said and cleared his throat as his face flushed.

Without waiting, I shot up to my feet and sprinted for the exit. The laughter I heard behind me spurred me to run faster and faster.

Images of the homes I had saw before filtered into my mind. A bed, a warm fire…a table to eat at.

"Netta!" I huffed as I reached the tent entrance and Netta lifted the blanket to look at me worriedly.

"What is it? Are you hurt?" Netta asked as she took my hands and searched my face but I shook my head.

"Bring everything," I breathed. "And follow me."

It had taken longer than I had intended to convince Netta to follow me with Luca and Brendan, but I had eventually gotten her to come. I just hoped that Kain was still waiting and hadn't changed his mind by the time we got back.

"Nevara, this doesn't seem right," Netta said nervously as she walked hand in hand with her sons, they walked with tired and bleary eyes from the sleep they had been awoken from.

"He is kind, Netta," I said reassuringly. "He isn't letting us stay there for free, he even got us jobs to make some money! All we have to do is save enough and then we can buy our own home."

"I know but…" she trailed off and I let out a sigh.

"It's better than the alley," I argued quietly and she couldn't deny it. Anything was better than the alley.

"Kain!" I waved as I ran over to him. He was still in the arena but looked as if he were about to nod off to sleep as he leaned against the side of the wall.

"Ah, you made it back," Kain said as he shook the sleep away. "This must be your family." His eyes lifted to Netta, who had bowed her head, her dark hair falling over her shoulder. His blue eyes focused on her for a moment and then a little longer before I let out a cough.

"I'm Netta and this is Luca and Brendan." Netta smiled as

she pushed the boys close to her side. "Nevara has told us of your offer and I must say that it's too kind. Something that I will remember and cherish for the rest of my life and my children's lives," she said and looked between her boys and then me.

"My home isn't very lavish but it's warm and comfortable," he said and smiled brightly at Netta, an expression I had rarely seen settled on his face.

"That is more than enough for us," Netta assured and Kain nodded.

"It's the flame man," Luca said, rubbing his honeyed eyes.

"The magic swordsman!" Brendan cried and they rush over to him as they tried to poke and view the swords that were attached to Kain's waist.

"Boys!" Netta scolded but Kain let out a bellow of a laugh as he hoisted both boys up in one movement so they both sat on each of his shoulders. Luca and Brendan let out squeals of delight and Netta let out a breathy laugh.

"Let's get going!" Kain said and he began to walk away.

Netta grasped my hand and placed a small kiss on the back of it, tears in her eyes as she mouthed *thank you.*

I gave her a toothy grin as I nodded and then we walked hand in hand together behind Kain as we made our way to our new home.

CHAPTER 5

 *ive years later...*

"That's it for today," Kain called out, and I slumped against the side of the wall, the midday sun burning down on the whole arena.

After about a year of my training, Kain had moved our lessons to midday as he wanted to spend more time with Netta in the tavern. I was fairly sure he just wanted to make sure that no one else flirted with her where she served as a bar maid.

I remembered chuckling when I came into the kitchen three years ago to find Kain and Netta kissing. They tried to play it off but eventually gave up when they saw that I knew.

They had been in a relationship since then and I was beyond happy for them. Luca and Brendan were even more thrilled that the mighty swordsman, known as Kain Manus was about to become their stepfather.

"What are you smirking at?" Kain asked as he came to

stand beside me, wiping the sweat off his forehead with the back of his hand.

"Just thinking of when you used to pester and follow Netta around all day like a lost puppy in love," I sighed dramatically and heat flushed Kain's face.

"You little brat, I did not do anything of the sort." Kain smacked me playfully on the head. He had also become a stepfather to me, even though I wasn't Netta's daughter by blood. He hadn't treated me any differently than Luca and Brendan which I was thankful for.

"What's she doing here?" A guard asked and my spine stiffened.

I had been coming here nearly every day for the past five years, apart from the days Kain had to go off and do work for his guild and all of the guards had grown used to me. Some would join in on my training and I would get into friendly spars and scuffles with them. But there were always new recruits to the guards that looked down on me like I was below them.

A woman who should be at home tending to her house and family instead of training to fight. Because that's what I was now, a woman. My body had definitely filled out in the last couple years thanks to the now constant supply of food and training. My form was now lined with lean muscles and curves and I was proud that I had created such a strong body that could hold out against an opponent.

"This is a public arena, I don't need to explain why I'm here," I said blandly and picked at my nails. Soot chose to fly down then and land on my shoulder, squawking loudly at the now red-faced guard. I smirked as I scratched the back of Soot's head.

I used to be terrified of the guards and how they would unleash their magic on the public and I wasn't the only one. The Commoners' District rose against the guards a few years ago and the King made it law that a trial must be held first before any sort of punishment would be made unless it was a necessity. He only did so to keep the peace, however frail that peace was.

"Who do you think you're talking to?" The guard was nudged then by the other guard beside him. Mark was his name if I remembered correctly, we had a few spars together and I knew him to be one of the more friendlier guards.

"Just drop it," Mark said to the other guard and then shot me an apologetic look. Even though the arena was a public space, the guards took up the majority of it using it as a space to go on their breaks and training.

"But…" The new guard was growing even redder in the face and then Kain pushed off the wall.

"I think he told you to drop it," Kain said in a low tone and the new guard blanched as he looked up into Kain's face. Kain was a soft and friendly man but would often change into someone you wouldn't want to mess with when he was angry. He was well known in the Commoner and Noble District as being one of the first swordsmen to graduate from Ashwood Academy and his name was revered but also feared.

It was a big deal that Kain and Derrick had been able to graduate from the academy because they were commoners. Apparently, Kain and Derrick had saved a hefty sum from some questionable mercenary jobs beforehand, which is how they were able to afford the tuition fee.

The guard seemed to consider what to do until he let out a string of curses and turned away.

"Being one of the first swordsmen definitely has its perks, huh?" Mark smirked at Kain.

"Well of course," Kain bellowed out a laugh, smacking him on the shoulder. "I heard the new graduates of the academy are getting cockier and cockier." Mark grunted and then nodded his head.

"That's because of the value of the magic artefacts," Mark added and my heart thumped in my chest at his words. "The prices of them seem to double each month, they're all looting the dungeons in their spare time."

Ever since magic was discovered, strange gates referred to as dungeons began to appear all over the kingdom. These dungeons lead to mysterious places filled with vicious and deadly beasts but were also filled with objects that had been enchanted with magic.

It could be something like enchanted armour or something crazy like a sword that could summon lightning. Or so I had heard. Once the nobles began to go crazy over the artefacts, Ashwood Academy became more and more popular with people hoping to learn magic so they could enter these dungeons and make some money.

You could get into the academy by other means though like if you signed up for a minimum duty of twenty years' service as a city guard or if you were referred on through a scholars program.

"The dungeons have been appearing more and more lately. We had to clear a double dungeon last week," Kain sighed and Mark looked at him in awe.

After the popularity of these dungeons began to rise, guilds began to form to conquer them. Kain was the leader of one of the top three guilds in the kingdom, the Ruby Guild. His was the first guild to form in the whole of the Ghislana Kingdom and had the most experienced members. The elite ten is what they liked to call his guild as it was made up of the top magic swordsmen, battle mages and healers.

The nobles never seemed to mention them much though as the Ruby Guild was made up of commoners.

"You were lucky the healer was able to fix your leg in time

after the last dungeon," I huffed as I remembered the bright red marks on Kain's leg as he arrived home last Wednesday. One of the creatures that was in the dungeons had torn his leg to ribbons but he wouldn't talk about it. Kain didn't like talking about anything that happened inside the dungeons, only that it was necessary to make money and feed hungry mouths.

"It will take more than a busted leg to keep me down," Kain beamed and I rolled my eyes.

"Well, just you wait, *old man*," I said and Kain narrowed his eyes at me. "By the time I'm through Ashwood Academy and in those dungeons, I'll be claiming all the artefacts before anyone else. You might even be able to retire." I smiled sweetly at Kain who looked like he wanted to throttle me. Mark stifled a laugh as he looked between the two of us.

"Well, she certainly has your fiery attitude," Mark chuckled. "She's definitely your daughter." My body froze and I looked up at Kain. Many people had mistaken me as his daughter from the sheer amount of time we spent together – I never knew how to respond.

"Yeah, I think she's a little *too much* like me," Kain chuckled and patted me on the head and my body relaxed. Soot pecked at Kain's hand and he let out a curse whilst I laughed.

Maybe it was because I grew up around Kain and Derrick and the rest of the guild that my persona and attitude became shaped by them. They were definitely a bad influence.

"Kain! Brat!" Derrick called for us across the arena. "The guild is waiting for us at the tavern."

"I told you to get rid of that damn bird!" Kain scowled as he slung his arm around my shoulders and I let him half drag me away causing Soot to squawk in anger and launch into the sky. There wasn't anything that would keep Soot from me, Kain knew I loved the raven but it didn't stop him from trying to smack Soot whenever it would peck at him or eat his food. I chuckled to myself the whole way to the tavern as I thought over all the bickering they did.

I wonder what everyone would think if they knew the Ruby Guild master often fought with a bird...that thought alone had me almost doubling over with laughter.

"What's with all the excited faces?" Kain asked as he sunk down in his usual seat at the head of one of the taverns rickety tables.

Derrick sat on the bench beside him and as I was about to take my usual seat opposite them, two hands encircled my waist and I was yanked backwards.

"Stop getting so big! You're making me feel so old," a familiar female voice whined in my ear. Victoria, or Vikki as she preferred now, cuddled me on her lap.

When Kain had first introduced me to his guild, it was only made up of him, Derrick, Vikki and Oryan. Kain and Derrick were the magic swordsmen who would deliver and take the brunt of whoever or *whatever* attacked them in the dungeons. Oryan was a battle mage who would use ranged magic formation attacks and Vikki would be there to heal them if they got hurt.

Vikki was one of the first to graduate the academy like Kain and had instantly taken a liking to me whenever we first met. She often told me that I had seemed like a stray kitten brought in by Kain and that she found me cute and scrappy.

"Can't...breathe..." I choked against Vikki's too tight hug and no one noticed it. Vikki's long brown curls hung down over my face like a curtain and the smell of lavender soap filled my nostrils.

"I think you may be cutting off her airways, Vikki," chuckled another familiar voice. Benji was another battle mage who had joined last year and was one of the nicer, more civilised guild members.

"Oh, she's fine!" Vikki tutted but released her grip on me anyway. I gulped down greedy breaths as Vikki continued to stroke my head. Sometimes I wondered if she really did see me like a real cat.

"Look what the palace sent out today," another guild member called Jamie said as he slid a flyer onto the table. Jamie was a magic swordsman who had graduated the same time as Benji but their personalities couldn't have been more different. Whilst Benji acted like a borderline noble, Jamie had an even more foul mouth than Derrick did.

"What's this?" I asked as I grabbed the flyer up and sank back into Vikki's grasp, not admitting out loud that her petting my head *felt good.* I focused on the jumble of letters on the page and focused on the words, remembering the years that Vikki and Netta had taught me to read and write along with Luca and Brendan.

"A once in a lifetime contest is to be held in the Grand Palace Arena. All registered guilds are to forward a non-magic challenger to compete in a winner takes all contest. The winner will be given a fully paid entrance fee to the Ashwood Academy and will also win 50 gold pieces."

I looked around the table and everyone had gone quiet as they listened. A non-magic person was someone who hadn't awoken their magic yet, which made sense. Anyone who had already awoken their powers could have only done so at Ashwood Academy.

"People of the public can view this event by purchasing their tickets from the Vendor in the city square in both the Noble and the Commoner District." Of course, they only added our district to make sure there was no complaints and also because they knew only a few people in the commoners district would be able to afford a ticket.

"Free admission to the Ashwood Academy *and* 50 gold pieces?" Kain said and the table turned to him. "Seems a little too good to be true."

"Put me forward," I said quickly and stood up to look at Kain. My heart thundered in my chest as I thought of winning the prize. This was just the push I needed to start off my swordsmanship career.

"I turn nineteen soon and was going to apply for the academy at the end of the year anyway! This is the perfect chance to get in for free! And fill my pockets while we're at it," I said and Kain lifted an eyebrow. "*Our* pockets, I mean," I corrected with a sweet smile that earned a chuckle from Oryan who sat beside Jamie.

"You will be going up against nobles and trained fighters, Nevara. This will be a chance for the winning guild to gain a lot of attention and influence," Kain said grimly and the table focused their eyes on me, even Vikki stilled behind me. I didn't back down.

"I won't let you down," I said confidently as I stared unblinkingly at Kain and then looked at the rest of the table. Some of the guild members weren't here but I would track them down on whatever errand they were doing and make them agree to it also. "I've been training for this kind of thing for years, you know I can do it."

Kain placed his hands under his chin as he stared at me, his eyes looking at me as if he were still seeing that dirt ridden, too thin child that I had been when we first met.

"I believe in you, brat," Derrick chuckled and Kain's eyes widened slightly as if he now saw me and the determination that I knew burned in my eyes.

I'm not that little thin homeless girl anymore, I willed him to see it.

"Anyone object to putting her forward?" Kain asked then, but the table remained quiet.

Throughout these five years I had trained with each and every member of this guild. I had sparred with the elite ten and learned the moves and techniques from each of them and honed all of their unique fighting skills into my own. They knew as well as I did that I was the only one they could find that would stand a chance against the other competitors.

"Let the brat fight!" Derrick roared as he raised his ale up into the air and the tavern exploded into sound. One by one the guild members lifted their mugs into the air and they all focused their eyes on me.

"Let the brat fight! Let the brat fight! Let the brat fight!" They chanted and I tipped my head back and laughed, my blood singing with the sound.

"The other guild members who aren't here would have agreed to this but it doesn't matter anyway because they would have been outvoted even if they didn't," Kain chuckled and reached over to put a hand on my shoulder and squeeze it. "Make us proud," he said and my heart swelled.

I would do everything in my power to win and put the Ruby Guild into the spotlight. I would make Kain and the rest of them proud and not let them regret their decision.

"You're putting Nevara forward?" Luca looked up from his book at the dinner table with wide honey-coloured eyes.

"Well obviously! Who else would they have put forward? She's the best choice," Brendan scoffed and I rolled my eyes at them. Since growing up, Luca had taken an intense liking to books. All day long his head would be buried inside one. History, fiction and all sorts of random genres had found home in Luca's bedroom.

Since Kain and his guild had been making more and more money from selling the artefacts they got from the dungeons, we were able to rebuild our home. The wooden walls were now made from bricks and the rooms were made bigger. We were even able to replace all of the old furniture with new and more modern items that had seemed way too fancy for my liking. I tended to keep away from the expensive display cabinet in the dining room in case I got too close and knocked it over.

I didn't mind what kind of furniture I had around me, as long as it wasn't broken then it would be fine. After all, there was once a time when recycled blankets was all I had to call home.

"I heard that the Sapphire Guild were putting forward a brute of a boy from the Noble District," Netta said quietly and I swallowed a forkful of chicken.

"It doesn't matter who they put forward," I shrugged and chugged down my cup of milk. I cocked my head as I read the title of Luca's book. *How yeast works and how it's made.* Yeast? As in bread making? I blinked as I read the title again.

"It's truly fascinating." Luca followed my line of sight. "You see, when the yeast..." Brendan groaned dramatically and Luca frowned at his outburst.

"No one cares," Brendan moaned and Netta smacked the back of his head lightly. "What? It's true! I don't want to learn about *yeast!* I want to know who else our brave sister will be up against."

"Well, it's not till the end of next month so most of the other guilds haven't chosen yet," Kain said after gulping down his mug of ale. "No doubt whoever is chosen will all be put through intense training from now until the contest."

"What about me? Do you have some ultimate training regime for me to follow?" I asked as I placed my fork on my empty plate and leaned back.

I rubbed the top of Luca's head and he leaned into me

slightly. The boys had grown up and become young men, but to me they were still those over excited little boys that used to follow me around everywhere like little puppies.

"I've left that up to Derrick," Kain said and my stomach twisted.

"*Derrick?*" I choked and I felt my eyes go wide. "That man is going to have me running laps with stones strapped to my body!"

"Come on, he only made you do that once," Kain chuckled and Netta shot him an unamused look and his laughter halted. "He was pretty serious about this Nevara. He asked me as soon as you left the tavern if he could train you until the contest."

I thought about Derrick and how he disliked me intensely in the beginning but soon warmed up to me when I showed him how serious I was about learning to fight. He was a magic swordsman but was the best at hand-to-hand combat and had trained me well throughout the years.

"I suppose…" I started and then sighed. "I suppose it's fine then if you agree with it." I was hardly in a position to argue when they were allowing me to fight in this contest with their guild name on the line.

"Good." Kain beamed a smile at me and the hairs rose on my neck. It felt as if I had just agreed to my death. "Because you are to meet him before dawn tomorrow."

CHAPTER 6

$\mathcal{I}$ looked down at the basket filled with different shaped rocks and then back up to Derrick's smirking face and blinked.

"You're not serious, are you?" I asked as I rubbed my tired eyes, hoping that this was all a bad dream and that I would wake up soon.

"Oh, I'm deadly serious," Derrick said as he stretched his arms above his head. "You're going to strap this basket to your back and we're going to climb the Sky Kissed mountain."

I stared at him again. This was definitely a dream – no, this was a *nightmare*.

The Sky Kissed mountain was located just outside of Ghislane and was called as much because it was that huge it really did look like it kissed the sky. It didn't actually reach the sky though. Thankfully.

"I'm going back to bed," I grumbled and turned on my heel to begin walking back to the city. It had taken around an hour to get here and the sky was bursting with orange and golden hues as the sun began to rise.

"Brat," Derrick called out and I stopped. "You've pretty much mastered all the moves and skills that we can teach you, but what you lack is power and stamina. You're going to have to fight round after round at this contest and have to be at your best at the beginning of each one."

"Well…" I began to bite my bottom lip as I thought on what he was saying, annoyed at the truth in his words.

"Doing this will not only increase your stamina and endurance but will also increase your strength. When you land those sword strikes in the contest, you're going to need a lot of strength to knock those nobles on their asses," Derrick said and I could hear the smirk in his voice, knowing that he was getting through to me.

It was true that I had pretty much honed my skills to be able to perform them without much thought, but he was right in saying I lacked stamina and strength. I hated that he had singled out my flaws and found a way to improve them.

"I'll even buy you stew at the tavern when we're done," Derrick added and my body froze.

Damn, he got me.

"And one of Kiera's pastries," I bartered and after a moment of silence I felt his hand clamp down on my shoulder.

"Alright, brat. You got yourself a deal," Derrick chuckled and began to strap the basket of rocks onto my back. When he first let go, I seriously thought I was going to topple backwards from the weight but I gritted my teeth and forced my body to stand straight. I wasn't a weak little girl anymore.

I looked up to where the peak of the mountain lay and took a deep breath in. *I can do this.* I affirmed in my head and began my trek. I kept my focus on the stew I would receive after this – that was more than enough encouragement to keep going.

~

THE FIRST LEG of the hike up the mountain was fine. I distributed the weight of the rocks evenly and was able to navigate through the thickening forestry with ease. Until, of course, the incline increased dramatically.

I grunted as I had to haul myself up a grassy ledge, my fingers grasping bundles of roots and stems of scattered plants. Sweat covered every inch of my body and my breaths came out in ragged gasps.

I knew this was going to be difficult but I had thought my body had strength to at least get me to the top.

As embarrassing as it was to admit, I knew I wasn't even a quarter of the way there yet and I was ready to wave the white flag of surrender. I hadn't pushed my body this hard in a long time, it felt good to feel the strain in my muscles again.

"It took me six months of trying before I could reach the top without my mana to support me," Derrick said as I finally collapsed onto my knees and fell onto my side. My hair stuck to my sweaty face and cool air burned into my lungs. "But you have less than two months to do it. If you can reach the top in that time then there is no question about you winning the contest."

Two months. I had two months of waking up before dawn and making this trek with my basket of rocks. The thought of it made me want to tie the basket of rocks around Derrick and push him off the side of the mountain.

"Do I…" I sucked in a jagged breath. "Do I still get stew and pastries?" I asked and Derrick tipped his head back and barked out a laugh.

"Yes, brat, you can still have your food," he said and bent down to sling the basket of rocks over one shoulder and lifted me up and over the other.

It was times like this that I was surprised by the strength

of one of the Ruby Guild members. When I sparred or hung around with them, they were always laid back or not using their abilities to the fullest – they knew they would most likely kill me if they did.

Seeing Derrick lift the basket of rocks like they were a basket of feathers made me do a double take. Would I truly become strong like that someday? I really hoped so.

DAYS PASSED and I rarely got past the spot on the mountain where I had failed before.

Weeks passed and I was able to clear a few steep slopes after a quarter of the way there.

A month passed and I was just under halfway there.

"I'm truly…" I gasped out. "Going to die this time." My body was on fire, each muscle feeling as if it was being stretched and split. I unclasped the rock basket and let it drop behind me with a thud and I fell on shaky legs, cringing at the way my sweat stuck my clothes to my body in a horrid and uncomfortable way.

"Your body is close to breaking point each day, yet you're able to get up again the next morning and push yourself all over again." Derrick handed me the water canteen, his face a mixture of curiosity and was that…jealousy?

"My body heals fast," I grunted out after gulping down the water. It was true, my body had always healed faster than others. Only on a rare occasion would I feel the painful muscle exhaustion that would come after a rough day of training and exercise.

Even after being battered and training to the point of collapsing, I would be back the next day, ready to do it all over again.

"Well, that's obvious," he huffed and I scoffed at his pouty face as I laid back down on the grassy ledge.

It was quiet for a moment and all I could hear was the slight whistling of the wind through the trees that littered the mountain.

Summer was truly here now as I felt the sun's heat warm my face.

After a moment I felt my heartbeat return to a normal rhythm; my lungs finally didn't feel like they were about to explode anymore.

"That mark still gives me the creeps," Derrick muttered and I looked down to see the lace of my shirt had come loose, exposing the old magic formation that lined the centre of my chest. A flash of bright red eyes hidden beneath a cloak suddenly rippled through my mind. I clenched my hands, forcing my mind to clear the image.

Soot squawked from above and I was surprised that he followed me this far outside the city. How many times had Soot followed me and I hadn't realised?

"It's harmless," I sighed as I sat up, grimacing at my throbbing limbs. "To be honest, when I try and recall the man who gave me it now…I can't remember him very well at all." And it was true. Beyond the bright red eyes and the fact that he was the one that branded the mark on my chest…all other memories of that day had become blurred.

It was as if I was looking through a dirty window and could only see a mess of outlines and shapes.

"Well, it happened before Kain and I met you," Derrick said and scratched at his chin. "But something about that formation isn't right. In all my time at the academy and in the dungeons, I've never seen one as detailed as that."

"Maybe once I get my free admission into the academy, the Archmages will be able to decipher it," I said smugly and he rolled his eyes.

The Archmages were the ones who controlled the academy under the King's order. Some of them were the first ever people to awaken their magic and had studied and mastered it to a point where their power was unrivalled. Even Kain and his guild didn't stand a chance against the power and knowledge they held. They pretty much acted as the peace keepers of the guilds.

"So, you're that sure you're going to win this contest, eh? I told you, you will only be sure to win if you reach the top. You've only got less than a month to go and you're only halfway there." He raised an eyebrow and flicked the end of my nose. I chuckled as I swatted at his hands but an unease settled in my stomach. It was the same feeling I always got whenever I thought on the branded formation on my chest.

Even though nothing had ever come of it, it had always felt as if it was - asleep. Dormant. Until the right conditions triggered it to awaken and that thought terrified me.

"Come on, we'll train at the arena for a little longer then I'll buy you some stew," Derrick said and helped me to stand up.

All thoughts faded as we made our way back down the mountain and I shook my head. The only thing I had time to focus on now was the contest and how I would definitely win it.

CHAPTER 7

*L*uca and Brendan were sat with Kiera and Netta in the Tavern. The place was unusually quiet as they waited for the shops to close and for the local patrons to come and drown their sorrows after a long day of working.

"Goodness, you're filthy!" Netta's eyes widened as she took in my sweat and dirt ridden appearance. "Go and get yourself cleaned up and I'll take you to trade square before the shops close to get you some new clothes." Netta had been pestering me constantly to get some new clothes other than the ones that Kain had once given me when we first met.

Over the years my clothes had gone through many repairs and washes and had definitely seen better days, but they were precious to me. They were the first gift that Kain had ever given me. My first set of clothes after the ones my birth mother had provided for me.

"I think you should listen to Netta," Derrick muttered as he sank down on the bench beside Brendan, ruffling his cropped blonde hair. "If you enter the contest in those clothes, they'll laugh you right out the doors of the arena."

I looked down at the clothes with a grimace. The shirt was a little too short as it ended just above my belly button. My breeches were a little too snug as they stretched against my thighs and ended a little too high above my ankles. I didn't even need to look at my boots to feel the many holes and scuffs that littered them.

"Ugh!" I groaned as I sat down on the bench. "Fine. Fine! But I'm not leaving until after my stew," I huffed as Netta's face lit up.

"You'll do it? Get new clothes?" She asked as if not sure she heard me correctly.

"Yes," I muttered quietly. Derrick smirked as he asked Kiera for two stews. She gave me a wink as she left, casting a smile to Netta.

Kiera and Netta had grown close over the years of working together and they became like sisters to one another. If anything went wrong, we could always count on Kiera. She had so many connections through owning a tavern that she could sort any problem or find anything you needed. She was amazing.

"I'll go get my coat," Netta said and I grunted in response, already feeling the energy draining from me. I hated spending money, *especially* on myself. This was going to be awful.

"LOOK AT THESE BEAUTIFUL DRESSES. Look at that lace!" Netta's face was pretty much pressed up against the glass of a dress shop in the trade square and I rolled my eyes at her.

The dress shop inside sat empty and I wondered if it ever made money. Commoners were too busy buying food for themselves and their family to even think about buying a fancy dress.

"Why in the world would I need a dress?" I asked incredulously and she pouted.

The shops were about to close and the setting sun warmed the back of my head. People milled around, looking in windows and chatting in groups and there was a nice kind of ambience in the air.

The summer was always the easiest time in the Commoners District as no one had to worry about frozen crops or trying to warm themselves when the sun set.

"Where is the armoury again?" I squinted as I searched the different shop fronts and Netta sighed as she linked her arm in mine.

"Over here," She pulled me towards the side of the trade square where a huge black bordered shop lay tucked in one of the side streets.

"Welcome!" An elderly man smiled from behind the counter in the back and my breath caught in my throat as I looked around the store.

I had been in here a few times when Kain or the other guild members needed their armour repaired or replaced and each time I felt the same. Overwhelmed.

The floor and the walls were stacked with rows and rows of different armour. There was heavy iron to sleek tanned leather and I never knew where to even begin to look. If this was only a commoners armoury, then what did the nobles one look like?

"Are you looking for anything in particular?" The man asked as he rounded the counter and I looked helplessly at him.

Understanding shone in his eyes and he smiled kindly at me, motioning me with a wrinkled hand to follow him. He lead us over to a corner of the shop where a few racks of darker leather armour rested in neat rows.

"I can tell from your build that you'll need something

close fitting and easy to move in. You're training to be a magic swordsman, yes?" He asked and narrowed his eyes at me. Despite his age, his eyes were clear and piercing, as if he could see right into my mind and see everything that I was and what I hoped to be.

"Yes," I breathed, a little taken aback. "How did you know?"

"I've been running this shop long before magic was discovered and have seen all different kinds of people."

"Different builds mean different professions and my eyes can tell what someone is from even the way they hold their stance," he chuckled and I looked down at myself, unable to see what his keen eyes could.

He shuffled along and pulled out a set of folded black leather clothes. He held up the chest piece and I felt my mouth drop open.

It was almost corset like in shape, bones holding its form with strong looking cord that would tie down the sides. The front of the breast pads was embossed with lines and a small crescent moon shape lay in between them, a silver detailed buckle just underneath.

A type of harness was added on the top with a smoky opal embedded in the middle and I had to admit that it was the most beautiful piece of armour I had ever seen. It was so unique and stunning that I couldn't stop myself from reaching out and brushing my fingers over the soft leather.

"Although it is armour, it's also an artefact that was found in a dungeon. An Archmage confirmed it has a slight elemental resistance and the leather is tough. Although we don't know what animal or being that the hide is from, it's near impenetrable with normal swords and arrows," the man said and I dropped my hands after a moment.

"All of that sounds amazing, but it also sounds expensive,"

I pointed out through tight lips and amusement lit up the man's eyes.

"I have bought and sold many magical armours since magic was discovered but I have always kept this set aside. Aside from the fact that it's female and there aren't many female swordsmen, it's also rare and unique. I've never came across anything like it so I guess I was selfish in a way when I didn't show it to anyone," he sighed and ran a wrinkled hand over the leather.

"Then why show it to me?" I asked arching an eyebrow because I couldn't tell if the man was sincere or just an amazing salesman.

"It's your eyes." He smiled and held up the armour again and pointed to the smoky silver opal stone that lay on the harness and then pointed to my eyes. "They hold as much power and uniqueness as I see in this stone," he said and I stared at him. My eyes *were* the same colour as the stone but was that really why he showed me this armour set?

I wanted to roll my eyes at his sales tactics but resisted. I looked to Netta who had remained quiet during the conversation but I noticed that she too looked captivated by the beautiful armour.

"How much?" I asked after a moment of deliberation and my stomach clenched in anticipation.

I had saved a few hundred silvers over the years from birthdays and winter celebrations but I had given the majority of my money to the people who still had to live in the alley. I had also made a deal with Kiera that if I cleaned the tavern before bed every night, she would give the leftover food and stale bread to the homeless people. She agreed of course, saying I didn't need to work for it but I did it anyway.

"In my eyes, it's priceless," he sighed and I clenched my hands at my sides. "But for you I'm willing to part with this treasure for ten gold pieces."

My mouth fell open. Ten gold pieces. That was more than the admission to Ashwood. More money than it would take to feed me for years. I knew the price for magical artefacts had risen but this was just ridiculous.

"No thanks." I ground my teeth as the man lowered the leathers, his eyes glittering with an unknown emotion. "Show me something I can afford. No artefacts." He should have known from the clothes I wore that I had no way near enough money for something like that. Was he trying to humiliate me?

"Wait," Netta said and I turned to her. "I've been saving some money since you saved me and the boys." Netta took a deep breath in. "Can you do it for eight gold pieces instead?"

"Netta, no!" I began to argue, appalled at the thought of Netta paying that much for me.

"This armour was made for you, girl." The man pointed out stubbornly and nodded to Netta. "I'm only accepting because I wouldn't want to see this on anyone else."

"Please let me do this for you," Netta begged and tears threatened in her eyes.

Since Netta moved in with Kain and fell in love with him, she had always thanked me over and over again for bringing us all together. I always told her not to thank me because they were my family now, I didn't need thanks for helping my family. It was all due to Kain anyway, not me.

"Netta…" I began but she clenched onto my arms, tears sliding down her face. "Fine! But I will pay you back when I win the contest." I scowled and she smiled brightly.

"You will do no such thing – now go try it on!" Netta pushed me towards the small changing room at the back of the shop and despite myself I let out a giggle. I was excited to see what the armour looked like and whether it would even fit me properly.

The man handed me the soft leather armour, a new white undershirt and a pair of black boots to match.

Whilst they went to the counter to talk about payment, I peeled off the older clothes Kain had given me and folded them neatly on the floor. They had served me well and I would pass them onto the people in the alley, knowing that they would find a new home there.

The new leather slid over my skin and after fumbling with the buckles and the cords at the sides, I finally managed to secure the chest piece. I tightened the cord of the trousers and then tied the laces of my boots.

Comfortable. That was the first feeling that came to mind. The armour fitted me like a glove, hugging and showing off my defined and well-trained muscles. I lifted my leg up into a kick and stretched my arms up and to the sides. It was flexible and breathable, perfect for training and fighting.

I finally looked up to the large mirror that covered the back wall of the changing room and froze. My days were filled with training and being busy so I never really looked at myself in a mirror over the last few years. Every day I would wake up, wash and tie my long hair back and leave. I had never even thought to look in the mirror before I left, not caring for my appearance.

"Is that me?" I asked the silence and lifted a hand to the mirror. Bright silvery eyes stared back and they indeed did match the stone that was now secure around my neck. My sun-kissed face – that had beamed from years of training outside in the heat – was now complimented by the darkness of the leather. The white shirt sleeves hung on my shoulders and left my arms free and easy to move – to strike.

Even though my arms were exposed to threat, I preferred not being suffocated in leather. If I needed more protection for the contest I could always borrow some arm braces from Kain.

I smoothed out a few of the loose black curls away from my face and looked at my reflection again. For the first time I actually thought I looked like a woman, not a snotty brat who lived on the streets. That girl would always be inside me…but now, I was strong. Powerful. Pretty in a 'could beat you up if needed' kind of way.

"Nevara! Let me see!" I heard Netta call and with one last look in the mirror I grabbed my old clothes and left.

Netta put her hands to her mouth and her eyes filled again.

"You look stunning," she whispered and my face flushed as she looked me up and down.

"Thank you again for this, Netta." I smiled and didn't mention the part of paying her back again because I didn't want to sour the mood.

"I told you that armour was made for you." The old man smiled, his eyes crinkling with emotion.

"You're too good of a salesman, old man," I smirked and Netta gasped.

"Nevara, don't be so rude!" Netta scolded but the man just tipped back his head and laughed.

"This young lady here was telling me you're entering the contest?" The man focused on me again, amusement still burning in his eyes.

"That's right," I said raising an eyebrow, wondering where he was going with this.

"I can't wait to see that armour in action. I'll be rooting for you, girl," he said and smiled kindly. Despite myself I smiled back at him. I was excited now, thankful to Netta for making me buy some new armour. It made me feel like I finally could be a part of the Ruby Guild. Like a proper magic swordsman.

Even as I fell asleep that night, I kept seeing myself in the armour again and again. I was close now. Closer than I had ever been before to becoming a magic swordsman, only the contest was left and I would leave no room for defeat.

I *will* win.

CHAPTER 8

I continued to get up every day before dawn and attempted to climb the mountain. Derrick would meet me there each time, pushing and motivating me to go further and further.

"This is the last day before the contest," Derrick said as we stood at the bottom of the mountain, the area now familiar. "You haven't been able to reach the top yet. Do you think you can do it today?"

My teeth ground together as I looked up and up at the mountain. After getting my new armour, I had indeed found it easier to scale the mountain. The leather had become like a second skin now, not interfering with my training at all. In fact, I would say it was improving how I was progressing.

"I have to do it today." I scowled in frustration as I yanked my hair back into a braid. I had run out of time. Between climbing the mountain in the morning and sparring in the afternoon, I had trained as much as I could.

But I still couldn't get to the top of the damn thing.

I would get around three quarters of the way there before my body fell limp and weak.

"Let's go," I said before I could doubt myself anymore.

The air was crisp and cool as the sun began to rise above the horizon. Summer was coming to an end now and autumn was beginning to show its head.

I loved seeing the leaves turn to brown and orange, the satisfying crunch they made when I would run through them. I remember a few years ago, Brendan, Luca and I had scraped together a huge mound of leaves and took turns diving into it. Netta wasn't impressed but we had hours of fun before Kain came home and was made to clean it up.

We reached the first steep grassy ledge and I hauled myself up it – a lot more easily than when I had done this the first time almost two months ago. The rocks clattered in the basket on my back but I was steady enough on my feet.

I carried on up the mountain, navigating through the now familiar trees and foliage.

A large boulder came into view, marking the halfway point and I felt excitement and nervousness course through my body. The tell-tale signs of exhaustion and muscle ache were beginning to creep in but I tried my best to ignored it.

"Keep up the pace, brat," Derrick ordered from behind me and I put a thumbs up in the air to which he laughed at.

I DIDN'T KNOW how much time had passed since we started our ascent but the sun was now creeping it's way higher into the sky. The air was getting thinner and I found myself gasping breaths into my now burning lungs. My legs ached and trembled underneath me and my shoulders were searing from the straps of the basket.

"Three quarters of the way, this is the furthest you've ever gotten," Derrick said and I began to slow down. My body threatening to collapse with each step. "Come on brat, I know you can push yourself more than this. You're far too stubborn to admit defeat on the last day."

Derrick's words ran through my head and I looked up at him as he walked beside me. The sun contrasted the dark swirls of the tattoo on the side of his shaved head and I remembered how I had thought he looked scary when I first met him.

His brown eyes were filled with concern as he watched me, wondering if I was about to collapse. He had come every day with me to this mountain without fail, he was as determined to see me complete this training as much as I was.

Knowing that spurred something deep inside of me, feeling how much he wanted me to win tomorrow filled me with determination because I knew that he didn't want me to win just to make the guild look good, he wanted me to win for *myself.*

I gritted my teeth and tried my best to ignore the burning feeling from all over my body. I gripped the vines on top of a grassy slope and dragged myself up, almost slipping but regaining my feet at the last minute.

"Look up, brat," Derrick called and with a gasp, I did. Up ahead the dense trees seemed to thin out and another grassy ledge jutted out of the earth but beyond that there was nothing but a rocky slope and a bright clear sky. It was the top of the mountain.

As I took another step forward my legs buckled beneath me and I crumpled to the floor, the basket of rocks crashing against my back. I let out a cry as blinding pain wracked my body from the sheer weight of them.

"Nevara!" I heard Derrick call and he began to help me up.

"No!" I gasped pushing weakly at his hands and he looked confused. "I...can do...this," I gasped out and tried to stand on my trembling legs. He took a step back but kept his arms out as if to catch me should I fall again.

After a few attempts, I was finally able to stand. The weight of the rocks still threatening to pull me backwards.

"You have come far enough, Nevara. This is practically the top so we can just call it quits now," Derrick ordered and I knew if he called me by my name and not *brat,* then he was definitely worried.

I grunted as I carried on, grabbing the thinning trees and plants to push myself forward until I finally got beneath the last ledge I had to climb.

The last obstacle before completing my training loomed over me and I wiped at the hot sweat running down my face. My muscles screamed as I grabbed hold of the roots jutting out the side of the dirt wall and lifted myself off the ground. I let out a sob as my feet dug into the earth of the wall, the pain in my body making my vision darken.

"Nevara, stop!" Derrick shouted worriedly from behind me but I couldn't stop now. I was so close, so damn close! I grabbed on to the patches of grass on top of the ledge and took a ragged breath. I could do this... *I could do this!* With a yell, I pulled myself up and over the ledge and landed with a thud on top of the soft earth that covered the peak. Cold air hit my face and it felt amazing against my burning skin.

I quickly pulled the basket of rocks off and crawled to the side of the peak and my breath caught in my throat. I could see everything for miles and miles.

Ghislane City covered the whole side to my right, stretching on and on in a wash of red brick stone and dark grey roofing. The palace stood proudly at the back, a mix of cream turrets and gold tipped towers; to the other side of the city was the open space of sprawling grassy plains littered with meandering rivers and towns that I didn't even know existed. With this view I wondered just howbig the Kingdom of Ghislana was. Even in the far distance I could see where the old port sat and was surprised to see a small merchant ship there.

I stared even further into the distance of the ocean that surrounded Ghislana and for a moment I let myself wonder about all of the other kingdoms I knew lay out there. What were they like? Did they have segregation and people suffering like there was in this kingdom? Did any of them even remember our kingdom?

"You are reckless," Derrick grunted from behind me and I shot him the biggest smile I could muster which he snorted at. "You did it, brat."

I did it.

A slightly hysterical giggle escaped from my throat at the same moment my legs and arms gave way beneath me and my vision turned black. The only thing I remembered before darkness engulfed me was the sound of a ravens caw.

"THE LANDS of the natural elements are where the Fae made their home. Cities for each element surrounded the main city Viridia. These cities made up the Kingdom of Arboria and was home to many types of fae including Undines, Seraphs..." My eyes opened slightly to find Luca cross legged on a stool beside my bed reading from one of his many books.

"Luca," I croaked and was surprised at how weak my voice sounded. I tried to sit up but let out a yelp as my body ached and burned at the attempt. Luca's eyes widened as he set down the book and pushed me back down onto the bed.

"Don't move," Luca commanded quietly and wrung a damp cloth from the bowl of water beside the bed, placing it on my forehead. The cooling sensation settled me instantly and I relaxed.

"How long have I been out?" I asked as the earlier events came flooding back to me.

"A few hours," Luca sighed and tucked his long blonde hair behind his ear. "Derrick was so angry when he carried you into the house over his shoulder." He paled slightly. Derrick was scary when he was in a good mood so he must have been terrifying in a bad mood. Derrick rarely got angry so I'm glad that I have yet to see it.

"Vikki has been healing you all afternoon. She only just left a moment ago after Kain convinced her to go," Luca said as he sat back down, his eyes were lined with dark rings from the countless nights I knew he stayed awake reading the stacks of books that littered his room. "He's angry at you too," he added and I let out a sigh, feeling that a telling off was in my near future.

"They have no reason to be angry and there was no need for Vikki to heal me," I mumbled and looked up at the cream-coloured ceiling.

In Ashwood Academy, the last class you could enter was to be a scholar. Scholars were to study everything they could about magic and how to use and improve it. They also studied deep into the materials and artefacts from dungeons and used them to create new things, such as a new product that was introduced lately called a healing elixir. Whilst there was a diluted version that Vikki must have given me to cure bruises, ache and fatigue there also whispers of a stronger version which was rumoured to cure any disease known to man, even bringing someone back from the brink of death. But, even if something like that did exist, I could only dream at how much gold it would cost.

"I know you heal fast, but you were in such a terrible shape when Derrick half dragged you through the door,"

Luca's voice trembled as he slipped his hand in mine. I gave a small tug and he crawled in the bed beside me, careful not to lean too heavily on my aching body.

Whilst Brendan and Luca were only a year younger than me, Luca was still as close and clingy to me like he had been when we were younger. Brendan on the other hand was a whirlwind of energy that was always out causing havoc in the city.

I brushed my fingers through Luca's soft hair and hummed a tune I had heard from the tavern one night.

"Be safe tomorrow, Nevara," Luca said quietly and my fingers stilled. "I know you're strong but the nobles…" He trailed off and let out a sigh. "I've read enough history records to know the nobles will do everything in their power to not let a woman from a poor background win something that the kingdom will see and acknowledge. Especially when they want to win it for themselves."

I was quiet for a moment as I pondered his words. I had been thinking the same thing, in fact I think just about everyone from the guild was thinking it. But in the end, the nobles weren't going to have any choice but to acknowledge me and my strength. A strength that I had been building day after day for years to attain, I wasn't going to hide it away now.

"Don't worry, I will be careful," I said quietly. "And I'll get into the academy for free, that means you can have the money I saved and get into the scholar class next year." Luca stilled beside me and looked up, his bright honeyed eyes burning as they searched my face to see if I was joking.

"You mean it?" He breathed and I smiled.

"Imagine what kind of library they have in the academy," I whispered and a grin lit up his face. "Better books than ones on *how yeast works.*" I wrinkled my nose and then we both chuckled at each other.

"Well, it seems you're doing much better." I heard Kain at the doorway and my smile faded as he narrowed his eyes on me.

He came to stand at the other side of the bed, his large muscular arms crossing his chest as he frowned down at me.

"I climbed the whole mountain," I said with a toothy grin and his lips twitched but stayed frowning.

Damn, he was angry.

He looked to where Luca was clutched to my side and his face softened slightly. After a moment of heavy silence, he finally let out a sigh and slumped down onto the bed which groaned under his weight.

"You could have really hurt yourself," he said quietly and I gulped at his disappointed tone.

"I know my limits, Kain," I sighed. "I may have gone too far this time but with the contest tomorrow, I didn't have a choice."

"It's because of the contest that you should have been more careful!" He yelled and then when Luca flinched, he pinched the bridge of his nose as he tried to calm himself. "What would have happened if you didn't recover enough before tomorrow? Or if you permanently hurt your body?" Kain asked in a more level voice.

"You know I heal fast," I argued as I began to smooth Luca's hair again. "I would have been fine for tomorrow."

"But what if you hadn't?" Kain pressed and I could tell it was taking all his strength not to yell again. "You need to remember that it is also the guild you are representing tomorrow, not just yourself. If you weren't in good enough health then our guild wouldn't have been able to participate." I froze. Dread pooled in my stomach as his words sunk in. He had trusted me when I had begged him to let me represent the guild, he had *trusted* me to be the one to go forward and win, not just for myself but for the fame that would befall the guild.

Even though I thought I knew my own limits I was being selfish when I pushed myself on the mountain. What if I had somehow managed to damage an arm or a leg? My future as a swordsman would be delayed and all the work I had put in would be useless.

"You're right," I said after a moment and Kain looked at me as if I had grown another head. "I was being selfish and didn't put the guild first." He searched my face and after a minute he pulled both me and Luca into his huge arms.

"You will always come first, not the guild you silly girl," he said softly and I gave him a small chuckle. We were quiet for a moment and I savoured the warmth coming from Kain's chest, this was the kind of hug I had been envious of when I used to see other kids from the city being held by their fathers. I closed my eyes and for a moment I just pretended. I pretended that Kain had always been my father, that I had never been homeless and this was how it always was.

"Are you feeling well enough to get up?" Kain asked and I was brought back to reality. I looked out of my bedroom window to see the pitch-black sky and cringed at how long I must have been unconscious for.

"Where do we need to go?" I asked. Where would he need me to go in the middle of the night?

A devious smile lit up Kain's face as he pulled us up from the bed and both him and Luca linked arms with me as they helped me walk. My body was already healing itself fast and I could easily walk myself but I didn't tell them that.

"There's something you need to see," Kain said and his smile grew bigger and I didn't know whether to be excited or scared as we left the house and walked out and into the night.

Whatever it was, I hoped it included food.

The chill in the air confirmed autumn was well and truly almost here. The trees that lined the city square were captivating with hues of orange and brown that shone in the moonlight.

"The tavern?" I asked as we turned the familiar corner of the square and approached the warmly lit building. Chatter and laughter filtered out the open windows and I felt my body instantly relaxing.

The tavern was basically my second home. If I wasn't out at training then I was in the tavern either helping to clean or hanging out with the guild or Kiera.

Kain glanced over his shoulder with a smirk at me whilst Luca's arm tightened around mine.

The wooden door of the tavern creaked open and the room fell into silence before a familiar head full of brown curls popped up out of the crowd, holding a large paper banner. Vikki's brown eyes twinkled as she started waving the banner around like a crazy woman and I could barely make out the words on it from the shaking. *Good luck Nevara*! The bright red writing on the poster said and then the rest of the Guild stood up from the table holding up familiar signs.

"Good Luck, brat!" Derrick shouted and the rest of the tavern held up their cups in agreement as everyone cheered and laughed. Heat flooded my face as everyone's eyes focused on me and I choked on a laugh.

"What is all this?" I asked as Kain shoved me forward and Vikki saw her moment to pounce on me and wrap me in her arms.

"It's just a little good luck party for the contest tomorrow!" She sang and hugged me even tighter in her usual death grip. Kain sat down at the head of the table and Netta appeared from the kitchen, giving me a warming smile.

"Don't think you're out of getting punishment for what happened earlier," Derrick snorted as he rubbed the top of my head a little too roughly. "I'll wait until after the contest til' I kick your ass."

"Looking forward to it," I grumbled and Derrick narrowed his eyes and let out a chuckle.

"Can't wait til' you're unleashed on those nobles tomorrow." Jamie smirked and Kiera laughed as she leant over the back of his chair, her brown eyes twinkling as she winked at me.

"I heard Han Dranson is being put forward by the Sapphire Guild," Ganya fake gagged as she tugged me out of Vikki's grasp and sat me on her lap.

Ganya was a battle mage just like her twin sister Dranya who now sat beside her, giggling at the two of us. They were the youngest of the guild but were strong in their linked magic formations. Being twins definitely had its perks, especially when you could share mana and create devastating magic formations with it.

"Han Dranson?" Benji wrinkled his nose as he took a sip of his ale. "I heard he was entering the Academy as a battle mage. I didn't think his swordsmanship would be decent enough to enter the contest."

The tavern had begun to settle down now, along with my heart rate. The table filled with all the Guild members and my body relaxed as I relished in how comfortable it was to sit amongst them.

"Well, the Sapphire Guild seems to think so," Phillip sighed as he put his arm round his wife Nancy. Phillip was slightly younger than Kain but had been a lifelong friend to him since before magic was discovered. He was a magic swordsman and his wife a healer that helped beside Vikki in the dungeons. They had two sons a little younger than me who would play with us when we were younger. As we grew older though they seemed to make ties in the noble community and often hung out with them whenever they could.

"So, you're saying that battle mages can't wield a sword?" Ganya growled behind me towards Benji and it was clear she had already drunk a little too much.

"Calm down Gan Gan." Jamie smirked and I felt Ganya still behind me. "It's widely known that battle mages only chose their class because they can't wield a sword like a magic swordsman can." His blue eyes danced with excitement as Ganya leapt up to grab him by the shirt and I almost toppled off of her lap. Dranya broke into giggles beside us and Ganya opened her mouth with what I knew was going to be a slew of not so innocent curses, but Kain cut her off before she could.

"Now that we're all here and *acting civilised*," Kain's eyes narrowed in on Ganya and she shrank back into her chair, yanking me back with her. She flipped Jamie off and he blew her a kiss that made me think she was going to leap at him again. "I think it's time for the gift," Kain said and I turned to look at him with surprise.

"Gift?" I arched a brow as the table filled with knowing smirks and grins. Kain slammed his hand down twice in some sort of signal and Brendan and Oryan appeared from where the tavern kitchen was located.

Brendan beamed at us all like an excited puppy as he quickly hurried over to the table, dragging Oryan by the front of his shirt.

"We just got here because *he* wouldn't stop talking to the blacksmith," Brendan scoffed and nodded at Oryan. "On and on and on he talked about–"

"What about the gift?" Kain interrupted Brendan's excited chatter and the others burst into chuckles, Netta patted her sons' shoulder reassuringly.

"The gift is right here," Oryan said as he slid a long object that was wrapped in a blanket onto the table in front of me.

"I made sure it was perfect before I brought it," he said proudly and gave me a wink.

"We've watched you grow up over all these years and seen you change from a tiny and frail child into such a strong and brave young woman," Kain said, his blue eyes twinkling with emotion and I suddenly found it hard to breathe. "It seemed like you just appeared out of nowhere and into my life—You even brought with you a loving family that I can now call my own. I couldn't have wished for a better daughter than you, Nevara." Kain finished and the table fell quiet.

Daughter.

He had never actually called me that before. My eyes burned as I watched tears spill over Netta's eyes as she gripped Kain's hands.

"You are our saviour, Nevara," she whispered and I felt a lump in my throat. I had never cried in my life. Not when my real mother died, not when I would get caught stealing and be beaten. I didn't even cry through all of the torturous training I had endured all these years. But now as I watched these two people in front of me, accept me as their daughter...as their family...

"Oh god!" Ganya cried from behind me and startled everyone at the table as she burst into tears. "It's just so beautiful! We all love you so much, Nevara!" She sobbed and the table burst into laughter, each one of them had twinkling eyes that said they weren't far off from crying either.

"You guys are just far too soft," I said jokingly as I tried to push back the heavy burn from my eyes. "If anyone saw how emotional the Ruby Guild was, you would become a laughingstock," I teased and the table booed at me.

I slid my hands over the table and took Kain and Netta's hands in my own. I smiled warmly and they squeezed my hands back in acknowledgement.

"Well, aren't you going to open your gift?" Brendan asked

impatiently as he came to stand behind me, his feet practically bouncing off the ground. I let out a chuckle as I pulled the wrapped object closer, my hands trembling slightly with excitement. I pulled back the cloth at one end and gasped at the silver hilt, embellished with swirls of metal ivy. The leaves were almost iridescent as they caught the lights of the candles that lined the walls of the tavern.

Slowly, I removed the rest of the cloth revealing a sharp silver sword with symbols engraved down its length that I had never seen before.

"It's a magical artefact that we tracked down a while ago. We were going to give it to you when you got into the Academy but thought you could use it for the contest," Oryan smiled proudly and my eyes threatened to spill again.

"We got it made lighter and smaller to fit your build," Kain explained. "It's re-shaped for you to wield it effortlessly."

"This is…" I trailed off, unsure of what to say. "This is too much, it probably cost a small fortune."

"Don't even think about rejecting it," Derrick grunted. "Now that it's been made for you, no one else could use it anyway."

"It's imbued with a magic formation that will activate when it senses your near death." Benji's eyes were wide with awe as he leaned forward to study it. "The symbols here make the formation but we don't know what exact protection spell is on it, only that it should save you from certain death." He smiled. "Well, only when you unlock your mana and are able to use it."

"So, it won't save her if she's hurt tomorrow?" Netta asked, her eyebrows creasing in worry.

"The contest will be watched by nearly the whole city! They won't let anyone get severely injured," Kain replied whilst squeezing Netta's hand.

"This contest is really only for the King to boast about how powerful his Academy has become and showcase the many magical artefacts he is able to bring into the city. The contest is just for a side of entertainment, that's all." Kain shrugged and I looked down at the sword again. I lifted it off the table and was surprised at how light it was.

"Entertainment or not, I'm going to win," I said quietly, then looked around the table. I smirked as I jumped up off of Ganya's lap and thrusted the sword in the air. "I will win for the Ruby Guild or may I be punished by training with Derrick for the rest of my life!" I shouted and Derrick choked on his ale.

"For the Ruby Guild!" The table shouted and they erupted into laughter at Derrick's reddening face. I clutched the sword in my hand, feeling as if it was a puzzle piece falling into place.

Ganya pulled me back down on her lap and pushed a mug of ale into my hand as we continued to sit at the table, laughing and discussing anything and everything. I smiled and enjoyed the company for as long as I could because I knew everything may change after tomorrow.

CHAPTER 9

"They really went all out for this event, didn't they?"
I said as I peeked around Kain's large frame as we
rode on horseback through the Noble District. I had peered
over the stone wall that separated the Commoners District
from the Noble District many times but it wasn't nearly the
same as actually being in it. The Noble District was clean and
well organised with its pristine cobbled floor and grey stone
buildings. Homes, shops and inns lined the streets and
coloured banners and flowers hung everywhere to celebrate
the contest. People wore extravagant and rich velvet dresses
and tunics and I found myself staring in awe at everything.
Even the air in the noble district seemed to be cleaner,
sweeter.

"I told you, they're putting on a show," Kain grumbled. I
leaned over as I tried to see the beautiful and glittering artefacts that lined the shopfront windows and I wondered if I
would be able to have a look around before we went home.
Not that I would be able to afford anything.

The palace gates towered ahead of us, and I almost
vibrated with excitement as we got closer. Never in my life

did I think that I would get close enough to see the palace gates – let alone get into the palace grounds. I clutched the hilt of my sword that now hung off my belt and it seemed to calm me.

"You clean up well, brat," Derrick smirked as his horse came up beside us. We came ahead of the Guild to make sure we got to the arena with enough time to prepare. The rest of my family would get a carriage later to attend the contest.

"Netta practically scrubbed me half to death," I muttered as I remembered this morning. Netta forced me into the bath and scrubbed my skin until it was red and then had dragged that blasted comb through my knotted black hair until she finally braided it down my back. "I feel too clean." I cringed and Kain and Derrick chuckled at me.

"Licenses ready!" A guard called out from the gate. There was a group of them that lined the wall and they narrowed their eyes as we got close. Whenever you graduated from the Academy you were given a license so you could join a Guild and enter dungeons; it was useful in situations like this.

"The contest doesn't start until this afternoon," one of the guards said and began to wave us away. My hand tightened around my hilt as I imagined thumping him on the back of his head with it.

"Ruby Guild." Kain shoved his license into the guards scowling face. "We're here so she can prepare for the contest." He nodded to me, and I gave the guards the best smile I could, but it was more a baring of teeth.

"Her?" The guard raised his brows in surprise.

"Yes, me," I confirmed through gritted teeth and it looked as if the guard was going to argue before someone beside him spoke up.

"Enter to the right at the back of the arena. Someone will come for you when it's your match," he said and Kain nodded to him before snatching back his license and moving forward.

"I don't know why it's such a surprise that a woman is entering the contest. There's so many females at the Academy." I sighed as I thought about the girls in the Guild and how strong and powerful they were.

"That's because there aren't that many female swordsmen," Derrick replied as we meandered down a small and well-manicured hill. "I've only known a handful of women that have graduated as swordsmen. Female bodies are just more suited to being a healer or battle mage."

"Well, I'm a woman and I've put you on your ass more times than I can count," I sneered and Derrick let out a bark of a laugh.

"That's because you're not a woman, you little beastie," he growled and Kain let out a chuckle.

The arena loomed ahead of us, and it was the same size and structure as the arena in the Commoners District, but this one was far more lavish. Golden mouldings and embellishments decorated its arches and green ivy climbed its sides. It was beautiful.

I could just make out the golden towers of the palace behind it and ached to see it up close. Maybe one day, if I win the contest then I may have a chance in the future.

"Well, if it isn't the Ruby Guild," a man called out and I felt Kain tense in front of me.

"Good to see you, Daniel," Kain said with a sigh and pulled to a stop outside the arena. We quickly dismounted and a guard led away our horses.

"I didn't know you were attending today," Daniel's tone was polite but his eyes watched us distastefully. I stepped beside Kain and viewed the large and round man. He was dressed in a fine blue velvet tunic with twinkling swords and daggers at his hips and thighs. I remembered seeing him a while ago and knew him to be the leader of the Sapphire Guild.

Kain had told me before that the velvet tunics that the nobles wore consisted of a magical artefact in the form of fabric that was as strong as leather. They could have just worn leather but of course, nothing says you have money than magical velvet.

"I'm here to put *my daughter* forward for the contest," Kain said as he dared him to say anything bad about me. Daniel fixed his narrowed blue eyes on me and his lips twitched.

"I didn't know you had a daughter." Daniel's eyes roamed over my body and I tried to suppress a shudder. I looked to his left and saw a guy around my age standing and viewing the confrontation, his cat like eyes not missing anything.

"You never asked." Kain shrugged and put his arm around me as we tried to side-track them to make our way into the arena.

"Are you sure you want to let her enter the contest? She will be up against a lot of strong men who won't hold back. The reward is too good to hold back against," Daniel warned and I narrowed my eyes at him.

"Don't worry," I sighed and flicked my braid over my shoulder as I met the eyes of the guy beside him. He was obviously who I was going to be up against. "I won't hold back either." And with that I turned back and pulled Kain and Derrick into the arena.

"What an asshole," I muttered and Derrick laughed.

"There's a lot more of them here," Derrick sighed and patted me on the back. "But I'm sure you can take care of a few idiots."

I smirked at him as we were led into one of the side rooms overlooking the arena. I pulled my sword from my side and looked over it. I twirled it in my hand and made a few lunges with it until I was confident in its weight.

"Let's hope that armour keeps up its defence," Kain sighed as he watched me, worry pulling at his features. "Those nobles are going to have the best swords out there."

"Yes, but they don't have this one." I smirked and twirled the sword in my hands again, mesmerised by the iridescent leaves that decorated its hilt.

"The main thing you have to remember is to keep on your toes and never stay still. Make it so they can't land a hit on you," Derrick advised and I nodded. I already knew that speed was my biggest advantage against opponents.

"The goal is to get them out of the ring right?" I asked and quickly looked out over the edge of the arena wall. The grounds were still being set up but I could see an outline of a circle drawn onto the dirt floor.

"Knock them out of the ring or make them surrender. That's the only way to win and move onto the next round," Kain explained.

Most of my opponents are going to be larger than me so I'm going to have to think of a strategy. I'll have to get them to lower their guards and dance just outside their reach with a flurry of attacks and dodges then as soon as they approach me, I'll take the opportunity to knock them back and hopefully out of the ring.

"Practice with me?" I asked Kain and he grinned as he unsheathed his sword. Now was the time to perfect this strategy, I had to make sure I had some sort of plan set before I went out there in front of everyone.

THE HOURS PASSED by as I practiced with Kain. I didn't try too hard, to reserve most of my energy but I still managed to knock Kain on his butt a few times.

"You're like a damned fly," Kain grunted as he landed on his behind yet again. "I feel like I'm trying to swat you but you keep coming back."

"That's the plan," I chuckled and helped him up.

Derrick had disappeared to try to find and meet up with the rest of the Guild and I could hear the crowds gathering in the arena. A nervous buzz of energy seemed to fill the air and I took a few deep breaths to steady myself.

"You're up in the first round, it's time to start moving." A guard appeared in the doorway and Kain came to clamp his hand on my shoulder.

"Ready?" Kain grinned excitedly and I clenched my hand around the hilt of my sword.

"Definitely!" I grinned back and we began making our way through a stone hallway that led down onto the arena floor. The place was now filled with chatter and cheers and I felt the sound reverberate in through my chest.

"Nevara!" I heard a woman scream and looked over to see the Ruby Guild seated in the middle area of the wooden benches and a smile spread across my face. Vikki and Ganya were fighting to see who could wave harder and I tried to stifle a laugh at the sight of it.

"Looks like you're up against the Emerald Guild first," Kain said and pointed over to the opposite end of the arena. A man was whispering into a younger guys ear, they looked deep in discussion.

I was about to question Kain about them before a sudden silence settled over the crowd. All of a sudden a trumpet played a short melody that seemed to make the arena intake a breath.

I had heard that haunting tune only a few times before, but there was no doubt on what it signalled.

The Royal Family.

"Introducing his Royal Highness King Embram, his wife Queen Cilia and their son, Prince Damon." The nobles in the crowd gasped and clapped as the three royals drifted onto an elevated platform at the side of the arena. The King was a large man with a head full of brown curls with a beard to match. The Queen was a slender woman with pale blonde curls and piercing blue eyes that I could see even from down here. The Prince plopped down on his seat, looking bored as he studied the crowd. I could already tell he was arrogant. He had his mother's pale blue eyes and blonde hair as it sat slicked back from his face. I wasn't so naïve that I wouldn't admit he was quite handsome – but he still seemed like a jerk.

His eyes fell on me and he leaned forward in his chair, his head cocking to the side as if he couldn't understand what it was he was seeing.

"Good afternoon to the citizens of Ghislana!" The King bellowed I tore my eyes from the Prince's quizzical gaze. "I'm happy to welcome you to this marvellous contest I am holding to showcase the talent of the young people of this kingdom."

"It is to show that even without magic we are still a strong and powerful kingdom!" He looked around the audience and I felt Kain sigh at the King's dramatics.

"The winner today will then be able get free admission into the Ashwood Academy and receive fifty gold pieces. This is no small prize! And to ensure that each fight will be fair, there will be a no magic rule along with a no killing rule. Contestants may injure and strike each other and there will be healers nearby to alert us if a near fatal wound has been dealt. Other than that, the goal is to push your opponent outside the ring. This is a contest to prove strength, so also prove your compliance to follow the rules or else you will be disqualified." The King's booming voice came to a stop and I felt the adrenaline rush through my body. This was it.

"Now, let's begin!" The King bellowed and the crowd erupted into cheers.

"The first round will be between Han Dranson of the Emerald Guild and Nevara of the Ruby Guild," the guard at the side of the ring called out and the crowd cheered even louder as we stepped forward. Many gasps and fingers pointed my way and I had to try hard to fight my annoyance.

"Are you sure you're in the right place?" Han called out as he sauntered into the ring and I rolled my eyes. The first round was going to be the one that everyone remembered so I had to make a statement to make the confusion about me disappear.

"Unfortunately for you, I am," I smiled sweetly as I unsheathed my sword. We stood a few feet apart and Han took his time retrieving his sword.

The crowd fell quiet as we faced each other and I felt his gaze taking in my sword and armour, a lazy grin appearing on his face.

"Begin!" The guard called – my blood spiked.

"I'm going to have to apologise for–" Han began to say something slimy before I cut him off. I darted low around his side and he jumped back, clearly caught off guard by how fast I was. This is what I had hoped for. He spun on his heel to face me and I took that opportunity to kick out my right leg and swipe his own feet off the floor. Whilst I still had the momentum, I turned and placed both hands below me to kick out with my feet to land directly in the centre of his back. He was big and heavy but luckily the speed of my attack had still surprised him. I managed to launch him forward with a grunt and he fell face first outside the ring, a cloud of dust erupting into the air around him from the impact.

I jumped back up onto my feet and wiped the dirt from my hands, sheathing my sword back in its place, slowly so I made sure Han and the crowd saw it.

"Didn't even need to use my sword," I smirked at him and the crowd grew silent. I could see them assess what had just happened as they looked from me to Han and then back at me again. A woman commoner had won the first round…in less than a minute.

"The winner is Nevara of the Ruby Guild," the guard announced and the crowd erupted again. I heard the Ruby Guild screaming and calling for me and I chuckled. I even sneaked a look up at the Prince to see him practically leaning over the ledge of the wall to see us. Gone was the bored Prince.

"You bitch!" Han yelled as he stormed towards me. "That doesn't count! The round hadn't even begun!"

"The round had begun and Nevara has won. Now go and join your Guild." The guard dismissed him and I smirked at Han. His eyes bore into mine and his fists clenched at his sides before he turned and stalked back towards the guy he was talking to earlier.

"The next match will begin in a few moments. We will call you when it's time for the semi-finals," the guard said and I gave him a nod before walking towards Kain, who was laughing his ass off.

"Well, that's one way to make a statement." He erupted into laughter again and this time I joined him.

"He had it coming," I said and took a drink from the water canteen beside the doorway. "He just wouldn't stop talking."

"Well, the other contestants are going to start taking you seriously now," he said as he put his arm round around my shoulder and leaned into my ear. "Seems you need to be a bit more careful." He nodded towards where Han and the rest of the Emerald Guild were standing, shouting as they casted angry looks my way. I smiled sweetly at them and could swear Han was about to storm over here before getting pulled away. I knew I shouldn't be making the nobles even angrier, but boy was it fun.

The next round was between the Sapphire and the Quartz Guild. Two rather large men faced off against each other and I could feel the angry tension that pulsated between them. I wondered if it was a Guild feud or if the two men just really didn't like each other.

They leapt at each other, roaring like wild animals as the round began and the clang of metal filled the air. The fight was drastically different than the one I had. The swords swung down brutally, and the crowd cheered with each hit, their own faces twisted into ones filled with bloodlust. I watched with a mix of awe and dread as they aimed to kill with each swing. I had never really sparred with someone with the intentions of causing intense harm and I think that was why I was so shocked as I watched the fight unfold.

The Sapphire Guild finally delivered a deadly hit to his opponent and a sickening thud echoed around the arena as the blade dug deep into the flesh of his chest. The healers immediately called the match and began to cart away the fallen opponent.

"That was brutal," I shuddered and Kain nodded.

"The winner is Samuel from the Sapphire Guild!" The guard called and the crowd went wild. Samuel smirked to the crowd as he thrusted his sword into the sky, blood still fresh and dripping from the blade. He was one to watch out for.

The next two battles went similarly to the last and was won by the Pyrite and Jasper Guild. My blood soared as I watched the brutal and bloody battles. The nobles certainly didn't hold back when it came to honour and fame within the kingdom. I wondered if they even needed the prize like I did? What was a free admission and fifty gold pieces to a rich person?

Then I wondered if this is what the King intended that the people took away from this contest.

Fear.

Most of the contestants were nobles and maybe this was the King's way of letting the commoners and the lower nobles know their place. It was as if he was letting us know that if we were to step out of line, then this is what we would be up against. The thought had my stomach churning.

"You're up against Xander next," Kain murmured next to me and my jaw clenched. Xander was from the Pyrite Guild and had won the third round in a bloody victory. He was huge and didn't hesitate as he struck down his opponent but there was one thing I picked up that I hoped I could use against him.

He was slow.

"Be careful," Kain warned quietly and I almost didn't hear him over the roars of the crowd. I gave him a confident grin as I walked over to the middle of the arena again where Xander was already waiting. His face was unimpressed as he watched me enter the ring to stand opposite him. Blood coated his dark skin and I clenched my hands at my sides when I saw it. I wouldn't be afraid, this is what I had been training for.

"These are now the semi-finals," King Embram called out. "The winners from the next two rounds will go on to battle against each other to determine who wins the contest. Begin!" He called and the guard signalled to us to go. I withdrew my sword in one quick flourish and angled it towards Xander.

"It's seems you're not a talker like the Emerald Guild was,"

I smirked and Xander remained silent as he unsheathed his own huge sword and his dark brown eyes zeroed in on me. His skin shone slick with sweat and I saw the small scars and cuts that marred his skin and realised they were similar to my own. This was a guy who had been training just as hard as I had been and had the wounds to show for it, which was strange for a noble.

I saw the left lunge before he had even moved, he had a tell in his left shoulder as it moved back ever so slightly before he made his move. I had been up against too many people to not be able to notice it. I dodged to the right and twirled behind him to land a shallow cut at his lower back. It was only now that I was so close to him that I could actually see how tall he was. He was almost three heads taller than me which meant landing a fatal blow was going to be even more difficult.

Xander let out a grunt of pain as he shot forward, facing me again and I had to fight the urge to feel guilty for what I had just done. I needed to stick with my original plan of trying to get him outside the ring, but it was going to be too difficult just to push him out like my last opponent.

Xander charged forward and I dodged again at the last moment and rolled forward to stand opposite him. He charged with a series of slashes that I nimbly dodged until Xander was red in the face and panting.

A plan formed in my mind then and I put it into action straight away. I took advantage of his breathlessness to slide across the ground to his left and I dragged my blade across his ankle and severed the tendon at the back of his heel. His bellow of pain made my gut wrench with guilt again but I couldn't focus on that. I knew he would hop off his left foot and that was the time to strike. He did what I thought he was going to do and I swung my right leg up from behind me to land in his gut and shoved him backwards. My foot crunched under the sheer weight of his body and I gritted my teeth as I watched him fall back out of the ring. The crowd erupted into cheer again and I cast a glance up to where I knew my family and the Guild were sitting. Ganya almost looked like she wanted to climb over the people in front of her to get to me as she screamed and cheered.

"The winner is Nevara from the Ruby Guild!" The guard called and I walked back to Kain, the pain in my right foot throbbing with each step. Curse Xander's large build.

"You're in pain," Kain pointed out and my eyebrows shot up.

"How could you tell?" I asked and he gave me a knowing grin.

"Your eyes narrowed every time you stepped on your right foot," Kain said and I scoffed. Eagle-eyed Kain missed nothing.

"It's nothing." I shrugged and took the water canteen from his hands.

"I'll get a healer," Kain announced and before I could say anything, he was gone. I sighed as I leant against the wall, my eyes skimming over the crowd. I focused on where the royals sat and realised all three of them were staring at me and mumbling to each other. The King and Queen looked as if they were looking at nothing more than the dirt that littered the arena floor whilst the prince looked like he was a cat who had just found a mouse. I sighed as I pushed off the wall to do an overly dramatic bow to them all and the King's jaw clenched before he and the Queen looked away. The Prince's grin grew even wider and he raised his eyebrows in delight.

"Nevara." A guys voice caught my attention and I turned to see Xander approaching me. My body tensed into defensive mode as my hand shot to the hilt of my sword. He shook his head and lifted his hands in surrender.

"What is it?" I asked bluntly as I relaxed my grip.

"I wanted to congratulate you," he said and I could have sworn he looked away nervously. His voice was soft and smooth compared to his gigantic and overbearing frame and I couldn't get over how different they were.

"You fought well," I said and had to fight a chuckle as he stuttered out a thank you. I held out my hand to shake his and he shook it gently, a small smile on his face. It was as if a mouse was living in a bear's body.

"Will you be attending the Academy this year?" I asked as I dropped his hand and he came to lean beside me. "I can tell you've been training hard."

"I was hoping to get a free pass in but yes, I will be attending," he said as he ran a hand through his close-cropped curls. He wore a grey velvet tunic with silver embellishments and breeches to match which complimented his skin tone beautifully.

"What would a noble need a free pass for?" I scoffed. The cost of his armour alone could have paid for twenty people's fee for the Academy.

"This armour is second hand from my brother. The money behind my nobility belongs all to my father and all he sees me as is the shadow of his favourite son," Xander mumbled as he picked at the silver thread of his tunic with a look of disdain.

"Then what makes you so sure you will be able to afford the Academy?" I asked with a raised eyebrow and he gave me a smirk that made him look adorable.

"Because then he will be rid of me which he would gladly pay the money for," he said and I barked out a laugh.

"Well, at least I'll know one friendly face at the Academy then," I said and he looked away nervously again before he nodded.

"You need to teach me how you can move so fast," he added and I laughed with a shake of the head.

"It's a secret," I teased – he narrowed his eyes at my smugness.

"Nevara," I heard Kain call out and turned to see him marching up to me with Vikki behind him. He shot a dark look between Xander and me and I rolled my eyes.

"Good luck in the finals," Xander said quietly, obviously not wanting to get on the bad side of Kain. "I'll see you at the Academy." I smiled and he gave me a quick grin before going up the stairs behind us that led to where the crowd was.

"Making friends are we?" Kain narrowed his eyes and I was about to say something smart before Vikki leapt on me. She immediately began examining me from head to toe.

"Her right foot, Vikki," Kain added with a sigh.

"Who's up next?" I asked as Vikki began to take off my boot and examine my foot. I looked over to where the two guys were approaching the ring, both caked in dried blood and sweat.

"Samuel and Walsh," Kain said and I remembered Samuel who was put forward from the Sapphire Guild, his match was extremely brutal. I'm surprise his opponent made it out alive.

"Let the match begin!" The guard called and the clang of metal filled the arena instantly. Both Samuel and Walsh looked as if they were consumed by bloodlust as they lunged and swiped at each other and I found myself cringing away from them. The sounds of their shouts and the sickening thuds of blades finding their marks had bile rising in my throat.

I felt Vikki place her hand on my ankle and an instant warmth filled up my right leg and I sighed as the pain began to disappear.

"It was only a small sprain." Vikki pulled herself up to stand beside me.

"Thanks, Vikki." I smiled at her and she waved me off as she watched the battle beside us.

Samuel let out a roar as he swung his two-handed sword in from the right and landed a clean hit to Walsh's side. A sickening crack sounded as the sword cut through to the bone. Gasps rippled through the crowd as Walsh crumpled to the floor and Samuel raised his sword to deliver to final blow.

"He's going to kill him!" I shouted and unsheathed my sword but the guards were there in an instant and held him back. Healers swarmed the ring and began to take Walsh away to heal him.

Samuel shrugged off the guards and lifted his bloodied sword to the crowd again and they erupted into cheer. My stomach twisted as I saw the guards look up to the King as if to see if they should take him away or leave him. The King's eyes narrowed in on Samuel, his mouth twitching as he gave a slight nod to the guards who returned to their positions along the side of the arena. They were letting him away with almost murdering someone? The King was going to let him fight me?

"This is bad," Kain muttered as he watched the scene unfold in front of us.

"He's going to kill her." Derrick appeared then at the bottom of the stairs and I began to grind my teeth as I watched Samuel bask in the cheer of the crowd, his eyes wild like an animal.

"I'll be fine," I said as I began to quickly stretch my muscles, my right ankle now fully healed thanks to Vikki.

"I don't like this," Vikki whispered. "You could always pull out. You know we have the money to get you into the Academy," she said and I gave her a small smile.

"I promised I wouldn't let the Guild down and that's what I'm going to do," I said as I looked at all three of them. "Plus, I really want to stab that damn bastard," I spat and Derrick grunted in approval.

"If anything goes wrong or you feel as if you will lose then just jump out of the ring. You're fast so you can do it before he catches you," Derrick instructed and I gave him a nod. Kain came over and placed his hands on my shoulders, lowering his head to level with mine as he looked into my eyes. I stared into those familiar blue eyes and felt myself draw strength from them.

"I can do this," I whispered and he searched my face and when it seemed like he saw I was telling the truth, he nodded and squeezed my shoulders.

"You need to get into the ring," a guard called over and I began to walk over. There was no rest between this round, they must want it over quickly.

"Well, if it isn't the little fly," Samuel spat as he wiped his sweaty forehead with the back of his hand. His bronzed skin was damp and dirtied from fighting on the dusty arena floor and he looked like a half wild beast, the complete opposite from the quiet person I saw standing next to Daniel outside the arena earlier. "That's what they're calling you. You're a damned fly that flutters around its opponents and it looks like I'm going to have to swat you down."

"I've been called worse things," I shrugged and unsheathed my sword. His answering grin chilled me to the bone.

"The winner will be determined in this match. Let's make it a good one!" The King bellowed and I gritted my teeth.

"You heard him, fly," Samuel chuckled as he wiped Walsh's blood off his sword and flicked the thick red liquid onto the floor beside us. Bile rose to my throat as I zeroed in on him. I was definitely going to kick his ass.

"Let the match begin!" The guard called and the crowd roared, the sound vibrating into my very bones. Samuel struck first which I knew he was going to do so I quickly dodged and twirled to end up behind him.

"There it is," he chuckled and lunged backwards. I dodged his attack again, but he stopped his swing in mid-air to quickly dart in the opposite direction and carved his blade deep between my shoulder blades. I hissed as I jumped to the side, surprised that he saw through my dodge.

"I told you I would swat you," Samuel chuckled as he began to circle me again. His steps light and precise as he watched everything I did. He must have watched me just like this in my previous matches, studying and noting the way I moved and evaded attacks.

I bit down on my cheek to suppress the pain in my back and the wetness that was growing there. I had to end this. Fast.

A sudden awareness filled me, and I felt an odd sense of someone near. I shuddered as I kept circling Samuel, knowing that no one else was near me apart from him…

What was this strange feeling?

I gripped my sword as I darted to his left and swooped down low with my sword, wanting to weaken his movements. The sword almost pierced the flesh at the back of his calves before he jumped forward and evaded me.

"I don't think so," he tutted and I growled at him. His eyes flickered with delight and he jumped at me with a series of lunges and swipes which I tried my best to dodge. His leg shot out catching my right ankle and I stumbled backwards, grunting as my back hit the floor. I had just enough time to roll as he brought down the sword to where my head would have been.

"Your bloodlust is quite overwhelming," I spat as I scrambled to my feet, my sword angling towards him again. This was bad. The pain in my back grew and I was beginning to sweat. I've fought people like Samuel before. Like Kain and

Derrick he seemed like he already had magic. Much like a magic swordsman he was quick and powerful and seemed stronger than a human should. But there was no way. This contest was strictly for people who haven't awoken their mana yet.

"Thinking of giving up?" Samuel teased and my hand tightened around the hilt of my sword. I should give up. I have sparred against Kain, Derrick and many other magic swordsmen but they have never used their full power on me. If by some chance Samuel has awoken his mana then he could very well kill me right here, right now.

You'll be admitting defeat. A voice in my head said. *You will be bringing shame to the Ruby Guild. To your family. You promised them you could do this...*

A sudden caw above me brought me back to my senses and my heart thundered as I saw Soot fly above our heads. His beady black eyes met mine and I felt like he was telling me I could do this.

"Get away!" Samuel hissed and swatted at Soot as the raven swooped low at his head. I took the opportunity and lunged forward, my blade piercing his right arm and I felt the resistance as it dug into his muscles and bounced off his bone. He roared as he jumped backwards with his sword now hanging limp in his right hand and he quickly trans-ferred it over to his left.

"That was a dirty little trick," he hissed, his green eyes burning with anger.

"It's not my fault you were distracted," I breathed and then winced at the pain radiating from my back. That familiar odd sense of someone close to me filled my senses again and I shuddered as a warmth spread out across the pain on my back, as if someone was embracing it.

I lunged forward again but he blocked it with his own

sword and I noticed that the movements were slower this time. Attacking his dominant arm had been a good idea.

I quickly poured all my energy into a series of jabs and slices, my sword cutting flesh and armour as he tried to dodge each one but his left hand couldn't keep up. His right arm was slick with blood now and his skin, like mine, was growing paler from the blood loss.

"You *bitch!*" He screamed. "I need to win this! Do you know how much money I have invested in this game!?" He hissed as he shot forward again, lunging more desperately now. I dodged and sliced him when I could, his armour was thicker on his chest but if I could just pierce it…

"Enough!" He screamed and he lifted his sword to me, levelling it with my face. His face was morphed into one consumed by fury and his eyes turned wild as they burned. "You need to die."

A crackle in the air sounded and everything seemed to turn into slow motion. Flames sparked from Samuel's hand and his sword was suddenly engulfed in flames. Heat licked at my face and then I heard my name being screamed from somewhere. There was no time to react as the flames engulfed my body. Searing pain shot up and down the left side of my skin and I screamed in agony. I dropped to the floor and began to roll, my instincts kicking in as I tried desperately to put out the flames.

A ravens cry sounded above the roar of the fire and I screamed and screamed, inhaling to smoke of burning flesh. That sudden odd sense of someone nearby filled me again and I felt the phantom-like hands embrace me. My screams felt distant to my own ears—as if it were someone else.

I suddenly felt people around me but I couldn't focus on them, the only thing I could focus on was the subsiding pain and the embrace of comfort that seemed to come from nowhere.

Rest now... A man's voice floated through my mind and I immediately relaxed despite my body still being consumed by flames.

My name seemed to echo around my consciousness until darkness finally came and I welcomed the cool void with open arms and I sank down into it until there was nothing left.

CHAPTER 10

"$\mathcal{I}$f they don't have that bastard executed then I'll do it myself," a familiar male's voice sounded from beside me and I felt the veil of darkness beginning to disappear. Was I still alive? I thought for sure when the fire consumed me that I was done for.

"The King won't let Samuel get away with what he did. Not when he went against the rules in front of nearly the whole city. Plus, the Prince made a show of stepping in to save her," another man's voice said and I tried to open my eyes, the light from the room blinding me and I groaned as I squeezed them shut again.

"Is she awakening?" A worried woman's voice asked.

"No. Vikki said she wouldn't be awake for a long time yet. She had to give her sedatives because she was screaming so much." The man's voice trembled and I recognised it as Kain's.

"I told the brat to leave if she was in danger! I warned her!" The other man seemed to growl and I knew instantly it was Derrick. The fog from my mind began to clear as the events from the contest came back to me.

"You're all being very loud," I groaned as I finally managed to open my eyes, blinking until they got used to the brightness. My voice was raspy and quiet and I had to swallow a few times before I could say anything else.

"You're meant to be sleeping," Kain said and I saw him press his lips into a thin line, but his eyes softened with what looked like relief. "Go get Vikki." Netta gave me a worried look before rushing from the room. I moved to push myself up into a sitting position but a sharp pain sliced down the left side of my body and had me gulping for air.

"Easy!" Kain yelled and pushed my head gently back down into the pillow. "You're nowhere near fully healed yet."

"I know it's a hard thing for you to do, but please don't move and do as you're told," Derrick sighed and my eyes narrowed on his.

"Since you said…please," I gasped and Derrick's eyebrows creased in worry. "I take it that Samuel was…cheating and had already awoken his magic," I said between breaths. The left side of my face burned and a sharp ache radiated through my skin with each word.

"When he released the flames on you, the guards jumped in to stop him. The Prince practically leapt from the balcony to help put the flames out that covered you," Kain said and my eyes widened at that. The Prince put himself at risk to help me? "Samuel went into a frenzy and took down a handful of guards but then Derrick and I stepped in and got him restrained enough for them to drag him away." I shuddered to think what Kain and Derrick did to Samuel, the glint in Kain's eye told me that it wasn't nearly enough than what he wanted.

"So…the winner?" I looked between Kain and Derrick and they both frowned at me.

"We just told you that you were attacked with fire and you're worrying about who won?" Derrick shook his head in disbelief. I nodded anyway as Kain pinched the bridge of his nose and closed his eyes. I wondered how long I had been sleeping. Kain looked like he hadn't slept in a long time, like he had stayed by my side since it all happened.

"Samuel was disqualified and you have won by default. But if you're hoping for a large celebration, you will be sorely disappointed. The King wants this whole event swept under the rug." Kain sighed and I smiled, the motion splitting something on my lip and I felt the warmth of blood trickle down my chin.

"Damn!" Kain hissed and grabbed a damp cloth and dabbed it gently on my mouth. "Where the hell is Vikki?" He shouted just as Vikki burst into the room. Her brown hair was a mess and her brown eyes red from crying.

"How are you awake?" She choked out as she rushed over to me. She began checking over parts of the left side of my body – I wished I could lift my head high enough to see just how injured I was.

"How bad am I?" I voiced my concerns and Vikki looked away quickly, her eyes glittering with more tears. I reached out my right hand, relieved that it didn't hurt like my other hand did and I grabbed her arm.

"How bad am I?" I asked again and she looked at me then, tears running down her cheeks.

"I tried my best to get rid of the burns, but they were too severe," she said quietly. "Every hour for the past two days I've been healing them and trying to set them but they…" she choked on a sob and I squeezed her hand.

"The burns can be healed?" I asked and she wiped the tears away from her face. Derrick placed a hand on the woman's back and I wished I could stop all the sadness that was on their faces.

"They can be healed but your skin…they're too severe to remove them completely," she explained and I understood.

Even though the burns could be healed I would be scarred by them.

"So, I get a few bad ass scars," I shrugged and then grimaced at the pain. "So what? They will make me look even more intimidating," I joked but none of them even cracked a smile.

"Get the mirror," Kain ordered after a moment of silence and Vikki hesitated before she left to walk to the other side of the room. I didn't recognise where I was but finally took in the fine interior and expensive looking furniture that surrounded me and guessed I was still in the Noble District.

Vikki came back with a large handheld mirror, her face pale with worry.

"I'm so sorry," she whispered and held the mirror above me. Nausea twisted in my belly as I looked at my reflection. The far-left side of my face was marred with bright angry red and pink burn marks and scars, the left side of my scalp was practically burned away and only had small patches of hair left on the side. I closed my eyes and gulped down the lump in my throat. Panic crept into my body as the image of the charred left side of my face seemed to permanently engrave itself into my memory – I took a deep breath.

The room was quiet as they waited for me to respond and the worry was almost palpable in the air. My eyes burned with tears but I couldn't cry now. I was never one to care for my appearance but there was something so shocking to see yourself in such a state. But I couldn't worry about it now, not when everyone else was in such a panic because they were worried about how I would react.

"I'm alive," I said and the words came out quietly. "I'm alive and I won. That's the only thing I will focus on."

"Nevara…" Kain trailed off and I shook my head, wincing at the pain.

"No," I rasped. "No more of this sad atmosphere, you're

all annoying me with all these hopeless expressions," I said waving my right hand. "They're just scars. That's all. Now go back to normal or I'm not sharing my winnings with you." The room fell silent and I refused to look at their sad faces anymore.

"You are a fearless little beastie," Derrick said with a chuckle and then slapped Kain's shoulder. "I knew it would take more than a little fire to bring you down."

"If your training didn't kill me, I don't know what will," I teased. I looked back to Vikki who was still crying so I reached up and brushed her tears away.

"Come on Vik, let's give them some time," Derrick said and put his arm around Vikki as he leads them from the room.

"I thought you were dead," Kain said quietly and my breath caught in my throat. I forced my head to turn and face him, ignoring the pain. Kain's voice sounded so quiet…so scared that I couldn't help but look at him. Kain had always been my role model. From the very first time I saw him in the arena, I was star struck. I knew I wanted to be just like him in that moment and have tried my best since then to do just that and make him proud of me.

"I'm not dead." It came out as a whisper and his eyes filled with tears. *Oh no.* I really didn't want Kain to cry. I've never seen him cry before and I definitely didn't want to see it now, because if he cried, I knew I wouldn't be able to stop myself from crying too.

"I saw you lying on the floor after the fire had been put out and I thought…" His voice broke on the last word as a silent sob wracked his body and my stomach churned with sadness. My eyes burned as I reached out with my right hand to rest on his shoulder, my body aching with the movement but I didn't care, I had to do something to stop Kain from crying.

"I should have been quicker to save you," Kain shook his head. "I should have known what Samuel was going to do," he choked.

"You couldn't have known, no one could have," I said. "Please stop crying," I choked out and the room was filled with nothing but the sound of Kain's sobs and my heaving breaths for a moment before Kain grabbed my hand and squeezed it.

"No more crying, Kain," I swallowed deeply. *"Dad."* I choked on the word and Kain's body froze. I had heard Luca and Brendan call him Dad for years but I could never get myself to say it. Not knowing if I was entitled to call him that or if it was ok. But it was the only name fitting for Kain. He has raised me, clothed and fed me, trained me…saved me. He was my father in every sense and meaning of the word.

"You, your mother and brothers are my world. I will do everything in my power to keep you all safe. My sword and flame are yours and will protect you for as long as you want them to. I love you, my loving, fierce and brave daughter," he said and a strangled whimper escaped my throat as I pulled him in with my right hand. He came as close as he could without hurting my wounds and gave me a soft hug. His whispers of encouraging words echoed around us as the bond between us strengthened like an iron lock. With Kain as my father, such things as scars barely mattered anymore.

Love. Something I always felt as if I were on the outside looking in on…but now, it was mine and I would do everything to keep and protect it.

CHAPTER 11

*D*ays passed as I became confined to a bed in a foreign room. I learned that I was in a healing tower in the noble district and that the King was paying for my stay. As he should because this was partly his fault. The contestants should have been more thoroughly checked that their magic hadn't been awakened before being allowed to compete.

I thought back at how the King had let Samuel continue to fight me in the finals even after his brutal match beforehand and scowled at the ceiling.

I wondered where Samuel was now? No one had heard if he were to be executed or not but by embarrassing the King I knew he wouldn't get off lightly.

I sat up in the bed, cringing as my newly scarred skin tugged and pulled with each movement as I walked over to the floor length mirror at the side of the room and studied myself. A bandaged wrap covered my breasts and a pair of soft white cotton trousers hung loose at my waist. The red angry burn scars were a stark contrast against the white and made them stand out even more.

I pulled my long black hair back over my right shoulder and studied the red and pinkish scars that covered the whole left side of my body and how they crawled up my neck to frame the side of my face.

Thankfully, Vikki had found a hair elixir and had been applying it to the bald and scarred patches of my head. I could already see about an inch of hair growth coming through again. She told me the elixir stated hair growth was to be expected within a day but I was still surprised at how fast it was working since I took it last night.

Having the scars on my body and face was enough to deal with, but the fact that my hair might have been permanently damaged really triggered something in me. My long black hair has always been a part of me. Through every moment of my life, even the blurred memories of my birth mother brushing my hair made it more sentimental and important to me.

My fingers skimmed over the black magic formation circle in the centre of my chest. I often forgot was there since it had been so long since I received it. It didn't even really bother me anymore – in fact, it had become a blurred memory of my life in the streets. An inky reminder of my time before I met Kain.

I thought back to the contest again and the final moments before the fire happened. I remember feeling as if someone was beside me – holding me and taking the pain away. I knew it wasn't possible, but the feeling was strange in a way that it felt familiar. Like phantom arms embracing me.

"Nevara," a voice called from outside the room and tore me away from my thoughts. I recognised it as one of the healers who had been helping Vikki take care of my wounds.

"Come in!" I responded and she appeared through the door with a small tray filled with meats and different vegetables. That was one of the best things about being in the Noble District. The food was incredible.

The now crumbling port was still allowing only a few select merchants to enter and trade under the strict scrutiny of the King. Of course all of the spices and exotic merchandise that was brought in was only traded in the Noble District. I don't think any of the commoners could afford the stuff they brought in anyway.

"A young man named Xander is here to see you," the healer said quietly. Kate, I think her name was. "Should I send him away?" She asked, her eyes darting to my scars and my bandaged chest.

"No, it's fine. Let him in," I waved a hand as I carefully sat down at the small table beneath one of the large open windows. I began chewing on one of the strips of beef and groaned at the aromatic spices that melted in my mouth.

I looked down on the bustling streets below. Nobles dressed in the finest velvets and silks went about their business. I wanted to chuck one of my carrots at them.

"You look like hell," Xander said from the doorway, his large build filling up the archway.

"That's not a nice thing to say to a lady," I snorted as I carefully swivelled in my chair, cringing again at the feeling of pulled skin. Xander saw the expression and his mouth tightened.

"Sit with me." I motioned to the empty chair opposite me and Xander obliged with large steps.

"He's a bastard for what he did," Xander hissed as he got closer to see my scars. He sunk down in the chair opposite and ran a hand through his short brown curls. "If I had been awoken, I would have killed him right there and then," Xander threatened through gritted teeth. His face became tight with anger as his eyes focused on the scars that covered my left arm like a glove and I instinctively pulled it back to my lap.

"What's done is done," I said after a moment as I leant back in my chair. "He's most likely to be executed anyway, so there's no point focusing on him anymore. I know I'm definitely not." I half lied. The scars were a constant reminder of my lack of strength against Samuel so I didn't want to focus on it. I have learned from living on the streets and losing my birth mother that there is no good from holding onto things from the past. They would only devour you from the inside out and plague the future.

"Still pisses me off." Xander sighed and watched as I ate a few more slices of beef, his face becoming softer and almost...nervous?

"I know flowers are typical for someone unwell, but I figured you weren't a flower type of girl," Xander said and I snorted.

"Flowers are of no use to me," I said and took a drink from the small cup of water Kate had brought in.

"That's why I got you this." Xander lifted a small, wrapped parcel and placed it on the table and I stared at it before looking at him.

"You didn't have to get me anything," I pointed out and placed the cup down. "We've only just met and don't know anything about each other. You do remember that I'm not a noble, right?" I said and Xander just let out a chuckle and rolled his eyes. A beautiful smile lit up his face and I couldn't help but smile in return, he seemed to have that effect on people. I thought it was funny how different his personality was inside and out of the fighting ring. When I first saw him at the contest, he was as huge and unmoving like a wall and fought mercilessly, but in person he was soft spoken and sweet. I think I could become good friends with someone like him, even if he was a damn noble.

"I told you I needed a friend at the Academy," he said and when I made no move to take the package, his mouth twisted and he pushed it even closer to me. "Just open the damn thing," he hissed.

Sighing I pulled the package towards me and was surprised by how heavy it was. I unwrapped the brown cloth to find a beautiful but lethal looking dagger.

I lifted it up in my hands and was in awe at the tiny row of white stones that lined the hilt of the dagger. As I twisted it in my hand, the stones seemed to be flecked with iridescent colours of orange and red.

"The stones are called fire opals," Xander said. "It was one of the first ever weapons I bought for myself without the help of my father." I stared in wonder at the gems that seemed to have fire trapped inside of them.

The same flames that devoured my body as I screamed and screamed until my lungs were filled with the scent of burning flesh.

I dropped the dagger to the table as I gulped down breaths. What was that? It felt as if I was back in the arena when Samuel unleashed his flames upon me. Sweat beaded on my back as my heart thundered.

"Nevara?" Xander came to my side suddenly, his hands burning like fire as they touched my own and I flinched away.

"The fire," I choked, pointing at the dagger. Had the dagger been cursed somehow? Cursed so that the holder experiences such pain and anguish? Xander's eyes followed my hand and then they clicked with realisation.

"The fire opals," His eyes widened and quickly covered the dagger with the piece of cloth that was beside the tray. "Oh crap, forgive me. I'm so stupid!" His eyes widened as he looked me over again. My body began to tremble as images and feelings of the contest flooded my mind entirely. I lost my grip of what was real and what wasn't as phantom flames licked and devoured the left side of my body again.

I had the vague sense of Kain entering the room and shouting at Xander and then calling for a healer but I couldn't speak. I couldn't do anything but give into what seemed like the never-ending flames that seemed like they wouldn't stop until it left nothing but ashes.

Burning. Burning. *Burning.*

The sound of a raven's caw sent a shock through my mind and the sudden *flap flap flap* of its wings made everything still.

A sudden coolness filled my blood and the flames began to wither away. My senses came back to me one by one and my eyes fluttered open. Black beady eyes stared at me and I jumped back in my chair to see Soot staring at me. His head cocked to the side as if to say, *are you ok now?*

"Nevara!" I heard Kain call as he tried to shoo the bird away. "What happened? Are you alright?" He asked as he grabbed my face, softly on my left side, as he examined me. Soot hopped over to stand on the table.

"The dagger," I breathed and my voice was hoarse. "I think it's cursed." The room turned to a shocked Xander who watched me with concern.

"Nevara..." He began and took a step forward. "It's not a cursed dagger. It's not even magical, it was made by a black-smith before magic was even discovered," Xander explained and looked worriedly at Kain. It was just an ordinary dagger? Then what the hell just happened to me?

"Vikki said that you might experience some...stress episodes after the incident," Kain said slowly and the words seemed to echo around the room.

"What do you mean?" I croaked out as I wiped the sweat from my brow.

"The fire opals from the dagger seemed to have triggered

the memories from the contest," Kain said, his eyes flickering with emotion. I sat back in my chair, my mind a swirl of thoughts and emotions.

"You're saying that every time I see fire that I'm going to become a screaming mess like I was just then?" I asked with a frown. There was no way... I was stronger than that.

"What you went through was extremely horrific," Kain said. "You're still trying to deal with what happened – even though your body may be healed now, your mind is still struggling."

I stared at Kain, then flitted my gaze to Xander and Vikki, who looked like she was going to cry again. Soot gave a squawk as he hopped closer, his wings fluttering as if to stroke my hand.

"I don't know what to say," I said after a few minutes of silence. "I think I might go to bed, if that's ok," I added, wanting to be alone to process all of this.

"Of course," Kain said quietly and placed a soft kiss on my head before standing up. "I'll be right outside the door if you need me."

"I'm so sorry," Xander said as he came closer. "I'll take the dagger away and I promise to never give you a gift again," he said and I gave him a small, weak smile. He went to retrieve the dagger and Soot flapped his wings and cawed at him. Soot pecked at his hand and Xander jumped back, swearing under his breath.

"Can I still have the dagger?" I asked quietly and Xander watched my face. I didn't want to seem entirely hopeless that I couldn't even be in the same room as the dagger. Xander seemed to understand that and after a moment he left along with Kain and Vikki. I retreated back to my bed and curled my legs up into myself. For the first time in a long time, I began to feel...weak. And that, it seems, hurt me more than the flames did.

CHAPTER 12

$\mathcal{D}$ays turned into weeks and before I knew it an entire month had passed of me holed up in a bed. My thoughts and memories plagued me every minute of the day and there was no escape from them.

Nightmares of flames and burning flesh chased away any grasp of sleep I could get and I knew I was in a downward spiral but I just couldn't shake the dark thoughts that seemed to linger in my mind, like shadows that seemed to grow with each passing moment.

Each day, Kain and a member of the guild would come and talk about what dungeon they had beaten and what artefacts they managed to obtain. I tried to listen and pay attention but my thoughts kept slipping back to flames and how weak I was and they soon left after they saw that glazed look slip over my eyes.

Luca sat beside my bed like he did every other night and was reading something to me. I had no idea what it was but the steady rhythm of his voice settled the onslaught of thoughts and memories.

I ran my hand over the small envelope that Xander had

brought earlier today and the dark doubts and thoughts came close to breaking through the calm. I held the admission letter to Ashwood Academy and I felt my fingers tremble around the ridges of the thick paper. My lifelong dream was sitting in my hands and for the first time since meeting Kain... I was unsure. Unsure if I was strong enough to truly train at the Academy and graduate to become like Kain and the rest of the guild when I have become so mentally lost after the contest. Flames flickered in my mind and they seemed to crackle and hiss the words, *you think you can go up against this sort of power again? Didn't you learn enough the first time I almost killed you, little girl?*

Soot cawed from beside me and smacked me with his wing as if he could read my thoughts. He seemed to shake his little head at me as if to say, *you are strong.*

A sudden tap to the window had Luca pausing his reading and both of us looked towards the side of the room. Another *tap tap tap* sounded as small pebbles hit the panes of glass. I slowly got out of bed and grabbed the dagger that Xander had given me from under my pillow.

I had wrapped cloth around the fire opals and that had seemed to stop the triggering of the horrific memories and I was glad because it was the first gift I had received from a friend that wasn't a part of the Guild.

My joints were stiff from staying in bed for so long and I cursed at my now weakening body, that same body that was used to vigorous training every day and now I was letting it wither away in a bed.

I peered down onto the street from the window and my eyes narrowed on a hooded figure below. My breath caught as fear prickled my spine. Was it Samuel? Had he somehow escaped the prison that was holding him until his execution next week? Was he coming to finish me off?

I was about to scramble away from the window when the

figure suddenly pulled back his hood to reveal a head full of soft blonde hair and pale blue eyes.

The Prince of Ghislana stood beneath my window.

He gave me a goofy grin and motioned for me to come down to him. I almost choked on my breath. The Prince was here with no guards and wanted me to join him.

"Is that... the Prince?" Luca asked with wide eyes as he turned to face me.

"He wants me come down," I said quietly as those dark thoughts came creeping back. Outside. Somewhere I hadn't been for a little over a month, it felt as if it was an entirely different world now.

The Prince was waving me down again and held up what looked like a bag of...pastries? I almost choked on a laugh. When was the last time I laughed? The motion felt foreign to me now.

A war raged in my head as I decided what to do. Do I go out to the Prince? Or do I crawl back into bed and into the darkness of my thoughts again? The bed seemed like the easier option but the former option caught my attention.

The Academy was starting in two weeks and if I continued to stay in my bed then I wouldn't be able to attend. I would throw away all of the training I had endured and my free admission that I had won from the contest would go to waste.

Won by default, the dark thoughts whispered but I pushed them away.

I froze as I looked down at the Prince again, his mischievous grin tugging something inside me. Something from the old me that loved adventure and excitement.

I took a deep breath and then gave the Prince a nod.

"If anyone comes then tell them I went out for a walk, I'm sure the Prince doesn't want people to find out that he has snuck out of the palace," I said to Luca who looked anxious.

"Are you sure you're well enough to go out?" Luca asked quietly as I pulled on my armour that had been sitting and collecting dust in the corner of the room. It seemed slightly too big now and I cringed at how I had been neglecting my body since the arena. After the first panic attack after the incident, my appetite had seemed to shrivel up and disappear. Especially anything hot.

"I'm fine, I'll only go and see what he wants." I smiled sheepishly as I went to the door of the room and then thought against it, the healers would only order me back to my room if they saw me leaving in the middle of the night. I went to the window and opened it before securing a spare cloak around my shoulders.

Luca looked pale as he watched me climb out the window and I gave him a small smile as I lowered myself down onto the ledge beneath me. My scarred skin pulled uncomfortably with the movement but I gritted my teeth and continued.

"Now this is entertaining," I heard the Prince chuckle beneath me and I scowled at him. As I put my foot lower it slipped on a loose stone and I was suddenly falling.

The air whipped past me and around my cloak and I saw Soot dive out the window with a cry. My room was on the third floor and I had only managed to climb down to the second floor before slipping. This was going to hurt. If it didn't kill me that was.

"Shit!" I heard the Prince beneath me curse as I closed my eyes. I was about to hit the floor and I braced for the impact but ended up falling onto something warm instead.

Both myself and the Prince fell to the floor as he wrapped his arms around me. He grunted as I fell on top of him and I felt adrenaline shoot through my body and I trembled and tried but failed to rise.

As I lay on top of the Prince it finally settled in my mind how absolutely absurd this whole situation was. If Kain

119

where to see us right now I think his head might have exploded.

"Are you alright?" The Prince panted quietly and I lifted my head from his chest to look into his bright blue eyes. They crinkled with concern as he took in my pale and thinning face, no doubt seeing the dark rings that now framed my silver eyes.

"Thank you," I breathed and felt his body warmth seep into my own. I rested a hand on top of his surprisingly muscular chest, his heart thundering underneath to match my own.

"I should've come to see you sooner," he murmured and I found no words to reply with but silently cursed myself at how weak I must now seem to him.

I pulled myself off of him and noticed how cold my body felt without his warmth. I quickly pushed the thought aside as I held out my hand and helped him up from the ground.

"Where are the pastries?" I asked after a moment of awkward silence and he let out a chuckle as he dusted off his velvet cloak. He pulled up his hood and did the same to mine as a few drunken stragglers passed behind us. He stayed close to me and ran his hand gently over the left side of my face, his own features filling with anger. I pulled my head back and bit the inside of my mouth to stop the dark thoughts from entering my mind. The taste of blood filled my mouth and the thoughts receded.

"I can't wait to see that bastard die for what he did to you," he whispered and all I could do was stare at him.

"I heard that you tried to help me in the arena," I said quietly after a moment. "I know your father wouldn't have been pleased at that, so thank you," I breathed and he winced, no doubt remembering the scolding his father must have given him for helping a commoner in front of such a large crowd.

"So… the pastries," I pressed and he shook his head whilst laughing.

"I want to show you something first," he said and dangled the bag of flaky pastries in front of my face to bribe me some more.

"I can't be gone long," I whispered as my eyes locked on to the golden deliciousness that he held in front of me and I felt my stomach begin to growl as if it had just woken up from a long nap.

"It's not far," he urged and held out his arm for me. After a quick glance up at the window, I linked my arm in his and grabbed the bag of pastries.

Now that I was actually outside I felt much better. I wouldn't go back to that room and hide in my bed anymore. I knew I needed to become strong again, even stronger than I was before because that's what I had always strived for. It was time to move on.

"Where are we going?" I asked with my mouth full of delicious flaky pastry that Prince Damon had said came from the palace kitchens. I can't remember the last time I had snacked on something sweet like this. The sugary taste tingled on my mouth and I shuddered at the happiness it brought with it.

"Classes start at Ashwood Academy in two weeks and my group and I will be attending," he said and I stopped to stare at him.

"*You're* going to the academy?" I asked in disbelief and he arched a brow at me.

"It took a lot of convincing my father, but he understands that becoming a swordsman will make our rule over the kingdom that much stronger if their prince has awoken his magic." A smug grin filled his face.

"Is your fathers magic awoken?" I asked and he shook his head as he pulled me to walk beside him again.

"He says that he doesn't have time but I know it's because he's too busy enjoying his nights with women and drink." He laughed humourlessly and my mouth opened and then closed again, unsure how to respond to that.

The streets of the Noble District were unfamiliar to me. We winded down roads and alleyways and I tried to memorise each path we walked through but lost count after so many. The streets were perfectly cleaned and well-kept compared to the Commoners District and I frowned at the stark differences.

We approached a small and quaint inn and I noted how clean and manicured it was compared to Kiera's tavern. Even the music that played from inside it was classy and boring compared to the hearty beats of Kiera's.

"You're bringing me to an inn?" I asked wearily and he rolled his eyes as he pulled me inside. Instead of going into the main bar area he quickly turned and pulled me up the stairs and I began to resist against his grasp.

"What are you doing?" I hissed as dread pooled in my stomach. Why was he taking me to the rooms of the inn? Had I been a fool to come along so easily? Even if I was weakened at the moment I would still fight like hell if I needed to. I felt the dagger harnessed to my thigh and I was suddenly thankful that I had secured it just in case.

"Don't flatter yourself, my friends are in here," he explained as we got to an unmarked wooden door and he thumped on it three times before standing back and waiting. The door opened slightly after a moment and two familiar brown eyes stared out at us. Xander. The door opened wider as his eyebrows shot up as he examined me.

"I didn't think he would be able to get you to leave your bed," Xander said gently and I remembered him earlier today when he had dropped off the letter from the Academy. He had tried his best to talk to me but my head had been too filled with thoughts to be able to keep a conversation.

"The Prince brought me pastries," I mumbled quietly as I quickly wiped the crumbs away from my mouth, earning a chuckle from the room.

"You can just call me Damon, no need for formalities." Damon said and my eyes widened a fraction at the realisation that I was now on friendly terms with the prince.

"So that's how to win you over? Sweets?" Xander asked in disbelief with a grin and despite everything, I smiled back.

"She doesn't look strong enough to take you out, Xan," I heard a female voice tease and looked past Xander to see a girl with bright red hair lean against the bed to the side of the room. She pushed off it and skipped over to us, her green eyes wide as she took in my face. "They look awesome! Do they hurt?"

"Don't be rude, Kitty." A guy with mousy brown hair grumbled from behind them, he sat cross legged in front of a stack of papers with magic formations.

"I'll introduce you," Damon said with a smirk as he pulled me to sit on the large plush sofa to the edge of the room. "You already know Xander Kenway," Damon said and Xander gave a small smile. "That is Kitty Beaufort and that is Harven Tern." He nodded to the girl and the guy who were just speaking and they gave me a smile and a wave. "And that over there is Alec." He nodded to the guy who was draped over a chair in the corner of the room, he lazily flicked through a small novel and didn't make any move to acknowledge me.

"As you can tell, he's a little unsociable," Xander added quietly and Kitty giggled. I watched the guy in the corner for another moment, his messy dark hair fell near his eyes as he scanned the length of the book. His skin was a beautiful, tanned colour that shimmered golden in the light of the lanterns in the room and I found myself mesmerised as I followed the contours of his chiselled face. His eyes swiftly lifted to mine as if he sensed me watching him and my breath caught in my throat at the unusual azure colour of them and how they pierced into me.

"It's nice to meet you all," I smiled nervously before I asked the question that was raging through my mind. "Why did you bring me here?" I finally tore my gaze away from Alec to look at Damon again.

"We're all going to Ashwood Academy this month so I thought we could all use friends whilst inside. Especially when the dungeon training begins," Prince Damon said. "Me, you and Xander are swordsmen, Kitty and Alec are battle mages and Harven is a healer. It's the perfect group." He shrugged and I swallowed deeply. They wanted me to be a part of their group. Even though I had failed the contest.

Even though I was now damaged.

"I'm a commoner," I pointed out after a moment of silence and Damon's mouth thinned. Dark thoughts flooded my mind as they seemed to call me other names like, *failure, weak...disfigured.*

"You're the damn best swordsman I have seen in a while. You had that Samuel bastard before he cheated and used his magic," Damon said and Xander nodded enthusiastically.

"You had me and my ass in no time," Xander added and I chuckled despite myself and I looked around at them again. Kitty winked at me and something began to bloom in my stomach. It felt like through all of the crap that happened with the contest, something good was beginning to come from it.

"I'll join your group if you promise me a bag of pastries each week," I negotiated playfully and Damon choked out a laugh.

"Deal!" He agreed with a grin and the group moved closer

and began to ask me about my training and about my different skills I had and I was finally beginning to feel like myself again. The nightmare of the contest was becoming like a bad dream and I wanted to move forward from it.

I made myself a promise to train tomorrow and start getting back into perfect shape before the academy began. My fear of flames...well I guess that would take longer to overcome but I'm sure if I kept at it, then I could get over that too.

The night flew by as I talked to my new friends, my eyes constantly drifting back to Alec and catching a glimpse of those bright azure eyes. My heart thundered every time his gaze met mine and a feeling I couldn't place twisted in my stomach. I found myself wanting to find out more about him and it made me even more determined to get better.

"You want to train?" Kain asked incredulously as he sat down beside me at the small table. I had been out well into the night before returning here to a sleeping Luca. I had woken up this morning feeling refreshed and motivated, something that I hadn't felt since before the contest.

I had said my goodbyes to Damon and his friends last night and we had all agreed to meet up again inside the Academy. Alec had grunted his agreement before he sauntered out of the room, barely looking my way as he left.

"I want to go back to the Commoners District," I said quietly. "I want to go home and get back to normal." Kain studied me for a minute before squeezing my shoulder.

"I don't know what happened to push you to do this but I'm happy it did." He smiled and Vikki came in with Ganya beside her. Kain pulled Vikki aside, no doubt to talk to her about getting me discharged from here.

"You're looking better today," Ganya grinned as she sat beside me and put her arm around my shoulders. Ganya was the only one who still treated me like she did before the incident and not like I was too delicate to be touched anymore and I loved her for it.

"I *feel* better today," I replied truthfully. Whilst the dark thoughts still lingered around the edge of my mind, they made no advances now. It was almost as if meeting Damon and his friends had given me enough strength to build a wall around myself mentally, keeping my head clear and focused.

"Netta is going to be so happy to see you again," Kain said as he came back over to me. Netta had come and seen me any chance she could but she still had to work at the tavern. Kiera, I heard, had given her all the time she would need off but Netta had told me she would feel guilty for not bringing money back for Kain and the house. Even though Kain made enough money from the dungeons, I understood completely how she felt. That no amount of money could ever repay what Kain had done for us, even if he refused any money we would give to him for our keep.

"I miss her," I replied, "and Brendan," I added as I thought of my younger brother and how he was doing in his new bakery job. When he told me that he managed to get a job in the bakery I remember desperately trying to hold back telling him that it was the same bakery I would often steal from when we lived in the alley.

"Well let's not keep them waiting then, shall we?" Kain smiled and Ganya pulled me up to head towards the door. I took one last look around the room and when I closed the door, it felt like I was locking away some of the darkness along with it.

CHAPTER 13

The remaining two weeks leading up to the beginning of Ashwood Academy was brutal. I reunited with my family and then threw myself headfirst into training. From dawn till dusk, I gave my all into getting my body back to where it was before the incident and then pushed myself even further. I refined all my sword and fighting techniques until they became second nature once more.

Every night I would go to bed, my body aching and burning from the pain, but I loved it. The pain seemed to make the darker thoughts drift even further away and it became my motivation to get up the next day and do it all again. I even climbed the Sky Kissed mountain a few times with Derrick just to prove to myself that I could still do it.

"Tomorrow is the big day," Derrick said as we sat down at our usual table in the tavern with the rest of the Guild. I wiped my sweat slick hair back from my face and gave a nod. Tomorrow was the first day of Ashwood Academy and I was excited if not a little nervous and scared. The one thing that I was really looking forward to was seeing Damon and his group of friends again. I hadn't made the hour journey to the Noble District since I left, but I wanted to be back to my normal self before they saw me again. The last time they saw me, I was in a very dark place and I didn't want anyone to see my like that again. Ever.

"Are you still not going to tell me how they awaken our magic?" I asked as Vikki lay her head on my shoulder. She softly stroked a hand down the left side of my face over my scars and I gave her a small smile. The scars became a part of me now. People in the streets and at the arena would often stare or do a double take but I didn't care anymore. These scars were proof that I almost died but made it out alive and came back stronger, I wouldn't hide them away anymore.

"The process is different for everyone, so it's better going in with an open and clear mind," she explained softly and I sighed at hearing the same explanation the Guild had given me over and over again. I was about to demand more information but saw Vikki's frown and thought against it. Vikki had also been in a bad place mentally since the contest, blaming herself for not acting fast enough and not being able to heal my scars fully. But everyone knew the limit to a healers ability, whilst they were powerful, there was always the chance of the wound not being healed fast enough or if the claws of death had already sunk too deep for them to be saved.

"I can't believe our little Nevara is going to the academy," Jamie sighed dramatically and everyone murmured agreements.

"I still remember the first day Kain brought you to train with us," Oryan said, sipping at his ale. "Tiny and scrawny thing that you were, we all thought you wouldn't be able to lift a sword let alone swing one."

"She still got a good few hits in at you though, didn't she?" Ganya teased and Oryan scowled.

"Are you all packed to go?" Kain asked and I turned to him.

"I don't have a lot of stuff, just my weapons and armour." I shrugged and his eyes softened.

"Here, I've been holding onto this until you were leaving." Kain chucked a heavy red pouch in front of me. "It's your winnings."

I lifted the bag and then bit the inside of my mouth, trying to keep the memories of the contest at bay.

"I don't need it," I said and pushed it back to Kain who frowned.

"It's yours," he replied, pushing it back.

"I won it for our guild, plus I don't want anything from the King," I said and I meant it. The King knew the risks of letting Samuel advance to fight with me and he allowed it anyway. Even if it wasn't his fault directly, I needed someone other than Samuel to blame because thinking of him…it stripped down my walls and left me wide open for the darkness to attack.

"Take it, buy more armour, weapons, food," Kain shrugged. "Buy whatever you want. You earned it." I wanted to tell him that I didn't earn it but I bit my lip and slipped the pouch down into my belt. I would take it for now.

"Now, let's eat!" Derrick shouted, a welcome distraction as the table dived right back into chatter and talk about the academy. I smiled as I tucked into my stew, savouring the comfort that being with the Guild brought as I knew I wouldn't be able to see them as much when I left. It had been a long time since I had been on my own, the last time was when I lived on the streets before Netta and Kain. But I needed this, the independence, it could only make me stronger. And that was what I wanted the most.

AFTER EVERYONE SAID their goodbyes to me at the tavern I walked home with Kain and Netta, chattering about the plans for tomorrow. When we reached the front door of our house I told them I wanted to take a walk around before turning in.

Netta gave me a kiss on the head followed by Kain and once they were both inside the house I turned and headed through the familiar back streets to a place I had once called home.

The alleyway.

"It's Nevara!" A boy called and the families began to peak their heads out of the tents that lined the floor to look and smile at me. Many were sat eating bowls of stew that I knew had been curtesy of Kiera's tavern and I smiled. I had visited the alley often throughout the years, always bringing whatever I had spare or just to talk to the people that were once my neighbours.

I took the pouch from my belt and went down the row of tents and handed out the gold coins, more for the bigger families and many of them embraced me or cried as I handed them out. A gold piece was enough to feed them for a year, get them new clothes or even shelter them somewhere at least for a little while. Hopefully, some of them might be able to find work with the money I gave them.

I wondered what the King would think if he knew the money he gave me was now been given to the poor and homeless. A smirk tugged at my mouth at the thought of his red and angry face.

I handed out the last gold piece and said my goodbyes, memorising all the different faces and smiles. I wouldn't be able to visit for a while but I knew the gold would help them immensely and that had made it a little easier to leave that night. Now all that was left was to sleep and then depart for Ashwood Academy in the morning.

My lifelong dream was coming into play, I was finally going to become a swordsman.

I just hoped the darkness that seemed to always encircle my mind would keep away long enough to see the dream become a reality.

~

I HAD a restless night of tossing and turning whilst drifting in and out of sleep. I eventually gave up at dawn and took a bath whilst everyone was still sleeping, enjoying the peaceful quiet. I took my time washing and combing out my long black hair and wondered if I should trim it as I studied the way it fell to my navel. After humouring it for a moment, I finally decided against it and braided it so it fell down my back.

I examined my face in the mirror, my silver eyes standing out against my sun-kissed face. The autumn was fully here now and I knew my skin would lose its colour soon. I touched the left side of my face where the pink skin that made up my scars was and ran my fingers over its soft and silky texture. I lifted my left arm and examined the same silky scarred flesh that covered it entirely. Luckily, the scars didn't affect my grip on my sword which was what I was worried about the most when I got back into training.

"They're so pretty." I heard Luca's quiet voice at my door and I turned to see him standing shyly at the threshold.

"I think most people would disagree with you," I chuckled.

"No! They are so pretty – *you* are so pretty," he said with a frown and I waved off his compliment with a chuckle. I didn't take receiving compliments well, mostly because I didn't know how to respond.

"Why are you awake so early?" I asked as I sat down on my bed and patted the space beside me.

"I haven't slept yet," he said lifting the book he must have been reading all night and I chuckled.

"I'm going to miss you reading to me," I said as I wrapped my arms around him, resting my cheek on top of his soft and messy hair.

"I'm going to miss you too." His voice wobbled and then I felt his body tremble with sobs and I held him closer.

"I'm going to visit as often as I can," I said, my own eyes threatening with tears. "Plus, you're going to be coming to the academy next year, right?" I asked and he nodded whilst sobbing.

"So, it's only a year and then we will be together in the academy! I promise," I said and that seemed to calm him down a little. We held onto each other as Luca cried. A breathy sob sounded behind us, and before I could look, Brendan had engulfed us in an embrace. The three of us wrapped around one another, and I held onto them. My silly and loving brothers.

When I was alone on the streets, these two had saved me along with their mother and Kain. I would do anything for them.

It was why I was going to the Academy; to become stronger and protect them, and not have to face the harshness of the world, the alley, ever again.

When their cries stopped, we got up and walked towards the kitchen where I could hear Netta cooking and talking with Kain. My heart thundered when I realised that I wouldn't be hearing their idle chatter in the mornings again until I graduated.

"You two look terrible." Kain chuckled softly as we entered the room, Brendan and Luca's eyes were big and red, evidence of their tears.

"I made a big breakfast to keep you full until you get to the academy," Netta said and she pointed to the table laden with food.

"You didn't have to cook so much," I choked as I took in the ginormous amount of food. Porridge, fruits, breads and oh my goodness *pastries.*

"Seeing as I won't be able to cook for you for a while… I wanted to do my best to…" She choked on her words and I came around the table to hug her. She crushed me to her chest as she sobbed and I rubbed her back.

"It's like I'm going away forever!" I chuckled and felt Netta's body shake with tears. "I'll visit every time I can and I'll write letters."

"Promise me you will be safe and take care of yourself," Netta whispered and I nodded against her head.

"I promise," I whispered and she pulled back and dried her tears, her honey eyes soft as she looked at me.

Kain remained quiet as we ate our way through breakfast, discussing the Academy and Brendan's time at the bakery. By the time I needed to go, they were all cried out and I hugged them closely as I tried to savour their warmth.

"Do you have everything you need?" Kain asked as he walked me to the trade square in the Commoners District where the carriages would be waiting to take me to the Academy. He placed my acceptance letter into my hands and I held onto it tightly.

"Yup." I grinned at him and he slung his arm around my shoulders. I had said my goodbyes to the Guild yesterday, my family this morning and now I knew I had to say goodbye to Kain.

"I don't want to say goodbye to you," I said quietly and Kain stared at me for a moment.

"Then we won't say goodbye," He smiled sadly. "But I will tell you to go into the academy with your head held high and dominate it. You are the bravest, most powerful swordsman I have ever seen and that's even before your magic is awoken. Become the best." he demanded and my heart thundered at his words, the boost of motivation had my blood soaring.

I pulled him into a hug and savoured the feeling as he held me tightly.

I climbed into the carriage and watched as Kain paid the driver and told him where to go. The horses began moving and I poked my head out of the window to wave at Kain, the sinking feeling hitting deep inside my stomach.

"Did you remember to bring the gold?" Kain asked and I hesitated a moment before answering.

"I gave it away to the alley." His mouth hung open for a moment before he gave a small chuckle and shook his head.

"I'd expect nothing less from you!" He shouted just as he disappeared out of view and my smile grew.

Once the view of the Commoners District turned into a view of forests and fields, only then did I let myself sit back and accept the reality of what was really going on.

And it terrified me.

CHAPTER 14

 $\mathcal{T}$ he silence inside the carriage was driving me insane, I had to stare out of the window.

We passed through small towns and sprawling emerald forests filled with the sound of birdsong and the creaking of trees. Seeing how much was really out here compared to the Commoners District…it made me feel tiny. There were so many more towns and villages in the distance and I wondered how they lived. Did they journey to the city often? Were their living conditions just like the Commoners District?

We passed crumbling castles and manors where the lords and some of the wealthier nobles once would have made their home. Ever since the civil war all the wealthy seemed to stay in their protected Nobles District.

Then I started thinking about the distant kingdoms that I knew lay beyond the island where we lived and began to wonder if I would see any of them in the future.

"We're only a few miles out now, lady," the carriage driver shouted and nodded his head to the opposite side of the carriage. I quickly moved to look out the small window and gasped. The Academy loomed ahead and I had no words to describe what I saw, only that it made the palace look withered in comparison.

Huge towers with spiralling bridges and turrets shot up into the sky, so high that I wondered how many floors were actually in the Academy. It was made of grey brick and the windows were covered with beautiful multi-coloured stained glass.

All along its high walls crept a twisting rainbow of ivy and roses that gave the whole castle-type building an almost dreamy feel to it. If I passed this building before, I would have mistaken it for the King's second palace and not an Academy.

"I've been here many times, but it still takes my breath away each time," the carriage driver said in awe and I agreed with him. This place was not something you could get used to seeing.

A huge forest surrounded the castle-like building and I could see a large lake off to the side.

As we got closer, I could make out different symbols and magic formations etched onto the dark iron of the tall fence that surrounded the grounds and I wondered what they meant.

A huge set of open black iron gates stood before us and as we passed under them, I felt a jolt of energy down my spine.

"What was that?" I gasped, a little breathless as I looked back at the gates through the rear window.

"Magic," the carriage driver shouted with a grin. So that was what the formations on the fence were, some sort of magic barrier.

As we pulled into the long driveway, I noticed it was filled with students, some in long black robes and some with just armour on like me. They all milled around, the sound of excited chatter and laughter filled my ears.

"Here we go, arrived safe and sound," the carriage man said with a smile and I thanked him as I hopped out. Some people turned to look at me as I retrieved my sword and dagger from the carriage and fixed them back into their sheaths on my belt. I gave a final wave to the carriage driver before turning and studying my surroundings. I had no idea where to go but making my way to the main building seemed like a good start.

I noticed that the crowd was mostly made up of nobles of all ages, their velvet tunics shimmering in the autumn sun and I wondered if they knew straight away that I was a commoner.

"Nevara!" I heard Xander's voice holler over the chatter and I turned to see his large form moving through the crowd with Kitty, Harven and Alec in tow.

"How did you spot me?" I asked as I gave them a warm smile.

"Kitty saw you in the carriage," he said and the girl quickly pulled me into a hug.

"Can you believe we're finally here?" She asked excitedly and I shook my head. I couldn't believe I was here. It felt like I would wake up any moment to find this was only a dream.

"Where's Damon?" I asked looking around the crowd.

"His Royal Highness is already inside with the protection of his knights, much to his displeasure," Xander snorted.

"He's probably trying to escape as we speak," Harven chuckled. I turned to look at Alec and watched as he scanned the crowd with a bored expression. He caught my gaze and gave a small nod of his head before looking around again. What a strange guy.

"Attention new students!" A man shouted from the front of the crowd and silence followed as we turned to him. "Please form an orderly line and approach the main building.

We will be receiving your acceptance letters and then placing you in groups to have a small tour of the academy."

"What about the awakening?" Someone shouted and the man who was dressed in long white robes gave a small laugh.

"The awakenings will be happening tonight, have patience," he said and a few nervous and excited giggles filled the crowd.

"I can't wait for our magic," Kitty whispered to me and I nodded. I've waited my whole life to get my magic awoken and it was finally happening, it was hard to believe.

We made our way slowly into the Academy building and waited for what felt like an eternity before reaching the foyer where I handed over my letter. Another man in white robes looked over the letter and then his eyes wandered over the burn scars on my face with a soft smile.

"I've heard how strong you were in the contest," the man said and the dark thoughts in my mind shuddered in response. "I can't wait to see what you can do when you have your magic."

I didn't know what to say so I nodded instead and he placed a small purple gemstone into my hand. I took it and walked back to join my friends again, turning the small gem in my hands and watched it cast shattered light onto the floor.

I took a moment to take a deep breath and make sure the walls in my mind were still intact before I calmed down. I glanced up to see Alec staring at me, a knowing look flickered across his gaze as his lips twitched. Almost like he could hear my thoughts.

"What colour did you get?" Kitty asked and I held up my purple gemstone. Harven and Xander had green, Kitty had red and Alec had purple. *Great.*

"Aww, I wanted to be in your group." Kitty frowned as she stared at my purple gem.

"It's only for the tour," Harven said, his green eyes studying the stone as he turned it over in his hand. "We should all be together again for the awakening."

"Do any of you know how the awakening happens?" I asked and they all shook their head, Alec leant back on the wall and closed his eyes as if he were napping. Why did I have to be stuck with such an ass? Did all this really bore him?

"I heard that it hurts," Harven frowned.

"I heard you have to drink a disgusting liquid to awaken your magic," Kitty said and I wrinkled my nose. I hoped not.

"I finally found you guys." Damon appeared to our left, breathless enough to make me think he'd ran to escape his knights. The Prince was definitely not what I expected him to be. I thought he would be a stuck-up spoiled brat that would hate on commoners like me but much to my happy surprise, he was none of those things.

"What group did you get?" Kitty asked and Damon held up a red stone. "Me too!" Kitty said excitedly and Damon turned to me and I held up my purple stone. His face crumpled slightly as he studied my stone but the look was quickly replaced to his usual smile as he met my eyes again. Was he disappointed that we had different coloured stones?

"If you would all now separate into your groups! Red and green over here and purple over there!" The white-robed man called and I waved goodbye to the rest of the group before following a slow-moving Alec to the rest of the purple group. There was around ten people in our group, all talking and chatting together as they waited for our tour to begin.

"Are you excited to awaken your magic?" I asked Alec after a moment of silence. Alec simply shrugged and pushed his hands into the pockets of his black breeches. I studied the way his black velvet tunic hugged his body and I could make out a slight definition of muscle underneath. This was a guy who had trained. *Hard.* His body had to be more suited to swordsmanship, so why was he wanting to be a battle mage? My eyes trailed up to the collar of his tunic and I spotted the swirls of black ink trailing up his neck. He let out a small chuckle and my eyes shot to his as he smirked at me. He lifted an eyebrow as if to say, *do you like what you see?* I turned away as my face heated and I bit the inside of my cheek in annoyance. I hadn't been looking at him in that way.

Not that Alec wasn't good looking, because he was. His tanned skin and dark walnut coloured hair complimented each other beautifully. His eyes were definitely captivating, I had never seen a shade of blue like them before and I found myself getting lost in them whenever he looked at me.

"Ah, the purple group, I am Archmage Syler." The Archmage was dressed in familiar long white robes which must signal the teachers and higher ups. Syler gave a slight nod of his head to us and the group quietened. "If you will all follow me, I will show you around the academy before we begin the awakening."

He turned and led us through a set of double doors. I quickly waved to the other two groups before I followed Alec into a huge stairwell. There was no ceiling as I looked up and gasped at the series of connecting bridges and stairs that lead to differed rooms and I knew I would get lost if I ever ventured there.

I had never been in a building like this. Even the healers tower in the Nobles District paled in comparison to this place. Huge arching doorways, tapestries and murals littered the walls and I found myself being drawn to the curious pictures they displayed.

"To the left is where all the battle mage classes will be held," Syler said and we turned around to approach a huge hallway to the left. Rooms and alcoves lined the walls and we stopped outside one of the wooden doors. Unnatural noises floated out and as we entered I flinched back at the bright rainbow of colours that filled the room. Students in black robes were casting magic formations into the air with sporadic flicks of their hands and I watched in wonder. The formations took form as glowing circles and symbols before they disappeared into an eruption of different elements.

"This is a four-star battle mage classroom. I'm sure you're familiar with the levelling system in the academy," Syler said as we all stared in wonder at one guy who released a fireball up and into the air, my breath caught at the sight of familiar flames. "You all start with no stars after you awake your magic and then once you learn how to wield it, your stars will increase until you reach five stars and graduate," Syler explained quickly. I had heard a little about the levelling system from Kain and the Guild but if this were only a level four class then I couldn't even imagine what a level five class would be like. The battle mages from the Guild never really practiced in the arena for safety reasons so I never got to see magic of this magnitude, only what Kain and Derrick used to do with their swords, but even that was limited. I wonder what it would be like in a dungeon when everyone could unleash their magic with no holding back.

"Next, we will move onto the swordsman classes," Syler said and we all shuffled from the room, I cast one more glance back as a girl unleashed a crack of lightning that splintered into the floor. Amazing.

We returned to the foyer again but this time we went to the right, down an almost exact hallway that the battle mages had and the sound of metal against metal made my heart thunder. This is what I'm here for.

We filtered into a class were students were paired off and sparring. I focused on a pair who were heavy with sweat and grunting with each lunge. One of them had a sword ablaze with flames whilst the other glowed with a green aura. The fire student shot forward and a flame roared towards the other student and I held my breath as the other student lifted his sword to create a wall of rock out of nowhere. I had no time to fear the flames as my mind spun at how amazing this all was and that green glow...he had the earth element.

I had heard there were different elements but I had never met an earth magic swordsman before, they were all normally healers or scholars. I watched as he retaliated with a row of sharpened stones that flew at his opponent before a roar of fire turned them to gravel.

My blood pounded as my hands clenched. I wanted nothing more than to lift my sword and join in the fray but I knew I couldn't. Not yet.

"This is a three-star magic swordsman class," Syler called out and then waved at the teacher who was viewing the sparring. "This is Archmage Perrion."

"Greetings new students." Perrion dipped his head and I felt his gaze shift over us, his eyes drifted to my scars and I flinched. I should be used to people looking at the scars now and I told myself I didn't care when I noticed them doing it but it seemed to be different when Perrion studied them. As my future teacher, it seemed like he might perceive the scars as a weakness and decide that they would make me inferior against the other students.

"I hope to see many of you in my classroom tomorrow," he said as his eyes shifted to Alec for a moment before he gave us all a small nod and turned back to his students.

"I can't wait to start his classes," a guy beside me whispered and excited chatter broke through the group.

"Let's return to the lobby," Xander called out and we left the classroom, it suddenly felt too quiet out in the hallway again. I cast a quick glance to Alec but his face remained impassive, bored as he followed the group. I wanted to smack him. Shake him. Do anything to get some sort of reaction from him.

"Up on the second floor is the scholar classrooms along with the libraries but unfortunately they are off limits to non-scholar students. We can't have everyone grabbing at old and delicate books so only those taught how to handle them are allowed in. However, there is a smaller library at the end of the hallway behind me which is open to all students." Syler smiled and then began to walk back through where the front entrance of the Academy was.

We passed out of the doors and down the steps to the right. We followed along a cobbled path that led up to another large building that had students in black robes coming in and out. It was very similar to the main building and I had to wonder how many students it housed inside its huge walls.

"This is the student accommodation along with the cafeteria," Syler said. "In here you will be given the key to your room—inside you will find the ceremonial clothes you will need for the awakening so please dress in them and meet me back here at sunset," Syler said and the crowd began murmuring excitedly as we began to make our way inside.

I followed the crowd in through the large wooden doors and up to a tall desk. A woman in white robes checked down a list for each of the groups and handed out keys and I took mine excitedly. I turned to tell Alec that I would meet him back outside after I got changed but he was already gone. Asshole.

I checked the number on my key, *room 166.* I followed the directions and found rooms *150* to *170* on the top floor.

Of course it was.

I quickly took the stairs two at a time before locating my room down a narrow hallway.

I took a deep breath as I stepped inside and looked

around. The floor matched the same dark wood from outside and the walls were covered in a soft beige paper. Two beds sat at opposite sides of the room along with two wardrobes and a matching set of dressers. I made my way over to one of the beds and found my name written on a piece of paper on top of a pile of folded white clothes. I lifted a pair of white undergarments and a large fur lined robe. Where the rest of the clothes? A key turning in the lock had me spinning around to find Kitty skipping into the room.

"It seems that Prince Damon pulled some strings to get us to room together," Kitty chuckled and then smiled brightly. I scoffed but was secretly glad I was sharing my room with someone I already knew as it skipped the awkward greetings that came along with it.

"Where's the rest of the clothes?" Kitty wrinkled her nose as she held up the strip of fabric that was to cover our torso.

"That's what I was thinking," I muttered and watched as Kitty shrugged and began stripping.

"You're going to put it on?" I asked in disbelief.

"You're not?" She scoffed. "I'll wear anything if it meant awakening my magic – plus the robe should cover us," she said and I couldn't really argue with that. I quickly pulled off my armour and pulled on the thin white material they left and scowled every time my eyes caught on it. I left my sword under the covers of my bed but attached my dagger harness to my thigh. Just in case.

Kitty let out a whistle through her teeth and I looked at her whilst I pulled the robe around my shoulders.

"What?" I asked as she stared at me.

"You are *ripped*. I mean, I have never seen a woman's stomach so muscular! How did you do it? Can I get mine like that too?" She asked as she poked at her own soft stomach and I rolled my eyes at her before I headed for the door, keeping my robe shut tight. Kitty giggled as she skipped beside me, not caring if her robe parted, which was understandable because she was flawless. She had pale freckled skin and soft red hair that fell to her waist that had even me giving her a double take. She winked at me when she caught me staring and I chuckled at her brazenness.

"You're all quite early," Syler said as we all re-emerged from the building and I caught Damon's eye and he smiled at me. Kitty dragged me over to them and I couldn't keep my eyes from drifting to their exposed torsos. Especially Alec's, his defined muscles were indeed framed by swirls of black ink. They formed all different shapes and I noticed an inked tree over his left peck and then the swirls travelled over to his right shoulder to form what looked like a ravens wing. He turned to face me then, his blue eyes dancing as the side of his mouth kicked up, he held up two fingers. Twice he caught me staring.

"I never heard anyone mentioning that we had to be half naked for this thing," Harven scowled as he hugged his thin torso, teeth chattering from the autumn chill and I was suddenly very grateful for the heavy cloak.

"I know you're all getting cold, but the ceremonial clothes are a sign of purity and is all apart of the awakening. We will now be going back to the academy so keep close!" Syler called out. "Anyone who isn't here now will be brought over by another Archmage," he said over his shoulder as he turned and began his way back to the academy.

"This is turning out to be quite exciting, isn't it?" Damon whispered as he walked beside me.

"Being led into a basement almost naked actually sounds like a bad idea," I pointed out and he snorted. I snuck a quick look down at the Prince's build and was surprised to see his own defined muscular body, not as formed as Alec's was, but pretty damn impressive.

Syler led us to the main room of the academy that was

situated at the base of the huge stairwell and lifted his hands to create a magic formation in the air. A grinding noise filled the space around us and the mosaic floor in front of us gave way to a large spiral staircase that lead downwards. Hairs raised on the back of my arms as I looked down to the darkness below. A brush of Damon's fingers on my back had me falling into step beside him and we emerged into an open candle lit cavern. It seemed as if it was carved out of stone and had been untouched for decades. Moss and unusual white flowers climbed the walls of the cave-like room and at the far end was a huge white tinted pool. It was ginormous and seemed like it could fit almost fifty people in it. I wondered just how it came to be here under the Academy.

"Before awakening your magic you must bathe in this pool and cleanse your skin. Your body must be purified before we begin," Xander said and the students slowly approached the pool. The water seemed almost *glowing.* Alec approached the pool with zero hesitation and lowered himself in. The other students took that as a go ahead and one by one the students stripped their robes and climbed in.

Damon, Xander and Harven climbed in and I watched as Kitty confidently stripped her robe and half dived in the water. I dipped my toes in the water and was surprised to find it warm.

"What are you waiting for?" Kitty asked and they all turned to stare at me.

"I can't swim," I said quietly. Growing up in the Commoners District there was no pools like the nobles had. There were lakes rumoured to be just outside Ghislane, but I never had time to go between training and working at the tavern.

"It's not deep at all, your feet will touch the ground," Xander offered encouragingly and I took a deep breath. I unfastened the cloak and swallowed a lump when the room went quiet. I didn't have to look up to know that the students were staring at the scars that covered the whole left side of my body. A hand appeared in my vision and I looked up to see Alec standing in front of me, his eyes twinkling as he watched my reaction. My eyes widened as I took his hand and let him help me into the water. After a fleeting sensation of panic, my feet touched the floor and my breathing calmed.

"It's not the scars they were looking at," he whispered as he leaned close and every nerve in my body heightened to his voice and closeness. It was the first time I had heard him speak and his voice felt like silk over my skin.

The group stared at Alec as he swam back beside Xander and I wondered if they had ever heard him speak too.

"I don't think the dagger is part of the dress code," Harven chuckled and I grimaced.

"You never know when you might need one," I pointed out and then sighed as the water's warmth surrounded me.

"That's a nice tattoo," Damon said after a long moment and my hand went up to the magic formation on my chest. Alec stared at it as an emotion passed under his eyes but quickly settled back into their bored glaze.

"I've had it for as long as I can remember," I shrugged.

"That's a bit strange." Damon cocked his head to the side. "You don't remember getting it? It looks like a magic formation," he pointed out.

"I've had it viewed by scholars and battle mages, but no one can work it out," I said and Damon raised his eyebrows in disbelief.

"That has to be the strangest thing I've ever heard," Harven said. "So, someone just marked you with a formation as a child? Who does that?"

I opened my mouth to tell them that my past hasn't always been so straightforward but Syler cut me off.

"We will call you out one by one and you will approach

the orb carefully," Syler called out just as a group of other Archmage's huddled into the room, carrying a beautifully carved wooden table with a large glass orb on top. My eyes flicked to Alec as his jaw tensed and his blue eyes blazed with fury. What the hell was wrong with him? "This orb is what will awaken the magic inside you and will tell us what affinity you possess. I will warn you that when you touch the orb you will fall into a dream-like state where some of you will have visions linked to your affinity. Please do not be alarmed when this happens, it is all very natural." He smiled kindly at us but I felt a chill tremble down my spine at the thought of it. "Your Majesty, would you please honour us by going first?" Syler asked and it was then that I noticed the two knights at the entrance of the room, red faced and breathing hard. Had they been chasing after Damon all afternoon? The students in the pool turned to watch him pull himself out of the water and I had to fight with myself not to look over his body again as he approached the orb. Everyone watched as he lifted his hands slowly to the orb and then his head hung limp as if he were asleep. The crowd fell silent as they watched their prince and I wondered what Damon was feeling. I saw the knights tense as they watched the Prince's body flinch and tremble.

"Breathe and try to relax," Syler said comfortingly and suddenly the orb lit up in a brilliant orange light that seemed to shine against the rocky walls of the cavern we were in.

"You have the fire affinity!" Syler called out. "A very powerful and fitting affinity for you, Your Majesty." Damon looked back at us with a grin. My breath caught in my throat as I stared at the bright orange glow, and I checked to make sure my walls were still up as I felt the dark thoughts push close at the sight of the flame.

"What class will you be attending?" Syler asked.

"Magic swordsmanship," Damon answered with a grin and Syler nodded and patted him on the shoulder.

Damon made his way to the side of the room as Syler called the next student up. One by one they all stood up and we watched amazed as the orb began to glow all different colours and I was in awe each time. Sometimes the orb wouldn't react at all and the students turned away with dejected expressions. I wonder what was inside someone to determine if they had magic or not. I really hoped I wouldn't end up like they had otherwise all my training would have been for nothing.

"Nevara," Syler called me up next and I took a deep breath as I pulled myself from the water and made my way to the orb. Each step I took towards the orb was a step closer to what I had trained my whole life for. I had dreamed about awakening my magic for so long now that I still couldn't believe that I was finally about to do it.

I lifted my hands above the orbs surface and could almost feel it drawing me closer, beckoning my hands to touch it. I flinched as my palms came into contact with the hot surface and a jolt ran through my body before my mind went dark.

"YOU'VE GROWN *a lot since the last time we met, little shadow." A man's voice echoed in the darkness. Where was I? Was this a dream?*

"In a sense... I guess you can call it a dream." The dark chuckled and then a flap of wings sounded.

"It seems that the raven has grown as fond of you as I have," the voice murmured and another flutter of wings shook the smoky darkness around me. I tried to lift my arms but realised I couldn't move at all. No...I couldn't move because I had no body.

Yes, I was definitely dreaming.

"Who are you?" I called out from my formless mouth.

149

"Don't you remember me? I was the one who gave you that mark on your chest," he said quietly as the same formation that was inked on my skin was now being drawn into the air, a dark aura surrounding it.

"Who are you?" I asked again and a pair of blood red eyes appeared from the shadows and the memory from when I was younger flashed through my mind. A figure stood with his hand to the centre of my chest.

"I told you there would be a time when I would require your help." The man in the cloak—the man from my childhood stepped forward from the darkness.

"It was you," I whispered breathlessly. "You gave me this mark... why?" I asked desperately, trying to finally understand its meaning.

"The prophecy tells of a priestess with the powers of shadows gifted by a Lesser Fae. Only she can reclaim the elemental stones and restore its power to the rightful rulers of magic," the cloaked man told me and a sudden sharp pain began to erupt from my chest.

"You are the one prophesied, Little shadow," the man said, his voice now tainted with need. "You will be the one to bring peace to the two kingdoms because you will become the priestess," he whispered and the sound was withered beneath my screams of agony as icy darkness spread its way through my body, ripping and tearing me apart from the inside.

"NEVARA!" I heard Alec's voice but I couldn't focus on anything other than the blinding pain that consumed me. All of a sudden I felt a shudder ripple through the air and something opened within my body, filling with the same darkness that was around me. It was as if my body was absorbing the dark shadows that surrounded me, a never-ending void that was being devoured by my stomach and there seemed to be no end.

. . .

"WE WILL MEET AGAIN SOON," the man whispered. The dark had no beginning and end, only me and the endless void that seemed to go on forever.

"NEVARA!" I heard Syler's voice crack through the darkness and I opened my eyes slowly to see the orb before me now full of a smoky darkness that seemed to flinch and ripple under the clear surface. The cavern was in a stunned silence as Syler looked between me and the orb with wide eyes.

"What's wrong?" I asked as I tried to remember what I had just saw and heard but my dark dream was just a blur of memories now. A hum of energy now pulsed in my body and I knew immediately that the new and strange sensation was my magic.

"It's the shadow affinity!" I heard an Archmage gasp behind Syler and they broke out into a heated chatter amongst themselves.

"Shadow affinity?" I asked Syler and he shook his head, his brows furrowed as he tried to process everything.

"We have only read bits and pieces from scrolls and books we managed to acquire through dungeons. They mentioned a shadow affinity and how extremely rare it is," Syler said, the students behind me began to chatter loudly about what was happening. "We have no idea what its abilities are…or anything about it, really." Syler looked again into the orb, his features twisting into one of awe as his eyes tracked its shadowy movements.

"The first recorded shadow affinity in Ashwood Academy's history!" Syler shouted and the room fell silent again. "You are all witness to an historic moment! Nevara here will only help to strengthen and improve our prosperous kingdom and Academy!" Syler's voice rang out and all the Archmage's began to clap and nod their heads behind him. The students then began clapping and my face flushed.

"What class will you be taking?" Syler asked with an excited smile.

"Swordsmanship," I said quietly trying to get this over now as fast as I could.

"Good! I can't wait to see how you perform." Syler clapped his hands and I quickly went to stand beside Damon who was watching me with wide eyes.

"I knew there was something different about you," Damon whispered as I tried to settle my overwhelmed thoughts. How did I manage to get myself a rare affinity?

"Air affinity!" Syler called and my eyes went to Alec as he stood with his hands now on the orb. His eyes were on me as Syler talked to him and I couldn't tear my eyes away from his intense gaze. "What class will you be taking?"

"Battle mage," Alec said quickly and when Syler nodded he quickly made his way over to me.

"Who gave you that mark on your chest, Nevara?" He asked, his eyes wide and accusing.

"I told you, I don't know. I've always had it," I said, unsure why he was bringing it up again. I looked down at my chest and my body went still.

The mark was gone.

"What the..." My voice trailed off as my hands slid over my now clear, unmarked skin and my eyes met Alec's again. He was looking at where the mark had been too, his gaze was dark and unyielding as it pinned me in place. I swallowed hard, a sense of dread flowering in my stomach. Without saying anything else, he turned and stormed up the stairs and left.

"I think he's jealous of you," Damon teased and I shook

my head. Strange things were happening and I think losing my mark was just the beginning of it.

AFTER EVERYONE HAD AWOKEN their magic, we were finally led back to our rooms and I quickly managed to half strip down before collapsing in my new bed.

"I can't believe I got a water affinity," Kitty sighed in wonder as she turned to look at me. "And I can't believe you got a shadow affinity. It's like I'm sharing my room with someone famous now," she teased and I groaned.

"That's just what I need," I sighed. "I just wanted to come to this academy, get my normal affinity, graduate and leave so I can make money. Now I'm going to be poked and prodded at by those old Archmages like I'm something to be studied." Kitty chuckled and nodded in agreement. I wished I could talk to Kain and the rest of the Guild to see what they made of this 'shadow affinity'. I wished I could talk to them just for a moment so I could settle the growing worry inside my stomach that told me all of this wasn't normal.

"Goodnight, Kitty," I said as my eyes began to grow heavy and Kitty grumbled a response. With a smile on my face, I quickly pushed aside all of my doubts and would deal with them later. I let darkness embrace me so I could escape the crazy day I just had and wondered if tomorrow would be any easier.

CHAPTER 15

I *was running through a forest. The twigs and the gravel bit at the bare soles of my feet but I didn't stop. I was searching for something—someone. Moonlight filtered through the trees ahead as I propelled myself faster, past the trunks and stones that lined my path. I could see it in the distance and knew he would be there waiting for me. The thought of him made me scream out his name, only I couldn't hear it. A different man suddenly loomed in front of me and he blocked my way.*

Alec.

He stopped me in my tracks as I tried to get past him. I needed to get to the place I was heading to, I needed to see him—but who was he? Why was Alec stopping me? Alec grabbed hold of me and began dragging me away, but I needed to keep going—I needed to see him—

"Nevara!" A voice hissed through my ear and I grumbled as I turned in my bed. I felt rough hands shake my shoulders and my eyes sprang open. Alec stared down at me and it was then that I realised I wasn't in my bed. I was outside in the forest that surrounded the Academy, laying on the grass.

"How?" I asked as I scrambled to stand up, trying to get my bearings as my head spun slightly.

"Your magic must have called you to the earth," Alec said as his eyes roamed over me and it was then that I realised that I was in my shirt and panties. My face blushed as Alec looked down and scowled as he pulled his black shirt over his head and handed it to me. I quickly wrapped it around my lower half and sighed.

"Why is nothing ever normal with me?" I asked quietly to myself as I rubbed at my face. "First the strange dreams and now this." I gestured to the forest around me. "I really hope I won't be walking around in my sleep from now on."

"Strange dreams?" Alec asked intrigued and I shook my head.

"More like nightmares." I shuddered and lifted my hand in front of my face, turning it this way and that. My magic was fully awakened now and I could almost feel it beneath my skin, like a current pulsing just below, waiting to be unleashed.

"How did you know I was out here?" I asked after a moment and he watched me as I searched his face, his dark hair shimmered against the sunrise – it casted splatters of golden light everywhere.

"I heard you yell my name," he smirked and my face heated.

"I did not!" I hissed.

"You did so," he accused with a slow perusal up and down my body. "Seems like you can't keep me out of your mind. I saw how you stared at me earlier and now you seem to call to me in your dreams." I gaped at him and a hysterical bubble of giggles escaped from my throat.

"I told you it was a nightmare, so I probably *did* see you

there," I smirked. "And I wasn't staring at you earlier, I was sizing up your body to look for your weaknesses." I half lied. He really did have a nice body.

"And? What weaknesses did you find?" He drawled as he took a step closer. My breath caught in my throat as my hands clenched into fists. This guy was the most infuriating and rude person I had ever met!

Unable to control my anger, I ducked low and swung out my right foot in an attempt to knock his legs from beneath him. He jumped back just at the last moment leaving me to narrow my eyes at him.

"I really get under your skin, don't I?" He chuckled and I lunged forward with my fist but again he easily deflected it with his own and I growled. The newly awakened dark mana purred deep in my stomach, begging to be let out and I used its drive to unleash a fury of attacks that even I had a hard time keeping up with. Alec parried them, landing his own attack as he lunged forward with an incredible speed and landed a kick to the back of my legs. I fell on my back with a grunt and Alec hovered over me, securing my wrists above my head and trapping my legs between his large thighs. I grunted as I struggled, embarrassed at how easily he took me down.

"Now, now, there's no need to get so angry," he murmured. He stared down at me, an expression I couldn't place crossed his features.

"Get off me!" I spat and he chuckled as he moved his free hand to travel down the left side of my face and I shuddered.

I hated this; hated feeling at the mercy of another person. Just like—just like Samuel. I choked. My eyes widened as a spider-like crack appeared on the walls in my mind.

"Easy," Alec whispered as he loosened his grip on my hands.

"Get off," I growled and my voice took on a dark edge.

Alec stared at me as if he was truly seeing me for the first time. I felt the newly awoken darkness pulse under my skin in a building pressure that was begging to be released and Alec's mouth twitched as he took me in.

"There it is," he whispered, placing a hand against my forehead. Suddenly I was back in bed, gasping and gripping the sheets as I sat upright.

A dream…it had all been a dream.

"Nevara, what's the matter?" Kitty asked half asleep as she looked over at me. Her eyes widened as her hands went to her stomach.

"I can feel it!" She cried. It was just like it had been in my dream, that buzzing and purring of mana in my stomach.

"It was a dream," I whispered to myself, pushing sweat slicked hair from my face. God, I was a mess.

"We finally did it!" Kitty giggled and hugged herself, embracing her new magic. I could only lay back down and stare at the ceiling and think. It felt as if my dreams were an omen of what was to come and it wasn't good news at all.

"Those were some weird dreams right?" Kitty asked and I snapped my head towards her.

"You had weird dreams too?" I breathed and she raised a brow at me, her red hair spilling across the pillow.

"In my dream I was swimming in the ocean, but I was being dragged down by these strange people…if that's what they were at all," she added on quietly and my mind spun. "It was just like the vision I had at the awakening."

"It must have been everything that happened last night," I chuckled sheepishly. "Probably all of the stress and excitement made us have weird dreams." I hoped I was right because those dreams I had were far too weird for me to make up on my own, especially the part with Alec. I remembered the feeling of his legs against mine and my blood heated with the memory.

Pushing the memory down, I pulled myself up and out of bed. There was no way I was going to let my mind wonder in that dangerous line of thought.

"Do you know where the bathing rooms are?" I asked Kitty as she sat up and stretched.

"The end of the hall on the right, I saw them yesterday," she said and I slipped from the room, making my way down the quiet and empty hall. It was a little after sunrise and I knew everyone would be awake soon. We weren't given a certain time for classes to start today but the Archmage's probably were giving everyone a chance to recover from the chaos of yesterday.

The bathing room was basic enough, with a couple of small cast iron bathtubs with a row of wooden basins and cloths. A large pipe connected to the baths, and hot water cascaded from them in tinted coloured hues. The basin filled as if like magic, and I spent a long time washing and letting my mind wander.

Wrapped in a fluffy towel, I looked over myself in the mirror. The magic formation was gone. I raised my hands to my chest, running my fingers over where it once was. My skin prickled as blurry memories of darkness and blood red eyes seeped in. I gripped the edge of the basin, took a deep breath before splashing water on my face—pushing away the darkness. The mark was gone. I don't have to think of it anymore.

At least that's what I told myself.

THE CAFETERIA HOUSED students like me, but even those of higher ranking. Some in their armour, training gear, whereas others wore the signature Academy black robes.

"I take it Kitty is snoring her head off up there?' I spun

around at the sound of Damon's voice. His knights and Alec followed behind him. I avoided Alec's gaze, especially after last night.

"She is indeed," I chuckled and fell into step beside them. The scent of food lured me across the room. Wooden tables with benches lined the room, a long counter spanned the far wall where robed men and women were placing out food. I immediately made my way over and began filling a plate I found with eggs, meats and then began piling a bunch of pastries on top of it. Oh goodness, this made last night's nightmares worth it. Damon coughed a chuckle from beside me but I didn't care as I found the nearest table and began tucking in.

"What is it with you and pastries?" Damon asked as he sat down opposite me, his own plate filled meats and eggs, Alec's was made up of a large bowl of porridge and a second plate full of boiled eggs—what a weird combination.

"Pastries are this kingdom's best creation," I said with a shrug and stuffed my mouth with food.

"You eat like a beast," Alec said and I frowned at him.

"In the Commoners' District, you eat like life depends on it because most of the time it does," I snapped at him and his eyes travelled over me.

"You were poor," he stated.

"I don't think that's any of your business," I argued between another mouthful of food.

"Well, the armour you're wearing along with those swords tell me enough to know that you're not poor now." Alec smirked and my hands clenched in anger. How *was* it that he got under my skin so quickly?

"You know nothing about me," I said through clenched teeth and levelled my stare at him.

"It appears that I know a good deal about you, *Nevara.*" The way he said my name made me want to punch him in the face, but a burning coiled low in my stomach.

I went back to angrily eating and Damon let out a breath.

"What the hell happened between you guys?" Damon asked and I cut him a look that warned him to stay out of it. Luckily Xander and Harven joined us then and diverted his attention.

"I slept better than I ever had in my life last night." Xander grinned as he sat down beside me.

"I could tell by how much you were snoring," Harven scowled and I chuckled at his tired eyes as he sat down beside Damon.

"Good morning students!" Syler's voice carried over the cafeteria and I noticed Kitty slip past him and hurry to grab her own plate of food. The room quietened and chatter ceased as everyone began to listen to the Archmage.

"I trust you have all slept well," Syler said and disgruntled murmurs broke out among the room.

"I can't believe I fell back to sleep," Kitty hissed as she slid into a chair at the table. She looked like she had rushed out of the room with her hastily braided hair and flushed face.

"In ten minutes, you will all make your way to the main Academy building and your respective teachers will be waiting to lead you to your first class," Syler said and excitement rolled over the room. "I hope you all have an enjoyable first day at Ashwood Academy. If you encounter any problems, please report it to me or any other Archmage you can find."

Syler waved a hand, dismissing the room, as his eyes met mine and motioned for me to meet him outside.

I sighed, brushing the crumbs off my lap before standing. I knew something like this would happen after it was revealed I had a rare affinity.

"I'll meet you guys at class," I said to Damon and Xander,

nodded to Kitty and Harven and completely ignored Alec altogether. If he was going to act like an ass then I wouldn't bother with him at all.

I made my way out into the crisp morning and found Syler standing beside a small water fountain as he waited for me.

"Your rare affinity has become the talk of the school," he said with a smile as I joined him.

"Great," I murmured. He studied my face and I realised it was the closest I had been to the man. He seemed like he was a middle-aged guy with grey curling hair that spilled out from under his hood. His brown eyes were soft and framed in wrinkles, age spots dotting his right cheek.

"The scholars and I were working all night to find as much information about your affinity as we could but unfortunately our libraries are lacking." Syler sighed and motioned for me to join him as he walked towards the Academy. "Even though it's been over a decade since we discovered how magic was awoken, we are still ignorant to many things that lies hidden within. Especially when it comes to the dungeons, but that discussion is for another time." He let out a low chuckle. "The elders of the academy have decided to keep a close eye on you to determine if your powers are to be a great asset to our school, or if you are dangerous."

"Why would I be dangerous?" I asked, my palms beginning to sweat. "Why would this affinity be any more dangerous than one like fire? If anyone knows how dangerous fire is, it's me," I said and met his eyes, letting him see the left side of my face and neck. It was evidence enough of just how destructive fire can be.

"I know you're not a danger to this school," Syler stated calmly after a moment, "it's just a precaution, that's all. If anything, we're all extremely excited to see what you can do."

There was a warning in the Archmage's words. Before I

could give it much thought, Syler gave me pat on the shoulder as he walked away.

Not wanting to think on it too much, I made my way in through the large doors of the academy. I walked into the huge main area again and frowned at the mosaic floor where we had ventured beneath yesterday.

"Ah, the mysterious shadow student," I heard a male's voice behind me and saw Archmage Perrion leaning against the wall to the right.

"Please tell me that name isn't going to catch on, because it's awful," I scowled as I made my way over to him.

"It is quite unoriginal," he chuckled and pushed off the wall. Perrion was younger than the other Archmage's I had seen, his brown hair was braided down his back and his dark green eyes seemed like they saw everything at once.

"How long have you been training? Your muscle definition is near perfect so it must be at least over five years." He studied me and I smiled proudly.

"That's correct," I nodded. "Kain Manus has taught me everything I know." A grin broke out across his face.

"Kain Manus was the finest damn student I had ever taught in this academy," he chuckled and patted me on the shoulder. "You've got big boots to fill," I knew that already. I was in disbelief that Perrion had taught Kain and wondered how old he actually was.

Chatter filtered through the room and I noticed Damon and Xander make their way over with around fifteen other males. All the girls seem to have joined the battle mage, healer, or scholar classes. I wondered if they were intimidated or scared to go up against the males—

I felt the smirks and stares; heard the whispers and sniggers before I saw them.

"Seems like we got another full class this year," Perrion called out as the last of the group gathered around him. "I want to let you know right now that you have until the end of the day to change classes. The swordsman class demands an incredible amount of strength and endurance and I will not tolerate anyone that falls behind," he gave everyone a levelled look.

"Excuse me," A voice interrupted from behind the group. Alec parted the crowd as he made his way forward. *What was he doing here?*

"What is it?" Perrion asked, his eyes flickering with something I couldn't place.

"I wish to change my class to swordsmanship and I was told that I was allowed to do so before the end of the day," Alec answered and my gut twisted. I was happy that I would be apart from this guy for the most part of the days at the academy but now...the thought of him being in the same class made me want to curse out loud.

"Good, join in," Perrion waved him forward. "Now the first thing we are going to do is go for a week's trek over the Marden Mountains. Go grab whatever you need; food and water will be foraged for, so you don't need to worry about that," When no one moved, he cocked his head to the side. "Did you all not understand me? I told you all only the strongest with the most endurance can train in my classroom, so before anyone steps foot into one of my classes I want to make sure I have the best of the best. You can change classes now if you're not up to this journey and please keep in mind that anyone that falls behind, will be left there. We meet outside the academy in half an hour. Go!"

"I guess the rumours about the terrifying Perrion were true," Damon murmured as we made our way back to our rooms.

"Why did you change to swordsmanship?" Xander asked Alec. That's what I wanted to know too.

"Circumstances changed," he said and I felt his eyes on

me. The thought of camping with him for the next week had even me contemplating changing to another class.

"Looks like you should back out now, shadow creep," a guy said and I froze. *Shadow creep?*

I turned around to face a group of guys, the one in middle I recognised. Han Dranson. My first opponent from the contest. He stood smirking as his eyes ran down the left side of my face.

"I guess I have to thank you for defeating me in the contest, it saved me from going up against Samuel and his fire," Han chuckled and the rest of his group grinned. *Samuel.*

"Shut up, Han." Damon warned and took a step forward whilst Xander took a step closer to me.

"What? I was just telling the truth! It could have been me that ended up with those ugly scars, so I'm thanking her for taking the hit," he mocked, his green eyes dancing as they seared into mine.

Darkness pushed against my mind, and I pushed back. Ugly scars. Samuel. They echoed as dread began to fill me.

Damon and Xander were arguing with Han, but their voices were drowned out over the roaring in my head. Tendrils of shadow began to purr and caress under my skin, begging for release—

"Easy" Alec murmured, as I felt his cool fingers brushed against mine. The cold like a band snapping energy throughout my body; darkness receding, coaxing calmness.

I met his eyes, his lips parted in surprise before his mask snapped back into place.

"Just make sure you remember that if you fall behind, you get left behind. Freak," Han spat and then turned to walk away.

"What is that asshole's problem?" Xander growled and I chuckled, my head suddenly clear and focused.

"It's because a commoner woman defeated him in under a minute." I shrugged. "I guess I hurt his pride."

I heard them laugh beside me – even Alec cracked a small smile.

I sat down beside the small water fountain and watched the sunlight ripple off the water.

"I'll wait for you here," I said to the guys.

"Aren't you bringing anything?" Damon quirked an eyebrow.

"I've got everything I need." I smirked, tapping the sword at my hip. Damon and Xander grunted, shaking their heads as they disappeared into the dorm building – leaving me and Alec alone.

"You travel light too?" Alec mused as he sat down beside me and I ignored the way my body reacted to his closeness.

"I don't need much to survive." I sighed and tipped my head back to the sun, its warmth heating my face.

"May I?" He asked and I turned to him as he gestured towards my sword. I hesitated and then unsheathed it from my belt.

The silver leaves and gems encrusted into the hilt glittered in the sun—the symbols catching my eye as the rays of light almost made them glow.

I jerked as our fingers brushed, earning a chuckle from Alec. He lifted the sword across his palms, studying the blade and its markings.

"It's a Fae sword," he mused, his hand gliding over the blade.

"Fae?" I asked curiously.

"Most of the magical artefacts found in your dungeons are made or owned by the Fae. This sword is actually considered a relic, it's inscribed here," he pointed to the symbols. *"This blade, guided by the raven, will unite what is lost."* My skin prickled at the dark silk his voice took on as he recited the words.

"How?" I stammered. "*How* do you know all of this?" I asked again in disbelief.

"I like to dabble in all things to do with magic." He shrugged, "I managed to find a few books on them."

I frowned and made a mental note to find out more about the Fae. If it was linked to magical artefacts and the dungeons then it was better I knew all I could about them.

"Keep the sword safe, it will protect you when you need it to," He said with a soft smile, then leaned over returning the blade back into its sheath, his fingers trailing over the exposed skin at my hip. I sucked in a breath as our eyes met.

"Looks like you two made up." Damon's voice rang out beside us and I jumped to my feet, my heart pounding. Alec's face was a mask of boredom as he got to his feet.

"I thought it was for the best seeing as we're going to be spending the next week together," he explained and I gritted my teeth. If this was how he wanted to play it then fine.

"Let's go," I muttered and began walking towards the Academy, trying my best to ignore the tingle that still lingered on my skin from his touch.

This was going to be a long seven days.

BY THE TIME we met up with Perrion again, the group had already lost about three students. They must have been terrified at the thought of seven days in the wilderness. Being a noble, they probably had never known the feeling of hunger and the helplessness that comes with having to survive each day with only what you can provide for yourself.

I wondered how many commoner students had applied this year?

For commoner's running their shops and providing for their families left little money and time to focus on anything else, especially enrolling at the Academy. I was lucky that Kain had given me the help I needed for this opportunity.

"Seems like we've already lost some people." Perrion chuckled and I noticed that he had changed from his white Archmage robes to a lighter leather armour. His dark brown skin glowed against the sun and his muscles flexed as he began to walk forward.

"It seems like I'm not the only person you stare at," Alec whispered and I flinched from his closeness.

"Follow me!" Perrion called out and began down the path to the entrance of the wall that surrounded the Academy.

"I was assessing his form, not staring," I scowled and Alec smirked.

"So, what did you assess about my form? You must clearly know now by the number of times I caught you staring at me," he teased. Damon and Xander walked ahead, as if they were trying not to eavesdrop.

"Your muscle density is incredible for someone who wanted to be a battle mage," I said after a moment as we approached the large iron gate just outside the Academy, "it seems like you've trained your body for a very long time. Being lazy doesn't leave you with a body like that."

"I told you I dabble in all things magical." He smirked at me and my heart fluttered at the sight of it. *Why did he have to be so good looking?* "I grew up in a forest, so I had to learn and adapt to many different things," I raised my eyebrows, surprised. There were numerous forests that surrounded the main city; so many questions flooded in—where was his family? How did he end up living amongst the Nobles?

Instead of asking, I whispered, "I know what it's like to fight for survival"

167

I turned my head and met his eyes; a soft look crossed his handsome face.

"Surviving only makes you stronger," he said gently, making my breath stutter.

"And it seems that you have survived and fought for a lot in your life, it's why you're so incredibly strong now."

I wanted to believe his words. With everything I had, I wanted to know I was truly strong—but that darkness that lived within me, it filled me with doubt. That darkness seemed to grow a little more every day—ever since the contest, memories of flames and shadow consumed me.

"Surviving leaves scars that you have to spend the rest of your life with." *Physically and mentally.* But I didn't say that last part. His brow furrowed, taking in my words. Before he could open his mouth to reply, Damon fell back beside us, and I was thankful. Any more talk about my past would give the darkness a bigger foothold in my mind, and I needed to conserve my strength to face what was to come.

"This is the furthest I've been out of the city." Damon said as he looked around the forest that surrounded the dirt path we were on.

"You're the Prince of this kingdom and you've barely left the city?" I questioned and he just gave me a shrug.

"The King is quite protective of his family if you had forgotten," he gestured to the two knights that walked behind us, a little apart from the group.

"But I saw so many towns and villages outside the city. Surely he must travel or at least acknowledge and help them with trade and such?" I pressed and Damon's jaw hardened. Alec chuckled alongside us.

"The King's vision doesn't seem to stretch too far past the nobles district." Alec smirked. "Anything other than making sure the higher ups are happy and rich doesn't seem to concern him." I looked at Damon, waiting for him to correct

Alec or at least argue the insults that he had just given his father, *the King* of Ghislana. But he did nothing.

"My father took over the throne after my grandfather and made some serious changes in relation to outside trade with other kingdoms. He grew greedy and when the tax was raised for citizens and the foreign merchants, he didn't think the people would rebel against him. When the commoners began smuggling in weapons with help from foreign kingdoms, he became enraged. Since then, he created the wall and seemed to isolate himself from the outer kingdom entirely…it's like he doesn't even acknowledge them most of the time anymore," Damon said quietly and I felt the darkness trickle under my skin at his words.

"So, he just leaves his own people to starve and struggle because of a rebellion that happened ages ago?" I asked shocked. I had been one of those people struggling to survive each day, hoping that the King would reach out with his generosity, but he never did. Kain had been the one to save us and even he didn't have a lot of wealth.

"I'm trying to change a lot of things in the palace, it's why I'm attending the academy so when I leave here, I will have the power over him to fix this kingdom," Damon said, running a hand roughly through his pale hair, tugging hard on the strands.

"It's not fast enough," I whispered, thinking of the alleyway. My friends. So many families and elderly living in tents. If I hadn't worked out the deal with Kiera to give them the leftover food from the tavern every night or give them whatever leftover coins I had—they wouldn't have survived. How many of them would have died already? How many children—

Bile rose in my throat at the thought. I mentally shook myself; I couldn't break, not here. I walked past the rest of the class and caught up with Perrion.

"How long until we reach the mountain?" I asked as I fell into step beside him.

"We should reach the base of it tonight, there's a town an hour from here that we will rest at before moving forward," He said, raising an eyebrow as he met my gaze. Images of the alley flashed into my head, the hungry and starving faces. I needed to hurry. I needed to train.

"I'll scout ahead and meet you at the town," I said quickly.

He searched my face and then seemed to understand whatever I was struggling with. He nodded and I didn't wait for a second longer before breaking out in a sprint.

The wind whipped against my face, tugging stray hairs from my braid as the burn in my legs started to ramp up. The breeze blowing away the shadows that flooded my mind.

I ran until my breath was ragged, my skin was slick with sweat and my lungs burned. I didn't stop. Not until the darkness had receded fully and then even more for good measure.

By the time the forest began to disappear and turn into open fields, I began to slow as cottages came closer into view. I gulped down air, wincing as my throat burned with each breath.

"Here," I almost choked on air holding back a scream. Alec had appeared out of nowhere, holding out a canteen with a small smile.

"What…" I tried to steady my breathing and my thundering heart. "Why did you follow me?" I asked incredulously. How had I not sensed him the whole way that I ran? I normally thought I had good senses and instincts, but I hadn't detected him at all.

"You seemed like you were angry when you left, so I followed to make sure you didn't do anything stupid," he said and pressed the small water canteen into my hands.

"Why do you care?" I asked as I drained the canteen. His eyes hardened and he looked away.

"I don't care," He grumbled, snatching the canteen back and storming further ahead. Well, friendly Alec didn't last long.

I rubbed the sweat from my face and unhooked the armour on my chest where my white undershirt was plastered to my skin. Glancing up my eyes met Alec's as he stared at every inch of my body, then smirked before turning on his heel and began walking again. I felt my cheeks heating. *Asshole.*

I realised as I walked behind him that he seemed unfazed by running such a long distance. I wouldn't have been able to tell he had run for so long if it wasn't for his skin slick with sweat.

"So tell me, do you feel better after running like a crazy person?" He asked over his shoulder. I scowled and looked away.

"I do actually," I said and fought the urge to stick my tongue out at him. His shoulders shook with laughter, as if he knew it. He ran a hand through his hair, I watched as his muscles rippled with the movement. Each dip and stretch.

A different feeling tugged inside me, it was headier and intoxicating.

"I've known Damon for a few years now," Alec said after a moment and he slowed down to walk beside me. "If there is anything I have learned since meeting him is that he is definitely nothing like his father. When he takes over the throne, which will hopefully be soon, the kingdom will be remade for the better."

"How did you and Damon meet?" I asked, my curiosity getting the better of me.

"That is a story for another day," Alec sighed and I didn't press him on it. If he didn't want to talk about it, he must have his reasons. "Do you think you will be okay making this trek?"

"I'll be fine. I would be a disappointment to my previous teacher if I wasn't." I laughed as I thought of Derrick and that damn mountain we climbed nearly every day for over a month.

Alec was suddenly in front of me, his hand tucking a strand of black hair behind my ear. My breath caught in my throat as his finger trailed from my temple, down my cheek.

"I've never seen eyes like yours before," Alec said and my heart thundered in my chest as he stepped closer, his azure eyes burning into mine. "You are like no one else I've encountered. Someone who's life has been filled with darkness such as yours…a normal person would have succumbed a long time ago," He whispered, his hand ghosting over the scarred flesh on my face. His skin like a brand where we touched, and the darkness reared its head.

"*You're* not normal." I breathed, and his mouth curled. Blood pounded in my ears as his breath mingled with my own; the smell of mint and earth, it was intoxicating.

"You were not planned," he said quietly, so quietly that I almost didn't hear it at first. His head suddenly whipped to the side as he squinted down the road we had just ran down. The rest of the class appeared way in the distance and Alec took a step back, the sudden distance making me feel oddly cold.

"Let's make it to the town and meet up with them," he said, his eyes twinkling. "I'll race you there," he shouted and before I could say anything he took off running.

"Hey!" I yelled, laughing as I ran. He ran with a catlike grace, every step propelling him forward effortlessly. I must have looked so sloppy in comparison. Each foot he placed was perfect and I began to mimic his every move. I copied how his footfalls landed, leaned into every stride—surprised when I felt my muscles straining less as I propelled forward faster.

Surprise coloured his features when I met his pace and ran alongside him, letting out a breathless laugh at his shocked gaze.

The town came into view then, a few scattered cottages along with a shop and stable and what looked like a tavern and I was relieved.

I pushed myself forward, my legs burning and breath sawing in and out, but Alec still beat me by a few strides.

"You copied my running form," he breathed and I fell onto a patch of grass just outside the town.

"I told you I wasn't just staring at you, I'm assessing," I replied breathlessly. He let out a grumble as he sat down beside me and the silence was filled by our ragged breaths.

We sat like that until the rest of the class joined us, in a comfortable silence.

"It seems like I'm the only one with low endurance," Xander choked out as he fell beside me and Alec, letting out a groan.

"You did good Xander." Damon patted him on the shoulder before sitting down beside him, his own hair and face slick with sweat. I smirked to myself, a little happy that most of the nobles seemed so out of shape.

"I'm sorry about before," Damon said quietly as he stared in earnest at me, his pale blue eyes vulnerable. "Everything you and Alec said were right. I'm trying to fix things but I'm not fast enough, I know people are suffering under my families rule and I feel helpless against it." My heart warmed at his words.

"I know," I breathed and patted him on his leg, "I'm sorry I let my emotions and my past get the better of me."

"Thank you," Damon whispered and then collapsed on the floor beside Xander. I tried my best to hide my laughter but seeing them exhausted from the walk had me laughing with tears in my eyes.

"It seems like you nobles rely on your horses far too much for you to be this exhausted," I laughed harder. "We haven't even reached the mountain yet!"

"I'm glad you find this hilarious, Nevara," Xander groaned and even Alec joined in the laughter.

"Ten minutes until we continue on," Perrion called out. "There's a well in the south of the town, make use of it before we leave! Anyone who believes they can't go on, I advise you turn and head back to the academy now before we go any further."

"Maybe being a battle mage isn't so bad," Xander said and Damon muttered an agreement.

"Come on, the water from the well will help," I said standing up and strapping on my leather torso armour again. I held out my hand to Damon and Alec helped Xander up, then we then made our way with the rest of the class to a small brick well beside the stable.

When it was my turn, I splashed water on my face and revelled in the cold taste as I drank deeply. Xander pretty much dumped the bucket of water over his head and groaned in relief.

"Much better." Damon half gurgled as he chugged down the bucket of water and I let out another chuckle.

"Take a good look." Perrion came up behind us and slammed his hands down on Xander and Damon's shoulders making them jump. He pointed ahead of them and we all looked up at the huge line of mountains just off to the distance and I wondered how I hadn't notice them yet. They stood as tall as the Sky Kissed Mountain, maybe even taller, and ran in a line, disappearing in the distance.

Damon was lost for words as his eyes widened.

"That, my new lucky students, is the Marden Mountains. It's a place where the healing scholars' journey to when they need to collect their herbs and other medicinal plants. Lucky for them, we will be collecting them this time," he said, giving us all a mischievous grin. "You know, the Prince of Ghislana would be exempt from activities such as this." He quirked an eyebrow at Damon.

"I don't want to be treated different than anyone here," Damon said, holding the Archmage's gaze before looking back to the mountain range.

"I like that spirit! But let's see if you continue to think that when we're halfway up." Perrion smirked and patted him on the shoulder before turning around with a chuckle.

"If this is only the beginning of his classes, what are we in for the rest of the year?" Xander gulped and I peeked at Alec, surprised to find that he was finding this as hilarious as I did. He caught my eyes and we both stifled another laugh before drinking more water and filling the canteen Alec had managed to sneak in.

The unease that was present at the start of the trip was fading the closer I grew to Alec, Damon and Xander. I had never had friends before, at least not my own age—except for my brothers and the Guild.

Friends. Comrades.

That's what we were now.

THE REST of the walk was uneventful as the sun lowered in the sky and the autumn cold began to pick up. As we neared the base of the mountain, Perrion led us to a small camping area the healers used when travelling and I was pleased to find out there was enough sleeping bags for us all to use.

Since beginning the trek, three people had dropped out and returned to the Academy leaving only around ten left in the class.

"So, who's going out to get the class's dinner?" Perrion

asked, retrieving a bow and quiver of arrows from the storage box located off to the side. It was one weapon I had never properly learned to use.

"I'll go," Alec said, taking them both and made his way to the edge of the trees surrounding camp.

"Do you think he needs help?" I asked as I crouched down beside Xander and Damon.

"Alec grew up doing this kind of thing," Damon said as he tried to figure out how to light the small fire in front of us.

I remembered him saying he grew up in a forest and I wondered just how he hunted. Maybe it was something I should learn to do, just in case. It seemed like a good skill to have.

"Can't you just use your magic to light it?" Xander asked and Damon raised an eyebrow at him.

"I have no idea how to use my magic," Damon said. "If you have forgotten, we only awoke our mana last night."

"Whilst you do that, I'm going to do some training," I said and excused myself, mostly just in case Damon started playing around with his fire magic. The idea of him testing his magic made me nervous, and even though I was comfortable around flames—it was only at a safe distance.

I found a spot away from where the group was setting up for the night and I began going through my warmups; stretching my body and pushing as far as my limits would allow, and maybe a little bit more.

The moon hung high in sky; the stars speckled across the darkness. I was just about to do a last round of fighting formations when I felt it. A small hum of energy.

It danced across my skin, tugging, and caressing for me to come. I looked back at the others, who didn't seem to notice it. Without even thinking, I was moving forward into the thick of the trees, following the lull of energy as it pulsed and beckoned.

Relying on the moonlight to guide my way, I kept my footsteps light until I came to a small clearing. The feeling grew warm and thick, and I braced myself behind a nearby tree. My hand brushed the hilt of my sword as I took in the scene before me.

Alec was crouched in the centre of the clearing, his head bowed over a small deer. The animal's legs twitching. How the hell did he manage to catch one so fast? Before I could intervene, he began murmuring something as he ran his hands over the deer's face. The feeling from before intensified, the heat becoming heavier, like a warm blanket on a winter's night.

I wondered what he was doing. It was clear that the magic was emanating from Alec, but I had never felt this type of magic before. Perhaps it was some sort of healing magic, the feeling between the two felt similar but Alec's seemed to be much stronger.

Alec lifted a small dagger he had strapped to his thigh and brought it down into the animal's chest. The magic swelled and I felt my body sway from the sheer power of it before it abruptly disappeared leaving me disorientated.

"Do you always lurk in the shadows and spy on people?" Alec accused, not bothering to look at me as he lifted the deer up and over his shoulders. I swallowed the lump in my throat.

"I felt magic in the forest and I was curious," I said after a moment, deciding I didn't want to admit I was worried about his safety.

His head snapped up at my words and he froze as he stared at me. Shock settled over his features as his mouth popped open.

"You felt that magic?" He asked, a slight tremble in his voice.

"Yes, I followed it out here. To you," I said and watched as the cool and bored mask slipped back over his features. His eyes still sparked with curiosity as he looked at me. I cocked my head to the side.

"What were you doing with the deer?" I asked and he began to move forward.

"What do you mean? I was getting us dinner," He raised an eyebrow and I frowned.

"Well, what about the magic I felt?" I pressed, annoyed at his condescending tone.

"The journey today has probably made you feel tired." He gave me a pointed look. "Did anyone else feel the magic?"

"Well, no—"

"You must have been mistaken then," he said abruptly as he turned away and headed towards where Perrion sat beside a huge fire. Asshole.

I stomped back towards where Damon and Xander sat beside a now small lit fire and scowled. I know what I had felt, it had been too strong not to be magic. I just knew it.

So why was he lying about it?

"What pissed you off?" Xander asked with raised brows.

"Who do you think?" Damon chuckled and nodded over to where Alec sat and began helping Perrion skin the deer. They were whispering to each other with hardened expressions and I wondered what they were talking about. When he turned and glanced at me I stuck my tongue out at him.

"How you became friends with such an ass, I will never begin to understand." I sighed and grabbed my sleeping roll from beside me and positioned myself far enough away from the fire as possible.

"It's a long story," Damon muttered and I bit the inside of my mouth in annoyance.

"I'm going to sleep, wake me up in a few hours and I'll keep watch," I said with a dismissive tone and snuggled down into the surprisingly comfortable sleeping roll.

"Keep watch? There's no enemies here," Xander said. "Plus the royal knights are here."

"The knights are here for Damon," I pointed out. "And there's a few people I need to keep an eye on," I casted a wary glance to where Han and the rest of his group sat laughing and chatting beside their own fire.

"What about dinner?" Damon asked after giving me a small nod.

"I don't want to eat anything that bastard caught," I said turning around and I heard Damon and Xander let out a sigh. I knew I was being petty but I couldn't let go of what had just happened in the forest.

The chatter and crackling of the firewood soothed me, like the magic I felt in the forest had and soon I fell into a deep sleep.

CHAPTER 16

The sun had yet to crest over the horizon and I was up training. I danced and lunged with my sword, sweat clinging to my skin as the rest of the camp slept. I swung and dodged my way across the open space beyond the sleeping area.

"It seems Kain has taught you well." Perrion's voice rang out, breaking my reverie, as he made his way towards me offering a canteen.

"I thought we weren't allowed to bring water with us?" I raised an eyebrow as I took a gulp of it, its coolness instantly soothing my throat and I handed it back to him.

"I only said that the students couldn't bring water or food, not me," he replied and I rolled my eyes. "Was that Derrick's three-fold lunge attack I saw you practicing earlier?"

"You remember Derrick?" I asked in disbelief as I placed my sword back in its sheath. I noticed the other students beginning to stir and wake up.

"Derrick was a student who was hard to forget." Perrion chuckled and I thought of Derrick; his appearance and intimidating expressions and I had to agree.

"I've learnt my techniques from all of the swordsmen in the Ruby Guild," I said proudly. "They've been training me since I was a child."

"Well then I can't wait to see what else you have in store," he said and gave me a knowing smile before turning back to wake the students.

"We begin our journey up these glorious mountains right now," Perrion called out and I watched with humour as Damon sat upright with his hair sticking out in every direction. "As we climb, I want you all to begin practicing your very first magical related exercise. Manifesting and circulating your aura."

"What's an aura you might ask?" Perrion continued, "Our mana is stored within the very centre of our stomachs." He patted his own stomach, above his belly button for emphasis. "When we begin to cycle the mana through our body from here, we form an aura around ourselves and into whatever weapon we may have. This feeds our body and muscles and pushes them to new levels of strength and endurance and is what allows us to merge our elemental affinities with our weapons. It's what makes us magical swordsmen."

"How do we cycle our mana through our body?" A student called out.

"I want you to all sit down and close your eyes," Perrion ordered and we obeyed. "Now, I want you to reach down inside yourselves and find your mana. Once you find it, you need to control it and mentally push it throughout your body. You'll know if you're doing it right," he explained and the group fell into a quiet concentration as we all began to search for our mana. The tingly feeling of magic crept over my skin as gasps sounded around the campsite. I focused on my own body as I mentally searched for my mana.

At first there was nothing, it was like trying to grab air. Then I found it, a mass of shadow deep in my core. Smoke swirled around it, and I tried to draw on its power—the darkness like ink as I tried to manipulate it and bend it to my will.

"Remember to breathe," Perrion called out and I flinched at how close he was, not hearing him come near. "Regulated breathing helps to circulate the mana."

I took a deep breath in through my nose and out through my mouth and repeated it a few more times. On the third intake of breath, I pulled at the mana inside me and found it reacted to my command and I got so excited that I almost lost control of it. I calmed my breathing and began to force the dark liquid down my legs and gasped as I felt the power and energy feed into my bones and muscles, forging them anew. I gave up on trying to circulate my mana any further because I was already sweating as I kept my command on it through only my legs.

I stood up, amazed at how light and powerful my legs now felt, a familiar energy running through them, begging to be used. I walked to the nearest tree and swung my right leg into a round house kick and bark splintered on contact, but I felt no pain.

"Remind me to not get on your bad side." Damon whistled as he came up next to the tree and inspected the dent that now rested in its trunk.

"This power is insane," I breathed, and lost focus on the mana with a curse. A sweat had broken out on my back, and my hands began to tremble.

"Not so easy is it?" Perrion asked, seeing my slip of power. "It took me nearly half a year to get the mana to flow around my whole body and then another half a year before I could keep it circling my body for more than ten minutes." He approached the same tree I had just kicked, inhaled, and then repeated the same kick I had executed. The tree fell with a crash, the trunk in two halves against the forest floor.

Students gasped, looking between the debris and Perrion in awe.

"That's amazing," I whispered, my blood pumping with excitement as I wondered if I would be as powerful as Perrion one day.

"That's power." He smiled. "Magic isn't only a flashy elemental show, the mana that strengthens us is pure and undiluted power. It is what makes up a magic swordsman. So keep practicing as we climb, let's go!" He ordered and the group followed close behind him, all focused on circulating their mana.

I welcomed that familiar burn to my muscles as we hit the incline and for a moment I was back at Sky Kissed mountain with Derrick barking at my heels and a chuckle left my lips.

"How can you be laughing?" Xander asked from beside me, his dark skin now slick with sweat and his breathing ragged. Damon was on my other side as he fought to feign normalcy as he also began to struggle.

"Just a funny memory," I said and added, "The month and a half build up to the contest I was made to climb the Sky Kissed mountain every single day with a basket of rocks tied to my back. Every day I pushed myself and failed until the day before the contest when I finally made it to the top – before collapsing." I chuckled. When they both remained silent I looked up at them only to see both their mouths were wide open in disbelief.

"You attempted to climb a mountain, every day for a month and a half *with rocks tied to your back?*" Xander asked, his eyes widening with surprise.

"Derrick was my trainer and he said that my sword skills were near perfect and only that I lacked core strength behind my hits. This was his solution." I shrugged and Damon shook his head.

"No one stood a chance against you in that contest, I

knew it from the moment I spotted you down in the arena," he grinned proudly and I raised an eyebrow at him.

"Is that why you nearly dived headfirst over the balcony to get a better look at me?" I teased.

"That and a few other things," he smirked back and I felt my blood heat under my skin.

"You're all falling behind," Alec grunted as he pushed past us and stormed further up the grassy bank where the rest of the class was.

"Ass," I whispered. Damon and Xander chuckled beside me as we pushed ourselves to go faster.

As we climbed, I kept trying to circulate my mana into my legs to help them against the gruelling incline and advised Damon and Xander to do the same.

We were about halfway up when Xander collapsed, his body drenched in sweat and his breathing coming out in strained gasps.

"Come on Xander, you're doing so well," I encouraged as I crouched down beside him.

"I can't—" he gasped out, wincing in pain.

Damon followed suit as his legs gave out. Glancing up to where the class was still marching ahead, I looked to the two boys, then over my shoulder. Damon's knights were a few feet behind, smirking at the prince—waiting for him for fail.

Think!

Panic began to set in as Alec appeared, producing a canteen from his belt and tipped their heads back to pour in water. Once emptied, he lifted Xander onto his back with ease. I knew Alec was strong but—

"Circulate your mana and carry him," he ordered with a nod to Damon before beginning the climb up to the class again.

I bent down beside Damon, his pale blue eyes stared up at me.

"Don't," he breathed. "Just leave me and join them yourself."

"That's not going to happen, *Your Majesty.*" I grinned as I took a deep breath and pulled at the dark pool of mana within and began to circulate it through my arms as I lifted him onto my back. It was just like the training I did with Derrick now, only instead of rocks it was a Prince. I wonder how my family would react if they saw me giving a piggy-back to the Prince of Ghislana. The thought had me giggling.

"Should I be worried as to why you're laughing?" Damon asked, his voice weak as he rested his head on my shoulder and I tried not to shudder as his breath tickled my neck.

"I was just wondering what my family would do if they saw me giving a piggyback to the Prince," I admitted. Damon was silent before a raspy chuckle left his lips.

"Thank you," he said quietly and I shook my head.

"You don't have to thank me, we're friends. Comrades even." I bumped my temple against his gently. "Plus, I'm kind of using you as training anyway so it's fine."

"You're crazy," he pointed out.

"Maybe," I admitted and we laughed some more.

We continued in silence as I focused on controlling my mana, manipulating it to flow into my arms and legs as I gained distance on the class in front of us. The midday sun was beating down on us through the canopy above, as I navi-gated the stones and roots on the forest floor.

"I envy you," Damon said suddenly and my mouth dropped open.

"*You* envy *me?*" I asked incredulously. "You are a Prince with more wealth then I could ever imagine and yet you envy me?"

"Wealth isn't everything," he said.

"It is when you're living day-to-day not knowing when your next meal will be." I snapped and his body tensed.

185

"I'm sorry." I whispered after I said it and felt him shake his head.

"I should be the one that's sorry," he said quietly. "I know how bad the Commoner District is. I first began travelling out there a few years ago when I learnt how to sneak out of the palace. It's where I first met Alec actually, I found him handing out food and clothing to the homeless in an alleyway." I stopped in my tracks. My whole body froze at the words that left his mouth as I envisioned Alec in the alleyway I grew up in, handing out spare food and clothes to the ones I considered friends. I would never in a million years think that he would do something as nice and kind as that.

"I made friends with him then and there and paid for him to stay at the same tavern I took you to. I have been supplying him with any gold, food or clothing that I can get my hands on so he can go out and distribute it to the poor. I knew they probably wouldn't take it if I was the one handing it out," he whispered and I gave a quick look back at the guards to make sure they were far away not to hear what he was saying. If the King found out...it wouldn't end well for the Prince.

"I'm sorry," I said and I swallowed the lump in my throat. "I blamed you for not helping the homeless and the people struggling when you have been doing just that. And I thought Alec was just a stuck up noble who's personality was awful," I said, my voice raspy.

"But you *were* right," Damon stressed. "What I'm doing isn't changing much. *It's not enough.* That is why I'm here, so I can get the power I need to make a change," he explained and then gave a playful tug on my braid. "And Alec *is* a stuck-up ass whose personality is awful, so you were right with that one." He chuckled and I laughed despite the awful feeling in my gut. I had judged them before even finding out the truth.

I was no better than the nobles who looked down their noses at the common folk.

"They must be setting up camp," Damon said and I looked up to see the class now on a flat plateau that seemed to be carved into the mountain.

My pace quickened as I felt the grip on my mana begin to slip. I had to rely on pure strength to make the last few steps up the incline. On the flat surface, my legs went out from beneath me. Damon landed with a thud beside me, both of us panting.

"Took you long enough." I heard Alec's voice say behind me but after hearing what he had done for the people in the alley, I couldn't find it in myself to be annoyed with him.

"Thank you, for the help," I gasped out and he looked at me surprised as if he was waiting for me to start yelling at him.

"There's a small stream off to the left of camp," he said before turning and leaving.

"Can you walk?" I turned to Damon who nodded before pulling himself to stand, groaning at the movement. He helped me stand and I met Perrion's gaze as he gave me a nod of respect as he looked between me and Damon. It was still late afternoon and I wondered if Perrion had chosen this closer camp so that Damon and I could catch up. He specifically said he would leave any that fell behind so I doubted it but held on hope that he wasn't completely ruthless.

Damon and I leaned against each other as we made it to the stream and we both collapsed into it, cold water sinking around our bodies in a cool embrace.

"That feels amazing," I groaned as I turned my face and opened my mouth to gulp down the cold water as Damon did the same. I turned back to face him, watching as he stopped drinking to roll onto his back, wincing at the movement. I rested my head on my elbow, relaxing as the cool water lapped against my back.

Water droplets cascaded down his face, along his sharp jawline. I counted the freckles that dotted over his skin, wondering when he'd been out in the sun long enough to get them.

I misjudged him. Despite where he came from, the wealth and luxury he was born into, he was a good guy. He wanted to help those who needed it most.

That is what a ruler should be like.

He turned his head, and his eyes widened at how close we were. My breathing hitched as his pale blue eyes melted from surprise to warmth. His breath puffed against my face— smelling of honey and roses. My gaze dropped from his eyes to his mouth, watching as his full lips parted.

"That's a very dangerous look," he said quietly, his voice thick and gravelly.

"What...what do you mean?" I breathed, unable to pull away from the addicting scent of him.

"It makes me want to..." His whisper trailed off as he leaned forward.

"Now wouldn't this be quite the story to tell the King." My body locked up at the sound of Han's voice and Damon jolted back from me.

"What are you talking about?" I asked, pulling myself to my feet. Han smirked, and it made me want to punch him.

"I'm talking about how the Prince and a common freak are getting very *comfortable* with each other," Han sneered.

"We're just friends you idiot, not that you would know what that word means," Damon said, rolling his eyes as he shoved past him and made his way back to camp, looking back to see if I was following.

I took a step towards Damon, but leaned towards Han

with a sneer, "You need to watch what you say before I leave you nothing but a bloody smear on the mountainside."

Han blanched, like he'd seen something in my eyes. The darkness beneath, swimming on the surface.

"Whatever" He snarled, as I pushed past him to join Damon. I didn't look back.

WE DIDN'T SPEAK of what almost happened in the stream that night and I finally gave into eating the left-over meat from Alec, not finding it within myself to still be angry at him—also because I was starving.

With a full stomach, I fell asleep after telling them to wake me so I could take my watch. Especially now since I threatened Han.

Darkness pulled me deeper as I dreamed of the feeling of hot breath against my lips, and the cool water of the stream against my back. But when I opened my eyes I found Alec staring back at me as I tumbled over the edge.

CHAPTER 17

J woke to the sound of footsteps, heavy breathing and found my eyes heavy and aching. When I finally opened them, the world was tilted and I looked down to see blood dripping from my hands. A scream bubbled in my throat as I began to kick and writhe against whoever was carrying me.

Han.

As soon as his name crossed my mind, I fought to pour my mana in to my legs and found the pool empty. "Shit" The person whispered, pressing me up against a tree. As I twisted to get away, I came eye to eye with Alec.

"Calm down!" He commanded, and my eyes darted around where we were. I didn't recognise anything, and I didn't know why Alec had dragged me away from the camp. I shied away from him.

"I'm not going to hurt you," He raised his hands and took a step back. "I think I'm the one who should be worrying for my safety."

"What do you mean?" I frowned, and he gestured to my body.

I followed his gaze and a gasp escaped my lips at the sight of my armour drenched in blood. I quickly searched for any wounds or cuts I had to cause so much blood but when I found none my body grew cold. The blood wasn't mine. "Who's blood is this?" I whispered.

"You really don't remember?" He asked and I shook my head. The last thing I remember was falling asleep and dreaming of—

"I found you passed out a little distance away from the camp surrounded by Han and his men," Alec gritted out, his eyes hard. "He must have somehow drugged your food because you were totally unresponsive when I tried to wake you."

Han must have planned my attack before we left for the hike. Bastard.

"What happened Alec? Who's blood is this?" I asked the question again and his eyes were unsure as he looked at my face.

"Han and his friends are dead," he stated and I let the words sink in as I held my breath— "You killed them."

"No," I whispered and shook my head. "I was asleep, I remember *nothing!*" I shouted beginning to feel delirious as my body began to tremble.

"I'm not saying that you meant to do it, I think it's linked with your affinity somehow," Alec said softly and stared at me as if I was some kind of puzzle he was trying to figure out.

"We have to go back. I need to figure out—explain to Perrion that it wasn't me," I stammered and I felt the darkness closing in on my thoughts as panic set in.

"What do you think Perrion will believe?" Alec hissed. "Do you think he will just believe that Han and his buddies just mauled themselves? Even after seeing you covered in their blood?" I swallowed deeply. *Mauled.* I had mauled them to death. "You will be executed and the King will probably drag in your friends from the Commoner District to say it was a planned rebellion against the nobles." I felt nauseous because it was something the King would love to do, any excuse to get rid of some more commoners tainting his kingdom.

"Damon wouldn't allow it," I argued weakly and Alec smirked.

"You really think he has the power to do that?" Alec countered and I found myself unable to argue.

"What do I do?" I asked weakly as the darkness began to close in on my mind again. It began scratching against my walls, waiting for its moment to—

"I grew up not too far from here." Alec's hand suddenly brushed against my face and I felt that familiar warmth and comfort like the magic I had felt the night before. "There is someone there who can figure out what happened to you and we can come up with a plan then." I nodded. I hated that I was running, hiding—that I was relying on Alec. But there was no other way.

"Can you walk, or should I carry you?" He teased as his eyes bore into mine. I scowled and made it all two steps before falling on the floor. The drug must not have worn off completely yet. "Carry it is." Alec chuckled and swung me up into his arms. My head was pressed against his chest where I could hear the deep thundering of his heart, his arms wrapped around my back and supported my legs. The nights events began to catch up with me, and I could feel my mind fraying at the seams.

"Sleep Nevara," Alec murmured against my hair and I relaxed into his body. I closed my eyes and breathed in his scent of mint and earth—sleep tickling the edge of consciousness.

"*Sleep.*" Alec commanded, in a tone that sounder both

louder and softer all at once. The strange magic wrapped around me as I slept.

I AWOKE with a jolt as an energy slammed through my body and I scrambled to sit up from where I lay against a tree. I looked around me to find that we were still in a forest and that I had been stripped down to my undergarments. There was a small river and Alec stood in the centre of it, his own chest bare as he scrubbed a bloodied shirt in his hands. I noticed my armour was washed and hung drying from a nearby branch. There were some dark brown stains on the chest piece and breeches, evidence of last night.

"I could have washed my own clothes," I muttered as I crossed my arms over my chest.

"You're welcome," he said dryly as he dunked his shirt back under the water before wringing it. "You should wash your hair before we continue," After a moment of deliberation, I slowly made my way over to the bank of the river, my legs still unsteady as I stepped into the warm water. Once submerged I looked around where we were. The trees were different here, they were greener and the way the sun reflected against them, they gave off a silver glow. The grass seemed greener too, patched with wildflowers here and there. Even the water seemed to thrum with a steady flow of energy—

Realisation hit. The forest was alive.

Buzzing with energy and magic and it sang into my bones, energising my empty mana pool.

"Where are we?" I asked.

"It's a little outside the kingdom," Alec said and it's then that I noticed that even he seemed different. His skin shimmered with an unnatural golden glow and his eyes, oh my goodness, *his eyes* were like azure-coloured gems.

"You're beautiful," I breathed, unaware at how ridiculous I sounded. I should be focusing on the reason we were out here in the first place. Figuring out a plan to deal with what happened at the camp...but I couldn't stop staring at him. From the cut of his jaw to his high and defined cheekbones, to every curve and line that defined the muscles all over his chest. Even the swirls and symbols of his tattoos seemed to glow and entice me.

"I think the drugs are still messing with your mind." He frowned as he eyed me wearily. The energy from the forest was making my body vibrate. I felt drunk on the magic.

"My mana," I groaned as my eyes locked onto Alec. It felt like I needed to explode, the energy was too much. Realisation clicked as Alec's eyes widened.

"You can feel it? The energy?" He asked and then cursed to himself. "You shouldn't be able to feel it—oh gods you're taking in too much." He began to pull me from the water, but I stopped him, letting the delicious energy take over and it felt like that time Kiera got in a new ale that tasted a lot like the icing she used on her pastries and I drank and drank *and drank* until it felt like a completely new person took over my body. It took nearly half the guild to drag me to my bed and force me to sleep, afraid of what I would do if I was let loose.

"Nevara," he warned in a low voice but then I heard his sharp intake of breath as I pulled myself towards him. I didn't care as I trailed my fingers over the hardened muscles on his chest and gasped when his own energy began to flow into me, dark and rich as it filled my blood and my head.

More.

My hands found their way up into his hair, tugging his face down to mine. He growled in warning, but I didn't care. His azure eyes burned with want as they travelled over my face to my lips, where they turned ravenous. I whimpered as he brought his mouth down onto mine, claiming. I tightened my hold against him, our chests brushing together. His kisses turned fierce, and when he deepened the kiss, I let go completely. I wanted it. *I needed it.*

"Alec," I whispered and he pulled away and stepped back. I whimpered at the loss of contact, at the loss of his energy and stepped forward towards him.

"Stop," he choked out as if he was struggling to hold himself back. "This isn't you, Nevara. This is the forest's energy that's making you do this," he said and I wanted to tell him that I didn't care and that I *needed* him.

"Get dressed," he scolded and clenched his hands at his sides, his eyes tight. It took me a moment to gather my thoughts before I pulled on my armour. I noticed Alec avert his eyes and turn around, he didn't even look back to check if I was following him before he ventured out into the forest.

"We will be out of the forest soon so try to control yourself until then," he snarled and it was like a slap to the face. I wanted to point out that he actually was the one to kiss me first but held my tongue. I winced at how the mana pool in my stomach had now become a raging ocean, overfilled and wild. I hugged my body as I tried to stop any of the trees or plants touching my skin. It felt like if I absorbed anymore energy then I might explode.

WE TRAVELLED for what felt like hours and I was constantly trying to fight the call of the forest, the temptation for me to let loose and bathe in its energy.

My hands kept drifting to my swollen lips, my mind at war with how I felt about kissing Alec. He was my first kiss. I can't believe it was with him, but it felt so... good.

"We're here," Alec said and his voice had softened a little as we neared a small grey stoned wall. A large silver gate stood proudly and it opened as we approached.

"What is this place?" I asked in awe as we stepped through the gate and into what looked like a small town. Homes lined the streets and were built with neat grey stone and ivy that climbed up everywhere. Perfectly cobbled path under my feet seemed like it was inlayed with chunks of crystal that shimmered in the sun. Water fountains were at every corner and statues of beautiful men and women lined the paths.

It was like an entirely new world compared to the city of Ghislane.

"I'll explain everything once we get somewhere safe." Alec said as he took my arm and pulled me through the streets. The lack of energy made me feel weak, but it was like my head was clear and I realised what had happened back at the river.

My feet stumbled on the cobbles, and his hand tightened on my wrist. I'd thrown myself at him. I groaned with embarrassment.

"We're almost there." He quipped, looking me over once then turning back to the path ahead.

We passed beautiful houses and shop fronts with signs written with weird symbols like the ones that marked my sword. Alec had said this place was at the far reaches of the kingdom, I hadn't even known another town as well kept as the Nobles District even existed. Especially one that made Ghislane pale in comparison.

We neared a small stone house lined with beautiful red roses. Alec knocked three loud thuds before entering and an elderly man was sat behind a desk. He almost toppled back as he scrambled to his feet, shuffling over to us, his eyes going wide when he saw Alec. He began speaking in a different language, the words bounced off my brain feeling familiar and bizarre at the same time. Alec spoke back to him in the same language and then they both turned to me. Was I dreaming? Surely this wasn't reality. Maybe I was still under the effects of whatever drug Han had given me and all of this was one messed up dream.

"This is my uncle, Fraser." Alec introduced the elderly man who smiled kindly. It was then that I noticed the man was extremely pale and seemed to have a glow to his skin like Alec did at the river. His eyes were the deepest of browns, almost black and they stood out against his skin.

He had strange growths on his neck that seemed to tremble as he spoke and I quickly averted my eyes whenever the man looked at me.

"It's very nice to meet you," Fraser said in my language and held out his strange, webbed hand and I hesitated before taking it.

"I'm Nevara," I said hesitantly and as our skin touched, jolts of energy passed between us. I quickly pulled my hand back as Fraser's eyes went wide.

He turned to Alec and the two began conversing in that musical language again. This time it was more urgent as Alec cast me a surprised look at whatever the man had said.

I dug my nails into my palms. Frustrated that I couldn't understand what they were saying.

Alec must have noticed.

"We will eat first and then discuss everything," Alec explained as Fraser led us through to a beautifully decorated study, that continued on into a dining room. A large table made from the trunk of a tree and stood atop ornate legs took up the centre of the room. I wondered how big the tree was before it was cut down.

Alec pulled out an intricately detailed chair, motioning me to sit down, then took the seat beside me. I glanced around the room, noticing a colourful herb garden on the windowsill beneath a large arched window.

Fraser was staring at me, I could feel it. Alec cleared his throat and my gaze returned to them.

"Explain."

Alec tried to protest, about eating dinner first. I cut him a look and gritted my teeth.

"Now."

The two men shared a look before Alec turned to me, a hard set to his jaw.

"Remember what I told you about the Fae?" He relented and I jerked my head back in surprise.

"The *Fae?*" I choked out. I tried to recall what he had told me about them and thought about how he told me that the Fae were the ones who made the magic artefacts and weapons from the dungeons. "What about the Fae?"

"The Fae hail from the Kingdom of Arboria, a place that's a long way from Ghislana," Alec explained. "They've lived in peace for centuries until an Fae named Penumbra, the exiled prince, grew hungry for power and wanted to reclaim the throne. He began creating gates that connected the Fae Lands to the humans and taught them how to awaken their magic. After a few years, the humans had begun entering the Fae lands and slaughtered every Fae and creature they saw and began looting their most precious artefacts and weapons." My blood grew cold.

"Why are you telling me this?" I asked desperately, my mind running wild with the information.

"Because my dear, you have just passed through one of those gates," Fraser said softly and I stared blanky at the old man.

"We're in a dungeon, Nevara. Although all they really are, is a doorway between our kingdoms," Alec said and I opened my mouth but no words came out.

"Don't you want to know why you have the shadow affinity, Nevara?" Fraser asked. "That affinity is rare and not many Fae possess it. Penumbra was one of the few who was blessed by the raven god with it in the past three centuries. He was the one who gave you that power."

"The mark on your chest," Alec elaborated, "it was a mark of his power that only awoke when you unlocked your magic."

My brain went into overdrive with the torrent of information. I slumped back against the chair, staring down at my hands before a laugh bubbled up in my throat. Tears filled my eyes, and I didn't know if it was from humour or hysteria.

I just wanted to go to the Academy. Not all this.

"Nevara," Alec said in a low tone but that only made me even more hysterical as I half laughed; half sobbed. The story played over in my head, and my head snapped up. Alec had said this was where he grew up. I turned towards him.

"So, you're telling me that you are…a Fae?" I asked and Alec nodded his head tensely. I felt the raging mana in my stomach twist and erupt along with giggling.

I turned to the side and vomited a thick black liquid that burned the inside of my body as it made its way out. I was done. The walls in my mind collapsed and the darkness swooped in to devour me.

"I want to go home," I sobbed as my world fall apart with each heave. Alec tugged my hair back and I tried to push him away.

"It must be the mana from the forest, she's not strong enough to handle it all," Alec said to Fraser. I couldn't concentrate as my body gave out beneath me. The darkness took over and consumed every piece of me, leaving behind nothing.

I was empty.

CHAPTER 18

$\mathcal{T}$he darkness didn't have a beginning or an end.

It had no sound and no air and was nothing but an endless void that only seemed to grow darker as time seemed to pass by.

A raven's caw echoed.

"I didn't think you were the type to give up." An ancient voice reverberated through my mind. "Penumbra forced me to split my magic between you both. At first, I was unsure what a poor human could do with the blessing of my shadows but as I saw you grow up and develop your iron-like will... I was surprised."

"I found myself watching you more often as you grew stronger than your fellow humans and that was even before your magic was awoken. Now your strength is mixed in with my shadows and they sing to me Nevara, it's like a voice I haven't heard in half a millennia."

Light broke through the darkness as a white raven swooped down.

It was Soot.

Except it wasn't.

The white feathers were stark against the darkness. I shied away from the brightness, wanting to stay in the dark.

"You are chosen now in more ways than one, my Priestess of Shadows," the raven raised its head as it spoke. "Penumbra wants you to bring the power of the stones to him, but now it seems you have enough strength to decide on your own who shall claim it. Maybe you will claim it for yourself."

"I will lessen the plague of shadows on your thoughts for now, but it will only be until you master them for yourself. You are strong and kind and will become the perfect vessel to do what needs to be done. Now go," it demanded and it swooped towards me and with a brush of its feathers against my forehead a blinding pain pulled me from the darkness.

~

"Gods, hold her still!" Hands were pressing me down. A high pitched scream made my eyes go wide, and it was then that I realised the noise was coming from me.

"Nevara." Alec whispered and I flinched at the closeness of his voice.

"Her forehead," Fraser gasped. "She's been marked by Ravenir."

"But she's human!" Alec furrowed his brows as my screams turned into whimpers and the pain on my forehead lessened.

We were in a different room now. I took in deep breaths, counting every inhale and exhale—pushing away the darkness, only to find it wasn't there. There were only tendrils of smoke whispering at the edges of my mind.

Alec and Fraser exchanged looks above me.

"What happened?" I croaked as I sat up, wincing at the pain in my stomach.

"What did you dream of?" Fraser cut in and I looked at him.

Dream? Did I dream of something?

A memory of white wings fluttered across my mind but other than that there was nothing.

"I didn't dream of anything," I said confused.

"But you were marked," Fraser began to say but Alec shot him a hard stare that made him stop. I wondered what that look meant. Why did he stop him from speaking?

"Tell me the rest of the story," I said to Alec and he frowned.

"I don't think that's a good idea," he said warily.

"I'm sorry how I acted before, but it was a lot to take in." It still was a lot, but I didn't mention that. "But I'm fine now, I need to hear the rest. Please," I added and he stared at me again before sinking down onto the armchair in defeat.

"To cut a very long story short, I'm guessing Penumbra gave you his powers so you would eventually bring the elemental stones to him." Alec sighed and pinched the bridge of his nose as if he was developing a headache.

"Elemental stones?" I asked.

"The elemental stones are just what they sound like. There are five in total: one for air, fire, earth, water and spirit. Although, the last one has been debated about," Fraser explained. "The stones control each of the Fae and now humans that share its elemental affinity. The one that controls the stone also controls the affinity wielder."

"Penumbra wants to get his hands on the stones to create an army under his control so he can take over the Human Kingdom along with the Fae Kingdom," Alec said, his eyes flickering with anger.

"Where are the stones now?" I asked as I took in all the information.

The locations of the stones have always been hidden. A

dungeon gate must have opened up near one, as the King is now in possession of the Fire stone." Alec sighed. "That's the reason I've been in your kingdom for the last decade. I've been trying to find its location and return it to Arboria."

I sat for a moment in silence, sorting through my thoughts and putting them away safely. How was I dealing with this so well? This information should have floored me but my mind was just taking in the information and dealing with it with ease.

"So the King can now control all of the fire wielders?" I asked horrified.

"It's been written in ancient books that only the Fae can control them so the King can probably only tell that the stone is very powerful and valuable. Like a child with a shiny gem," Alec smirked and I let out a sigh of relief.

"So... Why am I here?" I asked and the room fell quiet.

"Well, my brother seems to be cooking up a plan that consists of you delivering the stones right to him so I need to make sure you understand what the stones are and why they should be given back to Arboria where they belong," Alec said leaning forward.

"Your brother...as in, your brother the exiled Prince of Arboria? The Fae Kingdom?" I asked and was a little scared that I already knew the answer.

"Prince Alecin Corax of the Arboria Fae Kingdom, at your service." He smirked and I felt my body shudder at the weight of his words.

He was a damn prince.

AFTER THE SHAKING revelations were all out in the open, Alec and Fraser left me with time to get washed and dressed before trying to eat again seeing as last time we didn't get very far into the dinner before I went into hysterics and vomited everywhere.

There was a beautiful and ornate bathroom connected to the bedroom that had a similar design. A large copper bath took up most of the room, with a variety of pipes and a small wood burner in the corner. I turned on the tap, hot water flowing instantly, and soft puffs of smoke billowing from the burner in tandem.

A constant source of heat.

I sank down deep into the water and groaned as the heat eased into my muscles. I took the time on my own to reflect on the crazy day I had.

The Fae were real. Alec was Fae *and* a Prince. There were elemental stones that controlled the entirety of magic and I was somehow caught up in the middle of it all because of Alec's evil brother Penumbra.

I sighed and dunked my head under the water and stayed there until my lungs burned.

I grabbed a jasmine scented soap from the small shelf beside the bath and began to scrub my aching body and then my hair, cringing at the dried blood that was still matted into it.

Han.

That was something I still needed to sort out and find out if I actually did kill him or not. If I did then…I would have to deal with that later.

I quickly dried and managed to braid my hair before finding a white shirt and a matching pair of trousers on the bed. I pulled them on ignoring the fact that they were a little big and made my way downstairs.

Fraser and Alec were deep in conversation at the table and they smiled softly when I entered. The black vomit from before was now thankfully cleaned away and I felt guilty for whoever had to do it.

"You look better," Alec smiled softly as he eyed the loose clothes I wore and I noticed he wore something similar. Were they his clothes? Heat crept up my cheeks and I quickly sat down.

"I feel better," I breathed, "although I do have a question."

"And what's that?" Alec asked leaning back in his chair.

"Han and the others," I choked out. "Did I really kill them?"

"I was just discussing that with Fraser," Alec sighed. "There is a way to recover lost memories…but it can be quite invasive."

"What do I have to do?" I asked sheepishly, not liking the last word he said.

"Nothing too strenuous." Fraser smiled warmly. "There is a healer that is highly trained in the mind and deals with all kinds of memory problems. We can head out first thing in the morning." I looked between the two of them as I mulled over my answer but sighed when I realised that I didn't really have a choice.

"Okay." I nodded as a small woman came in with a tray and began to fill the table with all different plates of food that I had never seen before. I noticed everything was solely vegetables, there was no meat in sight. I didn't know where to begin.

"I think you'll like this one." Alec motioned to a dish made up of mixed vegetables with some sort of sauce over them. I took a bite and a burst of flavours erupted on my tongue as I took another mouthful, then another. It was sweet and savoury all at once.

Since living with Kain my food mostly consisted of stew and bread, not that I was complaining at all, but it just seemed so bland in comparison. This food… I just had no words to describe it.

"I told you." Alec grinned and when I finished one dish,

Alec would hand me another one until I was stuffed. I sat back feeling so content and full and Alec stifled a chuckle at me.

The evening passed in a blur as we spoke of upcoming events in the Fae lands—of places I had never heard of. Places I wanted to know more about.

"I'm going to take Nevara for a walk before we retire for the night." Alec said, as he pushed back from the table and offered his hand to me, which I took.

"Remember to meet up after breakfast tomorrow to visit Drisir." Fraser chirped, and Alec nodded before leading me out of the back door. The night air was oddly humid, but a cool breeze brushed my cheeks as we stepped out onto the cobbled path.

"You seem to be taking this whole situation surprisingly well," Alec stated. "Well, apart from the time you threw up everywhere." I winced at that and he only chuckled in response.

"I keep thinking I'm going to crumble at any moment but for some reason my mind is clear," I explained and Alec studied my face.

"Well, I'm thankful that you listened to what I had to say." Alec smiled and my skin flushed at the gentleness behind it. Images from what happened at the river fluttered through my mind and I quickly pushed them away.

I didn't need to think about that kiss now…or anytime really.

"Where are we exactly?" I looked around at the row of quaint houses that lined the street and spotted a large tavern at the end. Fae were huddled outside laughing, enjoying the festivities of the evening— I was taken aback by how normal it seemed.

"This is a small town called Undar which is on the border of the Aquaris City of the Mizurin Region," Alec said and my mouth popped open at all the words and places I didn't understand.

"This is only a town?" I gaped. I assumed it was a City from the wealth the occupants oozed, and how beautifully built everything was.

"The main City of Arboria is Viridia and is far bigger and grander than any of the other cities from the different elemental regions," Alec smirked. "The palace there is twice the size of Damon's."

"Elemental regions?" I frowned.

"In Arboria, the land is split amongst the different elemental affinities. The gods blessed each region with high amounts of raw elements so that the affinity wielders will have more power to draw on." Alec explained. "Like for instance, this is the water region Mizurin. Its lands are covered with lakes and waterfalls. It has the highest chance for rainfall and its air holds three times the amount of moisture."

I stopped walking as I tried to make sense of what he had just told me. I lifted my hand in front of my face and examined the drops of moisture that lay on the skin. I hadn't realised exactly how humid it was until I actually stopped and focused.

Alec's hand wrapped around my wrist as he began guiding my hand through the air and the moisture began to build on my skin.

"The Fae that live here are a race called Undine and they all have a water affinity, they need this moisture to help them live. The gills on their necks absorb it to help keep their mana reserves topped up." Alec explained and that's when something clicked in my mind. I thought back to when I noticed the strange growths on Fraser's neck and realised now what they were.

"That's incredible." I said as I examined the moisture on my hand once more before looking back at Alec.

"You have the same awe filled face that Damon had when I explained the Undine's." Alec chuckled as he took his hand back from mine.

"Damon knows about all of this?" I asked with wide eyes and he nodded.

"He hates the King more than anyone and I made a deal with him. I would help him keep relations between the Humans and the Fae when he became king if he helped me locate the fire stone." Alec shrugged. "Damon is one of the better humans I have met, he is still quite immature, but his heart is pure enough."

"You say that as if you're not the same age or as equally immature," I snorted and he raised his eyebrows.

"I'm 230 years old, Nevara," he said and I gawked at him.

"*What?*" I asked. He was lying...he had to be!

"The Fae age differently from humans. We can live for a few millennia before the earth claims us again." He shrugged and my mind spun.

"I bet you regret kissing me now, right?" He teased, his blue eyes dancing as heat flooded my face.

"I wasn't myself back at the river, you know that," I hissed at his brazenness, "and you kissed me first!" I added and stormed ahead.

"I was joking. Joking!" He laughed and held his hands up in surrender. "I didn't know you would react to the magic in the forest, humans shouldn't be able to feel it let alone absorb it. Even the Fae have a hard time feeling it."

"Then how come I did?" I frowned as I remembered the drunken state it had left me in.

"I'm adding it to the very long list of mysteries about you," he said and I let out a small laugh.

Our walk led us to a small garden, wildflowers blooming

beneath the stars with luminous petals. Alec steered me towards a bench and gestured for me to sit beside him. The smell of flowers filled the air as I tipped my head back, closing my eyes. If I wanted to, I could almost pretend I was back in Ghislane, outside the tavern—

"There's a prophecy," Alec whispered, and I turned to look at him. "That a priestess will come and use the stones to bring about peace to all of the lands. It was a story I heard growing up and thought it as nothing more than a mother's tale to her child. A legend." Alec tilted his head back and to the side, meeting my eyes, "But the more I get to know you I have to wonder if you're the priestess from the story. The one we've all been waiting for.

"When you woke up earlier tonight, your forehead bore the mark of our god. A small crescent moon with raven wings stretched out on each side." He tapped my forehead with a finger and chuckled. "If that's not a sign of you being her—well… No one had been marked by the Raven God in nearly half a millennia."

"But I'm only human, I don't know anything about this Raven God." I shook my head. "I'll help you find the fire stone, but I'm sorry, I'm not this priestess."

"You may be human by blood, but you remind me of the Fae warriors. Strong, brave and fearless." He leaned in as his hand travelled down the length of the scar on my face. I settled into his touch, a welcome feeling after a day of being so lost and overwhelmed with information.

"I wonder if you thought that about me even when I was puking my guts up," I murmured.

"Even then." He grinned, before blinking and standing up, holding out his hand. "We should get some rest, because it's going to be a long day tomorrow." I groaned in agreement as I got to my feet.

"I don't even want to think about whether I killed them

or not." I shook my head as we made our way back to Fraser's house.

"Whatever the outcome, we will deal with it and then make our way back to Ghislana as soon as possible," he assured and I nodded. After everything that's happened, the main thing I wanted to do was see my family again.

Back at the house, I found my way back to the same bedroom from earlier and collapsed onto the bed. The exhaustion from the day catching up with me.

I closed my eyes and pretended I was back at home, with Luca reading softly beside me, and soon enough sleep came for me.

CHAPTER 19

Fraser and Alec were sat at the table again when I came down the stairs the following morning. My dreams had been filled with Alec, and the kiss we shared in that damn river.

"Good morning Nevara," Fraser beamed. "I trust you slept well?"

"Yes, thank you," I blurted, as I felt my face flame as the memories of Alec surfaced. Alec cocked his head to the side, a knowing smile creeping across his face.

A plate of eggs and toast was already set out for me, and I quickly ate. Anything to take my mind off the dreams.

"I sent word ahead to Drisir so she could prepare for us coming," Fraser smiled softly and folded his hands on the table. "She's expecting us anytime now."

"Well, we might as well go and get it over with," Alec said and turned to me, his azure eyes searching my face again. "Are you ready to go?"

I nodded and quickly wiped my mouth before standing and following Alec and Fraser out of the house.

It was early morning and only a few Fae were milling

around outside. Some that we passed gave us weary glances, and it wasn't until the third or fourth stare that I realised they were aimed at me.

I studied one the females as we passed by. She didn't look much older than me, but had an ethereal beauty about her that set us apart. My brows furrowed as my eyes landed on her neck where strange growths—

"She's an Undine," Alec clarified as he followed my line of sight.

"An Undine." I repeated, trying not to shrink from his closeness as I casted a quick glance at Fraser who wandered behind us. It clicked in my mind then as I remembered the conversation with Alec the night before.

It was fascinating to me that these Fae had adapted to survive and use their affinities to the best of their abilities and it made my brain hurt as I tried to think of what the other elemental Fae must look like.

We suddenly stopped, and I craned my head to look at the sign that hung above us. The building was a beautiful sandstone structure, and on the sign were a cluster of Fae Symbols written in elegant script. I couldn't understand them, but they were striking.

Inside of the building, shelves lined the walls and a musty scent hung in the air. Ancient tomes and old looking books stood beneath a layer of dust.

A library.

I reverently hovered my fingers across the spines, careful not to disturb the dust. Lucas would love it here, falling headfirst into each and every page.

Alec beckoned me to follow him further into the library, skirting around tables and armchairs precariously placed here and there. A blonde woman rounded an aisle with a book in hand, and a smile graced her features when she saw Alec and Fraser.

I stood back, watching as they conversed and exchanged pleasantries in that foreign language.

"I'm Drisir, an Elder of the Town of Undar, and owner of this quaint library," The woman said with a wink, as she held out a slim had towards me. It was then I managed to get a good look at her—like Fraser she had those ethereal glowing qualities that I assumed all Fae have. She was also clearly and Undine with the pale skin, webbed hands and dark contrasting eyes. She carried an air of authority with her, something in the way she analysed me with her eyes that made me think she was currently assessing every move I made.

"I'm Nevara, it's a pleasure to meet you," I smiled politely as I took her hand and her red-lipped smile deepened.

"And here I thought all humans were savages! Seems like there are a few decent ones amongst you," she chirped and Alec tensed from beside me. I was lost for words.

"Drisir, we need you to perform a quick memory retrieval for Nevara. There was an accident amongst her kind and the memories seem to be lost," Fraser said quickly changing the conversation and I was glad. I guess if what Alec said was true, then all the Fae know is that the humans enter their world, kill without a thought and steal as much as they can. I thought of Kain and the rest of the Ruby Guild… Did they do just that? Did they know of the Fae? I made a mental note to make that my priority of finding out when I got back to Ghislana.

"I've never performed a memory retrieval on a human before," she stated as she tapped her chin with her webbed finger. "I can't say for certain how well the retrieval will go on a mind such as yours, but I will try my best." She smiled and motioned for us to follow her to a small room to the side of the library.

I cast a wary glance at Alec who gave me a sheepish smile.

Some help he was.

"Now you take a seat here," Drisir gestured to the armchair for me to sit, so I did. "I'm assuming the Prince would like to view these memories too, yes?"

I glanced to the side to see Alec stood by the door, a hard glint in his eyes as stared at me. The look was gone in an instant as he started towards me.

"Is that okay with you? If I take a look as well?" Alec knelt beside me, so our faces were almost level with one another. A smile pulling at his lips as I nodded and turned to look up at Drisir.

"Now close your eyes and relax your mind the best you can." Drisir instructed as she I felt her touch my head. I pressed back into the chair cushions and let out a breath, clenching and unclenching my hands against the arms.

"Relax." Alec whispered, as he interlinked our fingers against the arm. My breathing evened out.

"My god." Drisir gasped.

"What's wrong?" I tensed, opening one eye to peek up at her.

"Your mental shield is incredible," Drisir whispered. "It's like nothing I've ever seen... It's impregnable."

"The Mark of the Ravenir," Alec said, tightening his hold on my hand. "Right there."

"How is a human marked by the Ravenir?" Then I felt it, a small brush on a wall inside my mind. Drisir sighed, "You're going to have to let me in, Nevara."

"How?" I asked, sounding as if at the end of a tunnel.

"Picture a small door on the wall opening for me," Drisir guided.

"But what about if the darkness gets in?" I asked, my voice barely a whisper. Alec's hand tensed in mine, as his other brushed against my forehead.

"I won't let any darkness through it with me. I promise,"

Drisir said, her voice gentle. I hesitated, as cold fear sluiced over my skin. Alec's fingers began stroking back and forth against my temple, almost as if brushing it away. I relaxed back into the chair, focusing on him.

I concentrated on the wall around my mind, on creating a opening door and—

"Good girl," Drisir breathed as I felt her and Alec slip through the gap, an odd feeling settling over me. It was like an itch I couldn't reach. "I'm going to start looking for the memory now."

I nodded, not trusting my voice as I felt it then. Images started flashing behind my eyes, blurry and distorted; a black-haired woman holding a babe to her chest, then her lifeless body on the alley floor. A child cuddled in close to her cold body as guards came and took the body away.

A child crying out to the dark, alone.

I heard Alec curse under his breath. He could see the memories. *My* memories. I fought to keep my breath even.

More memories appeared; a child being beaten for stealing food from the bakery at the end of alley, to scrounging through trash to find something, anything to survive. To help others survive—my family.

"This isn't the memory we want." I said quietly, my face burning with shame.

"I have to follow the timeline, from the very beginning," Drisir whispered, brushing a hand over my hair. "I'm sorry."

I heard Alec's sharp intake of breath as the next memories surfaced. A man with a thick cloak over his face, red eyes striking in the darkness beneath.

"Penumbra." Alec ground out, his hand tightening against my own.

The scene became static and skipped forward to my first meeting with Netta and being welcomed into her family.

"It seems like Penumbra has removed the memory of them meeting." Drisir murmured.

"I didn't expect anything less from him," Alec sighed.

Memories began spiralling like wind in a storm—of Kain wielding his fire magic for the first time, to him taking in me, Netta and the boys. Flashes of us training every day, and memories of time with members of the Guild.

Tears rolled down my cheeks as I watched myself. The laughter, the chattering, the evenings in the tavern. I missed them so much.

The memories were coming faster now. Days leading up the contest and my body went rigid as I watched each round unfold all over again. Damon grinning down at me from the stands.

Sweat broke out on my forehead, my hands began to shake as Alec's thumb stroked the back of my hand. The final round with Samual shot forward in my mind, my breaths coming in ragged pants—

"Calm down Nevara. It's only a memory." Drisir urged. But she didn't understand. This memory was buried deep in the darkness for a reason.

Samual lifted his hands, and I started to scream as I felt it. Like a brand, the flames began licking at my skin.

"Shit!" I heard Alec curse as his hand cupped my face. I bowed away from the chair, my eyes clenched tight as I burned, and burned.

"Breathe Nevara! It's not real!" Alec pleaded, his breath against my temple as he pulled me against his body. He whispered soothing murmurs, pushing the darkness away. A bright light blotted out his voice, brushing away the dark on the back of white wings.

"It's Ravenir," Drisir gasped, as the room fell silent. "He's truly watching over her." She whispered, disbelief colouring her tone.

"If you want to stop this now Nevara—"

"Keep going." I croaked. After a moment I felt Drisir reach further into my mind, pulling forth more and more memories.

The weeks after the contest when I was nothing more than an empty shell, unable to overcome the darkness—how weak and trapped I had become. The night Damon appeared below my window, leading me to meet his friends.

To meet Alec.

I blushed, feeling my face warm, knowing he could see when I thought of how rude and arrogant, he was.

Alec chuckled, his breath against my ear, "You're not wrong."

Then came the awakening ceremony. The visions were Penumbra appeared again, but the images became more and more distorted.

"Bastard!" Alec gritted out.

Images from the dream I had after the awakening flew to the front of my mind. The night when I fought with Alec, how he pressed close to my body. Heat radiating from where he perched between my legs. I squirmed and could feel Alec's smirk against the side of my face.

Drisir kept looking, and I kept breathing, counting each breath. The forest from the hike with Perrion raised up in front of me, and a shadowy image began to form.

"This is it." I breathed, my hand pressing further into Alec's palm.

"I'm going to have to clear away the shadows, and I'm going to need your help." Drisir instructed, and I nodded. "When I peel back the shadows, I need you to not resist. No matter what you feel, your body is going to want to keep this hidden, so I am going to need you to fight against it." Another nod, and she began to swipe at the shadows. The feeling made me tense.

"Fight it." Alec whispered, and I did. The smoky tendrils began to disappear one by one, and I was left breathless.

Han and his group of friends were carrying me, half asleep and drugged away from the camp. Their vice-like hands digging into my legs and arms. Once deep into the forest they set me down on the mossy grass and stood over me.

"Not so tough now, are you, *bitch?*" Han spat and the rest of his friends smirked. Han dragged a small dagger down the side of my neck and I cried out as it made a shallow cut. "I've had these plans for you the moment I saw you in the arena," Han said, his breath wet at my ear as he leaned over me. Darkness began building in my chest as he gripped my chin and forced his mouth on mine, sloppy disgusting kisses as I tried to fight weakly against him.

"This mouth is so much prettier when it's quiet," Han smirked, "I wonder if the Prince will remember you when you're dead? I don't think so." His lips crashed back down onto mine, and I felt the darkness explode. Shadows erupted from my body, contorting and control was taken from me.

In my place now stood something more primal and animalistic.

Large shadow claws replaced my hands as I/It lunged for Han, instantly gutting him and blood shot out everywhere. His friends screamed as they ran into the darkness, and one by one I tracked them down. Bleeding them to death.

"By the gods," Alec whispered. I felt bile rise in my throat.

"What is that?" I whimpered as I watched my claws gut another one of Hans friends, clawing at him until he was unrecognisable.

"It's called a shadow beast," Alec whispered. "It's a rare trait that comes with the shadow affinity, it's only been recorded in books but no one has claimed it in a millennia. Not even Penumbra."

The screams filled my head and I gritted my teeth against the onslaught of memories.

"That's enough. I don't need to see anymore," I pleaded as the memories shifted. It was the day after the attack, and the sound of a river filled my mind. Alec was in the water, the energy like static around us where he pressed me against his chest.

I slammed the door to my mind closed, sealing the walls back in place, and my eyes sprang open. My heart was thundering.

"Well, that was unexpected." Drisir murmured. Whether she meant the shadow beast or the kiss, I didn't know.

I met Alec's eyes; his gaze was heated as he looked me over. Then cleared his throat and shook himself, letting go of my hand and stepping back. I felt cold suddenly.

I looked up as Fraser approached us and Alec glanced at him, then back at Drisir.

"I need you to look into as many records and references as you can about the shadow beast trait and record what you find. I'll send someone to collect it." Alec ordered, and Fraser nodded.

"What about what I did to Han?" I gulped, pulling my hands into my lap. I killed him, and his friends. I wasn't technically me, but—I shuddered to think of what would have happened if the beast hadn't appeared.

"I'll handle it," Alec said, his eyes hardening as he saw my shudder. "Perrion is one of my guards. I'll talk to him."

My mouth dropped open.

"Perrion is Fae?!" I squeaked. Remembering how the two whispered between themselves back at the camp, and how unsurprised Perrion was when Alec wanted to join the swordsman class.

"You said Perrion wouldn't believe me," I pointed out,

remembering Alec's words. "You said he would lock me up and then give me over to the King."

Alec paled at my words, and smiled sheepishly.

"I apologise," Alec looked down at me. "My words were harsh but I needed you to not go back to the camp because I truly didn't know what had happened."

"I have few of my most trusted allies are in the human kingdom, trying to track down the fire stone," Alec continued to explain and I didn't know what to say. My mind spun as I tried to remember everyone I had come into contact with and wondered if they were Fae or not.

"Are you ready to head back home?" Alec asked as he motioned to the door and I nodded immediately, there was nothing I wanted more right now other than to head home.

"Thank you for your help, Drisir," Alec said over his shoulder. The female's dark brown eyes crinkled as she looked between us.

"I don't think this will be the last time I see you, my dear," Drisir smiled, and I didn't know what to say so I smiled back.

Alec led me back out into the street, as Fraser stayed behind to begin the search in the library for the shadow beast.

On the walk back to Fraser's house, Alec tugged me towards a small storefront. Intricate armour and beautiful pieces of clothing and weaponry were displayed behind the glass.

I followed Alec as he led me inside, where he began talking to the Fae behind the counter. He was tall and beautiful, and smiled warmly as he lifted a wrapped box from under the counter. He said something to me in Fae, and I looked over to Alec.

"He says you resemble the full moon on a winter's night." Alec smirked as he grabbed the package, a blush covered my cheeks as the man winked at me.

Outside Alec chuckled as I looked up at him.

"What?" I asked, pressing my cool hands to my heated face.

"Nothing," Alec shrugged. "I just find it amusing how easily you get flustered."

"I do not!" I argued, scowling at him. He raised eyebrows, as he ran his tongue over his teeth. A challenge brewing in his eyes.

"Oh really?" Alec smirked. "Well then, let's discuss that dream you had of me after the awakening," He advanced towards me, teasing. "I seem to remember that you were laying beneath me while I—" I covered his mouth with my hand, my face burning with embarrassment. Mirth danced in his eyes.

"Ok! Ok!" I sighed. "I'm just not used to this sort of thing. I don't get many compliments because of… well, you know," I gave a lopsided smile as I gestured to the scarred skin down the side of my face. Alec's eyes softened.

"Everything about you is beautiful," Alec confessed, his eyes darkening. "This is only a sign of your strength; of what you went through and how you came out stronger and even more beautiful." His hand trailed down, over my scars, his fingers leaving a fire in their wake. A fire I could bear.

I tried to swallow, to do anything, as his eyes captured every inch of me before dropping to my lips. I ran my tongue across my lower lip unconsciously, wanting that energy again. The same that made us kiss at the river.

Alec was leaning forward, as a group of Fae passed us. He swung back on his heels as they bowed to him, and he ran a hand through his hair before turning back to me. The shutters on his eyes were back in place.

"I got your armour repaired." He said, pressing the parcel into my hands before turning and began walking again. "It seemed sentimental to you."

I clutched the box to my chest as I followed him down the cobbled path.

"Thank you." I whispered, surprised as his caring gesture.

"See, I'm not always an asshole." He grinned, and I blanched.

"I'm sorry," I murmured. Remembering he had seen my thoughts. "But you were kind of an asshole to me."

"I'm always an asshole, Nevara." He laughed, more loudly this time. I couldn't help joining in the laughter as we entered the house. I dismissed myself and headed upstairs to put my armour back on. It looked perfect now, like brand new.

Back downstairs, I noticed Alec had packed a small bag with food, water and some provisions. He gave me a small nod before we left Fraser's home without a backwards glance.

We made our way through the gates of town, and out into the forest. I took one last glance over my shoulder at the glowing lights. For some reason, my heart ached a little to leave. I wanted to know more about the Fae kingdom. I wanted to see its people, learn their language, their cultures.

But I was just human.

I turned and began walking to catch up to Alec.

And this wasn't my home.

CHAPTER 20

*T*he first day's journey went fine and uneventful as we walked and walked *and walked.* Before the sun began to set, we finally set up a small camp and I watched in wonder as Alec produced a small flame from his palm to light the fire in front of us.

"I thought your affinity was air?" I asked as I shuffled as close to the fire as I dared. The fear not as potent as before.

"The ability to control the elements fully is something only the High Fae, and those of royal blood can master." Alec closed his hand into a fist, extinguishing the flame. When he uncurled his fingers, three orbs circled one another. "A Fae of royal heritage can awaken up to three of the elements."

"Earth, Fire and Air?" I leaned in, watching the green, red and grey orbs float above his palm with awe. Realising then how powerful Alec truly was.

"My air element is the strongest. The most dominant of the three, but fire is a strong back up in combat, and earth is good for healing." Alec said as he shook his hand, the orbs disappearing.

"So, you really do dabble in all things magic," I gaped. "You know swordsmanship, battle formations and healing."

"I've had many years to master it all," Alec shrugged. "Though it still wasn't enough to stop Han." He gritted out, eyes burning with what looked like fury.

"It's not your fault." I breathed, leaning forward. Alec shook his head, staring at the fire.

"I should have stayed closer to the camp after Perrion and I spoke of our plans," he sighed. "You are the key to tracking down those elemental stones and keeping them out of Penumbra's hands... I can't let anything happen to you."

Silence stretched between us, only the crackle of the burning wood filled the void. Unable to bear it anymore, I unfolded my legs and stood up, walking a short distance away and unsheathed my sword.

Planting my feet, I took a deep breath and began swinging and lunging. A dance I knew all too well; every technique and skill honed since childhood.

"You're like a dancer with a blade," Alec voice carried from behind me. I had no idea how long he'd been standing there, watching.

"I can't take my eyes off of you." Alec stared as I turned towards him and his sword was ringing out against my own before I could register the movement.

He took in my surprise and lunged again, but this time I was ready as I parried his blow with a grin.

"You're better than most humans I've fought." Alec grinned as he spun his sword in his hand.

"I've had a lot of time to learn." I mused with a smirk, and he barked a laugh, his eyes darkening.

In an instant, he thrusted forward into a combo of offensive attacks, each move precise and deadly. Sweat began to collect on my brow as I parried and dodged the best I could, waiting for an opening.

There!

Dropping low, I passed under his arm rearing up behind, swinging my sword upwards. Before the blade could connect with his spine, Alec was facing me, deflecting the blow with ease.

"Push your mana into your sword." Alec instructed as he removed his shirt, pressing his hand against his stomach. "From here."

I tore my eyes away from his glistening muscles, mentally shaking myself.

"Isn't it dangerous? I don't know how to control it." I confessed, watching each of his muscles roll and twist as he circled me.

"I can handle you," He grinned, as his sword began to glow. "Don't hold back."

I took a deep breath as I focused on that dark pool within me, pulling and pushing it up through my body. Coaxing it down my arms, my eyes sprang wide as shadows began coalescing with the blade.

Excitement was short-lived as Alec lunged forward, a violent gust of wind slamming into me. It caught my shoulder as I made to dodge, knocking me back a few paces. I gritted my teeth as I swung my sword, concentrating on channelling the shadows to aid me, Tendrils of smoke whipped out from the sword's tip, clawing for Alec.

"Whoa!" I gasped, grinning. I focused as did it again and again. The crack of the shadow's making my blood thrum with excitement.

I felt powerful.

Alec struck out again, catching me off guard as a rush of wind sent me flying back. I rolled somewhat gracefully to my feet, flipping my braid over my shoulder and braced my hands on my knees, gulping in air.

"Every moment you can, you need to cycle your mana

through your body," Alec grabbed the canteen from his pack and handed it to me. "Your mana, like your mind, needs training. They go hand-in-hand."

I nodded as I gulped down cool water. Alec looked me over, his eyes finding mine.

"We will train every day until we arrive back at the Academy." Alec sat back down beside the fire. I lowered the canteen and watched the way the firelight casted shadows over the tattoo on his torso.

"Get some sleep," Alec said startling me. I blinked, to see his was staring into the flames again. "We leave at sunrise."

I laid down on my bedroll that Alec had brought, watching the flames dancing and the smoke disappear into the darkness.

Rolling onto my back, my mind wandered.

Ever since finding Kain, my life had been planned. I knew who I wanted to be—what I wanted to be. But now, I was just a pawn in Penumbra's plan.

What would happen if Penumbra got the stones?

War. Death.

At least to the humans.

Savages. That's what Drisir had called us, and maybe we were. But that wasn't entirely our fault. Penumbra had been the one to open the gates between the kingdoms, letting humans enter; aiding them in the status quo of kill first, ask questions later.

"Do you think it would be different is humans knew that the creatures in the dungeons were innocent?" I murmured, twisting to look at Alec.

"The gates can lead to anywhere in the Fae lands, some of those parts are forbidden and have been for centuries. It is where the Lesser Fae reside." He said, his eyes burning with something I couldn't place.

"Lesser Fae?" I asked.

"The Lesser Fae are more beast than man. Monsters." Alec met my eyes. "Boggans for example are native to swamp areas of our lands, like the Terra region. They are said to be carved from the earth itself and if you were to stare into their eyes for too long, you would become dirt like them." Alec added and I swallowed hard.

"What others are there?"

"Kelpies, Devas, Nymphs… There are too many to list in one night. Just know that they are bad by nature and are feared even by the High Fae." He said, and my mouth dried up.

Just what had the Guild been up against in those dungeons?

"Once we get the stone back from the King, I'll get the humans to change their minds. I'll make sure the Fae are seen as our allies." I stated. "That there can be peace between our kingdoms."

Alec returned his gaze to the fire.

"It is a fickle notion, but we must hope," He whispered. "Now sleep."

My glance lingered a little longer on his face, before I settled down in the blankets, letting the sway of the trees lull me into a deep slumber.

THE NEXT DAY we traversed through more of the dense forest. I walked beside Alec, inundating him with a steady flood of questions about the Fae.

"What's the King and Queen like? What about your parents?" I asked as we made our way down a particularly steep hill. Alec held out his hand, guiding me down the shale safely.

"My parents are loving, especially my mother," Alec

smiled. "I think that's why it hurt her so much when Penumbra rebelled and sought to take the throne." His jaw tightened, as he kicked away a branch with a little too much force.

"They were against my decision to come to the human lands. They didn't want to lose another son." Alec glanced over at me.

"But you still came anyway?" I met his eyes, wondering if I was asking too personal a question.

"If I am to be ruler of the Fae Kingdom, then securing the stones is a must. Without them, Penumbra will bring about war and bloodshed to both our kingdoms." He stated as I reached out, placing a hand against his arm.

"We will get the stone back." I said softly, and he gave me a small nod.

The slope levelled out and we picked our way through the brush.

"Do you have a plan to get the stone back once you've located it?" I asked, cursing as I stumbled over a bundle of roots.

"Some of my people demand that I invade the palace and force the King to hand over the stone, but I don't want unnecessary bloodshed," Alec said as he pressed a hand against my back to steady me. "Until I know where it is located, I don't have a plan."

Now knowing how strong Alec truly was, the idea of him taking on the King and his knights alone wasn't surprising. But the fate of the kingdoms were at stake.

"Then we need to find it. Fast." I said, and he smirked.

"That we do."

THE SUN MOVED across the sky as we traversed our way through the forest, and down the mountainside. Sweat stuck to my skin, my armour and shirt like a seal against my body. I'd spent every moment focusing on circulating my mana around my body, like Alec had told me. It was gruelling and made my head pound, a different strain from the feel of physical training.

"The town we passed with the class should be close," Alec broke my concentration, as I stuttered in a breath. "We can sleep at the tavern there tonight and return to the Academy tomorrow."

I made a noncommittal sound, following Alec until we reached the path leading us down into the town. No more brush, just a footworn dirt path I was more than happy to see.

Purple and orange mingled on the horizon as we reached the edge of the town. Few people lingered on the streets, those who did were bustling home no doubt.

Inside the tavern was loud, barmaids sliding between tables, holding trays aloft. I spied an unoccupied bench and collapsed against it. The warmth soaked into my bones, making me feel sleepy.

A scrape of wood against stone.

I opened my eyes as Alec sat down opposite, placing two bowls of stew on the table. I groaned at the first mouthful and proceeded to devour the rest. After days of living off seeds and bread, this was a welcomed change.

"It doesn't take much to please you, does it?" Alec chuckled as he took a sip from the ale he'd brought us. "A hot meal and you're like a purring kitten."

"If you add in pastries, then you're right." I teased, giving him a toothy smile.

"I'll bear that in mind." He grinned over the rim of his mug.

I pushed our bowls to one side, noticing he had only eaten the vegetables. Looking up at him, I raised an eyebrow, gesturing to the bowls.

"Didn't like the meat?" I asked.

"The Fae don't usually eat meat." Alec cleared his throat, lowering his mug. "We believe that animals are sacred, and only on special occasions do we choose to do so."

I looked at him, urging him to elaborate, and he did.

"We make sure their deaths are comfortable, to make sure their energy given is returned to the earth."

The magic from the forest. The night I found Alec over the deer, the quiet murmurs he whispered.

"That's what you were doing with the deer?" I pointed out. "You were comforting its passing?"

Alec nodded. "Yes, I didn't think anybody would sense it. Humans shouldn't be able to recognise it. But you—you did."

"Add that to growing list of mysteries about me," I joked, tilting my head with a smile. "I'm not normal apparently."

"Normal is overrated." Alec grinned, looking up at me through his lashes. "Besides, I'm eager to find out what you'll reveal next." With a wink, he stood up and motioned for me to stay put. I watched as he leaned over the bar, speaking with the barmaid. The woman shook her head, and I saw a muscle tick in his jaw, as she dropped a key into his hand.

Alec glanced over at me, holding up his hand as a single key dangled from his finger.

Just the one.

Without a word, I joined him as we made our way up the narrow staircase at the back of the tavern. A few woman stealing glances at Alec as we walked, some batting their lashes—all of which he ignored with a straight back.

Alec didn't speak until we reached a door at the end of the hall. Only when he pushed the key into the lock, and the tumblers clicked open did he speak.

"There was only one room left." I expected as much from the one key, but I followed him into the room and came to a standstill.

It was a basic room. A fireplace against one wall, a small chest of drawers under a solitary window, and against the other wall...

A single bed.

"I'll take the bed, you take the floor," I blurted, my heart thundering as I paced across the room. I turned and sat on the edge of the coverlet. Alec hadn't moved, but a smirk graced his face, his eyes dancing.

That tension was back again, that warm heady feeling was filling the empty spaces around us. I began pulling off my boots for something to do, when I heard Alec cross the room, unrolling a spare blanket on the floor.

"It's going to be strange going back to the Academy after everything." I murmured as I rolled onto my side on the bed. Alec's large frame took up most of the floor as he laid back, his hands propped under his head as he looked up at me.

"Now that you know the truth, it changes things, but Perrion is my guard and is a lot older than me— he can teach you more."

I was eager to get back to training, to see what else my powers could really do.

"Tell me more about the Fae lands?" I yawned, resting my head against my hands as I peered over the edge of the bed at him.

"The Kingdom of Aboria is made up of five regions." Alec began, turning his head so our eyes met. "To the east is Mizurin, where the those who hone the water element reside. To the north is Ventus, home of those with the air elementals." He gestured the cardinal points with his hands as he spoke, "In the west is Terra, home of the earth elementals, and finally in the south is Ignis, where you'll find the fire elementals."

"In the centre of the elemental regions is the Capitol where I live. Viridia." A warm smile crept across his face. "Its home to the World Tree, the centrepoint of all life. The gods planted it there to help supply the High Fae with mana."

My mind spun with questions. I didn't know where to start.

"When you say that the Fae reside in the Elemental Regions, do you mean High Fae and Lesser Fae alike?" Alec stared a little longer before he nodded, and turned his gaze to the ceiling.

"I would very much like to see all of those places one day. To spend my life trying to see it all," I yawned, snuggling down into the coverlet. My eyes were getting heavy. "There wouldn't be enough time—"

"Get some sleep, Nevara." He said, rolling so his back was to me. Frowning, I closed my eyes, wondering what I'd said to change his mood so fast. The warmth of the room, and Alec's steady breaths silenced my thoughts and sleep took me.

I WOKE IN A STRANGE ROOM, with my cheek pressed against a hard marble floor.

I pulled myself up to my feet and stared around the room. It was ornately decorated, the floor gleamed like obsidian and the far wall was encased in red silk curtains that billowed out into the open skies beyond.

A man stood, a silhouette against the red. He was dressed all in black, the clothes fitted against his body. The man turned towards me and I sucked in a breath.

"Penumbra." I breathed. Those red eyes I remembered so well, met my own.

I had only ever seen Penumbra from beneath a hooded cloak, but now that I saw him fully... he wasn't what I expected. His dark red hair brushed his chest, his body lean and muscled, and his face seemed softer in comparison to—to Alec.

The two didn't look alike at all.

"Penumbra." He bowed low, his voice like silk wrapping over my skin. I resisted the urge to shiver. "In the flesh."

"You have grown up well," He walked over, lifting a strand of my hair, letting it run through his fingers like water. "Very well indeed," Penumbra's eyes slithered over me. "I can see why Alec is so enraptured by you."

I shuddered as he leaned in, inhaling the hair twined around his fingers. Catching my eye, he grinned.

"Let me go," I whispered. My voice didn't sound like my own. The presence of this man made me shiver—his power. It was incredible.

"As tempting as it would be to keep you here, now is not the time," His breath grazed my ear. I sucked in a breath, hating the way heat bloomed in my chest. "I want to show you something."

Penumbra turned my body, pressing a hand against my lower back as he steered me towards the opening in the curtains. I blinked against the sunlight, until I saw it.

"An army." I gasped, bile rising in my throat.

"I won't make you forget this dream," Penumbra's hand splayed against my spine, as he pressed closer. "In fact, I would love for you to relay this information back to him." I heard the smirk in his voice.

"My dear brother." He sneered. "I want him to know that even without the stones, I will take both Kingdoms, and return the peace."

Darkness roared in my stomach. He was going to bring forth a war, no matter if he had the stones or not. Nothing would stop this.

"In the end you will bring the stones to me Nevara," He purred, as his other hand slid across my collarbone, his palm flattening at the base of my throat. His breath warm against my cheek. "Because after all, you belong to me."

My body froze as darkness erupted from my skin, as he pressed his fingers to my chin.

"There she is," He smirked, as he leaned in brushing his lips against mine.

"NO!"

Arms encircled me as I thrashed and screamed, tangled in the blankets of a bed.

"Let me go!"

Warmth covered my skin, as a hard body pressed against my own. My eyes sprang open.

"Nevara, calm down!" Alec's voice was urgent as I sucked in air. I felt his magic seep into my skin, calming my racing heart.

"Penumbra," I stuttered out. Alec's body tensed against mine as he leaned back to meet my eyes.

"You saw him?" His voice coloured with disbelief as he eyes darted around my face. I nodded. "The fact that he let you remember is a bad sign."

"He has an army already." I breathed, not realising I was shaking until Alec pressed back against me.

"There's been whispers of it, but I hoped—" He rested his forehead against my shoulder with a sigh. "Gods, I hoped it wasn't true."

"What do we do?" I whispered.

"Tell me exactly what you saw." Alec urged. "What happened?" I swallowed hard.

"We were in a room. It had black marble floors and red curtains. Penumbra was there, and he knew I was helping you," I said as I rolled onto my back, glancing up at Alec where he was looking down at me. "He showed me the army and made sure I would remember it so I could tell you, then —" I bit my lip. The phantom brush of his lips was still fresh in my mind.

"Then what?" Alec scattered my thoughts and I felt heat colour my cheeks.

"He said that I was his and he kissed me," I confessed and Alec stilled beside me. A sharp gust slammed through the room, making me jump. I looked up at Alec, his stare hard and full of fire. It was his magic.

"Stop!" I cried, grabbing Alec's arm, digging my nails in until he met my eyes. "There's no time to get angry, we need a plan to stop him!"

Alec didn't move, so I reached up wrapping my arms around his shoulders. Holding on for dear life, as if I could ground his fury.

"There's no time to give into anger, you need to save your people," I leaned back, met his eyes and hesitated before pressing my forehead against his. "And mine. Please."

I couldn't imagine what he was feeling right now, but I'd felt anger. I'd felt the worry and doubts of feeling helpless.

Alec's body shuddered, and the cyclone in the room eased, then stopped.

"We need the fire stone." He said, his voice ragged, I nodded.

We didn't move for a long time. It felt like forever as his eyes bore into mine, a small smile playing around his lips. Our bodies were pressed together, our breaths mingling. We were in our own world.

It was only when golden light cast through the window did the spell break, as Alec blinked and the shutters in his eyes had closed. He pulled away from me, clearing his throat as he went about clearing the floor.

I stood up, pulling on my boots and brushed my hair away from my face. Alec placed the blankets on the edge of the bed, before opening the door.

Before I could cross the threshold, his hand grasped my chin, tilting my face up towards his own.

"You're not his," He whispered, his thumb running against my lower lip. "Not if I have anything to do with it."

CHAPTER 21

e made it back to the Academy at lunch time because Alec and I had pretty much ran the whole way from the tavern. Once we made it through the gates, Alec lead me straight to Perrion's classroom and I felt a small sense of relief to be back inside the academy.

"You're back," Perrion said a little wide eyed as we appeared in his empty classroom. The students thankfully must be away for lunch in the cafeteria.

"She knows," Alec said quickly and Perrion's eyes slid to mine, he gave a small nod. "There's things we need to discuss. Now," Alec said in a low voice and Perrion noted the urgency and led us to a small room that must have been his office.

I stood back as Alec relayed everything that had happened to Perrion. It still turned my stomach when he mentioned my encounter with Penumbra.

"An army," Perrion whispered and his face paled. "Do your parents know?"

"I need you to send a messenger to tell them and urge them to ready our own armies and start preparing for war," Alec insisted and Perrion nodded. "We need to start pushing for the whereabouts of the fire stone. There's no more time to be secretive about it. We will meet with Damon later and put a final plan into action to retrieve the stone."

"I'll relay the message to your parents immediately," Perrion said. "I've told the elders that the students had died from an extremely unusual animal attack whilst we were up in the mountains. You will need to report to Syler and give him the same explanation," Alec nodded. Perrion then laid his right hand over his heart and bowed deeply before leaving the room, I was taken aback at the movement.

I kept forgetting that Alec was a prince.

"So me killing Han and his friends is covered up, just like that?" I gaped. It occurred to me then that I hadn't even thought out it. The killings.

Maybe it's because I had wanted to do it.

I pushed that thought from my mind and slammed my walls back in place.

"They deserved it." Was all Alec said as he made his way to the door.

We crossed the Academy until we found Syler in the main foyer. His eyes flew wide when they settled on us, and he crossed the room to meet us.

"Thank goodness you two are unharmed!" He exclaimed, placing a hand on our shoulders, giving a gentle squeeze. "What happened out there?"

"We heard Han and his friends yelling, so Nevara and I went to check on them," Alec lied, and I blinked at how easily the story fell from his lips. "We were unsure if the attacker was still nearby, so we ran and hid in the mountains. It wasn't until we stopped that we realised how lost we truly were and spent the last week trying to find a way back." Syler gasped, a hand covering his mouth.

"You two have certainly had an experience," He started.

"Take the rest of the day to settle back into the Academy and I'll report this to the elders."

Alec nodded and thanked the Archmage before taking my arm and leading me outside.

Once in the courtyard, I turned to look at him in disbelief, shaking my head.

"He believed that a little too easily," I whispered, and Alec gave me a smug smile.

"What can I say?" Alec leered with a chuckle. "I'm a charmer."

I rolled my eyes at him, laughing as I pushed against his shoulder playfully. Together we headed towards the cafeteria in search of food, and Damon.

The cafeteria was busy as students milled around and parted around Alec as he led the way to our usual table. Groups whispered and stared as we passed. Clearly the news of what happened to Han and his friends had spread, as had the news of our return.

"Nevara!" I heard someone call my name as a body collided with my own, Arms wrapped around me, engulfing me in a hug. Kitty pulled back and held me at arm's length. "I thought you were dead! Oh goodness, it's been awful staring at your bed every night wondering if you would come back." She sobbed.

My mouth hung open. I hadn't realised that this girl had felt like this. Friends wasn't something I was used to having, but I guess they were like family in a way.

I patted her on the back as I turned and met Damon's wide eyes. Dark circles were under his eyes, telling me hadn't been sleeping. He pushed his chair and stood up, in an instant his hands were on my face. The whole room went quiet as Damon checked me over before pulling me into an embrace of his own.

"Damon, I'm fine," I whispered, my face burning from the

weight of everyone's stares. He pulled back to look at me once more, smiling.

"I'm glad you're safe," He added, looking over at Alec. "Both of you."

Alec met Damon's gaze, a cold look passing between them before Damon turned away and dropped his hands, stepping back.

"I knew you couldn't have died." I turned to find Xander grinning as he reached over and squeezed my hand when I slid into my chair. "You're too stubborn."

I laughed as Alec returned with two plates of food and placed one in front of me, as he took the seat beside my own. Damon cast a curious glance between the two of us.

"What happened to you guys?" Harven asked. I noticed that he too had dark rings under his eyes.

All of them had worried and lost sleep. A warmth tightened in my chest and I swallowed hard.

"It was some sort of animal attack that got Han," I admitted. "Alec and I had heard them yelling and when we found them—" I hesitated, remembering their bloodied bodies. The lie we needed to weave. "We ran and ended up getting lost."

I felt bad for lying to them.

"That's crazy," Kitty said, her eyes wide.

"Well I'm sure if it was anyone else that got lost in the woods they wouldn't have made it back. You two are so crazy strong that I always knew you'd make it back just fine," Xander said with a small smile.

"Well, I was the one that got us back." Alec smirked. "Nevara lagged behind the whole time." My mouth dropped open as everyone laughed. I realised then, he had said it for their benefit, to relax them and ease some of the tension. I was grateful in that moment for it and wondered if the thought crossed his mind of how these humans truly cared for a Fae Prince. And they didn't even know it.

"I only lagged behind because you kept heading in the wrong direction." I laughed, keeping up the façade of our story.

Alec's blue gaze flitted to mine and narrowed. Kitty snorted as the rest of them laughed. Except for Damon who remained silent, his gazing bouncing between the two of us.

Just like that, we had eased back into our friend group like the last week had never happened. I glanced at Alec and caught his knowing smile and I knew deep down that this was a fake normality.

I wondered if life would ever return to the way it was before Alec…

I also wondered if that would even be something that I wanted.

Clouds had begun rolling in by the time we left the cafeteria, and a cold chill was blowing autumn leaves across the courtyard. We said our goodbyes to the others as Damon led Alec and me up to their shared room.

Alec leaned against the wall, his legs crossed over one another, his arms across his chest. I took the seat near the window as Damon sat on his bed.

"I take it you know about Alec then?" Damon looked over at me, raising an eyebrow.

"That I'm now lumbered with two annoying Princes?" I looked at them both in turn, the tension rolling off them in waves. "Yeah, I know."

Alec smirked at me, and Damon grinned.

"Then there's something I need to tell you." Damon looked between us both. His eyes darkening. "Samuel was scheduled to be executed yesterday, but when they went to retrieve him, his body was in shreds in his cell."

Alec pushed himself off the wall, brow furrowed as he crossed the room to me.

"What do you mean?" He demanded, placing a reassuring hand on my shoulder. "Someone got in there before his execution—and what? Killed him?"

"Not someone," Damon looked at my face, then to Alec's hand and looked away. "*Something*. His body looked as if it had been clawed up and charred. The cell looked like it been set alight."

I sucked it a breath. A small part of me was relieved he was dead and had suffered. Ironic that it was in the same fashion as what he did to me... but who did it?

Alec's hand tightened on my shoulder, and I glanced up to see his jaw harden, fury burning in his eyes. He noticed me staring and the cool mask slipped back in place as he gave me a small smile.

"The main thing is he's gone now." He said and I blinked, wondering if I just imagined the fury in his eyes.

"Tell me what happened now." Damon said, drawing our attention back to him, and Alec began to relay everything. The truth this time. Damon's face fell, then hardened.

"We need to make a plan," Alec demanded. "I need that stone by the end of the month."

"If what you say is true, then what use will the stone be? What good will it be against an army?" Damon groaned collapsing back on the bed.

"Out of all the elements, which is the most destructive? One that could make this Kingdom crumble?" Alec stated, and Damon twisted to face me.

"Fire." We all spoke in unison.

"If we can obtain the fire stone, we take away Penumbra's opportunity to control those who have the fire affinity," Alec pressed. "It's the only we hope have right now."

Damon got to his feet, flanking my body as Alec mirrored him on the opposite side.

"What's our plan?" Damon asked, his eyes never leaving Alec. I looked up between the two and sighed.

It was going to be a long afternoon.

WE SPENT the next few hours throwing around ideas of what we could possibly do to aid in stopping Penumbra but kept hitting the same wall.

We didn't know where the stone was.

Damon had sent one of the knights to inform Perrion that he was unwell and wouldn't be attending class. Alec had told him to use certain words, so that Perrion would know it was to do with the situation with the stone.

"What about an event?" I asked, and both turned to stare at me. "The King likes to show off his wealth. Like with the contest, the main point of that was to show off the magical artefacts and boast about the power within his grasp."

I cleared my throat as I continued, looking over at Damon. "What if you convinced him to have one of those elaborate balls?" I questioned with a smile. "I've heard you nobles love them."

Damon rolled his eyes as Alec snickered from where he sat against the wall on his bed.

"You persuade him by saying it would be a way to show-case the King's personal collection of artefacts," I raised my eyebrows, stretching my legs out on the floor. "We could enter under the guise of high-class nobles and when the moment comes, take the stone and flee."

"How in the Gods did you come up with that idea?" Alec was now braced on the edge of his bed, eyeing me up and down. I pressed my mouth into a tight line, frowning.

"I know how egotistical the King is when it comes to flaunting his wealth and power," I shrugged, looking anywhere but at his eyes. "We could have him bring the stone right to us."

"It's brilliant," Damon grinned before looking crestfallen. "But what if he doesn't bring the stone?"

"It's a gamble, but it's probably the best one we have," Alec's eyes met mine, before he grinned as well.

Damon got to his feet and began pacing back and forth. Alec watched his every step across the small space.

"It's the weekend tomorrow, so I'll be able to travel back into the city. I'll speak to father and convince him into throwing a ball." Damon decided, coming to a stop in front of me.

"I'll be travelling home too. I need to see my family." I added, and Damon nodded.

"You can share my carriage—"

Alec was on his feet in an instant, shaking his head.

"Your knights will report back to your father that you were in a carriage alone with her." A muscle ticked in Damon's jaw as Alec met my gaze. "I'll take you; I have some errands to run anyway." I nodded to Alec, and Damon's lips thinned. I cast a smile to Damon, but he looked away.

"Now we wait," I said. The two boys nodded in agreement.

My stomach grumbled as I made my way to the door, and I heard chuckles from behind me. Over my shoulder I saw Damon and Alec following, and I blushed, "Dinner?"

Both replied in unison, "Dinner."

Determination had settled in as we made our way down the hall. We finally had a plan in motion.

We would not let Penumbra win without a fight.

CHAPTER 22

*I*t was just after sunrise when I met Alec outside of the Academy. Exhaustion made my eyes heavy as I shuffled over to where he stood. I'd been up almost all night talking with Kitty as she updated me with what had been happening here.

Apparently, they'd sent out troops to track down whatever it was that caused the deaths of Han and his friends. I'd swallowed nervously at that.

She had then proceeded to gush and tell me all about her Battlemage classes, and I had to admit, I was a little jealous.

"You look tired." Alec teased as I yawned.

"I have a very chatty roommate," I sighed, and he chuckled as we made our way over the stables.

"Can you ride?" Alec asked as he gestured to the line of horses within.

"No." I admitted. I'd always rode with Kain when we travelled anywhere that warranted a horse.

Alec nodded and spoke to a stable boy, who left and returned with a beautiful ebony coloured horse in tow. I grinned as I reached up to scratch beneath its long mane.

"This is Fara." Alec peeked around the horse with a smile.

"A pretty name." I said, she nudged her head against my chest.

"She likes you." Alec smiled, his eyes soft. My heart fluttered as he led the horse out of the stables, and I followed.

Outside, Alec mounted the horse with ease, smiling down at me as he held out a hand. I hesitated, eyeing him and the horse.

"You know, we have been a lot closer than this..." Alec teased, and I froze. "Do you remember the river? How you threw yourself at me?"

"If I get up on the horse, will you shut your damn mouth?" I snapped, pressing my hands onto my hips, staring at him hard.

Alec tipped his head back and barked a laugh, composing himself enough only to nod and flex his fingers towards me. I took his hand as he pulled me up behind him, settling myself in place.

"And like I keep trying to remind you, you kissed me first." I mumbled, to which he made a non-committal noise in response.

Alec kicked his heels against the horse's flanks and Fara took off in a canter. I squeaked as I lunged forward, pressing myself up against his back, my hands clutching at the front of Alec's shirt.

"Ass!" I called out, which made him laugh even louder.

After a few miles, he slowed the horse to a trot, but I didn't move my hands. I let them trace over the muscles beneath his shirt. He tensed for a moment, then relaxed as I repeated the motion, feeling every curve and divot as he moved.

Feeling bold, I slid my fingers beneath the edge of his shirt, splaying both hands against his warm skin. I felt him suppress a shiver and make a gruff noise when my cold hands connected.

The heady feeling had filled my stomach again and my heart thundered in my chest. I let my fingers circle Alec's stomach as my mind wandered.

Years ago, Netta would always want to tell me about the love between two people, so I could prepare myself should the day ever come. I used to laugh and tell her it would never happen. That I didn't have time for that.

That my life revolved around my family and training. I thought I would spend the rest of my life like that, but then Alec came along.

He'd somehow began to chip away at the ice around my heart, and completely turn my world upside down. He knew of my past; of everything I'd gone through and still thought I was strong and beautiful.

The first time we kissed, it created a hunger in me I'd never knew existed. I gravitated towards him, wanting to touch—

Alec's muscles contracted under my hands, and his energy flowed down through my palms. A delicious comfort that made me sigh, resting my cheek against his back. The smell of mint and earth filled my nose, his heartbeat a steady drum. I followed the beats with my hands, up over his chest and he swore under his breath.

"Your energy is incredible" I mused, as he tensed.

"My energy?" He asked, his voice strained.

"Whenever I touch you," I ran my fingers up and down his chest absentmindedly. "I'm filled with a sense of calmness. Like the magic you used on the deer in the forest."

"Really?" He twisted slightly, looking over his shoulder at me. I lifted my head to meet his eyes.

"Like now," I pressed my palms to his chest and his energy flared in response. He grunted and roped an arm around my waist, manoeuvring me so I was sat straddled over his thighs in front of him.

We were nose to nose, my hands tangled in the bottom of his shirt. I stuttered out a breath at how close we were.

"I think that you should know, before I stop this horse, that unless you want a repeat of what happened at the river, I suggest you hold onto the horse and not me," Alec growled, eyes darkening as his eyes dropped to my lips before focusing on the path ahead. I dropped my hands to rest on the saddle between us. Realisation struck me as I looked up at him from under my lashes.

I liked Alec.

I wanted him in a way I hadn't wanted anybody else, and that terrified me. I knew that it would only lead to heartbreak.

I was human. He was Fae.

A relationship between us would be doomed before it even began.

ONCE WE REACHED the Commoner's District, Alec secured the horse to the post beside the tavern. I glanced up at the building feeling giddy, then turned to walk down the road and stood outside Kain's house.

My home.

"I'll meet you here at sundown," Alec called after me, and I spun around nodding with a smile, "Then we'll meet Damon at the Academy."

"Nevara!" Netta dashed out the front door, pulling me into a hug, weeping. "I heard news from the Academy, about the attack." She whispered, as Kain came up short behind her, his face pale. It was short-lived as he engulfed me into a hug of his own.

"We thought we lost you," Kain choked out. "The Guild and I, we were about to storm those mountains to track you down."

I glanced to side, noticing Alec was still stood a way up the road, a small smile on his face.

"You can thank him for getting me home safely," I gestured to where Alec stood, who had stopped smiling when Kain and Netta looked at him. "He saved me and helped get us back to the Academy."

"Thank you." Netta choked out as she bundled him up in a hug of his own. Alec's eyes flew wide as he patted her softly on the back. Kain placed a hand on his shoulder and smiled down at him.

Alec met my eye, a look I couldn't place crossed his features as Netta stepped back.

"Thank you for saving my daughter," Kain said, and Alec looked taken aback. "If there is any way I can repay you, I will do all within my power to do so."

I wondered, as I watched Alec, if he had met humans like Kain and Netta, who were open and kind. Or if he had only met those who were bastards in the Noble District.

"Forgive me," Netta laughed, wiping her tears with her apron. "Come in please, I'm about to make dinner."

Alec looked over his shoulder at me as Netta all but dragged him through the front door, sheer desperation in his eyes. I couldn't help but laugh.

"It seems you two are close." Kain asked, raising an eyebrow in the direction Alec had disappeared. "He's a good friend." My laughter ceased as he gave me a knowing wink and pulled out a chair beside Alec for me to sit down.

Thundering footsteps echoed down the hall as Luca rounded the doorway, his eyes going wide at the sight of me.

"Nevara!" Luca wept as he crossed the room. I stood up as

he threw himself at me, his arms wrapping tight around my shoulders as his body shook.

"Shh, it's ok," I whispered, as I stroked his messy blonde hair back from his face. "I'm here"

"Don't ever do that again," He sniffled. "We were all so worried."

"I won't." I choked out as he let go, I gave him a smile.

Netta called for Luca, and he and Kain disappeared into the kitchen. No doubt to help with dinner, I thought as I sat back down.

"They really love you," Alec mused. "And you them."

"They're my family, even if not by blood," I smiled, before grimacing at Alec. "I'm sorry I got you dragged in here, quite literally."

"I don't want to intrude on your time with your family." He looked over his shoulder at the kitchen door, then back to me.

"You're not," I said a little too fast, and Alec's eyes softened.

Netta came in then with Luca and Kain in tow, their hands laden with breads, stews and plates that smelled delicious.

"I had just finished cooking when you arrived." She said with a smile.

Once everyone was sat down, I poured a bowl of soup and placed it in front of Alec with a smile.

"It's vegetable soup. No meat." I whispered leaning in. Alec blinked and gave me a smile I'd never seen before, which left me breathless.

"Thank you." Alec said to Netta, who beamed at him.

Before she sat down, Netta disappeared into the other room and returned holding a small, wrapped package. She handed to it to me, which I took with shaking hands.

"What's this?" I asked, looking up at her as she grinned at me.

"Open it!" Netta encouraged and I raised an eyebrow before unwrapping the parcel to find a baby sized cotton vest.

"We found out when you left for the Academy." Netta whispered, her voice trembling. It clicked then and my eyes went wide as I looked from Netta to Kain.

"You're going to be a big sister again." Kain said, and I clutched the tiny fabric to my chest and laughed.

Netta turned to the side, smoothing her hands over her dress, showing her slightly swollen belly. I got up and embraced her, careful not to squeeze too hard.

"I'm so happy for you," I grinned, looking between them both. "Let's hope it's a girl so I can train her to be just like me."

"One Nevara is enough." Kain teased and laughter erupted around the table. Luca lifted a hand, rubbing slow circles on Netta's stomach with a smile.

"You can read to the baby every night, just like you did for me." I said to Luca, and he grinned up at me.

"Let's eat," Kain said as he pulled out a chair for Netta, then we all began to dig in

"I wish Brendan was here, you must go and visit him at the bakery after dinner, he's been worried sick like the rest of us," Netta said and I nodded.

"When do you head back to the Academy?" Kain asked between bites of his stew.

"Tonight," I said a little upset to be leaving them again so soon.

"Would you have time to come to the tavern before you go? The Guild is meeting up there later," Kain asked, his eyes pleading. I turned to Alec who gave me a small nod and I smiled at Kain.

"I can't wait to see them," I said and Kain gave a grunt of approval.

"I would prepare yourselves for them," Kain joked. I chuckled to myself imagining them squeezing me to death when they saw me.

I couldn't wait.

～

DUSK WAS COMING in as Alec and I meandered through town towards the bakery. A smile was plastered to my face and a warmth was a steady growth in my heart as I thought about my family once more and—

"You look beautiful when you smile like that."

Alec caught me off guard and I turned to face him; all words dried up in my mouth. The last dregs of sunlight cast a golden hue across his sculpted face, his eyes glowing as they met mine. His hair tousled from the wind, a stray piece fluttering in the breeze. I reached up to brush it away, as his fingers circled my wrist.

Half expecting him to pull away, I barely concealed a gasp when he pressed my palm against his cheek—that familiar energy tingling across my skin. With his free hand, he pulled me in by my waist, tilting my head up, placing a soft kiss on my lips.

"I didn't expect to meet someone like you," My head spun as he brushed his lips over mine again. "You drive me crazy every single godsdamned day."

I threaded my fingers into his hair, tugging him back down capturing his lips again, savouring the taste of him. Something sweet with the sharpness of mint. I shuddered against the feel of him, that hunger now being satisfied.

"I never expected to meet someone like you either." I whispered as I pulled back to look into his eyes. My heart thundered against my ribs. I knew I shouldn't be letting myself fall further, but I couldn't help it. Not when he kissed me or looked at me like that.

"We need to go see your brother now if you want to get to the tavern before we leave for Academy." Alec pressed another hard kiss to my lips, deepening it with a groan, before pulling away. His breath was ragged, and I was breathless, his eyes pinning me in place.

"If you keep looking at me like that, then we won't be going anywhere." His eyes darkened as he wove our fingers together and tugged me towards him. I really did want to see the Guild.

"That time I did kiss you first," He teased, his breath tickling my ear, I grinned, laughing. My mind still spinning from the kisses.

Sweet smells floated out the bakery door as we entered. It was the same, the same counter, shelves and I spied the doorway I snuck through for the bread that day.

"Welcome!" Brendan hollered, as he popped up from below the counter. "Is there anything—"

His eyes went wide and he rushed around the counter, pulling me into a tight embrace.

"I told them you were fine," Brendan mumbled into my hair. "That if anyone would survive in those mountains, it would be my sister." He leaned back, smiling at me.

"Brendan!" A gruff voice hollered from out the back. Brendan sighed, squeezing my hand with a smile before dashing out of sight.

"Do you have any silver?" I ask Alec and he gave me a slight nod. "Give me some." I batted my lashes and he raised an eyebrow at me as he pulled a small leather pouch from his coat.

"You've grown quite bold." He teased, placing the pouch

in my hand. His fingers lingering against mine before I headed over to the counter.

Brendan appeared around the door with that goofy smile I knew so well. One I had missed seeing whilst at the Academy.

"Give me all the bread you have," I left no room for comment.

"That would come to—" His eyes widened as I upended some of the coins from the pouch. Sliding an extra gold coin amongst the others.

"I owe the baker some money from a long time ago." I grinned, as Alec snorted behind me. Brendan shook his head before taking the coins and began bagging up the loaves of bread into sacks.

"Thanks for that," Brendan grinned, handing over the two sacks. "I might actually get some praise from the old man."

"No problem," I grinned as I pulled him into a hug, he walked backwards towards the door. "Are you coming to the tavern?"

"As soon as I finish up here." I nodded as Alec waved goodbye, and we promised to see each other soon.

Outside the bakery, I took a path I knew all too well, listening to Alec's footsteps close behind me. I turned and tossed the pouch back to him, which he caught with ease.

"You don't carry coins of your own?" He quipped.

"I don't care for money." I shrugged as he fell in step beside me. Wealth wasn't a currency when survival was a necessity. I'd seen what wealth could do to men. I would never been driven by greed of gold.

"I remember seeing the memory after the contest," Alec interrupted my thoughts. "Where you gave your winnings to the people in the alley." I turned to look at him, trying to gauge his reaction.

"That was very kind and selfless of you." He whispered.

The mouth of the alley loomed on us. Lines of makeshift tents and lights bordered the walls, some heads peeking out, speaking in hushed tones to their neighbours. Some ushering children under the blanket roofs.

"I was in their place once," I whispered, watching my old home flourishing with life. A unique kind, where harmony and friendship were the currency.

"Damon told me you visit often," I looked across to Alec with a soft smile. "To give them money and food."

"The idea of people going hungry or cold," Alec's face twisted in pain, staring down the mouth of the alley. "I can't stand it. Nobody in Arboria is left to fend like this."

A kingdom where no one went hungry, or cold. It sounded like a dream.

"Come on," I waved Alec forward.

Together we made our way into the thick of the alley. Noticing it then, how much the number of tents and people had doubled in size.

"No." I whispered, covering my mouth with a shaking hand. My eyes flitting from tent to tent.

"Nevara!" My eyes caught on an old woman. Edin. She'd been here for as long as I could remember. I dashed over to her, falling onto one knee.

"What happened here, Edin?" I breathed, looking around. "Where did all these people come from?"

"The King raised the taxes in the Commoner District," Edin sighed, bundling her shawl around her frail shoulders. She reached out patting my hand. "People couldn't afford to pay it, so they began joining us here. We used the money you gave us to help set them up with blankets and food, but it wasn't enough."

Darkness stirred in my gut as I felt Alec rest a hand on my shoulder. I glanced up and his own face was grim.

"I'll sort this out." I vowed, reaching into the bag, and

handing her a loaf of bread. She smiled up at me, patting my cheek with her hand.

"You're a beautiful soul, my girl." Edin whispered.

Loaves of bread ran out faster than I expected when Alec and I began distributing them down the alley. Alec had begun handing out coins when his sack was empty.

"How could he do this?" I snapped, crumpling the sack in my hands as we made our way back to the tavern. "These people can barely afford to put food in their stomachs every night, and now he's raising the tax?"

Fury rolled through me, making the darkness bubble under the surface of my skin.

"He's a bastard," Alec said, jaw hard.

"He's going to kill them," I hissed, my heart aching for those we'd left behind in the alley. "Some of them won't—"

"Easy." Alec whispered, his voice a warning as my he cupped my face in his hands. That calm and comforting energy seeping into my very bones. "I promise you that once we retrieve the stone, I will fix this."

"You would do that?" I breathed, looking into his eyes. "Even after everything the humans have ever done to your kind?"

"Those people in that alley are innocent," Alec's voice was firm. His thumbs caressing my cheekbones. "I could never let an innocent suffer, even if they aren't my people."

I leaned up, pressing my forehead against his, breathing him in before we began walking again.

"You'll make an excellent King," I whispered, bumping my shoulder with his, with a smile. He smiled in return, but it didn't quite meet his eyes.

"Let's hope I make it to King."

THE TAVERN WAS JUST like I remembered it. Dark wood tables circled the floor and a long bar stood against the adjacent wall. It was just as bustling as I remembered it too.

As the door fell closed behind us, a silence crept over the occupants before a scream echoed around the room.

"Nevara!" Ganya had shot up from her chair, pulling on my arm. I turned and grabbed for Alec's, laughing as she led us over to the table she had just vacated.

"How could you do that to us?" I barely got chance to sit down or let go of Alec before she tackled me to the floor, sobbing.

"I'm sorry," I said, meeting Alec's eye above her. He bit his lip, his eyes dancing with mirth. "I'll try and be more careful."

Strong hands lifted Ganya off me, then another set looped under my arms. Derrick.

"If you ever scare me like that again, I'm making you climb the Sky Kissed Mountain whilst you carry *me* on your back." Derrick bit out before he crushed into a bear hug. I wheezed out a laugh and wrapped my arms around him.

"I missed you." Derrick muttered. Tears threatened to fall as I stepped back beside Alec, who was watching at Derrick with an odd look.

One-by-one the members of the Guild welcomed me back with warm hugs and loud expressions of affection. I introduced them to Alec as we finally got seated around the table. A mug was pushed into our hands as Netta and my brothers joined us. Like the tavern, my heart felt full.

I glanced over at Alec. His jaw was set like granite and his eyes seemed distant where he stared across the table. Realisation dawned on me as I lowered my mug.

I'd brought Alec, a Fae, into a room filled with humans who had gone into what we knew as dungeons, had attacked his people and stolen from them. A wave of nausea filled me.

"I have a request," I blurted. The table fell silent as they all turned to look at me. I kept my voice level as I continued, "Please don't go into the dungeons."

Murmurs began between members around the table, quiet and some heated. Kain looked over at me and I swallowed. I knew in that one look he was wondering why; I'd seen it enough growing up.

"I can't tell you why, but please," I pleaded, meeting the eyes of Vikki and Derrick. Then up to Kain. "Tell as many of the other Guilds as you can, but I'm begging you to trust me on this."

Everyone fell silent and I sucked in a breath. Alec's hand was against my leg under the table. I wasn't sure when it got there, but the support was appreciated.

"There has been a raise in the tax Nevara," Netta whispered, looking up at Kain as she braced her hands on her bump. "And with the baby on the way…"

"If it's money you need, I can help," Alec spoke before I could take a breath, leaning forward. "I come from a rich family. Give me a list of your expenses. I will help you as best I can."

"I couldn't ask you to do that." Kain began, shaking his head. His eyes locking with mine as I stood up.

"I have never asked for anything. I've never demanded for anything," I began, my eyes pleading as I rested my palms on the table. "Please do me this one favour and don't go in the dungeons. Take Alec's help." I looked up at Kain, his eyes betraying him. I knew he wanted to know everything. Everything I couldn't tell him.

Kain's eyes closed as he took a deep breath in. Once he re-opened them, the look was gone as he nodded at me, then looked to Alec.

"It's done," Kain looked to everyone at the table, then locked eyes with me. Understanding and something else shining there. "Until you give us the go ahead, we will say out of the dungeons."

The others began to murmur their agreement, albeit some didn't sound happy about it. Tension released from my shoulders as I took my seat. Alec's hand found its place back on my thigh squeezing.

"Thank you," I whispered. Alec's touch warming me in more ways than one. I watched as the others went back to their ales and their conversations. Only Kain looked off to one side.

It may only be the one Guild I've persuaded to stay out of the land of the Fae, but it's a start.

WHEN IT CAME time to say goodbye to my family and the rest of the Guild, it was difficult. Even more so than the first time I left. Netta was the hardest to leave behind.

"If you need help, don't be afraid to ask for it." I said as I rubbed my hand over her swollen belly with a smile. "You need to relax more and make Kain do all the work."

Kain groaned beside us, and I shot him a look.

"I know, I know," Netta chuckled, hugging me tight to her. "I've been pregnant before you know."

Netta let me go as she pulled Alec into a crushing hug also. I made my way over to where Kain stood beside Fara.

"Thank you for agreeing to stay out of the dungeons," I whispered, looking up at him. "I'm sorry I can't explain why though."

"I'm sorry that I didn't agree straightaway," He smiled and stroked a hand over my hair and pressing a small kiss there.

"Take care of her for me please," I looked up, following Kain's line of sight to see Alec stood behind us. The words directed at him, who gave a solemn nod and then the two shook hands.

"I will."

Alec gave a small smile before mounting Fara and pulling me up in front of him. The horse began to walk forward, away from home.

"Take good care of Netta!" I peered around Alec's body, grinning as Kain and Netta waved in the distance.

The skies had turned twilight, hues of blues and purples coating the horizon in the distance as we rode on. Cold was beginning to seep in, and I was grateful for the heat radiating into my body from Alec's.

"Thank you for making them stay out of the dungeons," Alec whispered, his breath ruffling my hair.

"Thank you for helping them with your money," I responded with a smile as I tilted my head to the side, peeping back at him. "How do you have so much money anyways?"

"Well, I am royalty," He teased, chuckling. "But I just so happen to know your people pay a lot for magical artefacts, and I am able to get my hands on a lot of them."

I felt the rumble of his laugh reverberate through me and I grinned.

The kiss we shared earlier today had gone unspoken between us, much like the one we shared at the river. The more I thought about it, the more I realised I couldn't bring it up.

Love would never work between us. Between a Prince and a common girl.

So, I did the one thing I could.

I closed my eyes and leaned back against his chest, savouring his warmth. His closeness. Just him.

And pretended.

That we were two ordinary people, in an even more ordinary world, with feelings for one another that were anything but.

~

"You took your time getting back."

Damon was sat against the wall on his bed as we entered their shared bedroom. He got to his feet as I crossed the floor.

"I'm sorry it's my fault," I said with a sheepish smile. "I caught up with my family."

"We," Alec interrupted. Damon smirked, his eyes leaving me to meet Alec's.

"My father is going to hold a ball at the end of the month," Damon grinned, arms crossed over his chest proudly. "To showcase his most treasured artefact collection."

"How—" I started, and Damon held up a hand.

"There was something I had to promise in return," Damon ran a hand over his face with a sigh. "The ball will be an evening for me to find a bride."

Alec whistled and I stared at him as I sat on the edge of Alec's bed.

"Is marriage something you want?" I asked, pressing my hands to my knees.

"Of course not!" Damon shouted, pacing on the spot. "But I would have agreed to anything to make sure I could have him host this ball and bring those artefacts."

"You're right," I whispered, and Alec placed a hand on my shoulder. "I'm sorry."

Silence filled the room. Damon wouldn't meet my eye, I looked up at the ceiling blowing out a breath. Alec let go of my shoulder and braced his hands on the headboard, leaning forward.

"We need to practice," Alec ordered, his voice leaving no room for question. Only for us to listen.

Damon glanced over as I tried to catch Alec's eye. He wouldn't look at me. He just stared hard at something across the room.

"On the weekends we need to scope out the palace, to mark entrances, exits and where the artefacts will be located," Alec's jaw worked as his spoke. "To make sure we don't meet any obstacles."

Damon and I nodded as Alec continued. My body was sparking with adrenaline for what was to come.

"Once we the ball is over, we will make further plans." Alec left no room for argument.

This was going to be the biggest moment of my life—our lives.

The stone was what determined the fate of our future.

CHAPTER 23

*T*he next morning, I woke before dawn, unable to sleep from the never-ending thoughts plaguing my mind. I kept going over the plan in my head as I made my way through the Academy. It was deserted, only the whisper of my feet against stone for company.

I made my way across the courtyard, heading for the large circular track that sat behind the Academy. I placed my sword against a nearby tree and stretched out my limbs.

Alec and I would have to disguise ourselves as members of the nobility to play the part, to blend in. To find the location of the stone and find a way to get it out without being seen.

Thoughts of the ball, Alec, Damon all whisked away as my feet began pounding the dirt as I ran. My breath sawed in and out of my lungs as I continued to lap myself, over and over.

The sun had broken over the horizon and was shining down over the trees and creeping through the mountains in the distance. It was only then that I collapsed to my knees, sucking in air.

"That was impressive." A voice sounded.

I turned my head, looking through my sheet of hair to see Perrion walking towards me. I nodded at him as he sat down beside me on the grass.

Perrion unsheathed his sword and pulled a rag from his pocket, and began cleaning it.

"Alec informed me of the plan," Perrion looked up after a moment. I raised my eyebrows, wondering how Alec had got the message to him so fast.

"You're going to need better control of your mana before the ball," Perrion's voice cut through my thoughts as I looked at him. "I can teach you how."

"You know how to control the shadows?" I quipped, braiding my hair away from my face.

"I taught Penumbra when he was younger," Perrion began, and my head snapped up. "He wasn't always the man he is today."

I tried to imagine Penumbra as a child. If he was like Alec. Wondering what it was that changed him.

"I actually know of one of the traits that will come in handy at the ball," Perrion said, his eyes glittering. "If you can wield it."

"What is it?"

"Shadow walking,"

My mind spun at the possibilities. I had never really thought into much details about what I could potentially do with my shadow affinity. To actually be offered to be taught how to use one of the traits was exciting.

"How soon can we start training?" I asked, pulling myself to my feet. Perrion chuckled.

Excitement coursed through my body. I'd be able to help at the ball, I'd be useful. Alec had over two centuries worth of time to hone and perfect his elemental abilities. Damon knew the lay of the palace. I was the liability.

"A strong will," Perrion grinned, as he stood and sheathed his sword. "You will need it."

"I can do it," I bit out. I remembered training with Kain every day. Climbing the Sky Kissed Mountain with Derrick. *I could do this.*

"We shall see." Perrion smirked as he turned and walked into the forest that surrounded the Academy. He lifted a hand over, waving for me to follow.

"Sit under the tree canopy," Perrion gestured to the base of a tree when I reached his side. I sat down, folding my legs beneath me. "Begin to circle your mana."

I closed my eyes, following that familiar path in my body to that pool in stomach.

"I hope you managed to get some practice in with Alec the last few days," I snapped open my eyes to see Perrion smirking down at me. I felt my cheeks redden and I shut my eyes tight.

I heard Perrion's footfalls move further away, and I refocused my grasp on the pool in my stomach. That dark mass rising and coasting throughout my body. I was surprised when it began to flow with ease.

"Your shadow affinity works best at night, or in the dark, like in the shade of this canopy," Perrion explained, his footfalls pacing closer and further away in tandem. "Like with any elemental affinity, if the person wielding it is in close range to an abundance of its raw element, they can draw power from it."

I steadied my breaths, through my nose and out through my mouth. Storing away the information. I Began to manipulate the mana through my spine and up into my neck. The strain began to get worse the more I pushed.

"I'm struggling to reach my head," I gritted out, puffing breaths out between my teeth.

"The mind is always the hardest place to manipulate your

mana, even for the Fae," Perrion said and tapped his finger to my forehead. "The mind controls your entire body, and there are many pathways that exist from here,"

"It is much more difficult for humans as their mind naturally creates a barrier against the mana, as it thinks it's a foreign body, like when you're unwell." Perrion had continued his pacing as I cracked open an eye. "You have to teach your body, and your mind, to accept the mana there. Try to keep chipping away, pushing against that barrier. Only when you get your mana through with ease will we continue."

I nodded and closed my eye again. I straightened my shoulders and refocused my effort on circling my mana around my neck and the base of my skull. I coaxed tendrils of shadow against the barrier there. They brushed against it but didn't pass through.

I groaned as I pushed and pushed, the mental strain slipping each time. I repeated the process again and again. I felt sweat break out on my brow and between my shoulder blades.

I didn't hear when Perrion had left, but when I opened my eyes, a canteen of water sat at my feet and the sun had pass across the sky.

I gulped down the water and closed my eyes.

For the rest of the day, I circulated and focused on my mana. I was determined.

It was exhausting.

"So, this is where you've been hiding."

Damon's voice broke my concentration, and I cracked an eye open as he sat down beside me. He placed a tray of meats, eggs, and bread in front of me with a smile.

"I guessed you might have skipped breakfast." He murmured as I rubbed my eyes.

Clouds swept by on a soft breeze, the coolness welcome against my sticky skin. My stomach growled and Damon chuckled.

"Thanks," I mumbled with a small smile as I began tearing at the meat. Leaves surrounded where we sat, creating a blanket of rust, gold and greens.

"You seem to be taking all of this really well," Damon quipped and I glanced over at him. He was braced against his arm, his face tilted up towards the sun. "When Alec told me the truth about who he was, about the Fae, it took me a while to come to terms with it."

I chewed as I mulled over his words.

"It was a surprised at first, and trust me, I didn't take it well," My stomach rolled at the memory of Fraser's house. "But after being in the Fae Lands, and really getting to know Alec, it got a lot easier to accept."

I met his pale blue eyes to find him watching me, a glint of something I couldn't place in his eyes.

"You seem to be getting along with Alec pretty well." Damon cleared his throated and grinned. "More than when you first met at least, when you were at each other's throats."

I glanced down at my lap, feeling my cheeks heat up as I remembered the kiss we shared.

"Something happened between you two, didn't it?" Damon asked and my body froze.

"I don't know what you mean," I whispered as I met his eyes.

"I'm just concerned for you, that's all," he said, his stare cool. "I don't want you to forget. At the end of the day, Alec is still a prince—"

"And I'm just a poor girl from the Commoner District,

right?" I snapped, and his eyes flew wide. "I don't need you to tell me what I already know, *your majesty*."

"I didn't mean it like that—" Damon started, reaching out his hand towards me, but I stood up before he could touch me.

"I wouldn't want to taint your image by staying here, *prince*," I sneered, looking down at him. "Don't think I haven't noticed how you react when we're alone together."

Damon's eyes widened, his face flush. He opened his mouth as if to argue, or say something, but I didn't give him chance.

I spun on my heel and stormed across the grass, back to the Academy. Anger churned the darkness within, my eyes burning with unshed tears.

I knew it was hopeless to believe something could come of what was between Alec and me, and I knew I was taking it out on Damon, but I didn't care.

"Nevara, wait!" Damon called out behind me. I could hear his boots against the earth as he closed the distance between us. He wrapped a hand around my arm, spinning me to face him.

"Let me go," I warned him, my voice quiet.

"Please listen to me...everything I said back there," He begged, his eyes bouncing around my face. "I didn't mean it to come out that way. I'm sorry... I guess I just got angry because of how close you and Alec have become."

"Why are you angry?" I yelled, trying to yank my arm from his grip. I was tempted to punch him, but his knights lounged in the distance. "Whatever happens between Alec and I doesn't concern—"

"I'm jealous, dammit!" Damon whispered furiously as he shook me, and my eyes flew wide. He pulled me closer towards him. "Ever since I saw you at that contest, I haven't been able to get out of my mind." He bowed his head between us.

"Do you know how hopeless I felt when you disappeared with Alec last week? I was this close," He whispered, narrowing his fingers together in front of my face. "To storming those mountains, my position be damned, to track you down and find you... I couldn't sleep or eat."

"Please, you have to believe me." His gaze levelled with mine.

"And if I do, what then Damon?" I whispered. "You're still a Prince," I reiterated his words with a sigh. "Just let me go."

"Nevara," Damon's voice cracked as he pleaded, squeezing my arm.

"She told you to let her go." A voice boomed behind us, startling me as I flinched in Damon's grip.

Damon's eyes never left mine, even as Alec stepped up beside me and grabbed his wrist. I saw Damon's knights put their hands on their swords, ready to make a move, should Alec make the wrong one.

"I'm sorry." Damon whispered, letting go of my arm. His fingers brushing my skin. I turned away and stormed back towards the building that housed the dormitories.

I'd just dropped down onto my bed when a knock sounded at the door. I groaned when I realised Alec had followed me back.

"Nevara," Alec called out through the wood. I remained silent. "I'm coming in"

I heard the door click open and closed again, then his footsteps across the room.

"Are you hurt?" He whispered and I turned my face from the pillow to face him.

"If it weren't for his knights, I would have punched him." I grumbled and Alec's lips twitched.

"Do you want to talk about what happened?" Alec whispered as he sat on the edge of the bed, his hip pressed into mine.

"I'm sure you heard most of it." I murmured. "He was just kindly reminding me of where I come from."

"He likes you." Alec said after a few beats, looking down at me. "Do you like him?

"I thought I did, until…" I swallowed the lump in my throat.

"Until?" He pressed. I took a deep breath and almost said it. *Until I met you.*

"It doesn't matter." I sighed, pressing my face back into the pillow.

"Tell me," Alec urged, resting a hand against my arm.

"No," I mumbled into the pillow and Alec chuckled. He rolled me onto my back and hovered over me, caging me in.

"Tell me," He whispered. I could see it in his eyes, he knew.

"What if we make a deal?" I quipped and raised an eyebrow. "I'll tell you, after we get the stone back."

Alec leaned down, dipping his head towards my throat. He ran his nose up neck, inhaling with a groan and pressing a small kiss below my ear.

"Deal."

"And no more kissing," I trailed off, twisting my face so we were a hairbreadth apart. "It's far too distracting."

"Are you sure?" He breathed, teasing as he brushed his lips against mine. A whisper of a kiss.

"No" I croaked. Alec chuckled as he pressed one last kiss against my jaw before pulling away. I instantly missed his warmth.

"I agree to your terms," he said as he sat up beside me, his eyes burning. Heat swimming in their depths.

In that moment, I wanted to throw caution to the wind and pull him back down.

"Go get something to eat and meet me outside," He grinned, running his fingers down my arm to my hand. "We'll go over some sword techniques."

I nodded as he got to his feet, watching every inch of him as he crossed the room to the door. He looked over his shoulder when he got to the door, his eyes travelling the length of my body with a smirk.

The door clicked closed as he left and I rolled over, groaning into the pillow, screaming my frustration before composing myself and going in search of pastries.

TRAINING WITH ALEC had been frustrating. He'd kept to his word and went out of his way to not so much as brush a finger across my skin as we sparred.

Damon didn't turn up, not that I expected him to after what happened. He would only have be his *princely* self all evening at the ball anyways, seeking a bride.

"You're getting better at offensive attacks," Alec stated, as I swung my sword down on his one last time. "Usually, you just stay on the defensive."

"Well, it's a little hard to get a hit in when you strike so hard and fast." I frowned and Alec chuckled.

"Yes, but for a human you're fast," Alec grinned, nudging my shoulder. The one touch we'd shared all evening. "It's incredible. Use it to your advantage."

I bit my lip as I glanced up at him, relishing in the compliment and at the touch.

"So, what happens after we get the stone?" I asked. "What are we going to do about Penumbra?"

Alec seemed to mull over my question as we walked through the grounds of the Academy.

"The best-case scenario is that it deters Penumbra long enough for me to find the rest of the stones."

"What will Penumbra do when he finds out I helped you get the stone?" I whispered, wrapping my arms around myself.

"When I return to Arboria, I will leave guards to watch over you, and your family," Alec stopped and turned to me, his gaze hard. "To alert me if anything happens."

My stomach dropped at the realisation. Not if, but when.

"When you return to Arboria..." I repeated his words, my mouth turning dry.

"I have to return home and begin tracking down the other stones," Alec explained, his eyes flickering to my hands where they clenched and unclenched at my sides. "I need to ready the troops in case Penumbra decides to invade."

It hit me then. Alec was leaving.

The feelings I had for Alec washed over me like a wave, tightening my chest and laying heavy in my gut. I blinked away tears, focusing on wrapping those feelings in the darkness.

"Are you alright?" Alec asked as he grabbed my hands, lifting them between us.

I brushed my thumbs against his hands once before I looked up at him with a small smile. Hoping my eyes didn't betray me.

"I'm actually feeling a little tired." I mumbled, keep my voice level. "I'm going to head to bed. I'll see you tomorrow."

I slipped my hands from his and turned before he could say anything. Wrapping my arms around myself I walked away, with darkness as my constant companion as the sun began to set.

CHAPTER 24

*T*he weeks that followed seemed to blur together. It seemed like a lifetime ago that Alec and I had spoken about his leaving, but it still hurt anew whenever it crossed my mind.

Every day I would wake up before dawn to run a few laps and meditate, to begin circling my mana beneath a copse of trees.

Throughout class I would do the same thing, using every moment to concentrate channelling my mana against the barrier in my mind.

Every day I got a little closer to splinting a gap in the wall, small tendrils creeping through the cracks.

It was two weeks before the ball when the barrier came crashing down and the darkness flowed like water from a dam into my mind. I was sat cross-legged in the corner of Perrion's classroom. The other students were sparring with one another, Alec and Damon were off to my side faced off against one another. I had tried to start a conversation with both of them in the past few weeks, but I could never think of what to say.

With the darkness building inside me, I couldn't risk triggering the beast that clawed under my skin or the emotions that fed into it. Alec had told me that Fraser had reported back about the Shadow Beast, and that the only texts he found were vague and unhelpful.

The tendrils of shadow filled my mind and a mental snap reverberated throughout my skull as power roared in my ears. Flooding me from the top down, sweeping through the different pathways Perrion had spoke of, making my sense heighten and my skin buzz. I felt—

Powerful.

"Good Nevara," I heard Perrion's voice praise and I opened my eyes. I gasped at how vivid everything looked. Perrion's eyes were so defined, I could see the flecks of hazel in his irises. "It can be quite overwhelming at first, so take it slow."

The mana flowed beneath my skin, and I focused on my hearing. I could hear the birds singing outside the Academy and flinched as my focus shifted to the swords ringing out.

"Now I want you to dive into your pool of mana and force as much as you can into circulation," Perrion stated, and I gave him a slight nod. "That will be your next task. Practice the pushing of your mana around your body and holding it there for longer."

The storm that had been brewing and growing inside me over the past few weeks now lurked beneath the inky surface. When I reached inside the darkness, I felt it.

Something reached back.

My consciousness was pulled deeper, and in its place took the form of a beast made of solid night. The shadows crawled across my face, and as if from a distance I watched as Perrion's eyes flew wide and he began to shout to the rest of the room to empty as he took a step back.

The darkness caressed my mind, consuming every inch of me. It wasn't like when I witnessed myself kill Han and his friends. This was gentle. Powerful. More.

The dark gives birth to light and light recedes back to the darkness. I told you I would help you until you were strong enough to help yourself. You've done well, my Priestess of Shadows.

The voice echoed around the room. It was my voice, but it wasn't. It was ominous and foreboding, dark and beautiful.

Alec, Damon and Perrion stood by with pale faces, swords hanging from their grips.

It was like a puzzle piece had snapped into place, I felt whole, complete. I was darkness. It was me.

We were no longer separate. We were one.

I lifted my hand in front of my face, turning it this way and that. Admiring the claws and shadows as they danced over my skin, whispering.

"Was that… Ravenir?" Perrion gulped, awestruck.

No one spoke as Alec approached me, his face unreadable as he sank to one knee before me.

"Priestess," He bowed his head, his hair tumbling into his eyes as he placed a fist over his heart.

I gasped. The Fae Prince of Arboria was kneeling before me, a once homeless girl, from the Commoner's District. A human who his kind hated.

Yet still he kneeled.

Perrion followed suit and fell to his knee before me, his head bowed, and fist raised to his chest. Damon lowered his head in a bow where he stood.

I blinked as I felt the mana began to seep from the surface, retracting back into the pool within. The shadows receded and the claws became my hands again as I slumped to the floor, panting.

I felt reborn, the darkness now a living part of me.

"Now that was unexpected," Perrion breathed as the heaviness of the room lifted. Damon took a step forward behind them.

"A human Priestess," Perrion added in disbelief. "Did Penumbra know what she was when he shared his power?"

Alec stared at me a little longer before he spoke, his eyes dark as he watched me.

"I think it's because of the powers he gave her," Alec tilted his head. "That's why Ravenir chose her."

Something lit up behind Alec's eyes then and his gaze snapped to mine as he leaned forward.

"Do you remember that night on the bench in Undar?" Alec urged. "About the prophecy?"

I pushed up into a sitting position and leaned back against the wall. Trying to remember what he had told me that night.

"That a Priestess would come and use the stones to bring about peace to all of the lands," Alec answered, a smirk dancing on his lips. "I knew you had something to do with it."

"What is a Priestess exactly?" I asked, my head spinning now that the power had dispersed.

"A Priestess is someone who is chosen by the Gods to be their vessel," Alec explained, and my eyes widened when realising why they had all bowed before me. "A long time ago there used to be many Gods who chose their own Priestess', and they were treated with a higher respect and adoration than that of the King and Queen."

"There hasn't been one recorded in a long, long time," Alec added. "News of your appearance will shock the Fae."

"I don't think I can be what you're saying," I said as I ran a hand through my hair, shaking. "I'm a human for starters. How can I be a vessel for your God?"

Perrion rested a hand on Alec's shoulder, their eyes meet

in that strange silent conversation they have, then looked back to me.

"In the meantime, I don't think it's best we let this news spread beyond the four us," Perrion urged, looking between us all. "At least until we get the stone."

"I need to go tell the class some excuse for what just happened." Perrion got to his feet and crossed the room to the exit as Alec, Damon and I nodded. "Leave it to me."

Alec and Damon shared a look, before he turned to me, reaching down a hand to pull me to my feet.

"Let's go get something to eat," Alec kept a hold on my hand between us for a moment. "You look exhausted."

Damon cleared his throat and Alec dropped my hand as we turned to face him.

Between the sleepless nights and the mana depletion, my body ached for the comfort of my bed. I could still feel Alec's touch against my palm and I clasped my hands together tight, digging in my nails.

It was better this way, keeping that distance. After all, he was going back to his Kingdom soon. This way I'd be safe from the heartbreak that was evidently coming. This would lessen the blow.

On shaking legs, which I did my best to hide, I walked ahead of Alec and Damon out of the classroom. Their heavy stare like a brand against my back.

The corridor became a blur of windows, stone and people passing by. I missed my family in that moment. I missed Luca reading to me at night, how the Guild would join me for training every day and make me laugh at night in the tavern.

The longer I was away from them, the heavier my heart felt.

"Nevara," I heard Alec's voice cut through my reverie and turned to see that he stood alone. Damon was gone.

"What?" I sighed, as we exited the Academy into the brisk evening air.

"These last few weeks, you've been... distant," Alec began, his eyes filled with concern. "You didn't even go back to see your family last weekend."

I wanted to see my family. I just hadn't wanted to share a horse with Alec, that alone was what made me refuse to go. Not to mention that we had planned to scope out the palace last weekend, until Damon informed us that there was a council meeting in procession.

"I'm fine." I bit out, mustering up a smile. It must not have looked like one when Alec frowned at me.

"You're not fine," He accused, gritting his teeth. "I can't help you if you don't tell me what's wrong."

He was the last person I wanted to talk to what was wrong. I couldn't even talk to Kitty about it, as she didn't know about Alec being Fae. I was completely isolated.

"I'm fine," I reiterated, plastering a bigger smile on my face as I turned to walk away. "I'm just a little hungry. I'm going to get some dinner and head to bed."

"Dammit Nevara!" Alec cursed and I felt his arms go around me as he swung me up over his shoulder. His arms like an iron band over the back of my thighs.

"Alec!" I yelped, trying to dislodge myself from him as I felt his arms tighten around me. "Put me down!"

Alec's energy flowed into my legs, up over my behind and down my spine. It was cold, dark, and damp. So unlike the usual warmth I was used to from him. It was strange, I could almost taste it—

Alec was worried.

Before my mind could wonder as to why, Alec jolted me on his shoulder as he began to scale the wall surrounding the Academy. The ease in which he climbed was astonishing.

It was then I realised truly how strong and agile the Fae were, as Alec used the stone to propel himself up and over it.

"Where are you taking me?" I whispered, my braid whipping against the back of his thighs as he landed in a crouch on the other side.

Alec remained quiet as he navigated his was through the dense forest beyond the Academy walls.

We travelled for what felt like hours and the sky was turning dark overhead. Alec's scent had been invading my senses the entire walk; mint and earth, a heady mixture. I cursed my traitorous body for how quickly it relaxed against him.

He came to an abrupt stop in a thick copse of trees and pulled me over his shoulder. I slid down his chest until I was on my feet in front of him.

"You won't tell me what's wrong with you, so I had to do this," Alec whispered as he backed me deeper into the clearing. "You can't run from here, so tell me what's going on."

I sucked in my lower lip and bit down, the pain a welcome distraction from the flurry of emotions building in my chest. I turned around and gasped.

We were stood on a ledge, surrounded by trees on one side, and the ever-darkening sky on the other. A sheer drop off the edge.

It was beautiful. The lights of city twinkled like stars on the earth, mirroring the night sky. A scrape of metal caught my attention as I spun around to see Alec raising his sword, motioning me to do the same.

"We spar," Alec declared, a hard look in his eyes. "If I win, you will tell me what's going on. If you win, I will take you back to the Academy and let you keep living like a damned ghost."

I flinched at his words, the hardness of how they stung.

Bracing myself, I drew my sword and barely had any time to react as he lunged at me without warning. I rolled to the side just in time as his blade cut the air where I once stood, and our eyes met.

Fire burned beneath my skin as we met in a ring of swords, each attack echoing off the mountainside. My hands were slick with sweat as we fought on. Neither of us giving an inch, and the adrenaline seeped from my body as sadness crept in.

I used the darkness that accompanied it and pushed it through my body and down into my sword as I lunged forward. Shadows erupted from my blade, and I cried out as it struck hard against Alec's.

A boom ricocheted around the clearing, throwing Alec and I apart, our swords flying wide into the grass.

Alec watched my every move as I pushed up from the ground, both looked across to my sword then back to one another. I looked up to sky and sighed.

"You're going to leave." I whispered, a lump forming in my throat as my eyes filled with tears. Alec watched me with wide eyes as I sucked in a shaky breath, then he was on his feet in front of me. His hands cupped my face, forcing me to meet his eyes.

I had never cried. Never. Until now.

"This is why you've been so distant?" Alec whispered, his voice raw. I nodded as I felt the tears begin to fall freely.

"I don't want to lose you after we've become so close." I sobbed, unable to say the words I truly wanted to say.

I think I'm really falling for you.

Alec brushed my hair back from my face, ignoring the sweat plastered to my brow with a small smile.

"When I said I'd be going back, it didn't mean that I would never be coming back." He whispered as he caught my tears on the pads of his thumbs.

"But it won't be like this anymore," I choked out. "And I know that's selfish but it's why I've been distancing myself from you, so that it wouldn't hurt as much when you left." My voice cracked and the dam on my emotions cracked wide.

"When I had learned that Penumbra was working alongside a human to retrieve the stones, all I could imagine was tracking down that human and killing them," Alec said, and I froze at his words. "I was searching for the fire stone, and that human, but then I found you."

Alec's face softened as he pressed closer, our chests brushing together. He rested his forehead to mine, looking into my eyes.

"The moment Damon brought you to my room that night in the tavern, I couldn't get over how beautiful you were," He mused, his fingers caressing my cheeks. "Humans have always been so boring and dull in comparison to the Fae. But you... you were life itself. Even with your scars, the darkness that you had fled from, you still shone."

I gasped as he followed the pattern of scars down to my throat. His touch reverent and left a heady fire in its wake.

"On the night of the Awakening, when I saw the mark of my brother on your chest... that night I had come so close to killing you." Alec confessed, his fingers spanning across my throat, as his eyes flickered back to mine.

"My dream," I breathed, realisation hitting me. It was real. Alec was there that night.

"I couldn't do it. I knew I should for the sake of my Kingdom, but I just couldn't. I convinced myself if I got to know you, find out if you were a threat or not... then I found myself drawn to you more and more. When I found you that night with Han—" Alec's voice turned hard, and his hand stopped moving on my throat. He shook his head. "I have never hated myself more for not being fast enough to save you. The plan was to have Perrion bring us to the mountains so I could bring you to the Fae lands to convince you not to work alongside my brother."

"It wasn't your fault," I breathed, covering his hands with my own.

"It may not have happened by my hand, but I had a hand in it," He sighed, meeting my eyes. "But then that day at the river when you got drunk on the energies... I knew you weren't in your right mind, and I should have dragged you into town as soon as you—"

Alec's eyes burned, smouldering and I couldn't look away.

"When you touched me, I lost all rational thought," The hand on my neck curled around and tangled in the hair at the nape of my neck, our breath mingling in the space between our lips. "It was like some deep and primal emotion came over me. I had no idea how to control myself enough to get us to town."

"Since that day I haven't been able to get you out of my mind, and everything has only pushed me closer and closer to you," His body shook as his other hand wrapped around my waist.

"I will not leave you Nevara, because I can't."

I sucked in a breath and before I could even think about it, I closed the small distance between us and kissed him. I felt him still before he gathered me up in his arms, deepening the kiss with a growl. He loosened my braid, tangling his fingers there and I wrapped my arms around his neck.

A bright and intense warmth consumed us, the energy bouncing back and forth between us.

Alec broke the kiss, grinning as he ran his tongue along his lower lip before leaning forward and capturing my lips again with a groan.

My mind went static. No longer was he a Prince. No longer was he Fae and I only a human.

There was nothing but Alec as he held me tight.

We kissed until the stars filled the heavens and we made our way to the floor. Alec had pulled me into his lap, pressing kisses to my lips, my neck, and my hands. Each more gentle than the last.

The sky began to change colour as I fell asleep to lull of his heartbeat and sweet whisperings.

WHEN I WOKE UP, I found myself tucked in bed and I scrambled to sit up. I looked around my dorm room, Kitty's bed was empty, and I reached up to find my lips puffy.

Was it a dream?

"You're awake."

I hadn't heard the door open. Alec walked over holding a bowl of something steaming. He popped it down in front of me, then climbed onto bed beside me.

"I couldn't get you to wake up on the mountain, so I had to carry you the whole way back," He teased, propping himself on his elbow, grinning.

"Oh," I blushed. It had been real. "I'm sorry." I smiled sheepishly as I took a mouthful of what turned out to be porridge.

"You looked like you needed it." Alec said, his eyes perusing over me as I ate, and I shifted under his gaze.

"We're going to head to the palace today, but I'm afraid we will have to go in disguise." He mused, his mouth twitching.

"Disguise?" I asked, placing the bowl to one side, wondering what he meant.

Alec reached over, putting the bowl back in front of me. With a smile, he captured my lips in a soft kiss, lingering longer than necessary before gesturing to the porridge.

"When you're done eating, I'll show you." He chuckled, licking his bottom lip as he looked at me. I turned my attention to the bowl as I scoffed the porridge down.

Today was going to be a challenge to say the least.

CHAPTER 25

he last thing I expected sat on the desk in Alec and
Damon's room when I walked in. My eyes
widened when my eyes landed on the set of silver helmets
and armour.

"You're joking?" I spun around and looked between Alec
and Damon, my mouth agape. "We're going to be disguised
as knights?"

Damon was sat on his bed, his arms braced across his
thighs. He met my eyes as he shrugged a shoulder.

"It's the easiest way to get you in and out of the palace
without attracting any unwanted attention." I wrinkled my
nose, cringing over at the pile of clothing.

"You can't be serious," I shot them both an incredulous
look. Just knowing how uncomfortable and ridiculous this
was going to be.

Alec walked over to the desk, lifting a helmet from the
pile. He turned, passing it back and forth between his hands
before tossing it over to me.

"Looks like we don't have a choice." He grinned as I
snatched it out of the air.

285

Alec tore his shirt over his head, leaving his bare back to me. I blinked and averted my eyes to Damon.

"Where is the nearest bathing room?" I blurted, as Damon sunk back on his bed.

"You'll have to change in here," Damon said, a glint of a challenge in his eyes as a smirk played around his mouth. "My knights are down the hall, so we will have to climb out of the window."

"Fine," I scowled, snapping my eyes to them both. "But both of you turn around. I don't care if you're both Princes, if I catch you looking, I will punch you square in the face."

Damon chuckled but turned to face the wall. Alec on the other hand, he let his gaze peruse me from my boots to my face. Slow and steady until he met my eyes, then smirked, his eyes burning before he turned his back to me. My breath stuttered out as I moved to begin removing the corset part of my armour before letting it fall to the floor. Followed by my undershirt, pants, and boots.

I yanked the knight's armour on. The shirt swallowed my small frame and the pants needed to be rolled up for sure.

"This definitely won't draw attention to me at all," I drawled, rolling my eyes. Alec and Damon both turned to look at me, then burst out laughing. I wasn't skinny by any means. Years of good food and rigorous training had filled me out, but my curves and muscles were still not enough to fill out the knight's uniform.

"Can I help?" Alec asked with a grin, and I hesitated before nodding. He stood in front of me, his fingers deft over the hooks and snaps, tightening each one with precision. I was hyperaware of each drag and touch of his fingers against my bare skin. I was sure he was doing it on purpose as gooseflesh appeared in his touches wake. Flickering my eyes up to his, I watched as they danced, and a knowing smile appeared.

"Much better," Damon coughed, breaking the moment. I glanced over to him; his pale eyes dark as they bounced from me to Alec. I looked away, smoothing my hands over the uniform as Alec stepped away. It was still loose, but it would do.

I hoped.

Alec was first to lower himself out of the window and down onto the ground below. Scaling the wall and traversing the ledges down the two-story drop like it was nothing. Damon followed suit and even though wasn't as quick, he did it with ease. I suppressed a laugh at the idea of Damon sneaking away from his guards.

I peered down at Alec and Damon from the window. I took a deep breath and threw the helmet down to them before I kicked a leg over the ledge, straddling the sill before I lowered myself down. My legs dangling, nerves setting in as I found a foothold.

"This looks familiar," Damon chuckled, and I bit a curse out that would rival that of a sailor's tongue.

"I won't fall this time," I snapped.

"Unfortunately." He breathed and I rolled my eyes, making my way to the ground.

The relationship I had with Damon had been somewhat strained since our altercation a few weeks ago. We sparred together and ate meals together, but it was only the past few days that we began speaking again. I just wish we could be friends like we were before.

Alec handed me my helmet, as he secured his own on his head. He looked the part of a royal knight, and I wondered if I looked half as good.

I pulled the helmet on over my head, tucking my braid inside.

"Let's go."

~

THE CARRIAGE PULLED up outside the Academy and the driver opened the door for us. Inside the benches and walls were covered in plush velvet. Alec and I sat on one bench, and Damon sat opposite. He banged on the roof and the carriage lurched into motion.

"These things are awful," Alec curse tugging off his helmet and dropping it in his lap, frowning around at the carriage interior.

I pulled off my own helmet, swiping the sweat from my brow and blowing an errant hair out of my face.

"Keep circulating your mana," Alec urged, nudging his leg against mine. "It helps keep your body temperature neutral in tense situations."

"Is that how you always seem so unfazed by everything?" I asked, tilting my head towards him. "I've seen you climb mountains and not break a sweat."

"How long can you keep your mana flowing so that you're so unaffected by everything?" Damon quipped, crossing his arms across his chest. I wanted to know that as well.

"My mana is always circulated through my body," Alec shrugged, and Damon and I just blinked at him.

"I've been training to control my mana for centuries," Alec chuckled as he continued. "The more mana you flow through your body, the more your mana pool grows." He looked out the small window, then glanced back at me. "I can draw power from the Fae lands too."

"You remember the energies, right?" Alec caught my eye, grinning. I could feel my cheeks heating as I remembered kissing him at the river.

Damon frowned, looking between the two of us, unimpressed.

"You're not helping," I murmured as I closed my eyes and

took a deep breath. Letting the carriage fall away, I focused on coaxing a small tendril of smoke from my mana pool, expanding it as it flowed under my skin. Careful not overdo it like in class. I sighed as I felt coolness lick at my skin.

"Better?" Alec whispered.

I cracked an eye open and smiled at him.

"So much better."

Closing my eyes, I revelled in the coolness.

The power coating my skin.

The remainder of the carriage ride, Damon informed us of the layout of the palace, every entrance, exit and hidden passageway. My mouth had hung open the entire time, especially when he rattled off the different rooms and where they were located. I knew the palace was huge, but it sounded like a maze of rooms.

When the carriage came to a stop, Alec and I refitted our helmets as Damon straightened the lapels of his jacket. Even I had to admit that he looked handsome.

"Just don't say anything and follow me," Damon whispered as the door was pulled open and he lowered himself to the ground. Nerves fluttered in my stomach as we followed him out towards the palace.

It was a gigantic monstrosity of turrets, bridges and archways. Like the Academy it was built of grey stone, topped with spiralling towers, except everything was accented with gold. Gilded flowers wrapped around columns leading towards the entrance. A single leaf would enough to feed a family for a few years. I frowned, trying to focus on the sheer size of it.

"Remember that mine is bigger." Alec whispered, his eyes glittering from beneath his helmet. I blushed as we followed Damon inside.

We were lead through an ornate hallway, the walls laden with gold framed paintings of landscapes and portraits. Each one placed at intervals between expensive flame sconces. The double doors at the end swung open into a wide ballroom. A crystal chandelier hung in the centre of the room, above a white marbled floor. The ceiling was designed to mimic a summer sky with fluffy clouds. I had to admit, it was beautiful.

Mentally I shook myself, telling myself to focus. This was the last weekend before the ball and we needed to use this time to scout and plan.

I marked each of the windows and counted the number of glass double doors we passed through. Ones which lead out the gardens surrounding the palace, and the ones leading to alcoves and balconies.

Three thrones stood on a dais at the back of the room. One for the King. One for the Queen. One for Damon.

We circled around them, and I gave them a much wider berth, not wanting to get anywhere near them. Through a set of doors and down another hallway, we reached a door that was made of metal, engraved with different magic formations and locks.

Damon didn't need to tell me this was where the artefacts were kept. It was obvious. This was a vault.

Alec lifted a hand, reaching towards the door. His fingers twitched before he turned to us and nodded. I let loose a breath I didn't realise I was holding. It was in there. The stone.

"Prince Damon." A man's voice echoed down the corridor behind us as we were about to continue round the corner. I held myself as still and straight as possible.

"Maximus," Damon nodded, his back tense.

"I wasn't aware you were visiting today," Maximus said with a smirk. He didn't so much as glance at me or Alec. "Does your mother and father know you're here?"

Maximus was a middle-aged man with curling ginger

hair. There was nothing remarkable, but it was obvious he was a noble in the snobby way he carried himself.

"I was just about to go and visit them actually," Damon bit out, with a stiff smile. Maximus's mouth twitched as Damon edged around him and we followed suit. "I'll see you at the ball next weekend."

"Oh indeed," Maximus smiled, but it didn't meet his eyes. "We're all very excited to see who the next princess will be."

Damon nodded, before turning and striding down the hallway, his boots echoing on the marble. We kept pace behind him until we rounded a few more corners and Damon spun to face us.

"Make yourselves scarce and meet me back at the Academy tonight," Damon scowled, turning to continue down the hallway. I could have sworn I heard him curse, colourfully at that.

"Follow me," Alec ordered as he walked in the same direction Damon had taken but veered around the opposite corner. I obeyed and followed him through door after door until we stepped out onto a cobbled path.

The autumn breeze was crisp, night falling as we ducked behind a nearby hedge. Alec peered around another bend before leading me forward until we reach a small grove of trees.

"We will hide the armour here, as a backup escape plan," Alec removed his helmet and I followed suit. He tucked the outer-armour and helmets beneath the roots of a tree. "We steal the stone, and if there are any complications, these are here."

"You make it sound so easy," I whispered, wrapping my arms around myself as the undershirt fluttered against my body.

"It's only a plan B," He said, pulling me towards him. "Hopefully it won't come to that."

Alec hauled me over his shoulder and I bit my lip to conceal a scream as he scaled the wall and landed in an alleyway behind a row of buildings. It opened out into the main street of the Nobles District and Alec slid me back onto my feet with a grin.

"We'll get the carriage back to the Academy," Alec laced his fingers through mine as he led me through the crowds that littered the main square. Nobles glared in disgust, no doubt due to my lack of clothing, and I smirked.

"I think you're enjoying doing that way too much," Alec chuckled, and I stuck my tongue out at him, which made him grin and shake his head.

Once back inside the carriage, I flopped back against the plush seat and just breathed. Recounting everything I'd seen in the palace today, doing a mental inventory.

"I'll have to procure you a dress for the ball," Alec murmured, looking deep in thought. His eyes flickered to mine. "I already have a velvet tunic, so I don't need to worry."

"A dress?" I choked. I'd never worn a dress in my life. I'd always assumed my body was too masculine for one.

"Yes, a dress," Alec chuckled, raising an eyebrow. "You know, the things women wear to balls and other noble occasions."

"I've never worn a dress." I whispered, staring across the carriage.

"That's because you're a warrior." Alec's voice was soft, yet firm and I met his eyes. Respect and admiration shone there.

"Well, I think it would be difficult to fight in one." I pointed out with a chuckle.

"Something tells me you would surprise me in that respect," Alec grinned as he leaned towards me. "Would you like to choose one, or do you want me to get one for you?"

"You pick one," I blurted, blushing. "You or anyone else

really, would have more experience in dressing a woman for a ball. I'll leave it in your capable hands."

Alec's eyes danced and he opened his mouth as if to say something. Instead, he met my eyes as he ran a tongue over his lower lip, tipping his head back against the carriage with a quiet laugh.

Soon enough the lights of city disappeared and the forest became more dense, the road less smooth.

"My mother sent word," Alec broke the silence and my head snapped towards him. "She says that Penumbra has given them an ultimatum; they either surrender the throne over to him and no one will be harmed, or he'll take it by force and slaughter all in his path."

"What did your parents say?" I breathed, feeling as if the carriage had become far too small.

"They haven't replied yet," Alec sighed, pinching the bridge of his nose between his fingers. "I told my parents to wait until after the ball, in case we don't get the stone…"

His mouth pressed into a tight line as his hands curled into fists in his lap. If we didn't get the stone, we were surrendering to Penumbra or facing open war.

I reached over, covering his hands with my own. Trying to provide any sort of comfort I could.

"We will get the stone," I promised.

"We don't have a choice," Alec sighed. "It's either that, or we go to war."

"Welcome home, my Little Shadow."

The voice slid across my skin, and I didn't want to open my eyes. I knew if I did, I'd find myself in the black marble room belonging to Penumbra.

I wondered if I pretended to be asleep—

"I'm not so easy to fool," Penumbra chuckled and I opened my eyes slowly.

"You can read my mind?" I breathed as I sat up. He was lounging on a chaise as if he wasn't the monster trying to create war with his own family, his people, and mine.

"I can only read your mind when you're near me," He shrugged, fixing his red eyes on me. "And you think that I want war? That is the last thing I want."

"Then why are you doing all of this?" I stuttered as I gestured to the open window where I knew his army stood, waiting. "Why threaten war if it's not what you want?"

"My brother told you, did he?" Penumbra sighed as he pushed off the chaise and prowled towards me. He pressed a finger under my chin, tilting my face up towards his. "Tell me, has he warmed your bed yet?"

I ignored his words and clenched my teeth, not giving him the satisfaction of seeing me ruffled.

"Why did you threaten your parents with war?" I gritted out, hardening my gaze on his.

"Because I am hoping they will do the smart thing and hand it over to me without going to war, but I know my brother won't let them do that, the arrogant bastard he is," Penumbra sighed, his voice like silk. He twirled a strand of my hair around his finger lazily.

"What about the Human Kingdom?" I whispered. The humans wouldn't last long against Penumbra's army. Even with magic now, it would be futile against the Fae. "Will you give them the same choice?"

"I have plans for the humans," He tugged on the strand wrapped around his finger. "They have caused a lot of damage to my people."

"But you were the one who caused the rift between the humans and the Fae," I accused, glaring up at him. "Do the Fae even know that you were the one to open the gates between the lands?"

His gaze snapped to mine, fire burning in their depths, blazing.

"You think I'm the one who created those damned gates?" He demanded, an incredulous look on his face. The cool and composed mask no longer in place. "What exactly has my brother been telling you?"

"That you caused all of this. That you are a monster that caused the humans to go through the gates and blindly slaughter the Fae, and steal their artefacts," I whispered, as the hand that held the curl stilled. His hand slid into my hair and pulled with enough force that tingles spread out over my scalp and our faces were so close together.

"Sometimes the monsters are the ones who wear a shiny and beautiful appearance," He hissed, eyes boring into mine. "Did you even bother to find out the full truth before you decided to label me a monster? Or were you too busy having a pathetic crush on my brother?"

I sneered as I grabbed at his arm, trying to relieve the tension in his grip as a wave of energy shot through me. Complete darkness flowed over me, whole and consuming, and the room changed into the one I'd confined myself to after the contest. Anger and sadness washed over me, but they weren't my own.

"What happened to you?" I whispered, as I sucked in a breath. Dizzy from the flood of emotions. My voice caught. "Why do you feel so much darkness?"

The grip on my hair lessened, but he didn't move away as he studied my face. That cool mask fell back over his face and his eyes hardened.

"I didn't realise the power to read energies and emotions had passed to you," He pondered with a smirk as he released his hold on me entirely. The connection between us broke.

Penumbra straightened up as he looked down at me on my knees before him.

"Tell my brother that he has two weeks before my army marches on Arboria."

Penumbra turned, walking beyond the red flowing curtains, waving a hand over his shoulder.

"Wait!" I screamed. He looked back one last time, and I could have sworn I could see that sadness and despair swimming in his eyes.

I FLEW UPRIGHT IN BED, panting. I look around to see that Kitty was snoring softly in her bed and took time to calm my breathing.

What just happened?

I pressed my hand against my racing heart. What had Penumbra meant when he said that him opening the gates wasn't the truth?

I shook my head. Alec. I trusted Alec, and I would help him find the stone and stop this war.

CHAPTER 26

"*T*his is even more difficult than circulating my mana," I groaned, hands on my hips. It was what felt like the fiftieth time today, constantly following Perrion's instructions. And it was probably the fiftieth time I had failed. Miserably.

"Shadow Walking is the most difficult trait to master," Perrion chuckled, and I looked at him. "At first, Penumbra could only shadow walk a few steps. Even then, it took him a short while too."

"Was Penumbra always the way he is?" I asked after a moment, peeking over at Alec and Damon where they stood against the far wall.

A safe distance in case we had a repeat of the other day, and what seemed far enough away that Alec's Fae hearing didn't pick up on our conversation, if his passive face was anything to go by.

"Penumbra was always a good child," Perrion sighed, meeting my eyes. "He was reserved, always kept to himself, mostly due to his family and those High Fae who singled him out."

"Why would they do that?" I furrowed my brow, surprised to hear that the prince was bullied.

"Penumbra was born first, but only a few months after the King and Queen were married," Perrion stated, his brown eyes striking. "Penumbra was cast aside once Alec was born. Then the truth was revealed; Penumbra's father had been a Lesser Fae. From there things only got worse. *He* got worse."

"Who—What Lesser Fae was Penumbra's father?" I gaped, reeling from the revelation.

"No more story telling today," Perrion shook his head, waving a hand at me. "Keep practicing. Remember to reach out to the shadows with your own dark mana. Find the tether that connects the two."

"Easier said than done." I grumbled as I turned to face the shadow covering the weapon rack. I pulled at the dark mana in my stomach, pushing it into my hands. That familiar feeling of smoke coalesced from my fingertips, reaching for the shadow. The closer the tendrils reached, the more my head begin to hurt, a pounding beneath my skull.

Mana, I learned, didn't have a linear flow and I had to manipulate it to where I wanted it to go.

"That's it," Perrion urged, stepping up behind me. "Now connect with the shadow."

I gritted my teeth as pushed more tendrils from my fingers. It was like trying to funnel a river through the eye of a needle, like I'd seen Netta do time and time again.

Except her hands were steady.

Mine were not.

Tendrils brushed the edge of the shadow and I felt its emptiness greet my mana. I waited for a moment before it finally opened itself up to me like a door opening into a room.

"Now imagine pulling yourself into that darkness, using

your mana as a rope." Perrion whispered, his voice floating around the room.

I held onto that feeling of an open door and mentally thrust myself through it, pushing past the threshold and becoming one with the shadow—

"Damn it!"

The connection snapped and I pressed my hands to my temples, scowling. The pain throbbed throughout my skull.

"Like with everything, you just need to practice," Perrion explained, patting me on the shoulder. "And have patience."

I nodded, scrunching my nose and wringing my hands together. This sucked.

"What's that look?" Alec asked as he stepped up beside me.

"Just my horrible lack of control of my mana," I sighed, sliding my eyes towards him.

"From what I've seen, for a human, you're the fastest to get a good grasp on your mana," He said as he circled in front of me, reaching up to push a stray curl behind my ear.

"Not fast enough though," I whispered, as his hand slid down my jaw, cupping my face in his palm. My skin prickled at the sensation of his skin dragging over mine.

"You're doing amazing," He murmured as he dragged the pad of his finger over my bottom lip. I sucked in a breath, and he grinned. "Don't doubt yourself."

Perrion coughed, the noise echoing around the room.

"Class is over," He eyed Alec and me, at the space, or lack thereof between us. "So unless you want to put on a show for my next class, I suggest you head for the cafeteria."

Alec cut Perrion a look as he ushered me across the room. "Let's go," Alec whispered as we left the room.

Thoughts from my conversation with Penumbra still plagued my thoughts, and I kept wanting to bring it up to Alec, but every time I tried, my throat would clog up and my stomach churned. I didn't know if I feared his reaction or whether he wouldn't believe me and think I was actually giving Penumbra a chance.

But the thought of those sad red eyes haunted me.

"I'm exhausted." Xander grumbled as he threw himself down in a chair opposite me. Ever since I'd began at the Academy, we had all commandeered this table as our own. Though since training had begun, I had barely seen Xander, Harven and Kitty. We'd all become like ghosts passing one another with the odd greeting here and there.

Damon smirked over Xander who looked like he was about to fall face first into his food, or worse yet, off his chair and onto the floor. I chuckled, grinning at Xander who pulled a face.

"It's not my fault I don't have your energy," he said, pointing his spoon at me. "You never tire out."

I tried to speak, but Kitty chirped up beside me, nudging her shoulder against mine.

"You seem to be training from dawn till dusk every day," Kitty rolled her eyes, a small smile playing about her lips as she sighed dramatically. "I get tired just from watching you."

"You get tired from doing just about anything," Harven teased and I chuckled as Kitty stuck her tongue out at him. Everyone at the table began chattering with one another about their classes. Damon was watching me with a small smile when I felt a tap on my shoulder.

"Nevara?" I looked up to see one of the white robed Archmages and I nodded. "A package has been delivered for you. It is at the front desk if you could come and receive it."

I looked back to my friends at the table, meeting Alec's eyes as he gave me a small nod. Pushing to my feet I followed the Archmage through the cafeteria and across the grounds to the front desk. I didn't have to turn around to know Alec was only a few steps behind me.

The woman behind the desk handed me two small packages with a smile, before going back to her filing. I shrugged at Alec who returned the sentiment and we made our way outside and sat on a bench beneath a low hanging tree.

I pulled the card attached to one of packages,

Dear Nevara,

Happy Nineteenth Birthday! You probably forgot all about it, didn't you?

We though you might have. We miss you so much and can't wait to see you the next time you visit home so we can celebrate properly.

Please enjoy the gift and celebrate with your friends at the Academy.

All our love,

Netta, Kain, Luca, Brendan, and the baby bump. And of course, everyone at The Guild.

"My birthday," I breathed. I had completely forgotten. Today was the day Kain had stated was my birthday, the day he began to train me.

"It's your birthday?" Alec asked, and I blinked away my thoughts, nodding.

"How could you forget that?" He chuckled.

"I've been a bit busy lately," I pointed out with a shrug of my shoulder.

It's true, my mind had been focused on making it through the ball and retrieving the stone. I'd had little time for anything else.

Within the first package I found a beautiful handmade braid made of silver. At the end hung a small ruby in the shape of a heart, and as I held it up in the sunlight, light scattered and casted every which way.

I smiled. I'd only seen one of these before and it was tied around the pommel of Kain's sword. Netta had given him it as a symbol of her love for him, a reminder. Now I had one to remind me of my family's love for me. I looped it around the pommel of my own sword.

Alec's eyes tracked my movements, and when I caught his eye he smiled, then nodded to my lap.

"There's another one."

I smiled at him, then lifted the second card and squinted at the elegant handwriting.

MY LITTLE SHADOW,

I USED this ring to help control my mana when I was younger. I hope it can be of some use to you.

Happy Birthday.

PENUMBRA.

MY BLOOD FROZE as I finished reading the card, hands shaking.

"What is it?" Alec asked, and I didn't move as he took the card from my fingers. Moments later he tensed beside me.

I peeled back the velvet wrappings to find a small metal ring laid inside. A single black diamond was inset in the shape of an opal. Energy seemed to swirl in its depths.

"By the Gods," Alec breathed. "That's the Dark Forest's Heart."

"What?" I whispered.

"It's a stone my brother stole from the Dark Forest. A place forbidden in the Fae Lands," Alec explained, staring at the ring. A mixture of what looked like hate and something else in his eyes. "He used it to channel his shadow abilities."

"This could help us," I breathed, lifting the ring from the velvet. "This could help my shadow walking."

"No, absolutely not," Alec's hand shot out and covered mine, his eyes bore into mine as he shook his head. "Penumbra probably has a formation etched into it. It'll give him more control over you than he already does."

"No one has control over me, Alec," I scowled, pulling my hand from beneath his and closing my fingers over the ring. "He is trying everything within his power to win me over to his side, so what use would it be to send me a cursed ring?"

Alec's head snapped to mine, fire burning in his eyes.

"What do you mean 'he's doing everything he can to win you over'?" Alec said, his voice low and steady.

I swallowed, clenching the ring in my fist as he leaned in close.

"Last night," I whispered. "He visited me."

Alec's eyes hardened and a muscle ticked in his jaw.

"What happened?" He gritted out. A deadly calm mask dropped over his face.

"Pretty much the same as before," I shifted uncomfortably beneath his gaze. "Except this time, he tried to lie to me."

"Lie to you about what, Nevara?" Alec asked, his voice tight.

"He said that he wasn't the one who created the gates between our kingdoms," I breathed, his eyes sparking. "That I didn't know the truth."

Alec's jaw ticked again as he ran a hand over his face with sigh. I didn't dare move.

"He's already trying to manipulate you," Alec said and hesitated before caressing a hand over my cheek. "I'm sorry you hand to go through that again."

I released a breath I didn't realise I was holding and sagged against the back of the bench. I mentally shook myself, berating myself for thinking Alec wouldn't have understood. Penumbra was just getting in my head.

I covered Alec's hand with my other, holding it to my cheek as he leaned to press his forehead to mine. His scent of mint and earth consuming me.

"It seems like I will have to get you a bigger present now," He murmured as his thumb rubbed back and forth. I grinned.

"I like pastries," I suggested, and he chuckled.

"Pastries, got it." He whispered as he captured me in soft kiss, my body melting into his. Butterflies erupted inside my chest.

Alec pulled back and breathed the words against my mouth, his eyes shining.

"Happy Birthday Nevara."

THE NEXT FEW days consisted of more Shadow Walk training with Perrion, and each was more excruciating than the last. Though each day, I also spent hours eating my way through the many *many* boxes of pastries that Alec had somehow managed to have delivered to the Academy.

Now it was the day before the ball and I still wasn't able to successfully Shadow Walk.

I swung my sword towards Damon, venting my frustration and anger as we sparred. He dodged to the side before my blade sliced through his chest and he spun to glare at me.

"I think that you might actually be trying to kill me," He accused, narrowing his eyes as he thrust forward, I dodged to the side with ease. My training with Alec was really paying off.

"I'm sorry," I sighed as we called it quits and headed towards our water canteens. "I'm just pissed that I wasn't able to Shadow Walk before tomorrow."

Damon gave me a lopsided smile, pressing a hand to my shoulder with a squeeze.

"We'll still be able to pull it off Nevara," He stated. "Even without your Shadow Walking. We just need to stick to the plan, and everything will be fine."

"I know." I whispered, and I did. It didn't make it any less frustrating though.

We had gone over the plan so many times now, it was like muscle memory. Alec and I would be entering the ball room disguised as high-ranking nobles to blend in with the crowds. Then after the artefacts have been presented, I will create a distraction whilst Alec retrieves the stone from the locked room.

Then run. Fast.

I sheathed my sword and gestured over my shoulder to the door.

"I'm going to head back to my room to get washed, maybe practice a little more before dinner." I said and Damon gave me a nod before I turned and dragged myself back to my room.

THE WARM WATER of the bath had seeped into my aching muscles, but the annoyance of not being able to Shadow

Walk still pestered me. I dropped the towel beside my bed as I paced the worn rug. It would have been so useful for—

A quiet humming filled the air. I turned looking for the source as my eyes landed on the chest of drawers beside my bed. They had remained empty until recently.

The hum got more persistent the closer I got, and as I pulled the drawer open the humming grew louder until I closed my hand over the velvet bundle inside.

Penumbra's ring.

I turned it over in my hands. My own dark mana singing, reaching for it with invisible hands.

Alec's disappointed face appeared as I felt the urge to put it on. But I knew it would help. I clenched the ring in my fist—

With a groan I uncurled my fingers and slipped the ring on before I could change my mind. A dark energy jolted down my arm, striking at the depths of my mana pool leaving me gasping.

It felt like a bridge between the ring and my mana. A connection.

Calming my breath, I raised my hand towards the shadow casted over Kitty's bed and pulled my mana. It took no coaxing before it shot down my arm and encased my fingers. The rush made me stumble back before I refocused my mind.

Like with Perrion I felt my mana reach for the doorway in my mind, except this time it flooded through entrance. Darkness swallowed me up and the sensation of falling washed over me before I opened my eyes.

I looked over my shoulder towards my bed, then down at the shadow I now stood in.

I did it.

A laugh escaped as I held the ring up in front of my face and examined it once more. It had made it so easy that I wondered how I'd struggled before.

THE REST of evening I practiced Shadow Walking around my room. I melted in and out of the darkness like it was second nature now and laughed every time the falling sensation occurred and I popped back into existence. Retrieving the stone would be so much easier now, especially if anything went wrong.

A knock at the door had me yelling as I landed on my backside mid-Shadow Walk.

Alec's head peeked around the door and raised an eyebrow at me on the floor.

"What happened?" He bit his lip, his eyes dancing with laughter.

"You scared me!" I accused as I pushed myself to my feet.

"And what exactly were you doing to make you so jumpy?" He teased as he entered the room with a huge box in his arms.

"I managed to Shadow Walk." I said as I eyed the box.

"That was fast," He breathed with a raised eyebrow as he sat on the bed, placing the box beside him. "You were struggling yester—"

I watched as Alec's eyes fell to the ring on my hand and I lifted my chin.

"It helped me," I said. I wouldn't be ashamed of using something which would make sure tomorrow went without a hitch.

"I told you not to use it," Alec berated, his voice taking on a tone I'd never heard before. "What if he had in fact cursed it and harmed you in some way? What if you weren't well enough tomorrow?"

Alec's eyes hardened as they locked on mine, his hands clenching into fists in his lap.

"It's not cursed," I said, holding out my hand to show him. "And it helps. A lot."

"Then take it off." Alec said, his eyes snapping to the ring then back to me. "If the ring comes off then it's not cursed, and just maybe my brother does indeed have a shred of decency left. But if not, then you have been cursed and he's still the asshole I know him to be."

My heart fell into my stomach as I lifted my hand and tugged at the ring. *Please come off.*

I begged and begged and... nothing. It was as if the bridge between it and my mana had been bonded with steel. Each tug sent tremors down into my mana pool, making me flinch.

Alec sighed.

"Next time you should heed my warnings."

Penumbra had cursed me?

But I didn't feel any different, and my feelings for Penumbra hadn't changed. Though he was further up on my shit list for gifting me a cursed ring.

"Whatever," I waved off with my hand. "If I can Shadow Walk tomorrow then it's worth it."

I nodded towards the box on the bed.

"What's that?"

Alec smile turned smug as he leaned back on his hands.

"Your dress."

My mouth dropped open, but he held up a hand.

"I've informed Kitty that I'm taking you to the ball tomorrow and she will help you get ready," Alec grinned, tilting his head to one side. Clearly enjoying my reaction. "Kitty is the daughter of a baker in the noble district, so you needn't worry. She won't have any involvement in tomorrow's events."

I nodded, glad that Kitty wouldn't have any connections

with the attendees tomorrow. My face began to pale though as I looked back at the box. A dress.

"Thank you." I blurted out as I moved the box onto the top of the drawers.

"Aren't you going to look at it?" Alec pressed, resting forward with his elbows propped on his thighs.

"It will only make me more nervous." I admitted as I sat down beside him. He wrapped an arm around my waist, pulling me in closer.

"You don't need to be nervous, everything will be fine," He whispered into my hair as he placed a kiss to my temple, making me shiver as his energy coursed through me.

I glanced up at him through my lashes, staring at those bright blues as he tilted my chin up. His lips brushed against mine, every movement from the way his hands tangled in my hair to his tongue dragging across the seam of my lips, set me alight.

"You promised you wouldn't kiss me until after the ball," I murmured between kisses, and he grinned against my mouth.

"I think that ship has sailed," He chuckled as he pressed another sweet kiss against my lips. Almost like he couldn't help himself. I looked at him and bit the inside of my cheek.

Even though I knew deep down loving him would only end in heartbreak—

"You think too much," He whispered as he lowered his mouth back to mine with a smile. Something within me snapped and I fisted my hands in his hair and gave into him completely.

The kisses turned deeper, like he was mapping every inch of my mouth. His hands running through my hair and down over my face and over my waist. Like he couldn't settle on where he wanted to touch.

Alec's hands were cupped under my jaw as he leaned

back, his lips shining as his eyes burned into me as he looked me over.

"So beautiful," He whispered as he lowered himself over me, capturing my lower lip with his. Fire erupting over my skin as our legs tangled together and his hand slid under the hem of my shirt.

"You would not believe the day I just had—"

Kitty's voice echoed through the room as my eyes sprang open to meet Alec's. Panic and laughter danced there as he pulled back smoothing his hands over his shirt.

"I'll see you at midday tomorrow." He leaned down pressing a kiss to my cheek with a grin and I could feel my face burning. He hopped off the bed and crossed the room to the door. "Kitty." He nodded to her as he closed the door.

The room stood silent and frozen as I tried to wrap my head around what the hells had just happened. When reality caught up to me, I covered my face with my hands, hoping the ground would open up and swallow me whole.

"Oh my gosh, Nevara, I am so sorry!" Words began tumbling from Kitty's mouth. "I thought you were alone, then I saw you kissing and—"

"Kitty, stop!" I begged with a nervous chuckle.

"I am truly sorry," Kitty came over and sat beside me with a sheepish smile. "I didn't know you and Alec were together."

"We're not," I blurted, feeling my face flaming again. "It just wouldn't work with us that way."

The words spoken aloud sent a jolt of pain through my chest, even though I knew it was the truth.

"Oh," Kitty said, looking over at me with a grin. "Well, whatever it is going on between you two, I can promise he won't be able to keep his hands off you once I've worked my magic on you tomorrow."

Kitty waggled her eyebrows, and I couldn't help but laugh at her enthusiasm.

"I think anything will be an improvement," I chuckled, and she frowned at me.

"I don't think you know just how beautiful you are Nevara," Her eyes narrowed at me as I waved her away with a smile. "I'm going to make sure you see just how much tomorrow. Just you wait."

A mischievous smile lit up her face as she made her way over to her bed. Now I didn't know if I was more scared of the ball or Kitty's makeover.

CHAPTER 27

*T*hat night sleep didn't come easy, I tossed and turned with thoughts of what was to come. Doubt and nerves began to set in about the ball, and only when slivers of light began creeping through the window did sleep take me.

"Took you long enough to fall asleep."

That familiar voice roused me from my place on the floor. The cold stone seeped into my body as I looked up at him and scowled.

"Do you always have to put me on the floor when you bring me here?" I yawned, pulling myself up off the ground.

Penumbra was dressed in the same pitch-black tunic and breeches, his long hair falling in red waves to his chest.

"Unfortunately, I can't change where I summon you," He smirked, then raised an eyebrow at me. "Maybe next time I can put a few blankets down."

I ran my hands over my face with a sigh. Too tired for this, "What do you want?"

"Not in the fighting spirit today?" He mused as he stood up from the chaise and prowled towards me.

"I'm tired of being called here against my will." I bit out and he made a chastising noise as stopped in front of me. His eyes drifting to the ring on my hand.

"I see you liked my gift," He grinned, his eyes dancing with something I couldn't place. Then he blinked and it was gone. "Did it help with your training?"

"It doesn't concern you," I stiffened as he took my hand in his, lifting it to his mouth. He pressed a lingering kiss beside where the ring lay. His eyes never left mine as a dark heat burned through me.

I yanked my hand back, ignoring the way the heat ran across my skin like silk, consuming and—

"I haven't heard a response yet from my dear parents," His eyes met mine with a knowing look and he smirked as he walked over to a small cabinet, "or my brother."

Penumbra poured a honey-coloured liquid into a glass, swirling it around as he turned to face me.

"My army has begun preparations to march towards Arboria next week."

"You can't do this," I stuttered out, my blood running cold. I started towards him. "Why do you want this war? Is all of the bloodshed that will come with it worth it?"

Penumbra's eyes hardened as he lowered the glass from his mouth.

"If I can stop what is happening to my kin, then yes, I will go to war," He stated, eyes burning. "I would go to war a thousand times over if it meant saving them."

I stopped in my tracks.

"Who are you talking about?" I whispered, furrowing my brow.

"The King and Queen... led the humans... the lesser Fae," Penumbra's voice became distant and static as the room began to fall away.

"Nevara?" Penumbra's voice was low as his face flickered, concern swimming in his eyes.

I heard him call out again as the dream dissolved and only a thick blanket of darkness swallowed me.

~

"Nevara..."

A feminine voice dragged me from the darkness, and I opened my eyes to find Kitty peering down at me with a smile.

"Sorry to wake you, but I'm going to need to start getting you ready if you want to be on time for the ball."

I blinked as I pushed myself into a sitting position, rubbing my eyes. Sunshine shone through the window and my eyes widened.

"I slept in," I gasped, scrambling from beneath the covers. "I never sleep in."

Kitty giggled as I almost tumbled out of bed, the covers tangled around my legs.

"It's fine!" Kitty said, grinning at me. "Just go get washed up and we'll get started."

I nodded, throwing the covers aside and ran out the door, not wanting to waste any more time.

As I washed up, my mind wandered to my encounter with Penumbra last night. It seemed like he was about to tell me something important before everything dissolved. I shook my head, teasing my fingers through my damp hair. Now was not the time to be focusing on that.

I took a deep breath before I headed back to the room I shared with Kitty, and whatever she was about to unleash on me.

~

IT FELT like Kitty had brushed and pinned my hair for what felt hours, but the sun was already beginning to set and I found I'd enjoyed the day with her. Kitty had been gentle and careful as she teased in the curls.

"How are you so good at doing hair?" I asked as Kitty shuffled around me. Her hair was always so soft and sleek, like a sheet of fire with never a hair out of place. Only on days for class did she style it in two braids.

"I used to do this for my mother before she passed away," Kitty's eyes met mine in the mirror, a wistful smile on her face. "Whenever she and papa would go out, she would always teach me how to do her hair. She told me it would be useful skill in the future."

She brought her face level with my shoulder, grinning at me.

"Guess she was right!" She giggled, pinning up another curl.

"I'm so sorry about your mother," I whispered, and she nodded with a small smile.

"It's been almost four years now, but it only feels like yesterday," Kitty whispered as she stepped back, tilting her head to the side as she met my eyes in the mirror and clapped her hands. "All done!"

Kitty lifted a small hand mirror from her desk and held it up so I could see the back of my hair in it. I gasped. I hadn't been taking much notice, avoiding myself in the mirror as she worked. My usual messy hair was now pinned atop my head in a neat arrangement of curls and braids. Stray curls framed my face and for the first time I felt... pretty.

"Well?" Kitty asked, shifting from foot to foot behind me.

"It's incredible, Kitty," I whispered, meeting her eyes over my shoulder in the mirror. "It's so intricate and beautiful. I'm speechless."

A huge smile broke out across Kitty's face and in that moment, I was more thankful for her than she'd ever know.

"Time for the dress," Kitty clapped her hands, dashing over to retrieve the box where it sat on my drawers. "We'll have to meet Alec soon."

My stomach seemed to drop at the words. The very thought of Alec seeing me like this — it made me feel naked. Especially without my armour and weapons, it was like I'd be bare to the world.

Kitty placed the box on the bed, lifting the lid. Inside was dress of forest green that looked to be made of silk. Kitty pulled the dress from the box, and as it fell, the light caught against the tiny leaves and flowers embellished into the design. Each one strategically placed up the left side, in the same path of my scars.

Kitty motioned for me to undress and held the dress in place as I stepped into it. The silk whispered over my skin as she lifted it into place. I fingered the lace-like fabric that covered my left arm and hooked the end around my finger.

"It's beautiful," Kitty breathed as she stepped beside me, looking me over in the mirror. I turned in a circle.

The dress hugged my curves like a second skin, like water rippling on the surface of a lake. My right arm was bare and the silk at my chest plunged. The back swooped so low; it was pure magic it stayed in place at all.

"It feels like I'm naked," I chuckled, as I swished the fabric around my legs.

"That's because you're used to your leathers and armour," Kitty rolled her eyes with a laugh as she helped me into the matching green slippers. She popped back up with a smile as she made her way back towards the door. "Come on, we'll head down the carriage."

"Hang on!" I gathered up the dress as I reached into my discarded clothes and located the dagger in my boot. I hoisted the dress high and strapped it to my thigh. I let loose a breath, feeling a bit better.

Kitty raised an eyebrow as she turned and left the room. I followed her and her giggling down the hall.

~

"I CAN'T BELIEVE he would pick a dress like this in autumn."

We stood on the steps of the Academy as a brisk wind whipped over the courtyard. I shivered and hugged my arms around myself, trying everything to stop my teeth from chattering.

"I know that silk dresses are all the rage right now with the nobility, as it's material found in the dungeons," Kitty whispered, and my body went tense. I shuddered at the thought of a human stealing this fabric away from an innocent Fae.

We found Alec waiting by the carriage, looking out over the grounds of the Academy. He was dressed in an exquisite tunic with leaves embroidered down the—

I gasped, realising we matched. Had he done this on purpose?

He turned then and met my eyes. His gaze raked down my body, lingering on the dips and curves as he went. The look made my toes curl in my slippers.

"You look absolutely beautiful," He breathed, retrieving something from inside the carriage and walked towards me. He pulled a thick silk shawl around my shoulders, his fingers trailing down my bare arm. Heat broke out in their wake.

"As do you," I whispered as Kitty coughed beside us.

"Enjoy the ball," she said with a smile, nodding to Alec as she turned and re-entered the Academy.

Alec turned, holding out his hand as he stepped up beside

the carriage. I blushed as I gathered as much of dress in my hand and climbed up inside.

"What's wrong?" Alec asked as he sat on the bench opposite me.

"I can't move properly in this thing," I scowled, fidgeting in the dress. His eyes burned as he watched me move.

"That thing may just be the best piece of clothing I have ever purchased in my life," He smirked, his gaze lingering over my chest and waist where the dress was taut. "It really does leave little to the imagination."

My face heated again as his gaze travelled below my waist and I wrapped the shawl around me the best I could.

"Ass," I scowled, and he tipped his head back laughing.

"Here," He pulled a green domino mask from his pocket and handed it to me, a filigree of silk leaves covered the left side.

"What is this for?" I gestured to the mask, tracing my fingers over the leaves.

"It's a tradition," Alec grinned, watching me. "When the royal family hosts a ball for the prince for find a ball, it is a masquerade. To give fair maidens a chance, so the prince chooses from the heart."

He tilted his head to the side with a chuckle, nudging his boot against my slipper.

"It just so happens to hide your identity too, which is a bonus for us."

"So, you don't have to wear one?" I scrunched my nose.

"Do I look like a fair maiden to you?" He chuckled and I frowned.

"And I do?" I stammered. The thought of anyone referring to me as a fair maiden made me want to laugh.

"You most definitely do," Alec leaned forward on his elbows, his eyes lingering on my face. His hand reached out, trailing is fingers down over the leaves on my arm until his hand landed on my waist, tugging me to the edge of the bench. "And if it were my choice, I would have claimed you as my bride the moment I saw you in that dress."

Alec's knee slotted between my own, his free hand cupping my jaw, running a thumb over my lower lip. I held my breath as his eyes stared into mine.

"Too damn distracting," He growled as he shook his head, leaning back into his seat.

I spent the rest of the carriage ride trying to calm my thundering heart and cycling my mana to control the heat that burned where he touched.

THE CARRIAGE RATTLED into the Noble District, lights from the street and nearby houses flashed by the window. I took in a deep breath.

"Just act natural and you will be fine," Alec said, smiling over at me with a wink. "Leave all the hard work to me."

I nodded as I shifted towards the door, the dress pulling tight against my legs.

"Are you wearing a dagger on your thigh?" Alec asked, eyes widening as they looked from my leg to my eyes.

"For safety reasons, yes," I breathed as I shifted the fabric a bit more. It wasn't a total lie; I needed some form of defence should things go sideways.

"Good Gods," He whistled, his eyes turning into an azure fire. "I think you're going to be a little too distracting tonight, especially for me."

The carriage came to stop as he licked his bottom lip, then shook his head with a grin.

"Put your mask on now," Alec whispered and I secured the mask over my face, careful not to mess up Kitty's hard work. I ran my fingers over the leaves and realisation hit.

They covered my scars, something the King would recognise me for.

The palace was nothing like the last time we visited with Damon. It was lit up like a beacon and the courtyard was crowded with other guests piling from their own carriages. It was still early, but the sky was turning hues of purple and orange.

"Did you sleep well last night?" Alec asked as we joined a line of procession making our way towards the palace doors. I snapped out of my thoughts as I blinked up at him.

"What do you mean?" I chewed on my bottom lip as the line moved forward.

"I was worried about the curse on the ring," Alec smiled, folding my arm into his own the closer to the doors we got. "So, I placed a small formation on your door to help quieten the connection with my brother, so you could rest."

"Oh," I looked straight ahead, then glanced at him from under my lashes. He was frowning. I wondered why I didn't feel happy about it. I should be relieved the connection to Penumbra was lessened, but what Alec did... It didn't sit right with me. And I couldn't place why. "Thank you."

Alec smiled down at me, pulling me closer to his side as a burly guard at the door stepped up in front of us. His gaze bounced between us.

"Invitation?" He requested and Alec procured a golden card from inside his tunic. My hands began to sweat as the guard read over it, then waved us forward, "Go ahead."

"Remember that a lot of these humans have awoken their powers, so if they concentrate hard enough, they can hear and sense everything," Alec whispered against my ear, his breath tickling my neck. I focused on his words, his voice like honey. "It's time to pretend, fair maiden."

The hallway opened out into an opulent and grand ball-room. Bright velvet chaises and tables ladened with food lined the room. Women dressed in uniform circled the crowds with trays of wine and a small orchestra was playing on a raised platform.

Chatter and music filled the room in tandem with one another and as Alec steered us through the crowd, eyes fell on us. He stopped only to procure two glasses from a passing tray. Women were dressed in a similar silk that I wore but were a rainbow of colour as they danced and talked in groups around the room.

I didn't even realise anyone had approached until I heard Alec's voice.

"I'm Alec and this is my sister, Deanna," Alec smiled, gesturing to me.

"I'm William and this is my daughter Rose," The man said with a proud smile at his daughter. William and his daughter both had sun kissed skin, the latter had a dusting of gold making her look ethereal with a matching gold silk gown and mask. "I haven't seen you around here before. What business are you in?"

"I collect beautiful things," Alec's eyes looked from my dress to my eyes, smiling. It was anything but a brotherly look. I fought to push my mana into controlling the blush that threatened to cover my cheeks. "I trade in magical arte-facts. I actually provided most of which the King will be showcasing this evening."

"Incredible," William nodded, oblivious to the look Alec just gave me. "My family own a small boutique on the west side of the district. We actually supplied most of the dresses this evening, except yours."

"It's one of a kind," Alec mused, smiling at William. "My mother is a very skilled seamstress."

"Well, it is simply beautiful," William smiled as he met my eyes. "As is the lady wearing it."

I felt my face burn and bowed my head with a small smile.

"Please be silent as we welcome the King and Queen, and the Prince of Ghislana."

The King and Queen crossed the floor, dressed in the finest red velvets and silk, and took their seat on the thrones on the raised dais. Damon then entered, his eyes sweeping the room until they settled on me and Alec with a soft smile. He was dressed in a red velvet tunic lined with fur and he looked exactly as I imagined a Prince would as he took his seat beside his mother.

"I would like to welcome you all this evening to celebrate my son's choosing ceremony," The King called out over the crowd, gesturing to Damon. "Tonight, my son will choose his future bride, but before the dance begins, I would like to indulge you all in my collection of magical artefacts. Wet your curiosity if you will."

The King waved a hand and a group of knights entered, laden with boxes and glass cases of different sizes and placed them on the long table set out at the base of the dais. Alec released a breath as the knight lowered a particular box. He looked at me and gave me a quick nod.

"Please take a look at the power our Kingdom holds, and the potential of what we can become with the help of these artefacts!"

Knights began ushering curious guests into a line to get a closer look at the artefacts on show. Music began filtering through the room again as we made our way to the front. Excitement thrummed through me at the prospect of seeing what the King had coveted for himself.

In the first glass case was a double-edged sword which was worn and old, but from the care that was taken to preserve the hilt, I knew it was loved once. I wondered which Fae it had belonged to and if they had been alive or dead when it had been taken.

The thought alone made me shuffle faster down the line,

a sour taste in my mouth until we got to the stone. It was a large oval shaped stone that glowed red where it hovered in the middle of the case. My breath caught as the waves of energy hit me.

Alec pulled me away and I blinked. The energy falling away like dust. I'd never felt that much power before, not even from Penumbra's ring. I understood now why he wanted it so much. That amount of power would turn the tides of the threatened war.

"For the last of my collection I would ask for your utmost discretion," The King grinned as his voice carried over the room. From a side door knights entered wheeling in a large cage, and it wasn't empty.

A male with fiery red hair stood bound, his arms and legs outstretched. He wore only black breeches, his chest bare except for the chains that latticed over it, twining up and down his legs.

"These are the beast that roam in the dungeons," The King roared, his face twisting into a sneer. "They may wear a human skin similar to our very own, but when provoked..."

The King nodded to a knight who sliced his sword through the bars of the cage and across the male's torso. The man roared as his skin began to twist and shift. His skin began to change and, in its place, appeared rows of glittering red scales, then as quickly as they appeared, they disappeared. The crowd erupted into gasps and wails. My hand tightened on Alec's arm.

I looked up to see he had turned away from the cage, his eyes dark. My heart went out for him, it pained me to see this male treated with such cruelty. I couldn't imagine what Alec saw as one of his own was tortured.

We needed to free him.

"We have the power to dominate over these monsters and claim what is rightfully ours from their lands," The King continued as he gestured for the cage to be taken away. My heart sunk as I watched the Fae male disappear behind the door.

"Now that we've seen the strength of this glorious Kingdom, let's celebrate as your Prince chooses his bride"

The crowd erupted into cheers, but my mind was on the man beyond the door. Trapped.

Alec nudged me, and I glanced at him.

It was time.

The women were instructed to line up on the edge of the dance floor. I threw one last look at Alec before I joined them and watched as Damon came down the dais steps. He sauntered along the line of ladies, all of whom were offering him sweet smiles and some batting their lashes. I felt like we were all slabs of meat in a butcher's shop, waiting for the best to be picked off.

Damon came to a stop before me and met my gaze. I could feel my heart pounding in my ears as he offered his hand to me. I sucked in a breath as his pale eyes took in all of me.

What was he doing? This wasn't part of the plan.

"Would you do me the honour of the first dance?" Damon asked, a smile playing about his lips. I wanted to say no, to step back and hide away in a corner. But with Alec on the hunt for the stone, I couldn't.

Instead, I lowered into a curtsy that was anything but graceful. Copying what I'd seen the other ladies do, I slid my hand into his as he led me out onto the dance floor.

The music changed and the tempo became bright and upbeat. It made my blood sing as the notes rose and fell.

"I can't dance," I blanched as Damon placed a hand on my waist, tugging me closer with a smile.

"Just pretend we're sparring," He whispered, then took the first step leading me into the dance. I didn't know what he meant at first, but each step was like a thrust or lunge with my sword. Another kind of dance. I fell into step with him as he twirled me around the dance floor. A giggle escaped as Damon spun us around and around.

"You are truly magnificent when you laugh," Damon breathed against my ear as he pulled me in close, so close our bodies brushed together. The skirt of my dress whispering against his legs. As the music crept up to a crescendo, Damon spun me out and back into him before dipping me low to the floor. Our breath mingling in the space between us as the crowd erupted into applause.

Damon grinned as he pulled me upright and lifted my hand to his lips, brushing a lingering kiss to my knuckles.

I stuttered out a breath before dropping into another curtsy and re-joined the crowd.

"Now that was a sight to behold," Alec's voice near my temple made me jump and I spun to look at him with wide eyes.

"Well?" I asked and he nodded.

"I got it," He patted his tunic and I beamed at him. We did it. Now we just had to get out unnoticed.

"And the Fae too?" I whispered and his face tightened.

"No," He stated, his jaw tight. My mouth fell open.

"What do you mean, no?" I bit out, twisting to face him.

"It's too risky to release him," He whispered, still not looking at me. "It would alert the guards."

"But he's Fae," I pressed. "He's one of your people."

"He's Lesser Fae," Alec snapped. "He is not my people."

"I don't understand," I hissed. My stomach twisted with a sour feeling. "They're torturing him. We have to free him, Alec!"

Alec looked at me then, his eyes dark. A darkness I'd never see in him before.

"It's not worth jeopardising the stone," Alec stated, and I shook my head as I stepped away from him.

"Then you're not the man I thought you were," I ground out, and I knew my words had hit their mark as he tensed up and reached for me. I didn't care and slipped away before he could stop me.

There was a knight guarding the door as I pushed through the crowd. Damn. I circled around and slid up against the wall as close as I could to the door. Pressing a hand to my racing heart, I focused on the shadow in the crack under the door. I pushed my mana through my body and into the hand where Penumbra's ring was sat, watching as tendrils of smoke crept down the wall, reaching for the shadow. I felt when the connection snapped into place and melted into that familiar darkness.

Stumbling, I blinked away the shadows and steadied myself on the wall. A grin broke out over my face as I looked back at the door. I was in the hallway.

I did it.

It was deserted, but I didn't want to take any chances as I bundled the skirt up in my arms as I ran down the corridor towards the familiar metal door we had found during our first visit.

The door swung open with ease, clearly after Alec's recent visit for the stone. Inside the room was dark and the boxes and glass cases containing the artefacts were against the far wall. The Fae was in the far corner, and I covered my mouth with my hand. So many cuts and bruises littered his skin, a fresh cut seeped blood down over his face and chest.

I wasted no time unlocking the cage before cupping the man's face.

"Please wake up," I whispered, but the man didn't move. I shook his shoulders earning a groan as his eyes peeled open.

Fury descended over his face and he fought his restraints. I held my hands up in surrender.

"I'm just here to help," I whispered, looking over at the door knowing someone will have heard the chains rattling. "I'm going to set you free, but you need to be quiet."

The man regarded me with a look before nodding.

I looked around for anything to unlock the chains and my eyes fell on a key. I grabbed it and prayed it would work. The lock clicked on the first restraint as it fell to the cage floor. I followed suit with the rest.

"I don't know where the Fae gates are, but I know there is one to the east of here, in the Marden Mountains," I said, reaching out a hand to help him to his feet. Cringing against his weight as he limped and stumbled forward. "It's behind what looks like a castle."

"My sword," He croaked, and I looked at him confused before he pointed to the double-edged sword in the case from before.

I propped him up against the cage as I retrieved the sword from the case. It was so heavy.

The male shuffled up behind me, holding a hand to his chest as I placed the sword in his free hand. He whispered something melodic, and the sword began to glow. I stared in awe as his cuts and bruises began to disappear.

"You need to go now," I ushered him towards the door. "Before someone comes."

"You are just like he told us you would be, Titania." The man whispered as he fisted his hand over his heart and bowed his head. "I will never forget what you did for me this day."

I nodded, staring as he disappeared through the door and down the hallway.

Why did he call me—

A loud cheer rose up from the ballroom and I jumped into action, shutting the door behind me.

I turned and ran straight into a hard chest, a hand tugging me to one side. My hand drifted to my thigh before I looked up and realised it was Alec.

"What you just did could have ruined everything," Alec growled, and I levelled my stare with his.

"I wasn't about to sit back and let someone be tortured," I snapped, and his eyes softened as he sighed.

"I'm sorry," he said, and I frowned at him. "I should have freed him... I just got caught up with making sure the stone was safe."

Alec brushed his hand over my jaw, cupping my face in his palm. His eyes pleading.

"Please forgive me."

I stared at him for moment and hesitated before I nodded. It was easy to get caught up in the plan, but there was something bothering me that I couldn't put my finger on.

"I forgive you," I breathed and he gave me a small smile.

"I need you to hold onto the stone," Alec reached into his tunic as he pressed in closer to me. Shielding us from prying eyes. "The King won't make a scene about the Fae getting away, but he will no doubt make the men empty their pockets should he learn about the stone's disappearance."

Alec pressed the stone into my hand, the energy zapping through me.

"I need you to hide it until we're outside."

I looked up at him, gesturing to my dress.

"I don't have pockets."

Alec smirked as his gaze travelled down my neck until it landed on my cleavage. He leaned forward, running his hand down my neck, resting on my chest.

"I'm sure you'll find somewhere to conceal it," His breath

tickled my ear before he leaned back with a grin and stepped away.

"Jerk," I hissed as I turned to place the stone between my cleavage on the folds on the silk. Thank goodness for my curves, I mused to myself.

Alec bit his lip and grinned when I turned around, his eyes dropping once to where I'd hid the stone. I sucked in a breath resisting the pull of power radiating from the stone.

"I know it's taxing but bear it. It's only half an hour and then we will be returning to the Academy." Alec assured me and I gave him a small smile.

Once back inside the ballroom the heat became stifling, the stone pressing against my chest like a brand.

Don't fight it, My Priestess.

The voice echoed through my mind, and I looked around for the source, but there was only Alec.

The power thrummed against my skin as I sat down on one of the chaise seats. I took a deep breath, it was becoming too much and I succumbed to the voice and let the power in. A warmth spread through my body, my mana sang in response, and I relaxed against the back of the chair with a sigh.

"Feeling better?" Alec mused, leaning down towards me. "Perhaps you're not as susceptible to the power as I had thought."

"Maybe," I breathed out with a smile, shifting as the power sunk down further into my mana pool.

Whispers began to descend over the crowd as people began pointing towards the dais where a knight had appeared beside the King, speaking low in his ear. I watched as the King's eyes widen and his face turned red, satisfaction settled over me.

More and more knights began filing into the room, as couples still spun and danced around the floor. The weight of the stone felt heavier as the knights took up positions by the exits and windows.

"Let's go," Alec murmured, pulling me to my feet. I nodded as he led us towards the exit.

"Halt!"

A knight stepped up in front of us and my heart began to race.

We were so close.

The knight gestured for Alec to lift his arms to search him.

"It's just a precaution, but we need to check all items in your possession."

Alec frowned as he looked across to me, then back to the knight.

"I hope you can speed this along as my little sister is feeling quite faint," Alec said, and to add truth to his words I swayed a little on my feet. Alec reached out an arm, catching me around the waist to steady me.

The knight hurried his search and waved us out of the doors.

ONCE WE WERE SAT BACK in the carriage, it felt like I could breathe again. I watched as the palace became smaller and smaller out the little window and leaned back against the bench.

We did it.

"I can't believe it's over," I whispered, and Alec nodded. A bubble of giggles escaped as I threw my head back against the seat. Weeks of training and tension built up had just dissipated with that laugh.

"The King is a fool," Alec whispered. I looked back at him and could have sworn I saw him smile. "We were lucky the security was so lax. I bet he didn't think any of his precious nobles would steal from him."

"I'm so relieved," I sighed, pulling the shawl into my lap. "After everything… we actually did it."

"I'm also contemplating leaving the stone exactly where it is," he murmured, his eyes dropping to my chest. I flushed as his eyes darkened and I reached inside my dress, pulling out the stone.

Time seemed to still as we focused on the stone.

"Nevara… what did you do?" Alec's eyes were wide as his gaze left the stone to stare at me.

It had been red and glowing, thrumming with energy. But now.

It was dark.

Black.

Empty.

Alec reached over, fingering the top of my dress, and tugging it down. He sucked in a breath, his fingers tracing my chest.

I looked down and my own eyes widened as I saw the black row of symbols that were inked into my skin.

"Dear Gods, you absorbed its power."

CHAPTER 28

*A*lec dissolved into silence as we travelled the rest of the way to the Academy. Rain had begun pelting against the carriage. An omen, I thought, for what had happened.

"Alec," I whispered and got no response. Absorbing the stone's power was not part of the plan and panic was setting in. "Alec, please, say something!"

"I'm sorry," Alec blinked at me, then sighed as he sat back in his seat. "I'm trying to figure out what to do next."

"And?" I pressed. Nervous to hear his answer.

"The good news is that Penumbra and the King don't have the stone, "Alec's jaw ticked as his spoke, "The bad news is that you are no longer safe in the human lands."

My body stilled.

"What do you mean?"

"I mean, now that you have the power of the fire stone flowing through you, Penumbra will try anything to bring you back to him." Alec gritted out, his eyes snapping to mine. "You have what he wants, and he will stop at nothing to get you."

"I'll stay at the Academy," I said, my skin prickling. "I'll learn to defend myself, shield the stone's power—"

Alec shook his head, holding up a hand to stop me.

"You don't understand," Alec sighed, running a hand over his jaw, "Penumbra must have known something like this would happen. It's why you're linked with the stones and that damned prophecy."

Alec dropped his head in his hand, tightening his fists in his hair.

"Why was I so stupid for not seeing it?" Alec spat, looking up at me. "Penumbra will do anything to bring you to him, for instance using your family as leverage. The stone and its power belong to the Fae lands. I can protect you there, not here. I have to go home."

Alec leaned forward, capturing my hands in his.

"Come with me."

I sucked in a breath as his words echoed around my mind. My heart soared with what he was asking me to do, but my mind was also tugging me back down to reality.

"I've trained my whole life to get into this Academy, Alec," I whispered, tugging my hands from his. "I can't just up and leave to go hide in the Fae lands."

Alec's hands dangled in my lap as he stared at me.

"So you would rather stay at school that teaches you how to murder the Fae?" He snarled and I flinched back from his tone.

"You know my reason for wanting to stay," I whispered, clenching my hands into fists. "I will stay to learn how to control my mana and find a way to convince the humans to leave the Fae lands alone. I told you one day I would make our people allies, and I can't do that if I'm not here."

"But I can't stay here, Nevara!" Alec snapped. "My people need me back home. I've been gone long enough."

I leaned forward, holding his hands to my chest, looking into his eyes.

"Then trust me," I pleaded. "Trust me to remain here and look after the stone. Go help your people and visit me when you can. You need to keep searching for the other stones, right?"

"The other stones," He repeated my words and his eyebrows furrowed.

"Yes, the other elemental stones," I said, thankful he was listening to me. "The humans might find one and it's good to keep the relations you have here just in case."

In reality, I was terrified he would end up taking me to Arboria against my will. I knew he would do it if it meant keeping the stone safe.

I didn't breathe—didn't move at all as I watched Alec ponder over what to do, sweat building along my spine in anticipation.

"If you remain here, I will have to assign a guard to you at all times." Alec looked up at me, his eyes boring into mine.

"Yes! Anything you want!" I nodded, as his eyes dropped to the symbols above my dress.

"And you will have to travel to Undar each month so we can attempt to extract the power." He added and I was already nodding my head.

"I can do that." I smiled and he rested his forehead against mine. Relief swamped through me. I wouldn't be separated from my family or taken from the Academy.

"Nothing is ever simple with you, is it?" Alec mused as he pressed a kiss to my forehead. I smiled at him as a dark warmth stirred in my stomach, just beneath the surface of my mana power. I shivered at the power there.

Alec's fingers tangled in the hair at the nape of my neck, breathing me in. I knew being apart from Alec would be hard, but at least it wouldn't be forever.

I pressed a kiss to his mouth, a barely there brush of lips. Feeling the thrum of power come alive as Alec gathered me in his arms on the floor between the carriage seats, deepening the kiss.

My Priestess of Shadows.

The words whispered in my head, and I shuddered in Alec's arms against the silent promise it carried.

Fate was leading me somewhere, to be something, whether I wanted it or not.

THE SKY WAS STILL DARK when we returned to the Academy. Alec and I had stayed wrapped up in one another on the floor of the carriage as I reassured him between kisses that the Academy was the best place for me.

He had informed me that he would be leaving first thing in the morning as he wanted to tell his parents about the situation with the stone himself.

We were in Alec and Damon's room, waiting for the prince to return. I must have fallen asleep because when I opened my eyes, moonlight was all that lit the room. I sat up, searching for Alec, but the room was empty.

"Go outside," A voice filtered through the room, and I jumped to my feet. Dagger in hand I searched the room, trying to find the source of the voice.

"Go outside Titania." The voice came again, and my blood turned to ice. It was the Fae male from the ball.

Without hesitation, I hiked up my dress and tore out of the room, sprinting down the stairs and out the doors of the Academy.

"Now what?" I spoke into the night, the wind carrying my voice. I searched around, looking for the red-haired male. Only silence greeted me.

"Run now," The voice came, more urgent this time. "Climb over the wall and don't stop until you reach the lake's edge."

I ran forward, through the line of trees and stopped before the stone wall surrounding the Academy. Where was Alec? I could use his climbing skills about now.

Taking a deep breath, I began circulating my mana, pulling it through my body. Pushing it down into my arms and legs and I began to climb. With each foothold my movements became faster until I crested the wall. I panted and started to lower myself down but slipped and tumbled through the air.

"Use your shadows!" The voice yelled through my mind and at the last moment I threw out my hands as smoky tendrils erupted from my fingers. Instead of connecting with hard ground, I opened my eyes to find I was hovering just above it. Lifting my hands in front of me, I gasped when I saw the dark edges to my skin.

I had become a shadow.

"Hurry!" The voice shook me from my reverie, and I ran in shadow form, moving like smoke between the trees. Faster than I'd ever moved before.

The sound of lapping water got louder and closer, and I searched the ground for the Fae.

I came up short when I heard something.

"It seems my brother has become desperate if he sent the likes of you to retrieve the stone."

A man stood at the river's edge, facing the red-haired male who was half in, half out of the water, clutching his bloodied side.

The man turned and I smothered my gasp with my hand.

It was Alec.

"Penumbra didn't want to risk his men," The red-haired Fae gasped and doubled over. "I came against his orders."

My shadows trembled at mention of Penumbra's name, and that's when I realised who this male was. He was a solider from Penumbra's Army.

"Listen Titania," The Fae's voice wavered in mind, but his tone was insistent. "Listen."

"Pen is too late," Alec spat as he folded his arms over his chest. "I have the stone's power now. He's lost the upper hand in this war he wants so badly."

"We don't want a war," The Fae ground out. "All we want is for you to close the gates and leave our people in peace. The Lesser Fae don't deserve this."

Why was he asking Alec to close the gates? The red-haired Fae should know that this was Penumbra's doing.

"You people deserve worse than what was happening to you," Alec growled, stalking towards the male. "The gates I opened into your lands are just the beginning."

My body froze. Everything seemed to slow down.

Alec's words sunk into my mind—and my heart.

"The gates I opened..." My hold on the shadows dissolved. Failing to keep grasp of my mana as Alec's revelation shattered my very being.

"Please, there are children!" The red-haired male pleaded as Alec raised his sword to his throat. My body grew numb as my heart splintered.

"My brother probably already thinks you dead," Alec spat, venom dripping from his tone. "Maybe I will send your corpse back to him as warning."

Alec pulled his sword back. I couldn't move, my body locked up as I watched the scene unfold.

"Forget about me Titania," The Fae whispered in my mind, his voice soft and kind. Resigned to his fate. "You need to help Penumbra."

A scream built in my throat as Alec arced his sword

down, the blade slicing through skin and the sickening thud as the Fae's head toppled to the floor.

Alec turned, wiping his blade over his breeches. Then he looked up and froze as our gazes locked.

The man I had come to care about. The man I had almost come to love—everything he had told me was a lie.

You think I'm the one who created those damn gates? What has Alec been telling you?

Those were Penumbra's words when I had accused him of opening those gates. I had been so stupid and naïve to believe everything Alec told me.

Why lie?

Why did he open the gates?

My mind spun with questions as my eyes bore into Alec's.

I knew one thing for certain, I wasn't going to stop until I found out the truth.

ACKNOWLEDGMENTS

Firstly I want to thank all of you have purchased my book and supported me as a self-published author. It hasn't been easy but you guys have been there for me since the beginning and have made all the hard work worth it!

I also want to thank my family and my loving partner for all of their support and encouragement whilst writing this book. Especially my dad who has always been my number one fan and has always supported me in any decision I make.

Lastly, I want to thank the amazing friends I have made through in the book community.
Laura Metcalfe and Rebecca Lesurf, you two are literally angels sent from the heavens to help me. You guys worked so hard to help make my book the best it can be and I appreciate you both so much!

Thank you to everyone again and I can't wait for you to join Nevara in book number two!

Printed in Great Britain
by Amazon

86477586R00202